# Another Saturday Night and I Ain't Got No Body

Jennie Marts

ISBN-13: 978-1480211384

ISBN-10: 1480211389

Cover and book design by
THE KILLION GROUP
www.thekilliongroupinc.com

# *Dedication*

This book is dedicated to the three most important people in my life.

For Todd:
My love, my best friend, my hero, and my knight in shining armor.
Thank you for ALWAYS believing in me.

For Tyler and Nick:
The greatest accomplishments of my life.
My love for you is endless.

Never give up on your dreams.

The recipe for disaster began innocently enough with a phone call during a lazy summer morning while Sunny Vale sat on the sofa reading a book. Throw in a dash of dramatic eighty-year-old woman with a fondness for reality crime television, and mix with a midnight arrival of one hunky stranger. Spice it up with an automatic weapon, and the disaster entrée was nearly complete.

"Edna, are you sure it was a gun?" Sunny asked, used to her neighbor's tendency to exaggerate. She was anxious to get back to her latest romance novel and the bag of Cheetos she was munching on before the phone rang.

"Yes, Sunny, of course I'm sure," her neighbor replied. "I might be old, but I never miss a CSI. I'm telling you, I saw a man, with a gun, breaking into Walter's house last night!"

"Okay, I'm listening." Sunny licked the orange dust from her fingertips, and set her book on the coffee table. She looked longingly at the cover photo of the muscular, bare-chested pirate who held a sword in one hand and a raven-haired beauty in the other, her well-endowed bosom bursting from her corseted bodice. Heaving a boringly B-cupped sigh, she half-wished Edna really had seen a gorgeous gun-toting stranger. He might add some much needed excitement to her ordinary life. Not that teaching second graders how to read and write didn't have exciting moments, but it sure didn't compare to an affair with a sword-wielding pirate.

"Why were you up in the middle of the night anyway?" Sunny asked, now resigned to hear the whole story. So far, her Saturday morning consisted of coffee, Cheetos, and fantasizing about a pirate fling. Edna's story could only add one more facet to her exciting day.

"Because of that damn pepperoni pizza we ate last night. I got up around midnight and was looking out my kitchen window, chewing on some Maalox, when I saw this dark-colored sports car pull up in front of Walter's house," Edna said, referring to the house that sat between them. "Then this scruffy haired young punk climbed out and stretched like he'd been driving for a long time."

"Young, like a teenager?"

"No, young like you. Mid-thirties or so." Everyone seemed young to Edna, who had just celebrated her eightieth birthday by learning the Samba and going on a singles cruise. "Anyway, after he stretches, he reaches into the car and pulls out a duffel bag, then a gun that he tucked into the waistband of his jeans. Which, by the way, he filled out quite nicely."

Sunny chuckled as she pictured Edna in her robe and favorite pink, fuzzy slippers, the words Sassy and Girl embroidered on each in glittery silver lettering. She imagined her, peering out her kitchen window, her tongue working the chalky antacid from her teeth, as she checked out a hunky, mysterious stranger's arrival in the middle of the night. "So, did Walter let in this young, gun-wielding punk with the nice tush?"

"No, that's just it. Walter wasn't even there. This guy snooped around the house and garage then found Walter's hide-a-key by the front door and let himself in. And this morning, his car is gone, like he was never even there."

"Maybe Walter knew he was coming and told him to let himself in." Sunny shifted to pull her legs free from under Beau, her golden retriever, who was lying across them on the sofa. Both her legs and the dog were asleep, and Sunny and Beau each groaned as she stood and headed for the kitchen.

"I doubt it," Edna said. "I got to thinking about it and realized I haven't seen Walter in days. Have you?"

Now that Edna mentioned it, Sunny couldn't remember the last time she had seen their mutual neighbor. Walter's wife, Betty, died several years ago, and he seemed to finally be adjusting to life as a bachelor. He was an avid gardener and still quite fit for a man in his late seventies. The big white door to the garage behind his house often stood open all day, the radio set to an oldies station, as he putzed around the yard or tinkered at fixing one thing or another.

With the school year ending for summer, Sunny hadn't paid much attention, but she couldn't recall the last time she had noticed the garage door open. "I don't think I've seen him lately, either. Not even working in his yard."

"We usually have coffee once a week or so, but this last week I was so busy with those new Italian cooking classes, I never found the time. And now this strange guy lets himself into Walter's house. I just know there's something fishy going on here." Edna's voice climbed up an octave.

Sunny rinsed her coffee cup in the kitchen sink as she studied Walter's house. The yellow and white ranch style home looked peaceful, the gardens full of colorful flowers reaching for the June morning sun. A sudden movement caught her eye as a figure emerged from the corner of the house and stooped to look into Walter's front window.

"Edna, get away from that window!" Sunny cried, knocking on the kitchen pane.

Edna jumped and dropped the cell phone she had pressed to her ear as she looked over at Sunny, a startled expression on her face. "Gosh dangit, I dropped the phone."

Edna's voice sounded muffled as she bent to search through Walter's petunias. She didn't even have the gall to look guilty.

"Get out of Walter's flowerbeds!" Sunny yelled. Edna reached down and plucked the phone off the ground. She waved it at Sunny with a triumphant shake before putting it back against her ear.

"Edna, what are you doing over there?"

"I'm trying to gather evidence," she explained, as if Sunny were the ridiculous one versus the woman spying into her neighbor's window like a wrinkled, geriatric Nancy Drew. "His car is in the garage so he might be in there, hurt or bound and gagged."

"Well, what are *you* gonna do if he is? Break down the door? Get out of there. You're trampling Walter's flowers. I'm sure he's fine."

"Humph."

Sunny heard the older woman's grumble and imagined the eye roll that accompanied it, but Edna did get out of the flowers and start back to her own yard.

"I'm heading to the grocery store," Sunny told her, ready to move on from this ridiculous notion of a neighborhood break-in by a gun-toting hunk. "Do you need me to pick up anything for you?" *A fingerprint kit, a secret decoder ring, a sane thought, perhaps?*

"No honey, I'm fine. I just went yesterday," she replied. "But keep an eye out for this mystery guy and call me if you see Walter."

"I will." Sunny slipped on her flip-flops and noticed her purple toenail polish was starting to chip. So there *was* something to look forward to on a Saturday night, a home pedicure.

"I'll see you at book club Wednesday night," Edna said, referring to The Pleasant Valley Page Turners, aptly named for their small Colorado town nestled against the foothills of the Rocky Mountains.

"Great. I've almost finished the book. See you then." Sunny clicked off, grabbed her purse, and headed out the door. On the drive to the grocery store, she planned her shopping list in her head: milk, bread, eggs, more Cheetos, a bunch of Lean Cuisines, chocolate-chip cookie dough ice cream. That about covered it.

She had her cart half-full (or half-empty because she didn't have the ice-cream yet) when she spied a new product in the frozen food section. Opening the freezer door, she grabbed a couple bags of Mandarin Orange Chicken. Yum. She flipped the top bag over to check the calorie content, but the top had split open, and the entire package of small chicken chunks scattered across the floor. She stood stock still for a moment, and prayed no one saw or heard the chicken nugget explosion.

"Some people take them home before they open them," a voice behind her said.

*Oh, crud.* Sunny slowly turned around as she let the freezer door close with a *thwap*.

"The package was already opened," she said to, of course, a super-cute guy with an Owen Wilson style head of dark blond hair. Why couldn't she have flung chicken pieces at an old lady or a pimply teenager?

"Let me help." He scooted several chicken nuggets under the freezer with his foot. "I think I'm your only witness," he whispered and grinned.

*Wow. What a grin.* His left canine was just a little crooked, which made his smile look mischievous and boyish.

"Thanks. I've actually just been released on parole

for excessive chicken spillage and driving under the influence of severe humiliation. If anyone finds out about this, they'll send me back to the big house." Sunny followed his lead and nonchalantly slid two frozen chicken chunks under the large freezer with her toe.

She tossed the other bag of orange chicken into her cart and tried for a quick getaway. To her surprise, the chicken-hiding accomplice followed as she hurried into the first available aisle.

"I think we're in the clear," he said, sneaking a glance behind them. "And I don't think anyone followed us." He played along with the gag, and they both laughed. She tried not to look at the chicken nugget piece caught in the cuff of his khaki pants.

"Well, thanks. I guess I better get back to my shopping." She turned, and came eye to eye with a mega-shelf of tampons, douche, and maxi-pads. "Oh, I...um, I don't...wrong turn." She felt a blush crawl up her neck. Wheeling her cart around, she knocked over a 'special night of romance' display. Condoms, KY, and massage oil scattered across the floor.

"Do you always have this much trouble shopping?" Her follower grinned.

"Yes. No. I just needed some of this," Sunny mumbled as she chucked a bottle of massage oil into her cart. With a little wave, she pushed off down the aisle, weaving around the multi-colored boxes she left spread across the floor. "Thanks again."

Hadn't she just this morning been wishing for more adventure in her life? So maybe he wasn't a pirate, but a good looking guy was flirting with her, and she was blowing it by her clumsiness, and an oddly-timed need for maxis.

Cheeks burning, Sunny headed straight for the checkout. Of course, she picked the slowest checker in the universe. The one who has to methodically pick up each item and examine it before running it across the scanner. All the while, making meaningless small talk with the customer about their groceries. "Oh wow. I haven't tried this brand. Is it any good? What are you going to use this pork for? I'm always looking for a new recipe for 'the other white meat'."

*Well, I just left a full bag of processed all breast white meat coated in tempura batter defrosting under your back freezers, so can we move it along, lady?*

As Sunny reached her car, there was her new Super-Hero, the masked Chicken-Concealer, climbing into a classic, blue Mustang convertible. She ducked her head and concentrated on unlocking the car door and flinging her plastic sacks into the back seat. Frustrated at her rusty flirting skills, she debated if she should wave again or nonchalantly act like she didn't see him. Did she want to appear carefree and fun or sexy and aloof? Too late, he was already in the driver's seat and she was still standing at her car door looking like a dork. Again.

Half-way home, Sunny glanced into the rear-view mirror and noticed the blue Mustang right behind her. *Odd.* She turned the corner into her neighborhood.

Wait, he turned too. It took five turns before she reached her street, all of them with the Mustang turning right behind her. Her thoughts went from "Wow–what a coincidence," to "Maybe he lives here," to "He's a crazy stalker following me home to rape me in my driveway," with each consecutive turn. By the fifth one, she was reaching for her cell phone. Frantically digging through her purse, she accidentally knocked it into the passenger floorboard. She leaned over, reaching for the phone while keeping one hand and her knee still on the wheel. *Shoot!* A squirrel darted across the road in front of her car. Sunny swerved to miss the little rodent. The contents of her purse scattered under the seat and across the floor of the car. *Great. Stupid squirrel!*

She pulled up to her house, and the Mustang came

to a stop directly behind her car. Between the purse and the squirrel and Edna's paranoia creeping into her mind, Sunny had worked herself into a frenzy.

*Holy Crap! This is what happens when you flirt with a stranger in the grocery store!* Now she was going to be kidnapped and sold as a sex slave to some third world drug lord. Why didn't she carry that pepper spray that Edna gave her last Christmas?

Sunny jumped from the seat, threw open the back door, and scrambled for the contents of her bag. Hearing his car door slam, she looked up to see him headed her way. She grabbed a handful of things off the floor and stood to challenge him. She had come up with a Chap Stick, a tampon, and a spray breath freshener. *Damn!* Sunny flung the first two at him and hit him smack in the middle of the head with the Chap Stick. His hands came up in defense, but she squirted him in the face with the breath spray.

"Aaagghh!" He covered his eyes. "What the hell are you doing? Are you crazy?"

"You're the crazy, deranged, stalking rapist." She reached back into the car for whatever other weapon she could find. The first bag of groceries lay spilled in the seat, and she came up with the other package of orange chicken and heaved it at the stalker.

"Ouch! Holy shit, that burns! Cut it out!" Rubbing his eyes, he failed to deflect the flying bag of chicken, which hit him in the chest and split open. Tempura-battered chunks scattered onto the front lawn. "Stop! I'm not a stalker. I live here."

"You do not. I live here," she yelled back and grabbed for more groceries.

"Not here. There." He pointed to the yellow house next door to hers. "Walter's house."

Sunny stopped, her hand mid-throw, ready to launch a bag of egg noodles in his direction. "Walter's house?"

"Yes," he said. "I got in last night and just went to

the store to get some food." His eyes were red and tearing from the breath spray. He rubbed his chest where she'd beaned him with the bag of chicken.

"Geez. I just came over to see if you needed help carrying in your groceries." He headed across the lawn toward Walter's front door. "What is it with you and frozen meat nuggets?" he muttered.

"Sorry," Sunny lamely called out to his retreating back. "I thought you were following me." She tried to explain, but he had already gone in and closed the door behind him.

Feeling like an idiot, Sunny rummaged around the floor of her car and collected the assorted debris that had spilled from her purse. She threaded her four bags of groceries onto her wrist and weaved her way through her grocery dotted front yard. Why had she let Edna's crazy talk of mysterious men cloud her judgment?

She pushed open the front door, only to be knocked aside as Beau ran out into the front yard to see what excitement he had missed. The poor dog was in a frenzy as he raced around, frantically gulping down the scattered frozen chicken chunks. Leaning against the doorjam, Sunny realized that instead of throwing tampons at him, she should have been asking her new neighbor where her old neighbor was hiding and just what was he doing with a gun?

❀❀❀

The next morning, Sunny rang the doorbell of Walter's house, and chewed on her lower lip as she rehearsed her apology. The nugget guy was obviously Edna's mystery midnight man. Sunny figured she could ply her way into the house with a plate of warm brownies, then snoop around for clues to Walter's whereabouts. If for no other reason than to prove to Edna that her suspicions were unfounded and life was not as thrilling as the weekly crime shows she watched on television.

The front door opened, and all thoughts seeped from Sunny's head as her would-be stalker stood before her in nothing but a pair of jeans, rubbing his wet hair with a towel.

"Hi." He looked at her warily. "Sorry, you caught me getting out of the shower."

"Um...uh...hi," she stammered. She tried not to let her mind wander to him in a shower, soaping up those abs and that chest. Even though it was still early in the summer, his chest was already tanned. The smooth skin of his shoulder was marred with a quarter-sized scar that looked suspiciously like a bullet wound.

"Can I help you with something or did you stop by to torture me again?" he asked.

"Oh, gosh, no." The shower scene had her flustered, and Sunny thrust forth the plate of brownies. "I really wanted to say how sorry I am about that. It was just a misunderstanding. I saw your car behind me and I thought you were following me. And I let my imagination get away from me and I thought you were going to attack me. A single girl can't be too careful, you know." *Did she really just tell him she was single?* Her mouth was dry, she was talking too fast, and she couldn't stop staring at his chest. An inch long line of scar tissue ran diagonally across his left pec, and Sunny had an insane urge to reach up and run her finger along the pale white line.

She took a deep breath and tried to slow her words. "My name is Sunny, and I live next door. I made you some brownies and was hoping we could just put this whole crazy-rapist thing behind us and start over. I really am sorry."

"Warm brownies are a good start," he said, drawing her attention back to his face. He smiled mischievously. "In retrospect, I can see how you may have been scared when you thought I had followed you home." He stepped back from the door, with almost a look of 'I dare you' in his blue eyes. "Want to come in and join me for one? I've got milk."

"Okay, I guess, maybe just one." Sunny moved past him into the cool front room of the house and caught her breath as he reached behind her to shut the door. His arm barely brushed hers, and she could make out the tattooed shape of a shield across his forearm, the lettering too small to read. She hoped he couldn't hear the thump of her heart. She was both thrilled and a little scared to be in the house alone with him as she followed his faded jean-clad behind into the kitchen.

He set the brownies on the counter. As he reached into the cabinet for glasses, she couldn't help but admire his muscled forearms as she watched him flex. He turned and gave her a slightly cocky smile that told her she had been caught checking him out, and that possibly he had flexed on purpose. Sunny looked out the kitchen window, grateful that at least she hadn't actually begun to drool.

"The milk's in the fridge. Why don't you pour while I find a shirt?" He headed down the hall away from the kitchen.

Figuring it would take a few minutes to pull a shirt on over those amazing pecs, Sunny decided to look around and see if she could figure out where Walter was or what this guy was doing here. She quickly rifled through the mail sitting haphazardly on the counter. Nothing there but some junk mail and a notification that Walter may have already won two million dollars from Publishers Clearing House. *Wouldn't Ed McMahon be surprised if this shirtless guy opened the door? I'm not sure which would hit the ground first, the giant check or Ed's jaw.*

Sunny opened the fridge to a scant offering of milk, eggs, cheese, lunchmeat, and an assortment of condiments in the door. No clues there. She could live for a week on scrambled eggs and bologna sandwiches.

*Why am I letting Edna's paranoia get to me? Could I be this desperate for excitement that I'm looking for clues between the mayonnaise and a bottle of ketchup?*

She finished pouring the second glass of milk when her mystery man ambled back into the kitchen. He was still barefoot but now wore a washed-out blue t-shirt depicting a group of stick figures roasting hot dogs around a campfire and the caption, *IT'S ALL FUN AND GAMES 'TIL SOMEBODY LOSES A WIENER.*

"Nice shirt," she said and tried not to laugh at the juvenile humor.

"Thanks." He picked up a brownie and took a bite. "Nice brownies." His tone held an undercurrent of innuendo but she couldn't tell if he was flirting with her or not. He finished his first brownie, took a swig of milk, picked up a second one, and sat down at the round kitchen table.

"I'm Jake Landon, by the way," he said, before sinking his teeth into the brownie.

"It's nice to meet you," she said, meaning it. "So how do you know Walter?"

The smile fell from his face, and Jake's eyes suddenly couldn't meet hers. He stared out the window into the yard. "We're related."

"Related how?"

"Related, as in family. What, are you writing a book?"

Sunny leaned back, surprised at his snappish remark. "No, sorry."

"No. I'm sorry." Jake sighed. He returned his gaze to hers. "Look, it's a long, boring story. Let's talk about you, huh?" His smile was back, and he asked, "What do you do?"

She spent the next fifteen minutes regaling him with stories of second-grader high-jinx and the office gossip of fellow teachers.

"You must really love your job," he said. "Your face

lights up whenever you mention the kids. It's kinda cute."

Sunny blushed to her toes. *I must have skipped the chapter in the Man-Manual on conversation because nothing could be less exciting than some semi-adorable stories about kids to reel in the men.*

"What do you do?" she asked, hoping to divert the attention from herself and her obvious lack of clever conversational skills.

"Oh, a little of this and a little of that. Did I see you have a dog?"

"Yeah, that's Beau. He's my room-mate, cat-chaser, and garbage disposal all rolled into one. Do you have any pets?" She mentally kicked herself for starting another titillating train of conversation.

"Nope. Just me. I'm not home a lot, so it's hard to keep a pet."

"A little this-and-that requires long hours, huh?" *Okay, I can still be a little witty.*

"Exactly." He got up and put his empty glass in the sink.

"So, where is Walter?" she asked, trying for innocent nonchalance. "I haven't seen him around in awhile."

"I don't really know. I got in late last night, and I thought he would be here when I arrived." His face held a mixture of anger and barely disguised hurt. "He told me where to find the hide-a-key, so I let myself in. I've been waiting for him to show up."

"That's weird. Walter is always around. I can't even remember the last time I saw him."

"That is weird," Jake agreed. Then he deftly changed the subject and asked her to tell him about the neighborhood.

Sunny filled him in on who lived where and the inner-workings of the small cul-de-sac. He laughed at her description of Edna, whose house flanked his other side. Sunny didn't share Edna's late night observation of his arrival or her suspicions that he had a gun tucked into his well-fitting Levi's.

He chuckled. "I can't wait to meet her."

"She's a hoot. You'll love her."

Sunny relaxed into the conversation as they chatted like old friends. She liked the sound of his laugh, but still noticed how adept he was at changing the subject at any mention of his *suspicious* family relationship to Walter.

Glancing at the clock above the stove, Sunny realized over an hour had flown by. "I'd better get going. I didn't mean to take up your whole morning."

"I liked talking to you. It's nice to know someone in the neighborhood."

"If you need someone to throw frozen meat nuggets at you, I'm your gal."

He laughed as he walked her to the door. "Seriously, Sunny, I'm glad you came by this morning. Thanks for the brownies." *There it was again. Either he was flirting with me or he had a seriously sexy way of saying 'brownies'.*

"You're very welcome." Sunny headed across the lawn. Beau scratched and whined at the kitchen door. "See ya around," she called, as Jake waved and closed the front door.

She found herself grinning as she remembered how he caught her checking him out. Edna had to be mistaken. He obviously knew Walter somehow, and she never saw evidence of a gun or anything suspicious in the house. Although, she had only been in the kitchen and living room. *Maybe if I had asked to use the bathroom, I would have found his Hit-Man Aftershave in the medicine cabinet.* And he did have that scar which made her heart race a little, both out of fear and excitement.

Sunny let herself in and knelt on the floor to pet Beau. He was licking her face hello when suddenly the house was rocked with a violent explosion!

A piece of concrete crashed through Sunny's kitchen window, and glass rained down on her back as she flattened herself onto Beau. He whined beneath her, and she hugged his trembling body. *Or maybe that was me trembling.*

She waited a beat to make sure no other explosions followed then slowly raised to her knees. She ran her hands along Beau's sides and it appeared that neither she nor Beau were bleeding, which surprised her considering the amount of broken glass on the kitchen floor.

Sunny heard the crackling of fire before her head cleared the now shattered window. She peered out to see Walter's garage engulfed in flames. *Oh, no!* Her first thought was of Walter's classic convertible he kept in the second bay of the garage and how much he loved that car.

"Sunny! Where are you?" Jake's panicked voice called from the yard.

The kitchen door scraped along the broken glass as Sunny pulled it open. She felt the heat from the fire press against her as she stepped outside. "I'm here." Her voice was weak with shock.

Relief washed over Jake's face as he rushed toward her and pulled her into his arms. "I'm so glad you're okay," he said into her hair. "I already called 911."

His heart pounded against her chest, and she held

on tightly for a moment as she closed her eyes and breathed in his clean, soap scent.

Sunny pushed back and looked frantically around. "We've got to check on Edna!"

No sooner had she started to run across Walter's front lawn than she saw Edna stumble across the driveway, moving in the direction of Sunny's house. Her clothes were dusty, and she looked dazed. A trickle of blood ran down the left side of her face, stemming from a nasty gash above her eye.

"Edna, are you okay?" As Sunny wrapped her arms around Edna, she was aware of how small and frail the older woman really was. Edna's big personality couldn't make up for her petite shoulders that now shook in Sunny's embrace. Tears of relief blurred Sunny's vision.

"Yes, honey, I'm all right." Edna gripped Sunny's arms to steady herself. "The blast knocked me to my knees, and I think I bumped my head on the kitchen counter. Do you know what happened?"

"Walter's garage exploded," Jake explained, coming up behind them. "Are you all right, ma'am?"

"You!" Edna cried, staring at Jake in surprise. "Who are you? What are you doing here? Are you responsible for this?" Edna fired questions at him, her face a register of fear and shock.

"I'm Jake Landon. I've been staying here. Walter's my...relative," he said.

"Edna, it's okay. Jake's a friend," Sunny said. She had never seen Edna so upset.

They heard the sirens of the fire trucks, and Jake ran to the side of the house for the garden hose.

He sprayed water on the garage and their surrounding houses, including Walter's, to keep the flames from spreading. The fire trucks pulled into the driveway, and several yellow-coated men piled out, like clowns from a small car. They worked quickly in unison to put out the garage fire.

Edna and Sunny were wrapped in scratchy wool blankets and led to an ambulance that had pulled in behind the fire engines.

Within an hour, the fire was out. The two women watched, huddled together, holding hands, as the garage folded into itself and collapsed into a smoky pile of rubble.

❀❀❀

That Wednesday night, Sunny and Edna walked into Starbucks to the excited and shocked gasps of the Pleasant Valley Page Turners Book Club. Sunny had called Maggie and Cassie, her two best friends from college, and filled them in on the explosion at Walter's, but this was the first time they had all seen each other since the fire. The smell of dark coffee mingled with Maggie's expensive perfume as she hugged Sunny, but the real attention was showered on Edna as she limped toward the book club members.

"Edna, honey, are you all right?" Cassie embraced Edna and gently guided her to the table.

"Oh, thank you, dear. I'm sure I will be just fine." Edna eased into a chair, reveling in the role of the victim. She touched the large white bandage on her forehead. "The doctor insisted I needed stitches, but I told him I would be fine with just this little bandage."

Sunny rolled her eyes so hard she might have actually caught sight of her brain. *Hello. My house was rocked by the explosion too. Who's pulling out a chair for me?* Okay, maybe that was a little selfish, especially because while Edna stumbled from her home, bleeding from a head wound, Sunny had been wrapped in Jake's arms, pressed against his amazing chest.

Sunny shook herself to clear those thoughts from her head. Jake was smokin' hot, but his arrival to their quiet neighborhood, coinciding with Walter's garage going up in flames, still made her suspicious. What really worried her was the fact that Walter was still missing. Having a huge fireball on his property should have drawn him out of the woodwork. She had overheard Jake speaking with one of the firemen about a missing person's report being filed for Walter, so at least he had taken that step, but she still felt like he was hiding something.

Though tempted to blurt out her suspicions about Jake and the odd timing of Walter's disappearance, Sunny was afraid she wouldn't be able to talk about Jake without letting on that although she was suspicious of him, part of her still lusted after his body. And even if she played it up, Edna did get hurt, and Sunny didn't want to take the attention away from her.

"You look like you recently had a lobotomy," Maggie told Edna. Her usual sarcasm didn't hold much weight as she tenderly touched Edna's shoulder after sliding into the seat next to hers.

"I'll get us our coffee," Sunny told Edna.

"Oh thank you, dear," she replied with a heavy sigh, reminding Sunny more of Scarlett O'Hara than her elderly neighbor.

Sunny returned to the table a few minutes later to see no one had handed Edna an Oscar yet, but it wasn't from her lack of trying. She would have to settle for the frothy concoction of a mocha java chip frappucino with whipped cream and chocolate sprinkles that Sunny set in front of her before pulling up a chair next to Cassie's niece, Piper.

Sunny took a sip of her plain vanilla latte and tossed her purse into the multi-colored pile of bags under the table. Piper's gray backpack leaned against Maggie's expensive leather bag, which lay across Cassie's denim purse, a quarter-sized stain visible just under the strap. "So, what did you all think of the book?"

"It was sooo depressing," Cassie said. She tended to like upbeat books where everyone lived happily ever after. The mother of two, she had been married for close to fifteen years, and lived her own happily ever after with an adoring husband. They had met in college, and Matt had fallen for this fun, flirty, petite blonde with a mass of curly hair that framed her cute pixie face.

"It's about a kid who had a nervous breakdown. It's supposed to be depressing." Maggie flipped a lock of her long, dark hair over her shoulder, and took a sip of her latte. "Gosh, I had the best day today. I found a great parking spot, my hair didn't frizz, and I had the most wonderful nervous breakdown."

"I started to read it last week, but there was a *Sex and the City* marathon on cable and I just love those girls–they're so sassy," Edna said.

"How far did you get?" Sunny asked.

"Pretty far, a good twenty pages or so, enough to know Holden was a sniveling whiner who needed to grow up," she said.

"That's what the book is about, Edna," Piper said. "I loved this book."

Cassie's niece, Piper Denton, had come to live with her several weeks ago. She was finishing out her senior year of high school, and with her all black 'emo' outfits and dark eyeliner, Piper seemed to also be trying to figure out some of the growing up stuff.

Maggie stretched her long legs as she crossed one gorgeous high-heel booted leg over the other. "It felt like I was reading a blog from a sixteen-year-old kid who was venting all his anger at the world and grownups in general." With her lawyer's salary, she could afford to always dress to the height of fashion. Her tall, slim build, olive skin, and dark brown eyes cut an impressive figure in her power suits as she blasted defendants in the courtroom. Her gorgeous looks clashed with her piercing tongue and biting sarcasm. Her intelligence only fueled her dry wit, and her deadpan comedic remarks frequently had the group in stitches. Though Sunny couldn't help but envy how her expensive wardrobe fit her so well, the compassion and loyalty Maggie had for her friends made up for any fits of the green-eyed monster.

"I thought it was boring," Cassie said. "The kid smoked, drank, and basically hated everything." She snuck a glance at Piper, who wore a bored expression on her face as she stared out the window.

"I think our next book should have some more spice in it," Edna said. "I like those scenes with the hot stud who gets steamy with the busty girl next door. This book didn't have any shower scenes or mention a single 'throbbing member'."

"Yeah, well, I haven't seen a 'throbbing member' in so long that I forgot what they look like," Sunny said, and they all hooted with laughter.

Maggie smirked. "I think you'd recognize one if you saw it again. They still look like a worm wearing a turtleneck."

Edna giggled as she doubled over in her chair. "Oh stop. I think I peed a little bit."

Cassie smiled. "So, Sunny, what can we do to get one back in your life again? Sometimes they're fun to have around." A blush crept across her cheeks at her bold comment. "But only when you're older, and in love." She stared pointedly at Piper, whose attention was now riveted back on the group of women.

"Or older, and in need of love..." Edna added, a devilish grin on her face.

"What I *need* is another latte," Sunny said, as their laughter died down. Edna's mention of a shower scene had her mind returning to Jake's half-naked body and the fantasy of her, him and a bar of soap. Again, she considered telling them about her flirtation with Jake, but she didn't need to get involved with another man who was all wrong for her. It was easier to stay home with Beau and fantasize about an affair with her fictitious romance novel pirate.

"What you *need* is a man," Edna said. "It's been too long since you've even been out on a date."

"What does she need a man for?" Maggie asked. "As long as she can run a lawn mower, knows a good mechanic, and has a fresh supply of Duracells, she doesn't need one."

"Seriously, Sunny, when was the last time you went out on a date?" Cassie asked, ignoring Maggie's comment.

"Yes," Edna said. "Inquiring minds want to know."

Sunny fidgeted with a napkin as all eyes turned to her. "Gosh, seems like only a few weeks ago. You know, that date with what's-his-name?"

In truth, it had been months since Sunny had been on a real date. So much of her time revolved around her job as a teacher. The fact that she worked primarily with women, and didn't like to club-hop sorely diminished her chances of meeting eligible men. Life had sort of settled into a routine of working, coming home, walking Beau, then curling up on the sofa with dinner, a good book or a movie, and collapsing into bed around ten o'clock. Her only sister had moved out of the country last year in an effort to find herself, and she was lucky to hear from her mother once a month. Her weekends were spent around the house, cleaning, gardening or hanging out with her girlfriends.

Said girlfriends now watched her intently, and Maggie had that one eyebrow-raised look she got with defendants who weren't always telling 'the truth, the whole truth, and nothing but the truth, so help me God.' "Liar."

"Well, it seems like a few weeks ago."

"Girls, we've got to help her. Now my friend has a grandson–" Edna began.

"Stop," Sunny cried. "Don't go any further. I'm

perfectly happy to find my own man. I don't even know if I'm searching for my own man." Suddenly that vanilla latte was not setting very well as her stomach churned with the thought of a set up with one of Edna's friends' grandsons. She hated all this attention focused on her and her failed attempts to find or hold on to a guy.

"That's your problem," Cassie said. "I think Edna's got a point. You've had plenty of time to find a man on your own. And, frankly, you stink. If this were your job, you would be fired. In fact, you are fired."

"I'm fired from my own love life?"

"You're fired from managing your own love life," Cassie continued. "I hereby declare The Pleasant Valley Page Turners as the new managers of Sunny's non-existent love life."

"Wait a minute–" Sunny said, the latte now threatening to come back up.

"You've already waited minutes, hours, days, weeks, years. Forget it. We are now in charge. We will make it our mission to find you a man or else."

Sunny knew Cassie was used to leading troops of moms into getting fired-up for PTA projects and bake sales, but this was her life (or lack of life, it seemed) they were rallying around.

The girls seemed to eat up the 'Grand Pooh-Bah' Cassie's words as they nodded and edged forward on their seats.

"I know where they do speed-dating," Edna said. "I tried it once, but those men were only interested in my body."

Sunny almost spit out her mouthful of coffee. "I'm not speed-dating."

Cassie opened her planner. "I think you're on to something, Edna. Let's designate Saturdays as date days, and we each take turns setting Sunny up on dates throughout the summer. By fall, we should have a match. You've just started your summer break,

Sunny, and I know you've got a giant stack of novels you're planning to read, but you'll still have plenty of time to devote to finding Mr. Right."

*Finding Mr. Right? I didn't even know if I was looking for Mr. Maybe.* Things were really getting carried away here. No one was paying attention to her or to what she wanted. But what did she want? Her life was safe and quiet. Had it only been a couple of days since she had wished for more excitement? She feared she was about to get her wish.

Cassie's persuasiveness took over, and Sunny found herself agreeing to open up the next six Saturdays of the summer to let each of the women set her up on one blind date of their choice. In some odd twist of trying to include her, they even let Piper have one shot at matchmaking stardom. Maggie, always the lawyer, negotiated an extra two Saturdays, in case of illness, hurricanes, tornadoes, or other acts of God that might interfere with one of the Saturday nights.

So the evening progressed from *Catcher in the Rye* to a game of Catch Me If you Can, with Sunny as the prize.

❀❀❀

After leaving Starbucks, the Page Turners took in a chick flick, then ended the evening in their favorite pizza place downtown, destroying two large pizzas and a Caesar salad. The pizza turned Sunny's stomach queasy every time the topic of her dating life resurfaced, and she continually tried to veer the conversation back to the movie.

"That ending was so cheesy," Maggie said. Edna and Sunny had given her a ride home, and they sat in front of her house as she collected her bag and complained about the movie. "It was so unrealistic to have all that occur exactly in that order so he would just happen to see her again on that exact train."

"I liked it," Sunny said. "Sometimes all the planets do align just right, and you can have a happy ending."

Maggie's phone beeped, and she dug through her purse and pulled free her Blackberry. "Speaking of endings, it's the asshole himself."

Maggie's ex-husband, aka Chad the Cheater, had left Maggie and their teenage sons, Drew and Dylan, sixteen months ago on an ordinary Tuesday night. He'd tried to put a romantic spin on his affair, but when it was all said and done, Maggie Hayes, successful attorney-at-law, had been left for a Hooters' waitress named Sapphire.

Maggie now held up her phone and read the text aloud. "Sorry, won't be able to make Drew's thing this weekend. Sapphire and I will be in Mexico. Tell him I'll make it up to him later."

"He is such an idiot," she said. "Drew's *thing* this weekend is his high school graduation party but evidently Chad's *thing* comes before anything else in his life right now."

Sunny put a hand on her shoulder. "I'm so sorry."

Maggie sighed, and Sunny knew her heart ached for her seventeen year old son. Sunny hugged her, then Maggie got out of the car, slamming the door behind her.

Watching her beautiful friend cross the lawn, Sunny was struck with doubt over this blind date scheme. Both Sunny and Maggie had been burned by men, and if a gorgeous, intelligent woman like Maggie didn't have a man, what chance did Sunny have of finding not even a Mr. Maybe, but a Mr. Might Be Okay?

*Not bad.*

Sunny surveyed herself in the full length mirror that hung from the closet door. It was Saturday night, and she was ready for her first blind date. Maggie had called a few days before with the news.

"All right, I've got your first guy," she had said as Sunny answered the phone Thursday afternoon.

Sunny gulped. She thought it would take longer than a few days before the 'dating game' would begin. "I don't know if I'm ready."

"You'll be fine. You just have to start," Maggie said.

"Who is he?"

"His name is Blaine Bishop. He's a rich stockbroker who is a client of mine. He's divorced, no kids and did I mention rich?"

"What does he look like?" Not that looks were the most important part of a man, but a certain suspicious new neighbor had been creeping into her night time fantasies and a new hunky guy would be a great distraction.

"He looks like an attractive, rich guy."

"Nice. Any other details, besides his wallet thickness?"

"Sunny, would I set you up with a dog? No. He's tall, has dark hair, a great tan and he works out."

"Well, he sounds all right, I guess."

"Great," Maggie said. "He'll pick you up at seven on

Saturday night, and I'm sure he will take you somewhere snazzy, so dress up."

*My first date starts tonight with a man I don't know, going somewhere I've never been. How did I get myself into this?* She took a deep breath and threw her shoulders back. *I was looking for more excitement in my life, right?*

She wore the classic black dress and pumps for her date with Blaine that evening. She'd chosen a halter style dress to accentuate the good cleavage of her top half, and an A-line style to de-accentuate the bad cleavage of her bottom half.

It had been several days since the garage explosion. Edna had called a handyman, and he had replaced their broken windows and helped to repair the damage to their homes.

Sunny had seen Jake outside, paintbrush in hand, working to restore Walter's house to its original state. He wasn't allowed around the perimeter of the actual garage, but she was impressed that he was taking the time and effort to try to fix the side of the house where the fire had destroyed the paint job.

They still hadn't heard from Walter, and Sunny was actually starting to worry about him now. Jake's blue eyes took on a strained look the last time she asked him if he had heard any news on his 'relative's' whereabouts. He claimed there was no word yet. She still couldn't figure out what his game was. She had watched him flip through Walter's mail as he brought it into the house, but she had also seen him water the flower beds around the yard.

Walter took great pride in his yard and his flower gardens. The book club had met at Sunny's house the week Piper came to live with Cassie, and Walter had joined in that week because they had a read a book about the depression and he could offer some real life insight.

Walter had formed a grandfatherly bond with Piper,

inviting her to help with his flower beds and teaching her how to garden. Sunny loved watching Piper blossom under his grandfatherly attentiveness.

That spring, the two could often be seen quietly working side-by-side in Walter's backyard. His precious flowerbeds were now ravaged by fire and his lawn was patchy with burned-out grass in the areas closest to the garage. The grass was muddy and trampled as different sets of firemen had clomped around the burn site, and though they had dug through the rubble for hours, they seemed no closer to finding a cause for the fire.

Sunny's thoughts stole back to how it felt to be in Jake's arms as he held her after the explosion, but she worked to dampen them. She barely knew him and was still suspicious of why he'd shown up out of the blue and how he deftly changed the subject whenever she tried to ask him about himself or his relationship with Walter.

*Grrr!* Why was she thinking about Jake when her future Mr. Right could be on his way to pick her up right now? She hadn't been on a date in so long, maybe she was using the idea of Jake as an excuse to sabotage her evening's plans. But that wasn't fair to these women who cared about her happiness. Her friends were so hell-bent on this blind date idea, Sunny felt like she needed to at least give it the old college try. And in all honesty, she was a little excited to see who would show up behind door number one.

Dragging herself back to the present, Sunny dabbed on a little more lip gloss, then took a final look in the mirror. She decided to go with bare legs instead of nylons, and just to be daring on her first date, chose a black lacy bra and matching black thong panty. She felt sexy and racy and ready…

*Ding-Dong.*

*Oh crap. Not ready. Definitely not ready.*

"Pull yourself together," Sunny said out loud to her

reflection. Then she put what she hoped was a genuine smile on her face, walked down the stairs, and opened her front door to one of the most gorgeous men she had ever seen.

He stood before her, all six foot, three inches of him. His dark and wavy hair probably cost a small fortune to have cut so it looked like he was just overdue for another one. He had that scruffy five o'clock shadow thing going on, and wore an expensive, tailored suit over a light blue shirt open at the neck.

"Hi, I'm Blaine Bishop, Maggie's friend," he said with a smile that didn't quite meet his dark eyes. He gave her an appraising look, as he surveyed her from top to bottom, but he kept his face impassive so she couldn't tell if he liked what he saw.

"Uh, hi. I'm Sunny," she lamely answered, and stretched out her hand to shake his.

Before he could take her hand, a golden ball of fur ran to the door and leapt for joy that someone had come to visit him. Beau proceeded to sniff Blaine's shoes, his pant legs, and his crotch. Blaine did the keep-your-knees-together dance of non-dog lovers while he used his left hand to keep Beau away from his expensive inseam.

"Beau, get back." Sunny grabbed for his collar and pulled him back into the house. She snatched her purse from the hall table and pulled the front door shut, leaving Beau to whine and cry at their departure. "Sorry about that. He gets kind of excited when he meets new people."

As she turned from the door, Sunny noticed Blaine nonchalantly lean down and try to brush off Beau's blonde hair that clung to the legs of his black pants. *Definitely not a dog person.*

They crossed the lawn as he clicked his key fob, and with two quick beeps, he unlocked the doors to his silver Porsche Carrera. He opened the passenger door, and Sunny slid into the sleek, black leather seat.

Unfortunately, as she slid in, her dress had slithered up, and her bare butt cheek caught on the seat and made a small squeaking sound. Blaine had been in the process of closing the door as she quickly adjusted her dress, and she fervently hoped he hadn't heard or seen her dilemma. *Stupid thong underwear!*

Blaine opened the driver's door, slid into his seat (sans any peculiar fart noises), and started the car with practiced efficiency. He pulled into the street and headed toward the highway.

"Hope you like Italian. I thought we would try Maggio's, if it's all right with you." He named an upscale Italian restaurant centered in the downtown area.

"Great. I love pasta," Sunny replied, and thought, for a moment, she saw a smirk sneak across his face.

He shifted gears as they merged onto the highway, and she inhaled deeply, taking in the scent of leather and his expensive aftershave. It was a mix of woodsy musk and...and...poo? She wrinkled her nose in distaste, and wondered if maybe he had a spastic colon, or had Mexican food for lunch. She snuck a glance at his face, and saw he wore the same expression, and he looked at her with poorly disguised disgust on his face.

He thought that smell was her! It must have been that dang squeak when she got in the car. She shifted in her seat, and the smell of poo again wafted in her direction. Sunny looked down and *oh, no*! Her left heel had a big glob of dog poop stuck to it! When she crossed the lawn, she must have stepped in a fresh pile of Beau-B-Doo.

"Dang it. I'm really sorry, but I seemed to have stepped in a little dog poo on my way to your car," she said, her face crimson with embarrassment.

Sunny hit the button for the car window as she slipped her shoe off and proceeded to hold it out the window. "I'll keep my shoe out here until we get to the restaurant, and I can clean it off."

His look of horror as he glanced to the floorboard of his car then to her shoe as it dangled out the window was almost comical until he began gliding into the neighboring lane.

"Watch out!" she cried.

As he swerved back into his lane, Sunny's elbow bumped into the window frame which knocked the shoe loose and sent it careening into the oncoming traffic.

"Oh no! My shoe!" she cried. "We have to go back!"

Blaine pulled to the side of the road and flicked the lever to start his hazards flashing. "I'll get it," he said, with a sigh.

Sunny watched him retreat into the blinking hazard lights as she scrunched down into her seat in humiliation.

Within moments, he was back and dropped what was left of the shoe into her lap. "I think it may have been run-over."

A small whimper escaped her as Sunny regarded her beautiful black pump. The sides were smashed in, it was covered in dust, and the heel was completely missing. Since the heel was the source of the offensive doggie doo, at least that problem was now solved.

"Um, I'm sorry about your shoe." Blaine eased back into traffic as Sunny rummaged a tissue from the depths of her purse and began to wipe at the mess her shoe had become.

Not really knowing what else to do, they proceeded to the restaurant. Though humiliated and bummed about ruining her best black pumps, Sunny was also starving, and she couldn't very well back out now. She thought about what the book club gals would want her to do. She put her shoe back on as well as she could, so when Blaine opened the door of the car, Sunny stepped out and held her head high as she walked lopsided up the steps of Maggio's.

All thoughts of the shoe incident left her head as Sunny stepped through the doors and was engulfed in the heavenly scent of garlic and simmering tomato sauce. Maggio's was fabulous, and the sights and smells of the restaurant renewed her faith that there was hope to salvage the rest of their date. Blaine did have good taste.

"Reservations for Bishop," Blaine informed the Maitre D', who took one subtle glance at Sunny's feet before he turned and issued a "Follow me, please".

He showed them to their table, discreetly setting Sunny in the back corner chair so her feet would be hidden from the other patrons. She flashed a thankful smile at him as he passed her a menu and gave her a slight nod of acknowledgement.

Sunny loved Italian food and ordered the Tuscany Trio of lasagna, ravioli, and a portion of fettuccine alfredo.

"You certainly have a healthy appetite," her date commented, as he ordered a spinach salad with crumbled gorgonzola cheese. The waiter took their menus and turned toward the kitchen, but not before Sunny caught the small smirk on his stupid, twenty-something face.

She flushed. *Note to self. Next time, find out what your date is getting* before *you order.* Not knowing how to respond, she let it go and changed the subject. "So, tell me about being a stockbroker." Sunny smiled and tried to look interested.

That comment led to a forty-five minute litany of high finance, the stock market, and the world economy. Sunny was lost in his dialogue of numbers, and terms of annual percentage rates, and front and rear-load yields.

*Frankly, it all sounds like a bunch of rear-load to me.* She listened half-heartedly as she plowed through her dinner and several glasses of wine.

Sunny didn't realize how many glasses until it was

time to leave, and she stood up and began a one-heeled sway toward the door.

Blaine drove her home as he continued his diatribe of today's market value, interest rates, and blah, blah, blah. She tried to focus on the panel of the glove compartment, but the passing lights of traffic made her head spin and her stomach lurch.

They pulled up to her house, and again Blaine opened her door, and assisted her out of the car.

"You're a real gentleman, ya know that?" she slurred. "I had a really nice time tonight. Except for the dog poop, and my best black pump getting crushed, and all the boring finance talk."

*Sometimes I open my mouth and words pour forth before my brain has time to catch up and stop them.*

"Yes, well, we'll have to do this again some time." Blaine leaned forward to kiss her goodnight.

"Thanks for dinner," she replied as a small hiccup-belch escaped from her lips.

His kiss diverted to a gently pressed peck on the cheek, and he hurriedly made his escape back down the driveway.

Sunny noticed he avoided walking through the front lawn, and as she thought over the night, she burst into a fit of drunken giggles as she inserted her key into the lock. She shut the door, slid to the floor, and gasped for breath as her giggles continued.

Sunny's laughter died as she grasped the missing element of her entrance into the house. Where was her eighty-pound welcome wagon?

"Beau. Here boy," she called into the silent house.

She opened the front door, ran out into the yard, and yelled again for the dog.

"Did you lose this?" A voice called from the neighboring yard as Jake opened his door, and Beau raced out to greet her.

"How did you...?"

"He was in my front yard when I came home

tonight." Jake crossed the yard to where Sunny now sat in the grass, hugging Beau to her chest in relief.

"Oh Beau, you naughty dog," she scolded. Sunny tried to get to her feet and swayed slightly.

"Are you okay?" Jake took her elbow and put his arm around her shoulder to support her. She leaned into his chest and felt her body melt into the safe cocoon of his arms.

He began to walk her toward the front door when it suddenly hit. The gut-wrenching, oh-my-gosh feeling of 'I'm going to be sick–now!' She took two steps forward, fell to her knees, and heaved several glasses of wine and a large portion of Tuscany Trio into the azalea bushes in front of her house.

❀❀❀

Half an hour later, after she had taken a warm shower and brushed her teeth, Sunny found herself sitting opposite Jake on the couch in her living room. He had made her a cup of tea with a side of aspirin, and then dimmed the lights to spare her aching head.

"Feel better?" he asked.

"Yes, thanks." Neither of them were going to bring up the part of the evening where he had graciously lifted her from the azalea bush and discreetly pulled her dress back down over her bare bum cheeks she had been flashing him as she *ralphed* a hundred and sixty dollar meal onto her shrubbery.

He had actually been very considerate as he helped her inside, got her upstairs, and deposited her into the bathroom.

Now, Sunny sat facing him, her legs tucked under her as she curled into the corner of the sofa. The shower helped, but she was still a tad bit drunk, and the dimly lit atmosphere had her feeling safe and a little chatty. With her dog on the floor beside her, and a warm cup of tea in her hands, Sunny may have found herself sharing too many details of her life to a man she had only known a short time.

She told him about her college boyfriend, Mitch, and how he had dumped her after two years of being together, with her financing the majority of his schooling. She told him of her struggles with fad diets, and trying to always lose that extra fifteen pounds. She talked about her friends, and spilled the whole sordid story of the six blind dates and the hunt for a 'suitable match for Sunny'. She even ended up telling him every rotten detail of her date with Blaine. He stared at her incredulously when she got to the dog poo part, then he burst out laughing. By the end of the story, they were both busting-up.

"You are something, Sunny," he said, when she had finally wound down.

"Yeah, I know," she whispered, as they each realized how close they now sat. Her pulse quickened as she looked into his blue eyes. He reached up and gently touched her face. Tracing his fingers along the line of her jaw, his thumb came to rest on the edge of her lip, and he softly ran his thumb along her bottom lip.

Sunny drew in a quick breath, and a delicious warmth spread through her body. She tried to think rationally about what she was doing, but couldn't tear her eyes away from his. Her body betrayed her mind as she leaned closer, her lips yearning for the feel of his.

Slowly, he leaned in, his hand still cupping her face, and pressed his mouth to hers in a tender kiss. He kissed her once more softly, then the kiss turned more urgent as his lips parted, and his hand moved up to tangle in her hair.

Sunny's arms went around his shoulders, and she plastered herself to his body. He gently laid her back, his other hand splayed across her lower back, guiding her down as his lips continued to caress hers. His touch was whisper soft as he ran his hand through her hair, down her arm, and across her stomach, his thumb barely grazing the underside of her breast. Her body arched up to press closer against his as he trailed soft kisses along her throat and then...

The sun poured through her living room window as Sunny woke to find herself sprawled across her sofa, covered with the afghan that usually lay folded along the back of the couch. Her last memory had been of kissing Jake, then...*oh crud. I must have passed out as we were kissing. He must think I'm an idiot. Or a lush. Or an idiotic lush.*

A horrible thought crossed her mind. How far had they gone? She raised the afghan and sighed in relief to find she was still fully dressed.

*How can I face him again?* Sunny groaned at her own stupidity as Beau padded over and began to lick her face.

"I can't believe you ruined your Jimmy Choo!" wailed Cassie. "Those were great shoes."

"I can't believe you wasted that meal by hucking it into your bushes," Maggie exclaimed. "I noticed when I pulled up that your azaleas looked lovely. Barf must be a good fertilizer."

It was Wednesday night, and the book club gathered around Edna's kitchen table. She had made a marvelous chocolate cake, and they were indulging in cups of coffee and luscious chocolate icing as Sunny filled the group in on her date with Blaine.

Mortified, she had described the dog poo incident, and the girls had all screamed with laughter. When she had gotten to the part about puking into the azaleas, Sunny thought Maggie would wet her pants, she laughed so hard.

Maggie wiped the tears from her eyes with a napkin. "Okay, so maybe he wasn't the best match for you. I didn't really know him that well, but he was rich *and* gorgeous!"

"I think he was looking for someone a little more gorgeous than me," Sunny told her, "and classier and thinner."

"And with less poo adorning her outfit," Edna said, which set the girls off on another round of shrieking giggles.

The book club loved their weekly Wednesday night

meeting. They were lenient about finishing the book on time, but tried to read a different book each week. Usually their discussions veered from the books they were reading to happenings in their various lives. They listened to and supported each other through the day-to-day stuff, such as Maggie's divorce, and Cassie's recent acquisition of Piper. They rotated between Starbucks and their different houses, sometimes bringing brown bag suppers, while other times just having coffee and dessert. If a great chick flick was in town, like the week before, the Page Turners would venture out to the theatre, then go eat together. It was a loose routine of a tight group of women, and they all counted on their Wednesday night get-togethers.

"So, what's with the hotty in the house next door?" Maggie asked.

From Edna's kitchen table, they could see Jake in the backyard. He watched the firemen dig through the rubble of the burned out garage as they patiently excavated items that hadn't been destroyed in the fire. He had on his usual outfit of t-shirt and butt-hugging faded jeans. Another man had arrived about ten minutes before, and the two men had their heads bent toward each other in discussion.

"His name is Jake," Sunny explained. "He claims that he's somehow related to Walter." She hoped the other girls didn't notice the way her cheeks flamed when she said his name.

Sunny hadn't divulged the last part of her evening with Blaine, where Jake and she had done the lip-lock before she passed out on the sofa. Sunny wanted to keep that to herself for now.

"You're blushing," Cassie cried. "You like this guy."

Sunny swallowed a bite of cake. "Well, I don't know. He is really cute."

Edna was unusually quiet as she watched out the window and gazed thoughtfully at Jake. "I think there's something we should tell you." She filled the girls in on the night Jake had mysteriously arrived. They gasped when she got to the part where he had a gun tucked into the back of his pants.

"What do you think was in that duffle bag?" Cassie asked, wide-eyed. "Money?"

"Maybe it was Walter's body," Piper chimed in.

"Gross," Sunny said. "Why would you say that?"

"Edna said she hadn't seen him around in awhile. Maybe this Jake guy killed him and chopped him up and is taking his body parts out a few at a time to dispose of them."

"Girl, you watch too much TV," Maggie said, shaking her head.

"Hey, it could happen. Maybe Walter was secretly rich, and Jake murdered him for his money or to get his house. He is living over there now. Maybe he just made up that story about being related to him." Piper's words all came out in a rush.

Sunny thought about the strange look that crossed Jake's face as he talked about his family relationship with Walter.

"I think we need to get rid of cable," Cassie said. "What kind of late night television are you watching to give you these ideas?"

"I watch that stuff too," Edna said, coming to Piper's defense. "On all those true-crime shows, it's always the nice neighbor guy who everyone thought was so great until they began digging up skeletons in his backyard."

They all jumped as a fist banged on Edna's back door. Letting out their collective breath, they laughed uneasily over getting caught up in Edna and Piper's ideas.

Speaking of the handsome devil himself, Jake stood outside Edna's door, accompanied by a light-haired man wearing khakis and a wrinkled suit coat.

"Sorry to bother you ladies, but we need to ask you a few questions," Jake said.

"Have a seat," Edna offered, always the gracious

hostess. "Want some cake?"

"No, thank you," Jake answered somberly. "This is Tom Mansfield – he's a detective looking into Walter's disappearance. You may have seen him out here the last few days."

Tom nodded to the women. "Afternoon, ladies. Sorry to interrupt your visit. Jake tells me you all are pretty close with Walter. We still don't know what or if anything has happened to him. We did find some things in the fire, and since Walter has no family around here and you all seem to know him pretty well, we hoped you could take a look at them."

The detective pulled three plastic baggies from his pocket and placed them gingerly on the table.

Edna gasped and reached for the center bag that contained a charred belt buckle with a soaring eagle etched into it. "This is Walter's belt buckle. His wife, Betty, gave it to him for one of their anniversaries. He loved the Bible verse about soaring like an eagle, and she found this for him in a shop downtown. He wore it every day and showed it to everyone. He loved to joke about trying to soar like an eagle while surrounded by turkeys. I'm sure this was his."

"And I definitely recognize this as Walter's," Sunny said softly, as she lifted a bag that held a pearl handled pocket knife. "He got it on a vacation to the Grand Canyon with Betty when they were first married. He used it to cut string or slice through the tape on a box or when he helped with little things at my house. One of the blades is a screwdriver head."

Tears sprung to Edna's eyes as she fingered the bag closest to her. It held what used to be a gold wedding band, now grayed and covered in ash. "What does this mean?"

"We're not sure yet, ma'am," Tom replied. "We found some other odd things in the debris, but we haven't identified them yet. We still have a lot of unanswered questions. The explosion caused the fire to burn hot and fast so we haven't ruled out anything at this point," he said.

They all sat in stunned silence.

"We're still investigating the cause of the explosion, and the whereabouts of Mr. Mead. Nothing is conclusive yet, but we appreciate your time and help in identifying these items." Tom collected the baggies and placed them back into his pocket.

"Have any of you noticed anything suspicious in the neighborhood or with Mr. Mead's behavior of late?" the detective asked.

They all looked at each other, then Piper cried, "He's suspicious!" and pointed at Jake. "Have you asked him why he showed up in the middle of the night? Nobody knows him. How do we even know he is related to Walter? Did you know he has a gun?"

Jake appeared shocked, and a strange look crossed his face. Guilt, perhaps?

Tom turned to Jake with an appraising eye and a look of mistrust on his face.

"I think Mr. Landon and I will continue our conversation outside." He and Jake headed for the kitchen door. "Thank you again for your time, ladies. You've been a big help." He said this last with an appreciative smile at Piper, who flushed and looked at the floor, her bravado now gone after her brazen accusations.

The detective took Jake by the arm and led him outside. The women couldn't hear what they were saying, but it wasn't for lack of trying as the group jumped up from the table and plastered themselves against the kitchen door and windows.

They slunk back to the table as the men disappeared into Walter's house.

"I'm sure Walter is fine," said Cassie, the eternal optimist. "This could all be a mistake."

"Walter would never go anywhere without his wedding ring and that belt buckle. He had those things with him every day," Edna explained quietly. "I think something really happened to him, girls."

They somberly finished their coffee and helped Edna clear the table, all deep in thought with memories of Walter, imagining what could have happened. Maggie and Cassie had spent so much time in this neighborhood, they both had formed an attachment to the friendly widower.

Gathering their purses to head out, Cassie suddenly gasped. "Oh Sunny, I almost forgot to tell you. I set up your next date for Saturday night."

"What?" Sunny croaked.

"I know it's probably not the best time to talk about it, but Matt has an old football buddy who moved back to town. His wife left him, and he and his little boy moved back a few months ago. I think his folks live here in town, and they are staying with them. I remember him a little from high school. He was cute anyway. But Matt thinks he's a nice guy and seems like a good dad. His name is Hank, and I gave him your number. I wouldn't bring it up right now, but he may call you tonight. He wants to take you to a baseball game this Saturday, I think."

"Great," Sunny replied. "I can't wait."

"Now, give this Hank a chance," Maggie said. "You agreed to go on six of these. You can't give up after one botched date with Blaine the boring stockbroker." She smiled, and some of the mixed tension left the room.

"All right, you win," Sunny said, giving in.

"Just clean up the dog poo in the yard before he shows up Saturday night," Cassie said, and they all laughed as they filed out the door.

The next day, Piper Denton walked through the bustling halls of her high school. Graduation was two days away, and the noise level was deafening as kids banged locker doors, yelled greetings to each other, and ran from one class to another. She wished she were already on summer break like Sunny, but the older grades stayed in session an extra week after the elementary schools.

She inhaled the scent of stale classrooms and floor wax with an underlying odor of sweaty gym clothes. *High schools all smell the same.* She stopped at her locker and absently turned the dial of her combination lock.

Piper had known her share of schools. Her mother moved her from one school to the next after her father died in a terrible motorcycle accident. Piper had still been in grade school when she and her mom were robbed of the most important man in their life.

After losing the love of her life, Piper's mother led an elusive search to recapture her lost happiness. Her latest search had yielded a bald tattooed biker who went by the name of Spider. Piper's mother had unceremoniously dropped her at Aunt Cassie's door before she rode off on the back of Spider's motorcycle, spouting empty promises of coming back to get her soon.

The bell rang, and Piper found herself alone in the

hallway, staring into her half-empty locker. She pulled her English Lit book free, slammed the locker door, and trudged down the hall to class.

She tried to quietly sneak into the back of the class and into her desk. She had thought for years that she could will herself invisible and felt it work many times in the past.

It didn't work today.

"Thank you for joining us, Ms. Denton," her teacher said. "We're discussing the homework assignment. Have you finished reading the assigned book?"

As luck would have it, her English class was reading *Catcher in the Rye*. When Cassie saw the book in Piper's backpack, she had been so excited.

Piper had reluctantly accepted the invitation to join her aunt's book club, secretly happy, and feeling quite grownup to be a part of the coffee house discussions. She had never been in any kind of club, and she liked the feeling of being included. She liked Aunt Cassie's friends. Sunny was always nice to her, and Maggie cracked her up. She didn't know what to make of the old lady yet. She was funny, but didn't act like any other old person Piper had ever met.

"Yes, I've finished it," Piper answered the teacher. She didn't like the attention of the whole class looking at her.

In the seat next to her sat a boy with dark hair who she had noticed watching her at times when they were supposed to be studying. He was cute and athletically built. She had plenty of experience with boys looking at her, but usually in a more predatory way. This boy looked at her with kindness, and she sometimes felt him study her from across the lunchroom while she sat alone at a table, reading a book, and eating the sandwich Cassie had packed for her. When she would look back at him, he'd always look quickly away, engrossed in his lunch or his work. The way his cheeks tinged a slight red gave her a funny feeling in her stomach, and she found herself watching the halls or glancing around at lunch in search of his tousled dark hair.

"Would you like to share your thoughts on the book?" the teacher asked.

"Um, sure," she stammered. She tried to recall what the women had said about the book the other night at Starbucks. They had veered off topic, planning blind dates for Sunny, but she had such fun being included in the conversation and the plans.

"I think it felt like I was reading a sixteen-year old's blog who was venting all his anger at the world and at grownups in general." She hated being put on the spot and could only think to mimic Maggie's thoughts on the book.

She snuck a glance at the boy next to her and found he openly smiled at her.

"I agree," the boy said, without raising his hand. "I think Piper nailed Holden right on."

Shocked he knew her name and had spoken on her behalf, Piper could only stare down at her desk and try to keep a goofy smile from taking over her face.

"Well, thank you for your opinion, Drew," the teacher said. "Who else would like to share their ideas?"

Beginning a new thread of discussion, the class moved on, once again forgetting the new girl with the weird black clothes.

The bell rang, and Piper collected her things, and filed into the hall.

"That was good, what you said about Holden."

Piper looked up, stunned someone spoke to her, and found the boy walking alongside her.

"Oh, thanks," she said.

"I'm Drew."

"Piper."

"Yeah, I know. My mom is friends with your aunt. I think she had the same opinion about this book."

"Really? Who's your mom?" Piper asked, confused.

"Maggie Hayes."

"Oh, cool." She flushed at being caught using a quote from this boy's mother. Trying to come up with something to change the subject, she said, "Your mom's funny."

Drew smiled at the description of his mother. "Yeah, I guess she is funny sometimes. So I packed my lunch today. Mind if I sit with you?"

Piper grinned down at her feet. "That would be okay, I guess."

"Great."

They spent the lunch hour talking and laughing. Drew filled her in on the kids at school and who was going out with whom. He had a way of talking to her that made her laugh and feel at ease with him, and she found herself explaining why she showed up at a new school with only a few weeks left before graduation. She didn't explain that this was not the first time her mother had dumped her somewhere to run off with some guy.

"That sucks about your mom. But I'm glad you're here," Drew said.

"Me too." Piper looked at this boy and smiled. A true, honest, genuine smile, and she felt those funny butterflies once again in her stomach.

"I better get to class," Drew said, as the lunch hour drew to a close. "You want a ride home from school today?"

"Sure, I usually take the bus."

"Cool. Meet me by the bike racks in the front of the school. I have to take my brother to his soccer game, maybe you could come along, or I could take you home after I drop him off."

"No, I'll come with you," Piper said. "I like soccer."

"Cool," he said again. With another grin, he loped off down the hall, calling out a greeting to two boys who passed in the other direction.

*Yeah, cool,* Piper thought, and she smiled again.

*Maybe he's a spy.* Sunny fluffed out her curly blonde hair and gave it an extra squirt of hairspray.

It was Saturday afternoon, and her thoughts careened from her suspicions of Jake, to her imminent date today with an ex-football player, to how bad her roots were, and whether or not she was due for highlights again. She was a woman. That's what women do. They can spend four minutes on the phone with each other and cover seventeen different topics while loading the dishwasher and baking a pan of cookies.

The sound of her front door opening and a deep voice calling her name rousted her from her musings. *What the heck? Who lets themselves into someone else's house?*

Holding the can of hairspray outstretched in her hand, as if it were mace instead of Super Hold, Sunny's heart thundered in her chest as she cautiously descended the stairs. A huge bear of a man stood in the entryway grinning up at her.

"Hey. You must be Sunny. I'm Hank. Matt was right when he told me you'd be pretty," he said, good-naturedly. His gaze traveled up her body, appraising her curves, but his expression changed when he saw the hairspray can clutched in her hand. "Sorry if I scared you. I'm just used to small town policy of letting myself in."

"Hi, Hank," Sunny said, lowering the makeshift weapon. Relief flooded her as she realized that her intruder, although rude, was her expected guest. She relaxed her stance and smiled at Hank, as she took in his large frame and well-muscled forearms. He wore his light blond hair in a military style crew cut he probably hadn't changed since high school. He was good-looking and wore a big open grin. Though well built, he carried an extra twenty pounds, mostly in the belly, making him look like he had lifted more beer cans than weights.

"You ready to go?" he asked, his tone light, but the finger-drumming on the side of her door revealed his impatience. "They have a pregame show we don't want to miss."

Hank had in fact called Wednesday night about an hour after she arrived home from Edna's and invited her to attend a baseball game.

This seemed like a good idea for a date with someone she was meeting for the first time. She knew a little bit about baseball, and if the conversation lagged, she could use the game as a distraction. The last date had been such a bust, she was determined to try harder to make a connection with this one. Hank was good-looking and seemed friendly enough. Possibly too friendly, as evidenced by his comfortableness in letting himself into her home.

"Of course. I'm ready to go." She smiled and indicated the hairspray. "Let me just put this away." Sunny ducked back into the bathroom, tossing the can into the basket on the edge of the sink. She took one last look in the mirror and checked her teeth and nose for any unwanted tidbits. Taking a deep breath and praying for courage, she stepped back into the hallway.

Her jean shorts, pale blue tank top and sneakers seemed appropriate attire, as Hank was dressed similarly in long shorts and a sleeveless red and white sports tank that promoted the local baseball team, the Sky Sox. The sleeveless shirt only emphasized his enormous muscled arms.

Her driver's license, cell phone, twenty dollars, and a tube of lip gloss were stuffed in her front pockets so she wouldn't have the hassle of toting her purse around the game.

"We love your dog," Hank said, as he looked out the front door.

*We?* She scurried down the stairs to see what Hank was watching. On her front lawn, Beau nestled around a small boy of nine or ten who lay in the grass ruffling his neck and stroking his yellow fur. He laughed as Beau licked his face. The boy had on shorts and a red Sky Sox t-shirt. He wore his hair in a crew cut style that matched Hank's, whom Sunny assumed was his father.

"This is my boy, Hank Michael, Jr. We call him Mikey. I brought him along to meet you. He's a good judge when it comes to finding him a new mommy."

*New mommy?* She gulped. "Nice to meet you, Mikey. It looks as if you've already met Beau. He must really like you."

"I really like him. He's neat." Mikey's smile beamed from ear to ear.

She took Beau by the collar and led him back inside while Mikey climbed into his dad's black Chevy Avalanche.

Hank pulled the front door shut and slung his arm around her as they walked toward the truck. "Some men like those real skinny girls," he leaned down and whispered into her ear, "but don't worry; I like my women with a little extra train in their caboose." He finished his statement by giving her *caboose* a friendly pat before he opened the door of the truck.

Shocked speechless by his forwardness, she climbed into the seat, conscious of his obvious gaze at her behind as she did so. He slammed the door and jogged around to his side.

The drive to the stadium was spent with Hank explaining the full rules and regulations of baseball to both she and Mikey.

Their side of the conversation consisted of alternate "I know that already, Dad," from Mikey and assorted *ohs* and *hmms* from Sunny.

Her determination to make this date work sank with each know-it-all comment that uttered from Hank's mouth. He was a sports guy though, and sports guys loved to talk about every aspect of the game. He did include Mikey in the conversation, and she admired that Hank was taking the time to teach his son about baseball. Sunny couldn't help but smile as the groan that just emanated from the backseat proved this may not have been the first lesson Hank had imparted on the subject.

She was glad to pull into the arena parking lot. Most of the fans had already gone in, except for a few straggling tailgaters, their pennants waving from truck antennas, and the scent of grilled bratwurst in the air. Hank wasted no time bustling them into the stadium, and they found their seats with only a few minutes to spare.

"Who wants a hot dog?" Hank asked. Those words began a two hour feeding frenzy. Between the three of them, they had hot dogs, peanuts, cotton candy, nachos, M&Ms, five Cokes, and one beer for Hank. Memories of her last date and the meeting with her azalea bush helped make her decision to stick with Diet Coke an easy one.

Hank came back to their seats after another food run and plunked a new bright red Sky Sox baseball cap on Sunny's head. "There ya go. You look pretty," he said, with a wink. "Doesn't she look pretty, Mikey?"

Mikey looked over at her and shrugged. "Yeah, she's okay, I guess."

Hank put his arm around her shoulders and pulled

her to him. "See, he likes you already."

"Great," she mumbled.

"Hey, I also got you some more nachos, since you liked the other ones so much."

Sunny had enjoyed the nachos, but she usually stuck to one helping of nachos a month. She smiled, told him thanks, and took the plastic container of tortilla chips and oozing orange cheese sauce.

He looked so happy and eager to please her that she had to kind of like him. He reminded her of a golden retriever, a little bit goofy and annoying, but they tried so hard and were so cute, you still wanted to cuddle them. The references to their impending marital status and to her well-rounded caboose had to stop though.

Suddenly, half the stands were on their feet as a Sky Sox hitter put one over the back wall. Hank and Mikey were screaming and yelling, and Sunny got caught in the excitement as she jumped to her feet.

Unfortunately, she didn't have quite the hold on that little plastic container that she thought she did, and the nachos went flying.

As if in slow motion, she watched in horror as the cheese flew in a saucy spray to land in orange speckles across the backs of the two Sox fans who cheered in front of them.

The runner slid into home as the two men realized they had been assaulted by a curly- haired blonde with a container of nachos.

They turned to her in unison, one actually getting out the words, "Are you crazy, Bitc–" before they spotted Hank.

"I'm so sorry," Sunny cried, as she passed them a pile of napkins. Out of the corner of her eye, she could see Mikey doubled over with laughter.

"It's all right, Sunny. It was just an accident. Right, fellas?" Hank asked the two nacho cheese victims.

"Sure, it's fine," they grumbled. They wiped what

cheese they could reach off of their arms and shirts with the napkins she had handed them.

They all sat back down in our seats. Sunny looked over at Mikey who was still laughing. "That was hilarious," he said, before stuffing another handful of cotton candy into his mouth.

"Yeah, hilarious," she agreed, sinking low into her chair. She tried to focus on the game and eventually, after what seemed like (and was, in fact) hours, the Sox won five runs to two.

At this point, her stomach was cramping from all the greasy snack food she had consumed, and her arms and chest were tinged with pink from too much time in the sun.

They trudged from the stadium, making their way through acres of baseball hats and waving pennants. The kid walking in front of Sunny hit her in the head with a big red foam finger at least six times.

"Ya know, I like your name, Sunny," Hank told her as they piled into his truck. "It reminds me of my favorite drink, Sunny Delight. Are you delightful, Sunny?"

Her cheeks flamed, and she didn't know the proper response so she busied herself with the seatbelt and tried to get Mikey situated in the back.

Hank was still laughing at his own joke as he climbed into the truck and started the engine. "How about we go out for pizza? What do you think, Sunny D?"

She had heard many versions of nicknames, but this was the first time she had been referred to as a sugary orange sports drink.

She crossed her arms around her full stomach. "I couldn't possibly eat another bite."

"Dang. I was just getting hungry again. What about you, Sport?" He directed his question toward Mikey.

"I'd rather go back to Sunny's house and play with her dog," Mikey answered.

"Good idea," Hank said. "Sunny and I could probably amuse ourselves while you play with the dog." Hank winked at her and dropped his hand onto her upper thigh.

As they drove back to her house, she tried several subtle maneuvers to dislodge Hank's hand from her leg, but nothing worked. His giant hand gripped her thigh as if it was a football and letting go might cost him the game.

Since her mother raised her right, she invited them in, and put together a tray of tea and glasses of ice. Mikey and Beau wrestled in the backyard while she and Hank sat on the porch sipping iced tea.

Setting his glass on the table, Hank rose, grabbed her hand, and pulled her to her feet. "I want to show you something." He led her to the side of the house, her hand still gripped in his.

No sooner were they out of Mikey's sight, than Hank turned, pushed her against the house, and bent his head toward hers. Before she knew what was happening, he had his mouth crushed against hers, kissing her fervently while his hands roamed from her breast to her ample behind. *He had another think coming if he thought he was gonna be the engineer of that caboose!*

Sunny tried to shove against him, but he was like a giant bear, and she thought he must have misinterpreted her hands against his chest as passionate foreplay. Every part of him was huge, including the part currently pressed against her leg. She felt smothered and trapped between her house and this giant hulk of a man.

"Hey, Sunny?" a deep voice asked from behind them. Sunny had never heard anger in Jake's voice before and was surprised to hear it barely concealed in his tone.

Startled, Hank stepped back, and she squirmed free from her position against the house.

She had no idea she could be so glad to see a man that hours earlier she had considered to be either a criminal or a spy.

"Jake! Hi," she said breathlessly, moving to his side. "This is my neighbor, Jake, and this is my date, Hank."

"Nice to meet you." Hank engulfed Jake's hand in his meaty paw, but his smile didn't quite meet his eyes, and he seemed to hold the handshake just a few seconds too long. "Any friend of Sunny's is a friend of mine." He moved to Sunny's other side, and put his arm protectively around her shoulder.

"I came over to see if you were ready to help weed those flower beds you promised you would do this afternoon?" Jake asked her.

"Oh...uh...yep. Yes sir. How could I have forgotten about those flowerbeds? We better get right to those." She smiled apologetically up at Hank. "Sorry I've got to go, but a promise is a promise."

Hank looked crestfallen, but smiled in understanding. "That's okay. You go ahead. Mikey and I will go get that pizza."

He yelled for his son, and Mikey came running around the corner.

"We gotta go, boy. Tell Sunny goodbye."

Mikey gave her a half-wave and mumbled, "See ya later".

"Thank you for the baseball game," she said, as she dislodged herself from under Hank's arm.

"No problem," he said, and leaned down to plant another kiss on her lips. She turned her face just in time to receive the kiss half on the lips and half on the cheek.

"I'll be calling you soon, Sunny D." Hank gave her a final wink and a last slap on her rump.

Jake took a protective step closer to her as they watched Hank and his son pile into the Avalanche and drive away.

"Sunny D?" Jake asked with a smirk.

"It's his favorite sports drink." A smile tugged at the corner of her lips.

"He looked like he was trying to drink you up."

"No kidding. Thanks for rescuing me."

"You should be careful with him," Jake warned, his light tone gone. "He might seem like a big teddy bear, but that guy is one strong dude."

"I know." She thought of the trapped feeling she had while pressed against the house, and wondered what could have happened if they had been inside the house alone. "I'm glad you were there," she said, her voice soft as her eyes looked up to his.

"I'm glad I was there too, this time." He reached up to tuck a strand of hair behind her ear. "You sure you want to keep up this whole blind date idea? It could be dangerous."

*No more dangerous than the way my stomach just dropped when you touched my hair.*

Her mouth had gone dry, and she watched Jake's eyes darken as she bit her lower lip. She could forget this whole blind date plan and make Jake her pirate fantasy. Unfortunately, the thought that he might have something to do with the disappearance of her neighbor squashed her swashbuckling ideas, and made her wonder if the real danger was standing too close to her right now.

"I promised the girls I would try," she said. "And I'm sure Cassie wouldn't have set me up with someone who is truly dangerous. Hank was just a little overzealous today." She headed for the back yard to retrieve the glasses and pitcher of tea. "Thanks again. For being there. This time."

"Do you want to come over and have some dinner?" he asked as he walked alongside her.

Her stomach made an unpleasant gurgling sound at the mention of more food. "Ugh. I better not. I ate a ton at the baseball game."

"Okay. Maybe another time."

She looked into his blue eyes and tried to convince herself he was an innocent bystander in this whole mess, but then the image of his face when the detective questioned him flashed through her mind, and she could hear Edna's warning about seeing him with a gun.

"Yeah, maybe another time," she said.

His shoulders stiffened as he turned to head back toward Walter's house. "Yeah, no big deal. Another time."

"Hey," she called, not wanting to end their exchange on a bad note. "You promised to help me weed the flower beds? Was that the best you could come up with?" she teased.

He laughed, and the tension in his shoulders eased. "Hey, it was all I could think of at the spur of the moment. It worked, didn't it?"

"Yeah, it worked. See ya." With a last glance at his amazing behind, she stepped into the kitchen with the tray of glasses, and let the screen door slam behind her.

Although spending time with Hank had been a little fun, and she had enjoyed some of the attention he gave her, she felt nothing of the rush of emotions or heat that flamed her cheeks when Jake was standing near her. The last few weeks, she had been throwing caution to the wind and dating strange men, hoping to add excitement and find that right guy. But what if the right guy was next door and had just invited her to dinner? What if she knocked on his back door tonight and told him she had changed her mind?

Was that hope rearing up in her heart, or had it been so long since she had felt hope that she was mistaking it for heartburn caused by that extra hot dog she shouldn't have eaten?

Thoughts of passion-filled kisses with Jake warred with the fear that he really was dangerous and she could end up locked in his basement next to the rotting corpse of Walter. Her stomach lurched at the thought, and so instead of knocking on her neighbor's door, she chose a boring night of wishful thinking, kicked off with a handful of antacids.

*Ding. Dong.*

"Oh crap! They're here," Maggie said aloud, as she hit a few last keys and reached for the power button to turn off her computer. She had only meant to spend fifteen minutes at her computer, but as she so often found lately, those fifteen minutes turned into an hour and a half. She tried to stop herself, but she felt addicted and couldn't break free from the pleasure she secretly found at the computer keyboard. She pushed back from her desk, reached to smooth her glossy dark hair, and took one last glance around the room to make sure there were no visible signs to give away her secret obsession.

This Wednesday was her night to host the Page Turners, and as she walked into the living room, she saw everyone had arrived at once.

Maggie watched with amusement as Drew played host for the women, offering to take their purses and jackets to the guest room as if they hadn't been here many times before. She knew there was one guest in particular for whom he was putting on this show.

He smiled shyly at Piper and offered to take her jacket. She self-consciously shrugged off the black sweatshirt she wore zipped to her chin, and Cassie gasped at the shirt Piper wore underneath.

Drew grinned appreciatively. "I like that shirt," he told Piper, who looked at the floor, apparently uneasy with all the attention focused on her.

Piper had on her usual black pants and thick-soled black boots, but tonight she wore a v-neck t-shirt in pastel pink. Her dark hair had a little more of its softer, natural wave instead of the stick-straight look she usually achieved with the ceramic iron.

Drew departed for the guest room, laden down with jackets and purses, and the women moved into the kitchen.

Cassie grasped Sunny's hand and mouthed, "She's wearing *color*!"

Maggie didn't have Edna's flare for baking, but she did have a knack for picking bakeries. A Boston Crème Pie and a Triple Chocolate Torte sat ready on the table along with plates and cups she had set out earlier in the evening. She knew the girls loved their sweets, and the chocolate frosting of the pie glistened in the kitchen light. She moved to the sink and started the coffee brewing as everyone took seats at the table. Excitement filled the room, and she knew they were all anxious to hear how Sunny's latest date, the previous Saturday had gone.

"Well," Cassie said. "What did you think of him?"

"Who? Hank the Tank?" Sunny asked.

"Uh. Oh. You better start from the beginning," Cassie said.

"The beginning where he let himself into my house without knocking or the beginning when he brought his son on our first date or the beginning when he patted my rear end and let me know he likes women with big cabooses?" Sunny answered.

"Oh, he didn't." Maggie passed plates around, then sliced into the torte. "Who wants which kind of cake, and who wants a little slice of both?"

"Both," they all replied at once, then broke into laughter.

Sunny relived the date for her friends and laughed at herself when she told the part about spilling the nachos on the two guys in front of her. Cassie felt for the poor guys, but all Maggie saw was a lawsuit pending.

Unfortunately for Piper, she had just taken a drink of milk when Sunny said, "...and the nacho cheese dip flew up and landed all over these guy's –" Piper's unexpected laughter caused the milk to come flying out her nose. The table of women went silent in shock, then they all burst out, screaming with laughter. Cassie passed Piper some napkins and put her arm around her shoulder.

"It's okay, honey," Cassie said, with compassion. "That's happened to all of us."

"Yeah, but some of us have other liquids come out other places when we laugh suddenly," Edna said, which drew another round of giggles from the women seated around the table.

"Geez, what's so funny?" Drew asked, as he came into the kitchen. "I can hear you guys laughing all the way up in my room."

"Sunny was telling us about her last date, and Edna said something funny," Maggie said, as Piper reddened with embarrassment. She could see her son's focus shift from his mother's silly friends to the desserts sitting on the counter.

"I just came down for some cake." Drew reached for the cake server and cut himself a thick wedge.

"Help yourself," Maggie said. "Pull up a chair."

By the time Sunny had scooted her chair over to make room for Drew, he had already finished the slice of cake, not bothering with a plate.

"I was gonna see if you could spare Piper for awhile, and we could go for a walk?" he asked. He looked at Piper. "If you want to, I mean."

"Sure. I'd like that." Piper got up from the table and followed Drew to the front door.

"We'll be back in an hour or so," Drew called and pulled the door shut behind them.

Maggie blinked, looking around the table at the other women who wore amused expressions.

"When did this start?" Sunny asked.

"Within the last couple weeks, I guess. He brought her to Dylan's soccer game the other day, and they have been hanging out ever since," Maggie explained.

"Well, I love it," Cassie said. "She's the happiest I've seen her in years. She's been texting Drew and talking to him on the phone, and she walks around with an actual smile on her face. It's incredible. And the fact that she wore a colored shirt tonight is an amazing step. May the days of all black outfits rest in peace. Hallelujah!"

"Amen, sister!" Edna cried.

"She does seem happier," Sunny agreed. "Now that they left, I can tell you what happened after Hank brought me back to my house."

The women laughed and gasped at the brazenness of Hank and his mighty bulge.

"Good thing Jake stepped in when he did," Maggie said. "Or you might have been in real trouble."

"Yes, but how did Jake know you needed his help?" Edna asked. "Was he watching you? I still don't trust him. You need to be careful, Sunny."

"I agree," Cassie said. "He may be cute, but we really don't know anything about him."

"I don't trust him either," Maggie said. "It just seems too convenient that he moves in to Walter's house right at the same time the garage explodes, and Walter turns up missing, possibly dead. He is hot, but I work with lawyers. I've known plenty of hot guys in suits who could lie like a rug if it meant winning a case. I've seen men lie under oath, and men look you right in the eye and lie to your face."

She got up, collected the plates, and carried them to the sink. With her back to the other women, she rinsed and loaded the dessert plates into the dishwasher. Edna, Sunny, and Cassie looked at each other in grim silence. Maggie couldn't help but think about Chad the Cheater and how he had lied to her time and time again about his whereabouts and his days spent with another woman. Maggie didn't trust men in general right now, and her friends knew that.

"Well, speaking of men," Edna said, breaking the silence, "I've got your next date set up."

"You what?" Sunny sputtered, choking on the sip of coffee she had taken.

"I said, I have your next date for this weekend. I tried to tell you before, my friend Mabel has a grandson who is single. I called her, and we set up the date for this Saturday night. His name is Jeremy Rogers, and Mabel said he's a really nice boy."

"A really nice boy? How old is he? Twelve?"

"No, he's in his thirties and has never been married. Mabel said he makes a living playing computer games or something."

Crash!

The plate Maggie had been rinsing slipped from her hands and crashed into the sink, shattering into several pieces. "Damn it," she cried.

"Oh Maggie, let me help you." Cassie jumped up from her chair and went to Maggie. She gingerly picked the pieces out of the sink and deposited them in the trash can Maggie had pulled from the cabinet below.

Maggie knew the girls thought she'd been thinking about Chad, but actually the mention of the computer had brought up her nightly ritual, and she fumbled the plate in the soapy water.

"Maggie, I just loved that Boston Crème Pie," Sunny said, in an obvious effort to change the subject and divert Maggie's thoughts away from cheating men. "Which bakery did you find it in?"

"Oh, uh, the little one on the corner of Broadway, down from my office." Putting the trash bin back under the sink, she pasted a smile back on her face as she looked up. "I'm fine, girls. I got a little off kilter for a sec, but I'm back now."

She put her arm around Cassie's shoulder, and the women relaxed as Maggie's tension eased. "I'm awfully glad I have you girls to lean on though. Now, tell me about this new date for Sunny. Where is he taking her?"

"Mabel didn't say, but we gave him Sunny's address, and he'll pick her up at six on Saturday night. I would say dress casually. I don't think he has a lot of money. How much money could he make playing Pac-man anyway?"

The women smiled at Edna's reference to the eighty's video game, knowing the advances in the industry over the past several decades.

"I'm coming over Saturday night," Maggie said suddenly. "You told us all about this Hank the Tank, but I can't really picture him. I want to see the next guy."

"Oh, me too," Cassie said. "But I can't. One of the kids has a football game Saturday night. Dang it."

"I have Bingo Saturday night so I can't be there either," Edna said. "And this week, I'm going for the Double Diamond Board. They're giving away a hundred dollar cash prize *and* a ham!"

"Maggie, you will have to be our designated date eyewitness, and tell us what you think of Mabel's 'nice boy' grandson," Cassie instructed.

"I would love it if you were there," Sunny said. "It's always awkward right when they show up."

"Okay, I'll be there at five-thirty," Maggie said, then glanced up at the clock on her kitchen wall. "I wonder when the kids will get back."

🐾🐾🐾

The sun balanced over the mountains in gorgeous hues of pink and shades of blue, as Drew and Piper walked the few blocks to the neighborhood park. They walked in companionable silence, and at some point, Drew had reached over and intertwined his fingers with Piper's. Their joined hands swung slightly as they walked through the park.

Piper still could not believe that this cute boy was walking next to her and holding her hand. She felt like he must be able to hear how loud her heart was beating, and she worried that her palm would start sweating. As if he could read her mind, Drew squeezed her hand, and gave her an encouraging smile. She wondered if her thoughts were somehow written across her forehead because he always seemed to know what she was thinking.

The smell of freshly mown grass hung in the air as they stepped onto the small playground complete with swings, monkey bars, and a couple of slides.

Piper had always loved to swing, and she took a seat on the plastic u-shaped swing, and grasped the cool metal chains. Drew grabbed the edges of her seat and pulled back, only to release her into the air. He gave her several good pushes, her legs shot out, and her head fell back, her hair free, and a laugh escaped her lips.

Her swing finally slowed and Drew approached and stood behind her, his hands on the chains above her shoulders. She leaned back into his muscled chest, and he rested his chin on top of her head.

"I like to hear you laugh," he said into her hair.

She smiled and snuggled closer into his chest.

"Piper, I have a confession to make."

Her smile froze at his words, and her body stiffened. "Okay."

"I don't know how to tell you this, but I didn't *actually* read the *Catcher in the Rye.*"

She relaxed, and pushed off the swing to turn and face him.

"I only talked to you about it with stuff my mom

told me from your book club." He grinned at her. "And the worst part is, I got an A on my essay paper on it." He laughed and took off running, a teasing glint in his eye as if daring her to chase him.

"You cheater," she cried playfully, and ran after him around the playground, until he finally pinned her against the monkey bars.

Her laughter died as he drew nearer, and his expression became serious.

"I have another confession to make," he said as he looked into her eyes. "I only acted like I'd read it to impress you, so I would have a chance to talk to you." His finger stroked her cheek as he freed a loose strand of hair that had blown across her face. "I really like you, Piper."

She felt his warmth as he pressed his body closer to hers, contrasting with the cool metal of the monkey bars that seeped through the back of her thin cotton t-shirt.

"I really like you, too," she whispered. She raised her chin to meet his gaze.

They had spent hours talking on the phone and getting to know each other. But, so far, Drew had only held her hand. This was the moment she had laid awake thinking about every night since Drew had spoken up for her in class.

In an effort to steady herself and hide her shaking hands, she gripped the playground bar she leaned against. Her heart beat tripled in time and her mouth went dry. Finding it hard to breathe, she felt captured by the look in his eyes as they conveyed a message of want and need.

Drew's head dipped toward hers, and his lips lightly touched hers. A rush of desire flowed through her as he kissed her again, this time more insistent. His hands went around her back, and she pressed closer to him. Drew's knee moved between her legs, and they pressed closer still. His hands moved up and down her back, and Piper had never felt anyone treat her with such care or longing in her life. Hands gripping his back, she kissed him back as if her life depended on it. His lips parted, and she felt his tongue seek hers. He tasted of chocolate cake and smelled of cologne. Piper was in heaven, and could have kissed him for hours. She never wanted this moment to end.

*Bonk!*

Their teeth clashed against each other as a soccer ball bounced off the side of Drew's head.

"Dude, get a room!" a male voice called, followed by female laughter.

Drew looked down at her, mouthed "*sorry*", and pulled away to heckle the ball-throwing kid. "Troy, you jerk! What are you guys doing?"

Piper felt chilled as he pulled away from her. She rubbed her arms and already missed the heat of his body next to hers. He reached down, took her hand and held it lightly in his. Feeling his touch brought some of the warmth back.

"We're just walking back from the Tastee Freez and happened to catch you two mashing," the boy teased. "So, is this the girl you've been telling us about who you like so much?"

Piper froze and looked at her feet in embarrassment. She dropped Drew's hand. *How could I have been so stupid? Thinking he liked me when he was telling all his friends about some girl that he* really *liked.* The familiar feelings of abandonment crowded into her heart as she chastised herself for letting someone get close to her.

"Yep, this is her." Drew beamed and reached for her hand again, proudly holding up their joined fingers.

"Piper, this is Tara and Troy. You've heard me talking about Troy, my best friend and social ingrate. And Tara and I have lived on the same street since second grade. She's probably the closest thing I've got to a sister."

"Hi," Tara said to Piper, who was still stunned over Drew's declaration of his feelings for her. "I'm so glad we finally get to meet you. Drew has been talking about you non-stop ever since you moved here."

Piper looked toward Drew and smiled before she could stop herself. Looking back at Tara, she took in the girl's jean shorts, low top Converse sneakers, and brightly colored double layered t-shirts. "I really like your shirt," Piper said, then looked away and silently berated herself for such a stupid comment.

"Oh, gosh, I have tons of these. You can borrow some if you want," Tara offered, her smile filled with warmth.

"Oh, okay, thanks," Piper replied.

"Hey, we wanted to tell you Tara's having a Summer Luau party this weekend at her house to celebrate school being out. You guys should come," Troy said.

"It's a tropical theme," Tara said. "So dress Hawaiian. And Piper, you can tell your mom that 'yes, my parents will be there- all night.' I'm having a couple of other girls stay the night so you can sleep over if you want."

"Okay, thanks," Piper answered softly. She was stunned that this nice, pretty girl had invited her not only to a party, but to sleep over and loan her some of her clothes. Feelings of acceptance warred with her inner struggles of desertion, because she knew she didn't have to tell her mom anything about the party. Because her mom was gone, once again putting some guy above her own daughter.

"Well, we gotta go." Tara dragged on Troy's hand. "We'll see you guys on Saturday night. Piper, I'll get your number from Drew later and text you about sleeping over."

"Okay." Piper was filled with the unfamiliar sensation of pure happiness, and her throat felt full from the strange lump that was forming there. She swallowed, afraid to look at Drew, in case he could see the tears forming in her eyes.

"We better get back," Drew said. He pulled her toward his house. "Do you want to go to the party Saturday night? With me, I mean."

She swallowed again, shaking off the sentiment and resuming her tougher shell. "Sure, it sounds fun. I'll talk to Cassie about it."

"Great." Drew's face lit up as they walked through the park, the sun slipping behind the mountains at their backs. "It's a date then."

❀❀❀

"So, where did you and Drew head off to?" Cassie asked as she and Piper drove home that night. She had been dying to talk to her since she saw the teenage couple walk back in the door of Maggie's house. Cassie was shocked by the pink flush and the smile that kept popping up on her niece's face.

"Oh, we walked down to the park and played around on the playground," Piper answered.

Cassie knew this was an important communication bridge they were crossing and she tried to keep her tone light. "Sounds fun. I think Drew is a great kid, and he's very cute."

"Yeah, he's nice," Piper replied, then blushed and said, "and yes, he *is* very cute, too."

"I think he really likes you."

The darkness in the car must have freed Piper to open up, and she gushed, "Oh, Aunt Cassie, I really like him." She spilled the whole story of Drew holding her hand, and meeting the other kids, and being invited to the party. She described Tara in detail, and told Cassie she had asked her to sleep over. In a quiet voice, she even confessed that Drew had kissed her for the first time.

"Wow. You had quite a night," Cassie said, keeping

her eyes on the road. She was afraid if she looked at the girl, then Piper would see the tears that filled her eyes as Cassie burst with love and happiness for her. She wanted so much for her niece to be happy and free of some of the despair that seemed to be her constant companion.

Piper looked down into her lap and fidgeted with her seat belt. "Aunt Cassie, can I ask you a favor?" she asked quietly.

"Sure honey, go ahead."

"Um, do you think you would have time to take me shopping for some new clothes tomorrow? Maybe just like some shorts and a few t-shirts. I kind of like turquoise, and maybe yellow would be okay. And maybe a pair of flip-flops. Would that be okay?"

"That would be fine. Why don't we plan to go to lunch tomorrow, then head to the mall?" Cassie held her breath, hoping she hadn't pushed too hard by planning lunch and the mall in the same sentence.

"Cool," Piper said, then reached for the radio knob and turned the music up, effectively signaling their conversation was over.

Cassie smiled to herself as she released her breath. She tried to hold back the joy she felt for Piper. She worried her heart would explode with love for this daughter of her sister, and used the back of her hand to nonchalantly wipe away a tear that escaped her eye, as she drove into the night.

The smell of apples and cinnamon filled Sunny's kitchen Friday afternoon as she cut a slice from the warm pie she had just baked. She plopped a scoop of vanilla ice cream on top of the slice, dropped the scooper into the sink, and shoved the carton of vanilla back into the freezer.

By the time she carried her plate out to the deck and sat in her favorite lounge chair, the ice cream had begun to melt from the warmth of the apple pie and golden pools of cream and cinnamon formed on the plate.

Sunny put the first bite in her mouth and sighed with pleasure as the mixed flavors of warm cinnamon, cool vanilla ice cream and the tangy sweetness of the apples flooded her tongue. She chewed slowly, savoring the flaky crust and the gooey cinnamon filling.

She continued to savor each bite of pie and relished the warm June day. Closing her eyes, she turned her face to the sun and enjoyed the feel of the heat on her skin. *Oh, I* love *summer!*

On a whim, Sunny decided to take a piece of pie to Jake. But she had to ask herself, "Is that really the reason I had baked the pie? To give me an excuse to see him?" *Of course not. I am just in the mood for pie. I think.*

Thirty minutes later, Sunny walked across the backyard, freshly showered and smelling of perfume and shampoo. She carried a plastic dish that contained three pieces of apple pie.

As she approached the back screen door, she heard Jake's voice. He spoke rather angrily and since no one answered, she deduced he must be talking on the phone. *I know, I'm a regular Sherlock Holmes.*

She waited before knocking and listened to his heated words.

"Get off my back. I know why I'm here."

He paused as he listened to the caller on the other end.

"I haven't found out enough about her yet. She's not making it easy."

*She-who? Who was this 'she' he was talking about?*

"I know what I'm supposed to do. I've got the situation under control."

Jake turned and saw her standing on the doorstep.

"Hey, I gotta go. We'll have to continue this later." He listened another few seconds and replied, "You'll be hearing from me soon." He snapped the phone shut and pushed the screen door open to let her into the kitchen.

"Hey Sunny, I didn't hear you come up. Have you been standing there long?" he asked, warily.

"No, I just walked up," she lied. "Sorry to interrupt your call. Was it important?" she asked, trying to sound innocently uninterested.

"No, it's no big deal," Jake answered gruffly and then switched gears as he spied the plastic container in her hand. He smiled and raised his eyebrows at her. "What's in the dish?"

"Oh, ya," she faltered, a little undone by his smile. "I brought you some pie. I wanted to thank you for rescuing me. From my date. With Hank."

Sunny hadn't really seen Jake since the incident with Hank, several days before. She was still suspicious of Jake, but his grin and that tousled blond hair made her want to trust him. He smiled and nodded at her. "Anytime."

He took the container from her and peeled back one corner. His eyes closed as he inhaled deeply. "I love pie."

*Holy cow!* Sunny's knees went weak with desire, and she had a sudden vision of him sweeping the contents of the table to the floor, laying her back against it, then eating the pie off her bare stomach.

Where had that come from? Swallowing, she tried to pull herself back to the task at hand. Finding out what happened to Walter was more important than indulging in pie-eating sexual fantasies.

"So, what have you heard about Walter?" she asked, not very subtly.

"Nothing, really. They're still investigating the source of the fire and trying to locate information about his activities the past several weeks. Have you seen him acting weird lately or talking to anyone you don't know?"

They had quickly moved from Sunny trying to glean information from Jake to him questioning her. His rapid-fire questions sounded like an interrogation.

"No," she replied. "I haven't noticed anything strange. Walter just always seems to be around. He's working in the yard or fixing something in the garage. He's usually willing to come over and help me with a leaky faucet or with moving something." She felt a lump forming in her throat from thinking that something could have happened to him. "He's just a really nice old guy."

"Yeah, he's a real saint," Jake said bitterly, not quite under his breath. "What about any visitors? Have you heard him mention anyone new or talk about recent friends he's made?"

"The only thing I can think of is that he got a new computer at Christmas. I helped him set it up and got him connected online."

"Hmmm." Jake looked toward the desk in the

kitchen where Walter's computer sat.

Why was he asking about Walter meeting someone new? Was he worried Walter may have revealed the true relationship he had with Jake, or maybe that was just a ruse and Jake had just met him and was trying to cover his tracks.

Suddenly the strains of "*I'll Be Watching You*" by The Police drifted from Sunny's jeans pocket as her phone went off, startling both of them.

"What's that about?" Jake asked. He looked at her questioningly.

"Just me trying to be funny. I set that ring tone for Hank," she confessed. "He calls me all the time, and this way I know when it's him." She smiled sheepishly. "I just found a song that had a little stalker quality to it."

"Are you having trouble with him?" Jake's tone changed to one of alarm. "Are you worried he might hurt you?"

"No, but he's not getting the hint that I'm not really interested in him."

"Not *really* interested or not interested?" Jake leaned against the counter next to her. Sunny felt a zing of pleasure as his hip rested against hers.

"Not interested."

"Then you need to tell him to leave you alone."

"I know, but he's not getting the hint, and I don't want to hurt his feelings." *Yuck, my voice sounds way too whiney.*

"Who cares about his feelings? The guy is an ox. You need to cut him loose."

"Thanks, I'll work on that."

Jake had a point that she did need to be more assertive with Hank. But, she wondered, were Jake's comments out of friendly concern, or could he actually be jealous of the muscle-bound jock? And did she tell him about Hank in hopes he would be jealous?

Sunny needed to follow her plan of using the pie as

an excuse to spy on Jake and see if she could find out more information about why he was here. She pushed away from the counter and started toward Walter's desk. "Walter really was excited about this new computer."

Walter's desk was an old roll top with little cubbies and pigeon holes stuffed with a jumble of paperwork, rubber bands, and pens. Jutting out from one compartment was an envelope with the familiar letterhead of Wilson, Benton, Grant and Hayes. Maggie's firm! Sunny could make out the first part of the title, "LAST WILL AND TESTA..." but the rest of the wording was obscured by an envelope from the electric company. The will was jammed into a cubby amongst assorted bills and correspondence.

Jake closed the roll top by reaching across Sunny and brushed his arm against hers. Her mouth went dry from the sudden closeness of him. She could smell the musky scent of his aftershave and something minty.

Being this close to him made her realize how tall he was, and that she was alone in the house with him. She knew he could easily overpower her as he took her shoulder and steered her back to the kitchen table. "How about joining me for a piece of pie?"

The kitchen table, bare-stomached fantasy flashed through Sunny's mind, and she swallowed, trying to overcome the contrasting feelings of fear and flat-out yearning for this man. "I really need to get back."

She needed to get a hold of herself, to be in her safe house, and splash some cold water on her face. Plus, she was eager to get home and call Maggie about the envelope she had seen.

"So, who's lined up for this weekend?"

"Pardon me?" she croaked.

"Who's your blind date for this weekend?" he asked again.

Sunny had forgotten that she had told him about

the six blind dates. "A guy named Jeremy. He's the grandson of one of Edna's friends."

"Well, let me know if you need rescuing from this one," he teased. Then his tone took on a more serious note. "I'll be watching out for you."

"I better get going," Sunny said, trying to drag herself away from his blue eyes. He had once again moved close enough to her that if she tilted her head and leaned in a little...then maybe she could be kissing a murderer! *Eeek. Gotta go.*

"I'll see ya later," she said and made a quick escape to the door.

"Let me know how it goes with the grandson." He chuckled and followed her to the door. He reached out his long arm to hold it for Sunny, and she brushed against him as she walked through.

"And give that ox the old heave-ho. Really, Sunny, you need to firmly tell him to quit calling you." His voice was serious.

"Thanks, I will." She walked across the driveway toward her backyard as the familiar notes of "*I'll Be Watching You*" began to play again.

Her game of 'ignore it and it will go away' hadn't worked so far, so she picked up Hank's call and tried to follow Jake's advice.

"Hello," she cautiously answered.

"Sunny D!" Hank's voice boomed into her ear. "How's my favorite sexy blonde?"

"Well, I'm fine, Hank," she said. "But I think..."

"I'm calling to invite you over for a barbeque this weekend." Hank bulldozed over her in mid-comment. "I thought it would be a great time for you to meet the folks."

"I'm not quite ready to meet your parents," she stammered. "In fact, I'm not sure..."

"Oh, you're gonna love them. And I know they will love you. You're very different from my last wife."

"Hank, I can't. I've got other plans this weekend,

and I don't really see this working out."

"Well, dang. We'll have to make it another time then. Hey, Mikey's calling me so I gotta go. I'll call ya later, honey."

"But, I really don't think..." she began, but he had already clicked off.

*Way to be firm, Sunny.*

She snapped the phone shut and went inside, anxious to call Maggie and see what she could dig up from her firm on Walter's will.

"All right, so anything I tell you, or don't *exactly* tell you, is absolutely, totally one hundred percent confidential," Maggie said. It was Saturday night, and she had shown up around five so she and Sunny would have time to talk before *the grandson* arrived for their date.

Sunny had put together a plate of thin crackers and a circle of brie with pecans and warm melted caramel sauce drizzled on it. The smoky flavor of the cheese, combined with the sweet caramel and a salted cracker, was a flavor explosion. They dug into the warm brie and sipped on white wine. *Nothing like a little glass of wine to add that extra edge to a great first impression.*

"Fine," Sunny replied, anxious to hear what Maggie had uncovered about Walter's will, and if Jake had any real connections to him. "Top secret. Now, what did you find out?" She scooped a sugary pecan on to a cracker and tipped it into her mouth.

"Well, you know *I* can't really tell you anything about the document, but if *you* were to google any ancestry type website, you would find out that Jake really is related to Walter. And you would probably see that he really is his grandson," Maggie said.

Sunny felt a little spurt of joy at the knowledge that at least Jake was telling the truth about being related to Walter. "Why would he make such a big deal about being his grandson? Why not just come out and say that? What's the mystery?"

"That I don't know. I can neither confirm nor deny if this is true, but *if* a certain grandson were to be the sole beneficiary of his grandfather's estate, I *do* know what that means." She popped another cracker in her mouth and chewed twice. "Motive."

Sunny groaned. If Maggie had found this information so quickly, then it would only be a matter of time before the police also found out. If someone did murder Walter, she wanted the killer found. She just didn't want to find out it was Jake.

The doorbell rang, and Sunny gulped another mouthful of wine. She was wearing black jeans, black boots, and a form-fitting black t-shirt. Her black belt had a large silver buckle, and she had accessorized with silver drop earrings and a necklace with a large silver pendant. She had thought her outfit was sort of Matrix-y and befitting of a date with a guy who played video games for a living.

"You look great, by the way," Maggie whispered, following close behind her as Sunny headed for the door. "All black-very slimming."

The women opened the door to a tall, thin man holding a single red rose. He was that gawky kind of tall like he hadn't quite grown into his body yet. He wore round tortoise shell glasses and a thick shock of black hair fell across his forehead. He was really quite good-looking in a Clark Kent-cute-nerdy guy kind of way.

His eyes lit up, and he smiled widely, introducing himself as he held the rose out to...Maggie.

Maggie smiled back, obviously taken in with his charm and boyish good looks. She actually started to reach for the rose before she dropped her hand.

"Uh, sorry," Maggie said and backed away. "Party foul. She's actually your date."

His eyes shifted to Sunny, and he quickly tried to mask his disappointment.

"Sorry," he fumbled, his smooth entrance deflating like a balloon. "This is for you, I guess." He extended the rose to her, and Sunny watched a flush, as red as the rose, move up his neck and into his cheeks.

"It's okay. I know it's hard to get excited about the hamburger you ordered when you just saw a filet mignon go by," she said, trying to lighten the situation.

"Hmm," he said, distractedly. He smiled as his gaze drifted back to Maggie. "What?"

"Nothing. Come on in." *Stupid wine made me think I was a comedian there for a minute.*

The women moved aside, and they both did a quick tush-check as he headed for the sofa to take a seat. Maggie wiggled her eyebrows and grinned at Sunny.

"Sorry about the confusion," Sunny explained. "I'm Sunny Vale, and this is my friend, Maggie. We're both in a book club with Edna. Maggie just stopped by to drop off a dish." Sunny hoped her explanation for Maggie's presence sounded plausible. It was easier than telling him her friend just came over to check him out before their date.

"Nice to meet you both," Jeremy answered sincerely.

Maggie sat on the loveseat across from Jeremy and crossed her legs. "So Jeremy, tell us about what you do," she said, her litigating attorney voice coming through.

Sunny set the rose on the coffee table and perched on the arm of the loveseat next to Maggie, happy to let her friend take the lead in the conversation.

"Well, my company tests popular video games and designs—"

"Uh, excuse me," Sunny said as she jumped up and ran for the back door. She had just heard the unmistakable sound every dog owner recognizes as the 'pre-hurl heaving'.

Beau stood in the laundry room. He looked helplessly up at her, then lurched toward the back door. Sunny ran past him and flung the back screen door open while she urged him to please make it outside.

"C'mon Beau. You can make it, boy," she cooed.

The poor dog gingerly stepped through the door and made it the few steps to the grass.

"Everything okay?" Jake stood up from where he knelt in Walter's garden, a pile of weeds in the drive next to him. He came toward her, brushing dirt from his hands, but Sunny's attention was focused on poor Beau. His front legs were locked stiff, and his head was bent to the ground as his stomach pulsed with the rhythm of horrible spasmodic jerks.

With one final heave, Beau spewed forth a giant filmy pile of half-chewed dog food, pieces of napkin, and a ball of black fabric.

"What the heck is that?" Jake moved closer as they both peered in disgust at the pile, their heads tilted in unison as they tried to figure out what delicacy the giant dog had decided to snack on.

Jake started to chuckle as the dawning realization of what the dog had ingested hit them at the same time.

"Is that a thong?" Jake asked, now full on laughing.

"Oh Beau, how could you? Those cost eighteen dollars a pair at Victoria's Secret!" Sunny cried, not looking at Jake as humiliation heated her cheeks.

"That gives a whole new meaning to edible underwear." Jake doubled over with laughter at his own joke.

"Real nice," Sunny said. A smile played at the edge of her lips. *It was kind of funny.*

Beau looked up at her, tail wagging, his momentary gastric distress quickly forgotten. Then he bent his head to the mass of vomit, as only dogs do, ready to dig in and try it again.

"Aaaagh! No!" she shrieked. "Go on! Get away from that!" Sunny pushed Beau away and looked to Jake for help.

His eyes were shining with laughter as he reached for Beau's collar. "I'll hold him. Go grab a bag."

Sunny ran back into the laundry room and grabbed a grocery sack from the box on the shelf above the washer.

"I'll just be another second," she called to Maggie, who had moved to sit next to Jeremy on the sofa, their heads bent toward each other, deep in conversation.

In the back yard, Sunny used the Pooper Scooper to deposit the pile of hurl into the bag, tied the ends closed, and deposited it into the trash bin next to the house.

"Decided you didn't want to save those?" Jake smirked.

"I'm good, thanks." She smiled back, good-naturedly and bent to pet Beau's fuzzy head. "You feel better, boy?"

"So, you look really nice." Jake's eyes moved appraisingly up and down her body. Sunny tried to control the funny little shiver that ran through her as he did. "When's the grandson show up?"

"He's inside now being overwhelmed by the essence of Maggie."

"Aaahh. What does this one do?"

"He plays video games, I think," she answered sheepishly.

"What? For a living?"

"Well, I don't exactly know yet. It's something like that. I'll find out when I actually go on the date with him."

"Well, by all means, you better get in there then. He may have already plugged in his Xbox while he was waiting."

"Oh, shut up." She swatted at him playfully. "I don't know if I should go now. I feel bad leaving Beau alone. What if he...you know..."

"Upchucks another pair of panties?" Jake smirked. "Do you think he ate the matching bra?"

"Oh no!" Sunny gasped, and grabbed Beau's mouth, wrenching it open to peer down his throat. "You didn't...hey, wait a minute." Her eyes cut suspiciously back to Jake. "How'd you know there was a matching bra?"

"There always is, babe." He smirked again and reached for Beau's collar. "Go out on your date. Beau can hang with me tonight. We'll lie on the sofa and watch Airbud or something."

"Are you sure?"

"Yeah. We'll be fine. Come over and get him when you get home from your night out with Mr. Atari. We'll try to save you some popcorn." He said the last sentence over his shoulder as he walked toward Walter's screen door. Her loyal dog followed, looking up at him in adoration, as if Jake carried a piece of bacon in his pocket.

The sound of Maggie's laughter drew her back to the task at hand, and Sunny sighed before going into the kitchen to wash her hands.

"Crisis averted." Sunny smoothed down her curls as she stepped into the living room. "Sorry that took so long. Beau had a little digestive moment. He's going to spend the evening chilling at the neighbor's house."

"Oh, that's fine," Jeremy said, dragging his eyes from Maggie's smiling face. "We were having a great time talking. Maggie was just telling me all about her midnight–"

"You guys better get going," Maggie interrupted, suddenly on her feet. "Sunny doesn't want to hear all that boring stuff." She looked at Jeremy, her eyes imploring him to keep his mouth shut.

*Hmmm. Now what was this all about?*

He looked at her quizzically and then turned to Sunny. "Yes, we probably should get going." He glanced at his watch. "We don't want to be late."

"Late for what?" she asked, curious as to where he was taking her.

"Oh, it's a surprise," Jeremy said as he pulled the front door open.

Maggie handed Sunny her purse. "You're going to love it." Why she was wearing a devilish grin, Sunny wasn't sure.

"Maggie, it was a pleasure meeting you," Jeremy said, as he looked over Sunny's shoulder.

"The pleasure was all mine," Maggie said. Sunny whipped her head back to look at her friend, but Maggie was smiling openly at Jeremy.

"Hmm. Hmm." Sunny cleared her throat, and Maggie looked guiltily away. "Sorry," she mouthed as Jeremy stepped through the door.

"Have fun, you two," she said as she pushed them out the door. "I'll clean up and let myself out."

*That was weird.* Sunny crossed the lawn, this time on the lookout for any dog-turd land-mines.

Jeremy was holding open the door of a white Toyota 4Runner. Sunny climbed in and admired the tan leather interior. She appreciated the neatness of his car, no fast food bags or crumpled napkins on the floor, as he slid into the driver's seat and turned on the ignition.

"I like big butts and I cannot lie..." suddenly blared from the sound system, and Jeremy grabbed for the knob to turn the volume down.

"Sorry, forgot to turn that down." He was suddenly very focused on the steering wheel as he pulled away from the curb. Sunny looked out the window, so he wouldn't see her silently cracking up.

They made small talk about the weather and Mabel and Edna, and he asked a surprising amount of questions about Maggie. Sunny couldn't tell if he was just making conversation or if he was actually taking an interest in her friend. She didn't know how to throw Maggie's divorce into the conversation or her current distrust of the male species. If he only knew that Maggie had sworn off men for the next decade, he might be more willing to settle for the ordinary girl currently riding in the seat next to him.

They drove for about fifteen minutes, crossing through the edge of town and into a middle class neighborhood. The housing development was fairly new, with all the houses the same style in various shades of taupe, beige, and ecru trimmed in sage, tan, or mustard tones. They pulled up in front of one such beige home with several cars in the driveway and on the street in front of the house.

"We're here. This is my buddy, John's house," Jeremy said.

"So, are we going to a party or something?"

"Something like that," he answered mysteriously and climbed from the car. He hurried around the hood to open the door for Sunny while she collected her purse. "C'mon, it's gonna be really fun, and I guarantee you have never done anything like this before."

Sunny had visions of stepping into a house shrouded in darkness where a séance was being performed, or maybe they were going to a naughty nightie party and he expected her to model for him. She warily approached the house as he led her to the front door and let himself in, hollering, "Hey, John, we're here!"

They stood in a typical tri-level house, in a non-descript beige room with a brown sofa, a brown recliner, and a large screen plasma TV on the wall. The absence of decorative knick-knacks led Sunny to believe this was a single man's home. The living room opened into a kitchen area where she could see several pizza boxes and an open cooler sitting on the floor, full of ice and beer. Several ice cubes lay on the floor surrounding the cooler, dissolving slowly into random liquid pools.

Two sets of stairs were visible. The one going up was stacked with little piles of assorted books, shoes, and dirty socks waiting for the next person walking up the stairs to grab and take up with them. One lone track shoe dangled precariously off the edge of the step, barely hiding what might have been a sandwich.

The stairs leading into the basement were free of clutter. A framed poster of the Pink Floyd prism hung on the wall, and a significantly large bulldog lay across the top of the stairs, as if guarding the treasures that lay in the dungeons below. The dog watched them, moving only its eyes, as though lifting its head would take too much effort.

"Get your ass down here! We're just starting," a deep voice bellowed from the basement, and the dog did lift its head and utter a small whine. "And bring the lovely Priscilla, would ya?" His request was followed by male laughter emanating from several voices.

"Be right there," Jeremy yelled down as he headed into the kitchen. "Sunny, you want pepperoni, cheese, or supreme?"

"Um, pepperoni, I guess." *What the heck am I doing here? Who was this John, and why does he think my name is Priscilla?*

"Beer or Coke?"

"Got any diet?" Sunny still had enough wits about her to ask.

Jeremy had two paper plates of pizza stacked on top of each other and a bottle of beer jammed under his arm pit as he dug into the cooler. He extracted a Diet Coke, dislodging several more ice cubes that plummeted to the floor.

"Here, can you hold these?" He handed her the can of soda and the plates of pizza.

He stepped over the dog, took two steps down, turned and hoisted the fat pooch into his arms before he started down the stairs. "C'mon," he said over his shoulder.

Well, at least the mystery of the lovely Priscilla was solved. But what was she doing following some guy she didn't even know into a basement filled with male laughter? All she knew of the owner was he had big feet, didn't decorate or care about water stains on his hardwood floor, and fed his dog frequently. All for the allure of pepperoni pizza, and because Edna knew somebody with a grandson.

# 10

*Bzzt! Bzzt!*

The vibrating of his cell phone jerked him awake. Jake had been dreaming that he was being crushed by a heavy weight.

In reality, he was being crushed by an eighty-pound furry Golden Retriever. Beau had crawled up onto the sofa and sprawled across Jake's prone body while he dozed. Beau now lifted his head from where it had been tucked into the space between Jake's neck and shoulder.

Jake reached for the phone that bounced along the edge of the coffee table as it continued to buzz.

He flipped open the phone while trying to push Beau off his chest. "Hello," he croaked. The dog reluctantly stepped to the floor, circled the coffee table, and came back to rest his head in Jake's lap. One of Beau's ears flipped back, as if the dog were actually listening to the one-sided conversation.

"No, I'm fine. Just doing some research. What's up?"

"Yeah, I found the will. It definitely mentions me in it, but I can't find any place where it mentions her."

"I've tried to talk to some of the neighbors about Walter and his actions the last several months, but I haven't gotten very far. I'm not sure they really trust me. Yet."

"I know that, but some of the neighbors act suspicious of me already. I can't push too hard or I will blow the connections that I am making."

Jake absentmindedly patted Beau's head as he continued his side of the phone call. The dog whined as Jake's voice rose in frustration. "I *realize* this is a dangerous situation. I'm worried we may be running out of time."

"I'm still working on his computer and searching the house, but I haven't found much we can use. The man saved everything from old tin foil to eight track tapes."

"Don't worry. I'll let you know as soon as I find anything."

"You don't have to remind me how dangerous she is. I remember."

"All right. I'll be in touch."

"Bye."

Jake stood and stretched, his muscles sore from sleeping on the ancient sofa and bearing the weight of the dog. Said dog seemed to have wandered off, and Jake picked up his empty paper plate and soda can to carry into the kitchen. As he went in search of his canine house guest, thoughts of the conversation with his boss replayed in his head.

He had been surprised to see he and his mom mentioned in Walter's will. *I didn't think the old man even acknowledged that I was alive.* The old bitterness surfaced, no matter how hard he tried to forget.

He knew he needed to put his personal feelings aside and focus on figuring out what happened to his grandfather and the woman Jake was afraid he was involved with. As angry as Jake was, he wasn't sure he wished her kind of vengeance on anyone, even Walter.

Jake tossed the trash into the wastebasket under the sink and whistled for the dog.

"Here, Beau. C'mere, boy," he called as he wandered from room to room.

Beau made his entrance from the hallway leading to the bedrooms. He proudly held a new found treasure aloft in his mouth.

"Whatcha got there, boy?" Jake asked, as he reached for what looked like either a very old flannel shirt or a rag used to clean the bathroom.

Beau recognized this game and raced around the room, pausing only to look back to make sure Jake still chased him. And he did.

He chased that dog all over the house, trying in vain to retrieve the cloth treasure. At one point, he had it, but then lost the game of tug of war, and Beau took off again. Jake did have it long enough to recognize it as a flannel shirt and to wonder if the hardened brown splotches that ran down the sleeve were dried blood.

Seeing the possible blood stains ramped up his heart rate and created more questions in Jake's mind. What had Walter gotten himself into? Had the woman Jake searched for hurt Walter, then staged the explosion of the garage to cover her tracks?

Jake hadn't taken the time to fully explore the garage before the explosion, and he pushed back the guilt of wondering if he could have found his grandfather inside, possibly hurt or already dead. He picked up his efforts to capture the shirt, but that only increased Beau's commitment to keeping it.

"You win," Jake cried as he collapsed on the floor, the green shag carpet rough against his outstretched arms. He closed his eyes and was catching his breath when the offensive, crusted- and now wet with slobber-material dropped onto his chest. Jake's eyes fluttered opened to see Beau's giant head leaning toward him, a drop of slobber clinging to his lolling tongue as warm breath panted into his face.

Jake grabbed the shirt and rolled just as the slobbery drop left Beau's mouth and descended to the carpet below.

He held the shirt gingerly in one hand as he carried it into the kitchen and got a trash bag from the box under the sink. Jake had hoped this was just an old work shirt and the brown stains were paint, but upon closer examination, Jake was fairly certain the sleeve was covered in dried blood. His worry and frustration deepened as he chastised himself for not getting here sooner.

He dropped the shirt into the bag, tied it closed, and then grabbed his car keys before he opened the back door for himself and Beau.

The dog raced outside and ran around the yard, sniffing bushes and spots of grass as Jake carried the trash bag to his car and locked it into his trunk.

Heading back into the house, the dog at his heels, Jake looked up to see the curtains in Edna's kitchen drop quickly back into place.

"That nosy old woman sees everything," he whispered to Beau. "Now, if I can only get her to trust me..."

Following Jeremy into the basement, Sunny prepared herself for a lot of things. What she wasn't prepared for was walking into a room filled with six people and eight computer stations. The room was decked out in so much technology, it looked like NASA.

As they walked in, a few of the men looked up and gave Sunny appraising glances, but the others were too intent on whatever action was happening on their screen to notice her.

The basement was a large room with one side a typical living room complete with couch, coffee table, and television. The other side of the room was a wall of shelves with a counter that ran the length of the room at about desk height. Four cubbies were spaced along the wall and laptops or PCs were set into each one.

In the center of the room, four cheap, particle board desks sat back to back to make a large workstation. Each desk also had a computer on it. Rows of cords and wiring snaked across the floor connecting computers to power strips and wall sockets. Some of the cords were duct-taped to the floor while others ran pell-mell across the room as if they were the tentacles of a giant computer beast.

Three men and one woman sat at the desks in the center of the room. Two other men sat at the far cubbies against the wall.

"Hey, everybody. This is Sunny, my date for the

evening." Jeremy nodded at her as he placed the overweight pooch on the floor beside the first man who sat at the desks against the wall. "Sunny, this is John, the owner of this fine establishment, and the proud papa of our beautiful Priscilla here."

John reached out to shake Sunny's hand, and she passed the plates of pizza to Jeremy. John wore an open, friendly grin and had a warm handshake. "Nice to meet you. Thanks for filling in tonight," he said, as he slipped one foot from his flip-flop and absentmindedly began massaging the dog's back with his bare foot.

"You're welcome," she said. "But Jeremy hasn't filled me in yet on what we're doing here this evening."

"We're playing an MMORPG," said one of the men at the desks, "and we need to get started."

"A what?" Sunny asked.

"A Massive Multi-player Online Role-Playing Game," said the woman, with a roll of her eyes. "They like to use technical jargon."

"I'm Rachel," she continued, "and this is my husband, Mike, and his brother, Bill." She pointed first to the dark-haired man who sat next to her, then across to a younger version of the dark-haired Mike.

"Bill and Nick work with me at the office." Jeremy gestured to the two men at the desks. "Bill brought Mike and Rachel into the game."

"This is our bi-monthly date night," Rachel said. "We've all played this game every other week for over a year now. It's something fun to do together and a date night away from the kids for Mike and I."

"The guy sitting behind John over there is Tim." Jeremy waved to a short, heavyset man with thinning blond hair.

"Nice to meet you, Sunny," Tim addressed her with a nod. "Have you ever played World of Warcraft before?"

"No, I've never even heard of it." Sunny heard Mike

let out a groan behind her. “But I like games, and I’m a quick learner.”

“Well, you better be, because we’re all waiting for you two so we can start our raid,” Mike said.

Sunny looked blankly at Jeremy who had set the pizza and beer on the counter and was setting up the two laptops closest to them.

“It’s easy, Sunny,” Jeremy assured her. “You’ll catch on really quick. Here, have a seat.” He pulled out the chair between himself and John and gestured for her to sit. He moved the two laptops closer together.

Sunny was intrigued by this game idea and everyone in the room seemed to think it was fun. Feeling a little intimidated by the closeness and experience of the group, she listened intently to Jeremy’s instructions.

“World of Warcraft is a game played on many different realms. Everyone in this room has built a character and has played long enough to build up to be level eighty players,” he said.

“Is that good?” she asked.

“Yes, that’s very good. That means they’ve done countless quests and fought a ton of battles. We meet here every other Saturday night and play the game as a team with a bunch of other players online. We’ll do a ten-person raid tonight so we’ll battle together until we reach a Boss, or a really big dragon, then we’ll fight him and take him down together.”

Sunny was fascinated by the images on the screen. The colors of the computer-generated world were vibrant blues, greens and purples, and the details of the castles and the trees and the animals were wonderful. Jeremy brought up a character on her screen of a dwarf with long reddish-blond hair wearing a purple shirt covered with gold stars, holding a shield and a mace. A black panther paced in the background behind the dwarf.

“I’m going to let you play one of my characters

tonight," Jeremy said. "This is Hesiod. He's a hunter, which means he specializes in ranged attack, which is bows and arrows and things you throw."

"Cool. He looks kind of like Gimley from Lord of the Rings."

"Yes, he does. That's because Gimley was also a dwarf. Now, this beautiful beast behind him is his pet. Her name is Cocoa Puff." This elicited a few snickers from the men around her, but Jeremy ignored them and continued his instructions. "I've set her so she will attack anyone who comes near you."

"Go, Cocoa Puff!" Sunny cheered. "But what if I get near one of you? Will she attack you?"

"Good question, but no. We are all in an alliance together, and you or your pets can't hurt any of your friends or your alliances you're doing the raid with. You won't fight us; you can walk right through us if you want."

He clicked on a box labeled ENTER WORLD, and Sunny's dwarf suddenly stood in a village looking at a water fountain.

"Wow. This looks just like Belle's village from *Beauty and the Beast*," she said, only to elicit another groan from one of the dark haired brothers.

"My character is Stroszec, who is also a dwarf, but I'm a Paladin, which means I'm a Defender of the Light. I specialize in..."

"Killing puppies and punching kittens," John filled in.

Sunny looked up at him horrified as the men in the room broke into laughter.

"Be prepared for plenty of Junior High humor with this crowd," Rachel told her, good-naturedly.

"He's teasing you," Jeremy said. "Really, I'm speced for Retribution, so I carry a two-handed weapon, and I hit people *really* hard."

He used both his mouse and Sunny's, and she watched as their characters ran through the woods to a copse of trees where a group of assorted characters stood in a large huddle around a doorway that glowed with a bluish light.

Jeremy pointed out each character as he introduced them to her.

"So, this enchanting creature is Rachel." He pointed to a tall, svelte woman dressed in blue and gold with long, flaming red hair. Quite the opposite of the cute, chunky five-foot two blonde who sat across the room.

"My character's name is Aliya and I'm a Mage, so I stand in the background and cast spells while my brave husband goes in and fights." Rachel smiled over at her husband, who was currently wearing a scowl. "This is Mike's character, Zeus." She pointed to a tall, dark haired man whose outfit was adorned with spikes and skulls. "He's a Death Knight, so he uses diseases to fight with. His brother is Prometheus, he's the one next to him in blue, and he's a healer. John's character is a healer, too. John and Bill will help heal us when we get hurt in battle and restore our health levels."

"Tim's character is this little gnome that looks kind of like him." Jeremy razzed his friend. "His name is Bankerboy, which is clever because he is a loan officer at the bank, and he's a warlock. In the game, not at the bank. So he creates soul stones to give you so you can come back to life if you die."

"Good to know." Sunny was a bit overwhelmed by all the information, but loved how they were so into the characters and the game setting. She tried to keep track of the names and the traits of each player.

"Nick's character is a Night Elf Druid who can change into different animals. He's our Tank so he'll change into a huge bear, go into the fight first, and start killing everything in sight."

"Okay. I think I've got the gist of it. Who is this other woman?" Sunny pointed to a blonde woman dressed in blue and purple. She was holding a bow, and a white tiger prowled near her.

"That's Kynsya. She's a human hunter, and that's her pet, Chaos," John explained. "We don't really know who she is. Anyone can join your raid if you don't have enough people, and she asked to play with us tonight. I hope she knows what she's doing." He looked pointedly at Jeremy. Sunny got the feeling not everyone was overjoyed at her joining the fun tonight.

"John's our group leader so he can let other people into our raid," Jeremy said. "Kynsya is good. I've played with her before."

"Are we ever going to start?" Mike asked.

"Let's do it," Jeremy said. "It's on like Donkey Kong!" he cried to the others in the room before quietly telling Sunny, "I'll help you as we go along."

The characters all grouped together, stepped through the portal, and the raid began. Jeremy showed her how to move forward and shoot her weapon at monsters. Mostly she just wandered around lost trying to figure out how to move her character. Sunny's pet killed more monsters than she did.

"Hey, look, if you press the space bar, you can jump," Sunny said, excited with her accidental find and pressed it to jump her character up and down several times. Evidently, everyone else in the room knew this trick because no one seemed to achieve the same level of excitement she did.

They spent the next two hours strategizing their game plan, going on quests, fighting different battles, and moving their characters from place to place.

Sunny spent most of her time trying to find the battles, figuring out how to shoot her gun, and getting herself killed. The healers spent a lot of their time restoring her health each time she died. Jeremy tried to help her, and John and Rachel gave her a lot of helpful tips. Most of the others tried to pretend they didn't know her.

In the battles, Jeremy's character tried to protect Sunny and so did, surprisingly, the new character to their group, Kynsya. She stepped in and saved Sunny several times, including once when she was facing the wrong direction.

The game had a dialogue box in the corner where people could talk to each other and none of Sunny's comments were flattering.

As a grade school teacher, she was used to comments like, "You gave it your best!" and "I can see you're really trying." And simply "Good job!" The comments Sunny got were, "Why do you keep *#!*#! jumping up and down?!" and "Try not to get killed this time!" and "Fight or get out of the way!"

The only 'good job' Sunny got was "Good job getting yourself killed *again*!"

She was repeatedly called a Noob and Sunny leaned over to Rachel to ask her what that meant. "Do they think I'm playing like a girl? Is Noob code for Boob?" she asked.

"No." Rachel laughed. "Noob is short for new-bie because they can tell you're new to the game."

"Basically, it means you suck," Mike said.

Rachel elbowed him in the side. "Be nice."

"Well, she does," he mumbled. "You shouldn't have shown her how to tell a joke. I was fighting three monsters and she was right beside me and all she did was jump up and down and tell me a knock-knock joke."

It was a fairly complicated game, and Sunny couldn't remember all the keys and functions to fight and do damage.

"I swear I don't even know how I caused an 'aggro'," she said, but evidently her actions drew the giant dragon they were battling to attack and kill their whole raid, including the healers.

"Well, that was just great," Bill grumbled.

"Sorry you guys," Sunny said weakly. "You all were doing a really good job."

Her positive reinforcement comment was met with

grumbles and sighs as they all began to shut down and pack up their equipment.

"I think we're gonna head out." Jeremy guided Sunny toward the stairs before a lynch mob could form. "I'll come by and pick up my stuff tomorrow."

"It was really great meeting you all. I had fun playing your game with you," Sunny called as they headed up the stairs.

John followed them up, and Sunny thanked him and apologized again for the whole dragon killing them and ruining the game thing. She had a surprisingly good time tonight. She loved watching the interactions of the friends in the room and how they worked as a team in the game. Her ego was a little bruised at how poorly she had played, but she *was* a World of Warcraft virgin, and the others had been playing for years.

"Don't worry about it. You added a whole new level to our game, Sunny." He smirked at Jeremy. "See ya Monday, Bro."

The ride back across town was fairly quiet. Sunny tried to reassure Jeremy what a fun time she had, despite her obvious lack of gaming abilities. She thought he must have had a whole other idea of how this night was going to go in his head.

They pulled up in front of her house, and Jeremy looked at his watch. "It's only eight-thirty. It's still pretty early if you want to do something else."

In all honesty, the allure of going into her house, taking a hot bath, and curling up on the sofa was pretty strong, but Sunny felt like Edna had tried so hard to set up this date the least she could do was give it another few hours. Plus Jeremy was kind of cute, and he seemed like a nice guy.

"Okay. What did you have in mind?" she asked.

"How about we go back to my house and watch a movie. I have a big screen TV and a pretty extensive movie collection. I think I even have some popcorn."

"Sure, let's watch a movie." That's probably what she would do at home anyway. "Why don't I get my car and follow you over so you don't have to drive me home again."

"I don't mind at all."

"It's silly for you to leave once you're already home." Sunny pushed open the door and climbed out. "I'll just follow you." This also worked better for her, so if the date started to go south, she could make a quick getaway.

Sunny got into her car and backed from the driveway, giving a longing glance to her house and the comfy afghan she could be curled under. Gazing at Walter's house, her thoughts suddenly had Jake curled under that afghan with her, and they weren't watching television. She envisioned that hot bath and leaning back into Jake's soapy slick chest.

Sunny followed Jeremy's truck out of the neighborhood and tried to refocus her thoughts on her current date. She didn't want to disappoint Edna, who had been really excited about Sunny meeting the grandson of one of her oldest friends. Jeremy had certainly been a huge step up from the last two dates she had been on, and he was trying.

Besides, who knew how long Jake was even going to be in town? He could go home to wherever, or he could be going to prison for murdering her neighbor. Sunny resolved to put 'dangerous' Jake out of her mind and focus on 'safe' video game guy, Jeremy.

They had driven into a newer, upscale neighborhood, and Jeremy pulled into the driveway of a large, beautifully landscaped house. Sunny parked on the street and met him at the front door.

He ushered her into the foyer of a large living room tastefully decorated with man-sized, comfortable-looking furniture, nice artwork on the walls, and a thick Berber rug on the floor in front of an immense gas fireplace.

Jeremy led her through the living room into a huge kitchen decorated in shades of maroon and gray, with gleaming black appliances and shiny Corian counter tops.

"Wow! You have a gorgeous home," Sunny told him as she planted her rump in one of the stools pulled up to the center island.

"Thanks. My mom did a lot of the decorating."

"That's nice. You two must be very close."

"Oh, we are. My parents divorced when I was in grade school, so growing up it was just my mom, my brother, and me. My mom is awesome. You want some wine?"

"Sure." She watched him smoothly slide wine glasses from a rack under the counter and pull a bottle of wine from a small wine cooler. He poured two glasses and set one in front of her.

"So, action-adventure or chick-flick?" he asked. "I've got a ton of movies to choose from."

"Comedy." She picked up her wine glass and followed him into the living room. A large flat screen television covered one wall and recessed shelving flanked either side of it. He did have a huge selection of movies, and she poked through his section of comedies and chose one with Hugh Grant. His dry sense of humor could always make her laugh.

Setting her wine glass on the coffee table, she surveyed the room. Plush throw pillows and blankets dotted the sofa and loveseat. Jeremy turned on the fireplace and dimmed the lights so they had all the ambience of a romantic mood.

They sat next to each other on the sofa, and Sunny pulled off her boots, curled her feet under her, and dragged a throw across her legs. "This is nice." She smiled at Jeremy.

"Yeah."

They settled in to watch the movie, and it only took Jeremy about half an hour to awkwardly get his arm around her shoulders. She snuggled into his side. This really was nice. Romantic lighting, a little wine, a flickering glow from the fireplace, all the right setting, so when Jeremy leaned in to kiss her, she threw caution to the wind and leaned right back.

"Ouch. Sorry." Their noses collided as their exuberance resulted in a facial collision.

He smiled apologetically and came toward her again. This time Sunny held still, and his hand came up to hold her face as he gingerly kissed her. He tasted like wine as their lips parted and his tongue explored hers. Sunny eased back on the sofa and his arm that had been around her got pinned between her shoulder and the cushion.

He groaned as he pulled his arm free, and she shifted to give him more room. Her legs got tangled in the throw as she shifted again to push the blanket to the floor. He continued to kiss her, and his left hand moved slowly up her leg, across her hip and grazed the side of her breast before circling behind her back and cupping her shoulder. His kisses moved from her lips down to her neck, and Sunny sighed with pleasure.

"Jeremy, when did you get home?" a female voice asked from the hallway as the light snapped on.

"Mom?" Jeremy croaked.

"Mom?" Sunny asked. "You live with your mother?"

"No. She's just…staying with me, I guess."

"Yeah, right." Sunny quickly readjusted her blouse and grabbed her boots.

"No, really…" Jeremy stood and tried to do some readjusting of his own.

Meanwhile, his mom had fled back into the kitchen, and Sunny thought she could hear her laughing as she called out, "Sorry, honey. I didn't know you had company."

"I'd better go." Sunny made her way to the door, boots in hand.

"Sunny, let me explain…"

But it was too late. She slipped through the door, calling, "I'll see ya, Jeremy. I really need to get home to check on my dog anyway."

Sunny ran barefoot across the grass, threw her boots in the car, and started the engine. Pulling away, she took one last look at his beautiful home, and shook her head. *No wonder he has such a great house. He lives with his mom.*

❀❀❀

Sunny pulled her car into the driveway, got out and headed for Walter's house, still barefoot. She hit the top step as the front door swung open to Beau and Jake, one holding a beer and both wearing sloppy grins.

"I've heard of a guy knocking your socks off before, but I've never actually seen it happen." Jake passed her the cold bottle as he looked down at her bare feet.

"Thanks." She took a long pull and wondered how she could feel so relaxed around Jake. "It's been an interesting night."

"C'mon in. I've got to hear this."

So, once again, Sunny found herself on the sofa with a drink in hand and a cute guy sitting next to her. But this felt different. She was comfortable with Jake on one side of her and the dog curled into her other side.

Sunny didn't know why Jake was so easy for her to talk to. Was it the fact that he was a stranger and she knew he wouldn't be here for long? Or was it a deeper connection that she felt for this man? What drew her to him despite the danger that oozed from his every pore?

And he was dangerous. Whether he had killed Walter or not, this man had seen danger. His cool surfer boy attitude didn't mask the keen intelligence in Jake's eyes.

Sunny didn't fill him in on every aspect of the

evening. She kept the part where she made out with Jeremy on the sofa to herself, but she told him all about showing up at this strange guy's house and how this group of people were playing an online game together.

"Have you ever heard of a game called World of Warcraft?" she asked him.

"Sure. I even have an online account and several characters."

"You do?"

"Yeah, I love it."

"Have you ever done a raid?"

"Tons of them."

"What level are you?"

"Level eighty."

"Wow. You must be pretty good."

"You have no idea." He said this with an evil grin, and she narrowed her eyes at his double entendre. Sunny had plenty of ideas and dreams and fantasies of how *good* he just might be.

"Well," she said, her mouth suddenly dry. She took a drink from the cool bottle of beer in her hand. "Do you know how to jump?"

"You mean by hitting the space bar?"

*Dang! I guess everyone knew about that.*

She had fun telling him all the details of the game. He laughed at her 'Noob' status and groaned when she explained how she got the whole raid killed by drawing an agro-attack from the 'Boss'.

"So, you say another character helped you? Why do you think they were doing that?" he asked.

"Oh, I don't know. I figured they felt sorry for me because they knew I was a Noob and they remembered how it felt to be a beginner and need help. Why?"

"Just wondering," he said casually, and then changed the subject. "So, how did you leave in his car and end up coming home in yours?"

She told him about Jeremy's invitation to watch a

movie at his house, and how she followed him over so he wouldn't have to drive her back later. She gushed over his beautiful house, told him how Jeremy had said his mom helped him to decorate, and how close he said they were.

"I should have known something was up when I checked out his movie collection. I was expecting rows and rows of 'tech guy' stuff like X-files and Star Trek, and I guess he did have a ton of Vin Diesel action flicks, but he had quite a large selection of romantic comedies. I mean, how many guys have five Hugh Grant movies to choose from?"

"Hey, that guy is funny. He cracks me up," Jake said, in Jeremy's defense, which earned a raised eyebrow from Sunny.

"Well, he does."

"Okay."

"Besides, what does his movie collection have to do with anything?"

Sunny explained how they were *sitting* on the sofa when Jeremy's mom called from the kitchen, and about her sudden realization that her date for the evening still lived with his mother. Hence her subsequent barefooted flee from the house and eventual shoeless landing on his front stoop.

"That's hilarious. I wish I could have met this guy," Jake said. "Can I come over for the next one? I want to have a better mental picture when you're telling me about it next time."

*He was assuming there would be a 'next time'? Hmmmm.*

"Speaking of your dates," Jake said, suddenly taking a more serious tone, "how's it going with Hank the Tank? Is he still calling you all the time?"

"Um, I guess." Sunny didn't really want Jake to know that Hank still called her daily. "I tried to let him down easy, then I flat out told him I didn't want to go out with him anymore," she reluctantly admitted.

"But he doesn't get the hint; he just keeps calling me like I haven't said anything."

"Have you told him to stop calling you?"

"Pretty much. I don't want to be mean."

"Sunny, you have to be firm. It sounds like this lunk-head isn't getting the message."

Beau must not have liked Jake's stern tone, because he got off the sofa and came up behind him to nudge his arm up with his snout. Jake must have been startled by Beau's wet-nosed nudge. He yanked his arm up, effectively spilling his beer down the front of his shirt.

"Damn." Jake cursed, and both of them jumped up to keep the spilled beer from getting on the sofa. "This is my last clean t-shirt." His voice was muffled as he pulled the soiled shirt over his head.

Sunny sucked in her breath as she took in the full view of Jake's tanned abs and his muscled chest. *Damn was right.* Had the temperature in the room just increased by ten degrees?

Jake turned and took her arm, pulling her closer to him. "I'm serious about this, Sunny. I'm worried this meathead might be getting too attached to you. You let me know if you have any problems with this guy."

His face was set in a look of concern, and all of a sudden, the room felt much smaller. His half-naked body seemed much closer. Her breath caught as she lost herself in his eyes, and he bent his head closer to hers.

She could smell the scent of beer on his breath and could almost feel his warm lips against hers. Sunny's body ached with a yearning to be against his, and she rested her hand on his bare chest. He shivered as her fingertips touched his skin. His arm encircled her waist, and his hand flattened against her back drawing her closer to him. His lips were feather light as they brushed against hers, then he pulled her against him and his mouth took hers with a devouring hunger. Sunny's body responded with an urgency she didn't know was in her. Her hands ran up his chest and her arms encircled his neck. She filled her hands with his thick soft hair and pulled his mouth deeper into hers. There was none of the awkwardness she had felt while trying to kiss Jeremy. This was pure passion she felt as she gripped Jake's bare shoulders.

Suddenly, he jerked upright, his back arched and he let out a strangled groan.

Jake was in obvious pain, and as she pushed back from him, Sunny realized the source of his pain were the claws of the four-legged creature who had jumped up on his back in order to not be left out of their embrace. Jake looked over his shoulder as Sunny pushed Beau from him. Angry red scratches formed where the dog's claws had raked down Jake's back.

"Oh, man, that hurts." Jake winced, but the next instant laughed as he playfully pulled Beau's head against his shoulder. "You worried you were being left out, boy?"

"I'm so sorry! Are you okay?" She couldn't believe that he was playing with the dog instead of being angry that Beau had scratched him.

"Yeah, I'm fine. Don't worry," he assured her, "this body has seen much worse damage than a few dog scratches."

The break from Jake's embrace and that subtle comment about Jake's unknown past brought her to her senses. Though her body ached to feel Jake against her again, her head told her she needed to slow down, do not pass Go, and do not collect two hundred dollars.

"Ya know, I should probably go," Sunny said. It took everything in her to get up from the sofa. She was so drawn to this man, but she had made mistakes before and there was still so much she didn't know about him. She considered just asking him if he did something to hurt Walter, but part of her was afraid that once the truth came out, she wouldn't be able to be with him again. Was she willing to risk not finding out the truth just to kiss him again?

"Really? You don't have to. I'm fine."

"It's late and we should probably get home." Sunny knew she needed time to think and sort out her feelings. She walked to the door before her body betrayed her and jumped him. "Thanks again for watching Beau tonight, and I'm really sorry about your back. I hope you're okay."

"I told you I'm fine. And I will watch Beau anytime." He held the door for her, and Sunny escaped, still barefoot, into the cool night air. "Hey, Sunny," he called from the doorway.

She stopped and looked back. His lean body was silhouetted against the light coming from the house, and it took all she had to not run back and throw herself into his arms. "Yeah?"

"You *can* trust me," he said softly, looking into her eyes. Then he stepped back into the house and closed the door behind him.

Maybe, but right now, she didn't think she could trust herself.

Peaceful is what Piper felt as she sat in the saddle astride a large brown gelding. She turned her face to the sun and sighed as the horse plodded up to the open barn door. She loved the feel of being atop the steed, the reins in her hand, and the way she moved in sync to the rhythm of the horse's stride.

She and Cassie had spent a lot of time talking, and Piper felt herself open up more and more to her aunt. One evening, as they sat on the back deck together, Piper had confessed her dream of learning to ride. Two days later, Cassie had surprised her with six weeks of riding lessons at the Lazy G Ranch. Piper had thrown her arms around her aunt and gushed out her thanks before she even knew what she was doing.

This was Piper's third week of lessons since summer had started, and she had been having the time of her life. She reveled in the cool morning rides and the scents of dusty earth mingled with horse and manure. She remembered this feeling from before her dad had died, when times were good and she'd been happy.

Life with Uncle Matt and Aunt Cassie had settled into a routine, and the time she spent with Drew was both thrilling and comforting at the same time. She sighed again as she recognized this feeling as *happiness*, and she let herself enjoy it just for now, in this moment.

"You gonna sit up there and daydream all

morning?" a deep voice drawled, which brought her crashing back to reality.

Piper looked down into the grinning face that tipped up to her from beneath a straw cowboy hat and smiled at the gorgeous cowboy who had taken hold of her horse's bridle.

"Nope." She kept her head down to hide her blush as she swung her leg over the horse's rump and freed her toe from the stirrup. "Just enjoying the ride."

"You look like it," the cowboy said. "You're doing really well, Piper. You really seem at ease with the horses."

"Thanks, Levi." Piper blushed again, unused to praise. He had been her instructor the past three weeks. He and his father owned the ranch where she had been riding. Piper had been on the lookout for a candidate for Sunny's date the past several weeks and had decided Levi would be a good match. She had shared her idea with Cassie that morning as they drove to the ranch. Cassie wanted to check out Piper's choice so the two of them set up a reconnaissance mission to spy on the hunky cowboy as he went about his morning chores on the ranch.

Cassie had admired Levi's muscled wiry frame as he hauled a bale of hay to the corral and easily tossed it over the fence. He spoke gently to the horses as they plodded over for their morning meal.

"He is really cute," Cassie whispered to Piper from their hiding spot behind the edge of the barn. "And those Wranglers show off his great butt!"

"Aunt Cassie!" Piper's eyes widened in shock at her aunt's comment.

"Well, they do," Cassie said, and they broke into giggles as Cassie tried to hush Piper.

Her aunt had given her the thumbs up, so as Piper brushed the dust from her jeans, she nonchalantly asked him, "So Levi, are you single?"

"What?" The cowboy looked up in surprise.

"I mean are you seeing anyone right now or would you be available to go out with someone?"

"Well," Levi croaked, a blush creeping up his neck. "I'm really flattered Piper, but I have a policy against dating my students."

"Your students? What?" she asked, confused. "Oh, not me! That's gross!"

"Well, thanks a lot."

"Sorry. That's not what I meant. I was wondering if you would be interested in going out with this woman in my book club. She's my aunt's best friend, and she's blonde and cute and funny, and don't worry, she's old like you."

"Well, that does relieve my mind. And what makes you think this blonde, cute, funny woman, who is old, like me, would want to go out with a cowboy?" he drawled lazily.

Piper explained a little about the book club and their mission to set Sunny up on six blind dates.

"They trusted me to pick one of the dates, and you seem really nice, and you have a job, and you're like cute and all."

"For an old guy, you mean?" he clarified. "Does she like to ride?"

"I don't know. Probably, like I mean, who wouldn't? She's really cool, though. I know you would like her. So what do you think? Are you free this Saturday?"

"Well, you do have me intrigued," Levi said, taking his hat off and scratching the side of his head. "You've got me just curious enough about this Sunny to want to meet her. I guess I could bring her out to the ranch and take her horseback riding for the afternoon."

"That would be great. I bet she'd really like that." Piper beamed up at him. "I'll give you her number."

She plucked his cell phone from the holster on his belt and with practiced ease entered Sunny's name and number into his contact list. "I'll tell her about you tonight at book club, so wait until tomorrow to call her."

"All right, but if this turns out to be a disaster, you're cleaning out stable stalls with me next week after your lessons."

"Deal." She laughed and waved to Levi, who leaned back against the horse, his hat tipped back on his head.

"You're gonna like her! See ya next week," Piper called as she ran toward the car waiting for her in the driveway, her cowboy boots kicking up dust behind her.

The boots had been a gift from Uncle Matt, who had proudly presented them to her on her first day of lessons.

"You need some boots if you're gonna ride horses," he had said. "Hope these will work for you. Cassie told me your size."

"Thanks, Uncle Matt." Piper hadn't known what else to say, she was so flustered at the unexpected gift of kindness from her uncle.

Now, she stomped the dust from her new boots as she opened the car door and slid into the seat.

"How's my cowgirl?" Drew leaned in to give her a hug.

"Awesome," she replied, still amazed that this incredible guy was her boyfriend. Her insides went gooey as he nuzzled her neck and placed a warm kiss below her ear. She turned to him and rubbed her cheek against his soft hair. She didn't know what shampoo he used but she loved the way his hair always smelled like Jolly Ranchers.

"You gotta be hungry after ridin' the range and rounding up all those cattle," he teased. "Where do you want to eat?"

"Surprise me," Piper said. She leaned her head back against the seat and smiled as Drew put the car in gear, then reached for her hand to hold as he drove away from the ranch.

Ten minutes later, they arrived in town while Piper filled Drew in on her conversation with Levi and her thoughts on setting him up as Sunny's next blind date.

Drew suggested a little deli downtown with patio seating, and they sat outside enjoying an Italian sub sandwich, some chips, and the summer sunshine.

Piper was in the middle of a story about a girl from her last school when she saw Jake's blue Mustang pull up and park on the street across from where they sat. Jake got out and pulled a black garbage bag from his trunk before hurrying into the building across the street.

"Hey, look." She nudged Drew to look in the direction of her nod. "There's Jake, you know, Sunny's neighbor, the guy Edna saw with the gun. I wonder what he's doing down here."

The stucco-sided building Jake had entered was a mix of office suites with a sign out front listing the three businesses within: Aliya Salon and Day Spa, Madame Zia, Psychic and Tarot Card Readings, and Jerry Finney, Private Investigations, Inc.

"Well," Drew said, "he's either getting his palm read, his back waxed, or he's meeting with the private detective."

Piper laughed and took another bite of the sandwich they shared. She chewed slowly while she puzzled over Jake's sudden appearance.

They finished eating and were tossing around possible explanations when Jake emerged from the building and hurried to his Mustang.

As he reached for the door handle, he looked across the street and stared directly at Piper. He kept his gaze steady on hers for a full beat, his mouth set in a tight line before shaking his head, getting into the car and speeding away.

"That was scary." Piper released the breath she had been holding.

"C'mon," Drew said. He gathered up their trash and

dumped it into the garbage can before he grabbed her hand and jogged across the street toward the office building. "Let's go see what he was up to."

They stepped through the doors into the cool interior of the adobe style building. A wide hallway ran through the center of the building. Wooden benches and large potted plants sat in the hallway consistent with the mission style of decorating. Two office fronts lined each side of the building. The salon had full windows and encompassed one whole side. Through the windows, four chairs were visible and in one sat a blonde woman in the midst of a highlight, half her head covered in folded aluminum foil squares. Two pedicure chairs were visible on the other side of the room, a dark haired woman in one, her head tilted back against the head rest as her bare feet sat in the bubbling tub of water.

"He wasn't in there long enough to get his haircut," Drew said.

"Or a pedicure," Piper teased. "They take like an hour."

"That leaves these two choices," Drew said as they turned to face the other two store fronts, both with their blinds drawn so they couldn't see into either office.

The first door was purple with mystical designs of stars and moons. The window was painted with a large eye, and the words surrounding it boasted, FULL PSYCHIC READINGS IN UNDER AN HOUR. LET MADAME ZIA 'SEE' WHAT THE FUTURE HOLDS FOR YOU.

The other door was plain, but the window had another painting of an eye, remarkably similar to the first window. However, surrounding this eye were the words, ***Jerry Finney, Private Investigations, Inc.***

"That eye is weird. They must have gotten a two-for-one deal," Piper said.

"Let's try this one first." Drew reached for the door of the private detective.

"What are you doing?" Piper asked in a panic.

"Just follow my lead."

Drew pushed open the door to find a non-descript room with a desk in the middle, two chairs set in front of it for clients, several file cabinets, some motel artwork on the walls, and two floor to ceiling bookshelves crammed with books and crime magazines. At the desk sat an average looking man of medium build with brown hair, wearing a blue open neck button-up shirt, jeans, and small reading glasses perched on his nose. He looked like an ordinary guy who would blend into any crowd. The reading glasses would have completed his dullness, if not for the shoulder holster with a gun strapped to his side.

He looked up when they stepped into the office, Piper bumping into Drew's back as he stopped suddenly.

"Can I help you two?" the man asked.

"We were hoping to get a psychic reading," Drew said.

"Sorry kids, you got the wrong door. Stupid eye is always throwing people off."

"Oh, sorry to bother you."

"No problem. You ask me, don't waste your money."

"Thanks," Drew said, as the two backed out of the office and pulled the door shut behind them. They had spent less than a minute in the private eye's office, but it was long enough to see the black garbage bag Jake had been carrying perched on the side of Jerry Finney's desk.

The sweet scent of cinnamon filled the kitchen as Cassie pulled the apple turnovers from the oven. It was her night to host book club, and she had baked up a storm earlier that day. A luscious chocolate cake sat on the counter, and Sunny nibbled on a cookie from a plate of Oatmeal Scotchies that sat next to her as she perched on a kitchen stool.

Cassie and Matt lived in a spacious brick house with three bedrooms on the main level and a full basement with two bedrooms downstairs. Her decorating style was a cross between cottage and country with lots of comfortable pillows, candles, and flower arrangements. She wanted people to walk into her home and feel like they could kick their shoes off and curl up on the sofa.

Cassie treasured the roles of wife and mother, and she was always taking care of someone or hosting an event at her house. The rooms of her home were usually filled with the smells of baking and the laughter of her kids and their friends.

The book club loved to sit in Cassie's large kitchen around her big oak table. She had spacious countertops filled with cookbooks, candles, baskets of paperwork and a big stoneware cookie jar that never sat empty.

In one corner of the kitchen sat a large fireplace, and Edna was balanced on the edge of the flagstone hearth. She also was eating a cookie and feeding little bites of it to Oswald, Cassie's little Welsh Corgi. Funny how the dog always seemed to sit next to Edna at every book club function.

Maggie had yet to arrive, and Piper sat sideways in the leather recliner next to the big picture window in the living room. Her feet dangled off one side as she pretended to read a book, but she looked around every time a car approached in anticipation of Drew pulling up to drop off his mom.

"They're here." She jumped out of her chair to check her hair in the mirror.

"Makin' sure there are no bats in the bat cave," Edna said, as Piper tipped her head back to do a quick nose check.

"Exactly." Piper laughed as she realized she had been caught in the act.

Edna shook her head in mock despair. "The length we girls go to for our fellas."

"But they're worth it." Piper gave her a smile and opened the front door to Drew.

"Hi, Drew," Cassie called. "Where's your mom?"

"Hi, Cassie. She's in the car answering her Blackberry."

"More like her 'Crackberry'," Sunny said. "I swear she's addicted to that thing."

"It's gotten worse lately. She's always on it," Drew said.

"Geez. How could someone spend so much time texting on their phone, I wonder," Cassie teased, looking from Piper to Drew.

Piper ignored Cassie's sarcasm. "We're going to sit on the deck for a few minutes." Leading Drew by the hand, she pulled on the sliding glass door. "Call me when you're ready to do the book discussion or when Sunny's going to tell us about her date."

"I can only stay for ten minutes. I'm picking up Dylan from soccer practice," Drew said.

Cassie smiled as she watched the two step onto the deck and sit next to each other in the glider swing. She turned to look out the front window to Maggie's car where her friend's dark-haired head bent forward as she typed furiously on her small black phone.

"That woman is always working," Cassie said out loud, before she headed back in to the kitchen to pour herself some iced tea.

❀❀❀

In her car, Maggie Hayes was doing anything but working. Her fingers feverishly worked the tiny keyboard as she responded to the latest text she had received.

It read, I can't seem to get u off my mind.

I've been thinkng about u a lot 2, she texted in return.

Will u still meet me 2nite? Same place, same time?

I will b there.

Can't wait.

Maggie couldn't control the secret smile that stole across her face as she closed the phone and held it to her chest.

With a contented sigh, she opened the car door and headed for Cassie's house.

❀❀❀

Sunny ran her fingers over the cover of the book. "I just love Jane Eyre." Sunny preferred for the discussion to be centered around a fictional love story, rather than on another botched attempt at finding her a match.

Drew had left to get his little brother and the women were gathered around the table to discuss their latest book club choice.

"Okay, so Jane Eyre, Jane Schm-eyre, who cares. I want to hear how the date went," Piper said, reaching for another cookie. "We've spent twenty minutes talking about the romance of a pretend character when we have a real romance I want to hear about."

Sunny laughed, knowing she was outnumbered. She told the group about her latest date, including the mix-up at the door, and how disappointed Jeremy was when he realized he wasn't going out with Maggie.

"Oh, he was not," Maggie said. The other girls were listening intently, but Sunny couldn't help but notice the little smirk that played across Edna's face as she watched Maggie reach for another cookie.

"What's that face for, Edna?" Sunny asked.

"Oh, nothing." Edna grinned. "Nothing the rest of you won't have to figure out for yourselves. If you'd all watch more CSI, you wouldn't even have to ask me!"

Cassie waved away Edna's comments. "I'm too busy to watch television." She gestured for Sunny to continue. "So, what happened then?"

The girls laughed like crazy as Sunny told them how Beau had barfed up her thong panties and then *oohed* and *ahhed* over the suspicious date that led into the basement. Sunny skipped most of the details of the online game. She hit the highlights of how Jeremy's friends thought she sucked, and how she ruined the whole raid by getting them all killed by a dragon.

She spent more time describing the details of how Jeremy's house was decorated than she had when she told Jake about it. But, this time she revealed to the girls that she and Jeremy had been kissing when his mother made her unannounced appearance.

"So you just ran out without letting him explain?" Piper asked.

"What's to explain?" Sunny answered. "He's a great guy, but he still lives with his mom."

"Maybe she really *was* just staying with him,"

Maggie offered.

"I don't know. It kind of felt like we kissed because it was the expected thing to do. It wasn't anything like the passion I felt later when I kissed Jake."

"Now we're getting to the good stuff," Piper said.

Cassie gasped. "You kissed Jake?"

"Well, I was standing right next to him, and he wasn't wearing a shirt, and he's got these great…eyes," Sunny said.

"Where was his shirt?"

"Beau nudged his hand, and he spilled his beer on it so he had to take it off."

"Did he spill beer on his pants too?" Maggie asked.

"No." Sunny laughed. "His pants stayed on."

"Dang," Piper said.

"Look, we just kissed, and then Beau interrupted us. I basically ran out of Walter's house," Sunny explained. "I feel guilty for kissing two men in one night." She looked pointedly at Piper. "I got caught up in the mood with Jeremy, but it's like Jake has this thing that draws me to him. Like I have a fish hook in my belly, and every time I'm near him, it reels me in closer to him."

"Real close," Edna muttered.

"I am attracted to him, but I still feel like he's dangerous. I know he's not telling me everything. In fact, he's told me nothing."

"Listen, Sunny, I realize Mr. Hotty-Pants is gorgeous," Edna said. "But I still don't trust him. I've got my eye on that one, and something just isn't right. What if the guy you kissed is the same guy who killed Walter?"

"I know. I know." Sunny covered her face with her hands.

"That night, when you were playing dungeons and dragons, I saw Jake bring a black garbage bag out of Walter's house and lock it in the trunk of his car. Now what kind of trash is so important you lock it into the backend of your car?" Edna asked.

"Maybe Sunny could distract him, and we could sneak out and check the trunk to see what's in the bag," Maggie said, a wicked gleam in her eye.

"You won't find it," Piper said.

All eyes turned to Piper, and Cassie's eyebrows shot up. "What do you know about it?"

"Well..." Piper obviously enjoyed the spotlight of having the group's full attention. "I've been waiting all night to tell you."

Piper regaled the group with her tale of seeing Jake with the aforementioned black garbage bag and Drew's sly detective skills at ferreting out where Jake had been.

"That was dangerous," Cassie admonished at the same time Maggie was declaring, "That's my boy." Cassie glared at Maggie, who shrugged.

"Are you sure it was the same bag?" Edna asked.

"How many black garbage bags tied together in a knot do you think Jake has locked in his trunk?" Piper asked in exasperation.

"Touché," Edna said. "Sunny, I think you need to stay clear of Mr. Sweet-Buns."

"I'm so confused," Sunny said. "I can feel there's something dangerous about Jake, but at times I also feel completely safe with him. Plus, he did rescue me from All-Hands Hank."

"*I'll Be Watching You...*" As if on cue, Sunny's pocket began the now familiar notes of Hank's ringtone. She pulled the phone out and pressed the button to ignore the call.

"What's that about?" Maggie asked.

Sunny had kept most of the details of Hank's repeated attempts to drag her down matrimony lane from the book club. She knew he was Matt and Cassie's friend and had wanted to tread lightly with Cassie, so as not to hurt her feelings. "I didn't want to tell you about this, because I know he's your friend and all, Cass, but Hank is kind of creeping me out."

"What do you mean? He's not my friend. Matt knew him in college, but he hasn't seen him in like, ten years. What's going on, Sunny?"

Sunny gave in and told the Page Turners about Hank's frequent phone calls, and his stubborn denial of Sunny's repeated turn downs.

"I haven't told anyone this, but I've been getting calls in the middle of the night, and when I answer, they don't say anything. They just listen for a few seconds and then hang up," Sunny said quietly.

"Why didn't you tell us?" Cassie asked and took Sunny's hand.

"I didn't want to worry anybody. At first I thought it was a mistake or a wrong number, but now it's happening more often, and I'm starting to get a little scared."

"Don't you have Caller ID?" Maggie asked.

"Yeah, but the number comes up as blocked."

"It could be Jake, trying to scare you," Edna said. "He seems like the type to know how to block Caller ID."

"I don't think it's Jake," Sunny said. "But I don't know if it's Hank either. It feels like someone is calling to check and see if I'm home."

"Sunny, I had no idea," Cassie said. "I knew Hank was a little pushy, but I didn't think he was dangerous. Don't worry, I'll take care of this." Her chair scraped loudly as she pushed it back from the table. She squeezed Sunny's hand, then with a fierce look on her face, strode from the room, yelling, "Matthew Paul Bennett, get in here."

"Don't mess with Cassie," Maggie said. She smiled at Cassie's retreating back. "Matt's going to get an earful. Seriously, Sunny, from a legal standpoint, next time he calls, you need to firmly state, 'Stop calling me'."

"Jake said the same thing."

"Jake knows about the calls?"

"Not the calls I'm getting at night, but he knows that Hank has been calling me a lot. He told me to flat out tell him to quit calling me."

"That's right," confirmed Maggie. "If you don't tell him to quit calling you, then you don't have a case once the police get involved."

"The police?" Matt said as he walked into the kitchen, Cassie on his heels. "I'm sure there's no need to get the police involved. It sounds like Hank just really likes you, Sunny."

He moved to stand behind Sunny's chair. "Listen, I'm really sorry Hank's been bugging you. I haven't seen the guy in forever, and you're not hurting my feelings if you don't want to go out with him. I'm a little worried about your late night hang-ups, but I doubt it's Hank. Let me talk to him, okay?"

"That would be great, Matt," Sunny said. "I hope you're right. Maybe some women like all this attention, but he's a little over-zealous for me. And, I'm not ready to step in as Mrs. Hank II."

"I'll talk to him and make sure he knows you're not interested in going out with him again." Matt reached between Sunny and Maggie to snag a cookie from the plate on the table.

"Thanks, Matt."

"No problem," he answered around a mouthful of cookie. "The real issue here is when can I get a piece of that cake?"

"I was just about to cut it." Cassie took the cake knife she had sitting on the counter and sliced into the rich dark chocolate. She sliced several pieces and expertly slid them onto dessert plates as Piper retrieved the coffee pot and commenced refilling half-empty mugs. Matt took the plate with the largest piece and disappeared back into his den, and the women settled back around the table.

"So, what I'm wondering," Maggie said, licking the

thick chocolate icing from the side of her fork, "is if you're going to go out with Jeremy again?"

"No," Sunny said. "He did call on Sunday and left me a message to call him so he could explain. He seems like a great guy, but..."

"But, what?" Cassie asked.

"But a great guy to be friends with. I don't think we have that chemistry. And then there's the whole living with his mother thing."

"Well, I can solve that one." Edna reached for her purse. "I'll call Mabel and ask her."

She dug through her enormous handbag, piling assorted items on the table as she searched the depths of her purse as if hunting for buried treasure. A crossword puzzle book, a mini-umbrella, a stick of deodorant, a dog-eared romance novel, a can of pepper spray...her pile grew as she mumbled, "I know my 'sale' phone is in here somewhere."

"Edna, it's called a 'cell' phone," Piper corrected and peered into Edna's bag, then tilted her head to get a better look at the cover of the romance novel. Flaming red hair spilled down the heroine's back as her buxom chest heaved forth from a sheer peasant blouse. Her leg wrapped around the waist of a hunk of man-flesh dressed remarkably like a pirate. Evidently Sunny wasn't the only one with a weakness for a good pirate romance.

Cassie smacked Piper's hand as she reached for the paperback.

"Well, I call mine a 'sale' phone because I got a hundred and fifty dollar phone for nineteen ninety-nine with a new two year activation agreement. Ah-ha!" Edna triumphantly raised the little touch screen phone she had unearthed from the depths of her bag. Oswald whined as he stood on his hind legs and delicately nosed her purse as if she would next pull a delectable doggie treat from the bag.

Always the sucker for brown eyes, Edna gave

Oswald the remaining corner of the cookie left on her plate as she scrolled through the contacts and looked for Mabel's number.

"I'll put her on speaker." Edna touched the appropriate squares on her phone. Piper giggled as they listened to Mabel's ringback tone of "*I'm Bringing Sexy Back,*" then Mabel's cigarette-hardened scratchy voice stating, "This is Mabel and I could die any day now so if you're bothering to leave a message, it better be important."

"Hey, you old bat," Edna said loudly into the phone. "You couldn't bring sexy back even if Justin Timberlake personally delivered you on a silver platter. Call me."

"Sorry, gals." Edna touched the little screen to disconnect the call and lock the phone. She dropped the phone into her purse and scooped the piles from the table back into the bag. "I'll let you know when I hear back from her."

"So, I guess I have a free weekend," Sunny said, happily.

"Not so fast," Piper said. "I've got your next date set up for this Saturday."

"You're kidding?" Sunny asked, a bite of cake halfway to her mouth.

"I am not. Keep the day open on Saturday because you are going horse-back riding with a hot cowboy," Piper instructed.

"First of all, how do you know a hot cowboy, and how did you get him to agree to a blind date?" Sunny asked incredulously. They had included Piper in the original plan, but Sunny didn't really think she would come up with a thirty-something blind date for her.

"Just how hot is he?" Maggie asked.

"Oh, he's hot all right," Cassie said and wiggled her eyebrows at Maggie. "Let's just say boots, tight Wranglers, and a cowboy hat, and leave it at that."

"Let's not leave it at that," Sunny said. "Who is this

guy, and since when do you know any cowboys, hot or otherwise?" She looked expectantly at Cassie.

"He's my riding instructor," Piper explained. "I told him all about you, and he said he's 'intrigued', so he wants to take you riding on Saturday."

"Oh, great. You told him I was intriguing? How am I gonna pull that off?" Sunny slumped back in her chair. "I'm the least intriguing person you know."

"Look, I checked him out at Piper's last riding lesson," Cassie said.

Maggie laughed. "I bet you did."

"Not like that." Cassie tossed cake crumbs across the table at Maggie. Oswald jumped up and licked the floor where the crumbs had fallen, his tail wagging in a cake-induced frenzy. "Well, okay, a little like that." She giggled.

"Well, I *am* intriguing," Edna said, "and I love horses and hot cowboys. Can I come with you on this one, Sunny?"

"You want to come *with* me on my blind date?" Sunny asked.

"He's not like a stalker cowboy," Piper said. "He's cool."

"I'll be your back up," Edna said. "I don't know that you're the best judge of character lately. I can be your voice of reason."

The table was silent for a moment as the women all looked at each other before breaking into hysterical laughter.

"What?" Edna asked. She was the only one not laughing.

"Why not?" Sunny said. "You can come along as my chaperone so I don't get all crazy and jump the hot cowboy. What's his name anyway?"

"Levi."

"Of course it is," Sunny said with a smile. She reached across the table and took Piper's hand. "Thanks honey, I think a day spent learning to ride a horse sounds fun. I mean really, how hard can it be?"

The warm water sloshed as Sunny stepped from the tub and a lone pool of soapy bubbles meandered down her wet leg as she reached for a towel. Sunny smiled as she thought of the fun they had had earlier in the evening at Cassie's, talking about books and boys, and eating chocolate. The bathroom clock read ten-thirty, and the worries of the book club, stalkers, and blind dates seemed to swirl down the drain with the diminishing bathwater. Beau stood up from where he had been curled in front of the door sleeping as she had soaked in the tub. He stretched, then padded over to lick the scented moisture droplets from her lower leg as she toweled dry.

"Go on, Beau." She shooed him and reached for one of the assorted bottles of lotion piled in a basket on the back of the toilet tank.

Sunny smoothed layers of moisturizer into her arms and legs and breathed in the scent of 'Moonlight Path'. She smeared Oil of Olay onto her face and dabbed a thick ivory wrinkle-reducing cream around her eyes.

She pulled on her robe and felt the smooth satin adhere to the drops of moisture she had missed on her back. Reaching for the door, she heard her cell phone ring out the familiar strains of Beethoven's Fleur de Lis.

The cool night air rushed at her as she ran from the steamy warm bathroom across the hall to where the phone sat on the bedside table.

The readout told her Jeremy was calling, and she wrapped the robe tighter around her waist and flipped the phone open.

"Hey, Jeremy," she answered hesitantly.

"Hi, Sunny. I'm glad you're home. I'm sorry to call so late. I just got home from work, but I really wanted to talk to you about the other night."

"That's okay, I'm still up." Sunny sat on the edge of the bed.

"Listen, I know how things must have looked, but if you would have just let me explain instead of running off."

"Okay, go ahead and explain."

"I was as surprised to see my mom there as you were."

"Why? Is she not usually home on Saturday nights?"

"Actually, she *is* usually home on Saturday nights, at her *own* home in LA."

"Her own home in LA?" Sunny repeated.

"Yes, Sunny. My mom lives in Los Angeles. She came up for a spur of the moment business trip, and she usually stays with me when she's in town. She hadn't had time to call me and was beat from her trip, so she let herself in and went up to the spare room to crash."

"She stays with you at your house, that you own and live in by yourself?" Her voice squeaked a little on the word 'yourself'.

"Of course. I can see how it looked a little funny, but I haven't lived with my mom since I was nineteen. If you would have stayed and let me explain, you could have met her."

"Jeremy, I'm so sorry I over-reacted. Now I'm embarrassed."

"It's okay. I can understand how you got the wrong idea. As a matter of fact, my mom thought it was hilarious."

"Oh, great. Well, she sounds like a good sport. Is she still here?"

Beau padded into the room and with a heavy sigh, plopped himself on the floor in front of the bed, his heavy hind end resting on her left foot.

"No, she headed back to California this morning," he said.

"Jeremy, I'm really sorry again. I'm embarrassed I ran off, but it probably worked out better this way. I wouldn't want us to have done something we regretted later just because we had some wine and a romantic fire going."

"You thought that was romantic?" he asked. "Good to know. That would help in case I have to suffer through some more of those Hugh Grant movies my mom left here last time she visited. But it doesn't sound like I'll be doing that with you, huh?"

"No, I don't think so. I think we would be better as friends. I'm really sorry."

"Don't be. It's not the first time I've heard the old 'let's be friends' thing." He laughed. "Seriously, I thought you were nice too, but I guess I'm looking for a little more as well."

"Okay. So I guess I'll see you around then."

"Yeah, okay. Goodnight, Sunny."

"Goodnight." She closed the phone and thought about Jeremy as she absently rubbed Beau's furry back with her right foot. He was a cute guy, and he had seemed fun to be around.

The phone rang again, and she absently flipped it open without checking the Caller ID readout. "Hello."

Sunny's foot stopped in mid-stroke on Beau's back as she heard the familiar silence on the other end of the line.

"Who is this?" Her body was tense as Sunny strained to listen for a voice or any recognizable background noise. Her hair was still piled in a knot on top of her head, and a droplet of water slithered from a loose ringlet. It ran down her neck and between her breasts, and a deep shiver ran through Sunny's every nerve.

"I want you to quit calling me," she stated firmly, remembering Maggie's instructions. "Don't ever call me again."

Sunny snapped the phone shut and tossed it away from her. It bounced twice on the bed and landed by the pillow as she concentrated on slowing her breathing.

Suddenly, she felt Beau's body tense under her foot. A low growl emanated from his throat. His head came up as he stared at the open bedroom window, and the sheer curtains blew inward with the night breeze.

Nerves already on edge from the mysterious phone call, she now felt a fresh jolt of fear race through her. Sunny stared at the window, her body alert as she watched and listened for what had triggered Beau's response. The light was on in the room, so the window only reflected her dark pink walls with the black night in the background.

Sunny realized she was holding her breath. Forcing a loud exhale, she wiped sweaty palms down her robe. *It's fine. I'm fine. I was strong and told him to stop calling me.* She sucked in a deep breath. *Calm down.* Beau growled again. A chill rippled down her spine. What was –?

*Oh, Lord help me!* A large black-gloved hand reached through the curtains!

Beau shot from the floor and flew at the window growling and barking.

Sunny let loose a blood-curdling scream. The hand jerked back and disappeared.

She sat frozen in place on the edge of the bed. Beau placed both of his front paws on the windowsill as he continued his frenzied barking. She thought she heard a scrambling across the shingles of the roof, but couldn't be sure.

Seconds passed as she continued to stare at the open window, then suddenly she heard a fierce pounding on the front door. She jumped and let out a shriek as Beau raced past her and ran down the stairs, now barking at the front door. She slowly got up from the bed and inched out the door toward the landing at the top of the stairs. Her legs felt as though they walked through molasses, her body stiff with terror.

In the movies, the heroine would have grabbed for a weapon: a baseball bat, a tennis racket, even a lamp. But Sunny stood frozen and listened to the pounding on the door, mesmerized by the way the front door knob moved as someone furiously shook it.

The pounding stopped and she heard a voice yell, "Sunny! Open up, it's me, Jake! Sunny, are you okay?"

Beau stopped barking and let out a whine. Her paralysis broke, and Sunny stumbled down the stairs, a sob escaping her throat as she reached the door. She fumbled with the deadbolt, pulled the door open, and flung herself into his arms.

"My God, Sunny! Are you all right?" he asked, holding her firmly in his arms. "I heard you scream and Beau barking. What happened?" He tried to pull back to get a better look at her but her arms were locked tightly around him. Her legs turned to jelly.

She sagged against him and he reached down to swing his arm under her legs to lift her up. He carried her to the sofa and sank down into the cushions, Sunny still cradled against his chest. He reached behind them, then she felt the softness of the sofa quilt as he pulled it around her, tucking her into a warm cocoon.

"Geez, you're shaking like a leaf." He pulled her in tighter and rubbed her back.

Sunny looked at him then and saw he was shirtless. His hair was rumpled as though he had been sleeping. Something about the start of the blond whiskers on the side of his face, and the way his eyes looked into hers with such worry and concern, sent a new kind of warmth through her that no quilt could accomplish.

It dawned on her that she was naked beneath the little silk robe. She looked down to see that her robe had slid open so the full top of her left breast was exposed, the silk hem of the robe only being held up by the crest of her nipple.

Sunny raised her eyes to see that Jake had now also noticed her exposed flesh, and the look of worry in his eyes dissolved into one of desire.

Her arms curled tighter against his neck and her mouth found his. He pulled her close and she felt a deep stirring as her bare flesh pressed against his. His lips were everywhere as they kissed her mouth, her neck, and the top of her breasts. Her breath came in shallow gasps as her head dropped back, and she arched up, giving him a larger palette of exposed flesh to feast on.

"Sunny! Sunny! My goodness, are you all right?"

Jake and Sunny jerked apart as Edna's voice came through the partially open front door. She pulled her robe together and pushed up from his lap as Edna barged into the house. She made quite a sight in her flowered robe and pink slippers as she stormed the entryway, a can of Mace in one hand, and a black Taser gun in the other.

"Get away from her!" she yelled at Jake, wielding the Taser. "I am not afraid to use this!" She held her stance, but her eyes moved to Sunny. "Sunny, darlin', are you okay?"

"Edna, I'm okay." Sunny went to her, her legs still wobbly, and threw her arms around the older woman.

"I'm okay," Sunny assured her again. "Jake came to help."

Edna looked from Sunny to Jake and back to Sunny again. Sunny nodded and Edna lowered her arms and dropped the can of Mace into the big terry cloth pocket on the front of her robe.

"What the hell is going on, Sunny? I thought I heard you scream, and Beau was barking like you were being attacked. I would have been here sooner, but I couldn't find my damn gun, so I settled on this one and rushed over. Where *did* I leave that thing?" Edna muttered the last question more to herself, sticking her hand in the other pocket of her robe, as if her revolver might be hiding there.

"Edna, I'm all right now. Jake came over because he heard me scream too."

Jake stood slowly from the sofa, and she saw that he hadn't had any trouble finding his gun. The black metal handle stuck up conspicuously from the back of his jeans, and Sunny wondered how she had not felt that a moment ago during their embrace.

He turned and slowly approached them, as Sunny's eyes tracked from the gun at his back to the open top button of his jeans. The denim sides formed a vee against his tanned abs, and her legs suddenly didn't seem quite as strong again.

*What is wrong with me? Someone tries to break into my house and I go crazy over Jake coming to my rescue and start making out with him! I must be in shock.*

Sunny reached for the back of the loveseat as her knees threatened to buckle, then Jake was there, his strong arm around her, holding her up and guiding her back to the sofa.

"Well, what in the name of heaven were you screaming about?" Edna wanted to know. Her eyes were sharp. As Sunny looked up at her, she could tell Edna wasn't missing much, from Jake's bare chest, to his open button fly, to his arm around Sunny's shoulders. "And what is Mr. No-Shirt doing over here with half his pants on?"

Sunny's face burned with shame, but Jake's eyes were amused as he gave Edna an appraising look. Before he could respond, Sunny blurted out, "A man tried to come into my bedroom through my window."

Both of their heads shot back toward Sunny. Jake's eyes went from amused to hard as he took in the whole room with one sweeping gaze.

"Why didn't you tell me sooner?" He looked down at Sunny with exasperation. He headed for the front door, reaching behind him to pull the gun free. "You two stay here and lock this door. Don't let anyone in until I come back."

He looked pointedly at Edna. "Keep an eye on her." Then he was out the door, pulling it firmly shut behind him.

"Why would someone do that?" Edna asked, more to herself than to Sunny. She picked up the quilt from where it had fallen to the floor and again wrapped it around Sunny's shoulders. Edna sat next to her on the sofa, taking Sunny's hand and rubbing it between her own.

Edna peppered her with questions as she fussed over tucking the quilt around her. "What is going on here, Sunny? Are you really okay? When I walked in you looked like a kid caught with her hand in the cookie jar. Are you falling for this guy? And why is he running around acting like he is in charge? And where is his shirt?"

Edna took a breath and looked Sunny in the eye. "And I *told* you he had a gun! Now do you believe me?"

They both jumped as they heard Jake knock loudly at the front door and call for them to let him in.

Edna looked at her first, one eyebrow raised, and only after Sunny nodded her consent did she get up and let Jake back into the house. He locked the door behind him, then ran up the stairs. Sunny noticed for the first time that he was barefoot.

They heard him move from room to room upstairs, opening and shutting doors, then he came down the stairs and headed through the dining room, continuing his search for any other signs of the intruder. They listened as he stopped in the kitchen, opened the cupboard door, then heard the faucet running. Sunny's heart melted as he walked back into the living room, no gun in his hands, only a glass of water he held out to her.

"Okay, start from the beginning, and tell me everything that you can remember," he said.

She took a sip of the cool water, then set the glass on the edge of the coffee table. Sunny told them everything she could think of, stopping only when Jake had a question.

"Why doesn't your window have a screen?" he asked.

"It does. I just take it off when it's warm, because there's a little flat spot on the roof outside the window, and I love to sit out there in the summer. You've seen me, Edna." Sunny looked to the older woman for acknowledgement, and Edna nodded in agreement.

"Could you see any of his hand or arm? Was his skin color white, black, tan, fair? Did you see any moles or freckles on his arm?" Jake asked this time.

"I couldn't tell. It was a hand with a black glove and a black sleeve, so I couldn't see any skin. It was a big hand, meaty, ya know? So, that's why I'm sure it was a man."

While Sunny had been talking, Beau had come to lie at her feet in front of the sofa.

"It all happened so fast. I don't know if he would have run if Beau hadn't flown at him, barking his head off. I've never seen him like that."

"He was protecting you." Jake ruffled the yellow fur around the dog's big head. He pulled Beau's head up to look in his eyes as he crooned, "Good dog, Beau. You were a good dog."

"Do you have any idea who it could have been?" His gaze left the dog's and looked questionably into hers.

"No," Sunny said softly.

"How do we know it wasn't you, Mr. Barefoot-Show-Up-to-the-Rescue-with-a-Gun?" Edna asked, scowling at Jake.

"Me?" he asked, shocked.

"Yes, you." She pointed at his chest. "And how do we know you're not responsible for these calls she's been getting in the middle of the night, too?"

His eyes narrowed as he turned to Sunny. "What calls?"

"I've sorta been getting some weird heavy-breathing hang up calls," Sunny admitted.

"On your home or your cell?"

"Both."

"Why didn't you tell me?"

"Why would she tell you?" Edna snapped. "You expect her to come over to some strange new Mr. Half-Dressed-Neighbor and knock on your door to tell you she's getting prank calls?"

Jake and Sunny both just looked at her.

"I'm just saying…"

Jake turned back to Sunny. "When's the last time you received one of these calls?"

"Right before I saw the hand at the window."

"Great. Well, we're calling the police. You need to have a report filed on the calls and the possible break in." He grabbed the phone from the side coffee table and held it out for her. "Call 911."

Sunny did as instructed and was informed a police cruiser would be by shortly.

She went upstairs to pull on some pajama bottoms, a t-shirt, and a bra. She pushed her arms through the sleeves of a zippered sweatshirt. As she came down the stairs, she heard Edna and Jake talking.

"Will you stay with her?" Jake asked Edna. "Make sure she tells the police everything about tonight and the phone calls, too."

"Should we even tell them my suspicions of you?" Edna's voice carried a hint of a challenge.

"Sure, tell them all about me." His voice carried a hint of amusement.

"Wait. Where are you going?" Sunny asked, coming

into the living room. Cold fingers of fear crept up her spine.

"I've got some stuff to check into at the house. Don't worry. I'll be right next door." He stood from the sofa and picked up the glass of water to return it to the kitchen.

Flashing red and blue lights pulsed through the front window as the police cruiser pulled into the driveway. Sunny heard the back door click shut as Jake slipped through it... just as the front doorbell rang.

Edna opened the front door and escorted two officers into the living room. They took in the dog, Edna and Sunny, and the black Taser gun resting on the coffee table.

"You ladies okay?" asked the younger of the two officers. He was tall, well-muscled, and had short dark hair. His teeth were white against his tanned skin and his dark eyes expressed concern as he held out his hand.

"Are you a real policeman?" Edna gave him the once over...then a second over. "You look more like one of those Chippen-Dale Strippers who dance at bachelorette parties. You sure you got the right address?"

"Edna!" Sunny admonished.

The young officer smiled at Edna. "Yes, ma'am. I can assure you that we are real policemen. I'm Officer Steve Royce and this is my partner, Officer McCarthy."

Officer McCarthy was all business as he nodded and took a small notebook from his pocket. "Nice to meet you. Can you tell us what happened?" He looked to be in his mid-fifties and wore his hair shaved close to his head. His body was lean and also well-muscled.

"Well, seriously, look at the two of you. Haven't you cops heard of donuts?" Edna muttered.

She ushered the group into the living room, and the women sat on the love seat across from the policemen.

Sunny repeated her story to the officers and answered their questions, which were remarkably similar to the ones Jake had asked. Edna's earlier comment about Jake running around acting like the police crossed her mind, and Sunny wondered if Jake was possibly in law enforcement. That would explain why he had a gun. She would feel so much better about having a policeman's lips on her breast than a criminal's.

Edna told them about Hank's repeated phone calls, and his obtuseness about Sunny not wanting to continue dating him.

"Now, Edna. We don't have any proof that it was Hank at my window." Sunny hated to stick up for Hank, but also didn't want to get a single dad in trouble if he was just enthusiastic in his dating technique. She shrugged at the policeman. "But, at this point, I think it's a possibility and you should probably check him out." Silently she wondered if she would rather her intruder be the over-zealous guy she did know or the scarier possibility of it being someone random who she didn't know.

Officer McCarthy continued to visit with the women while his partner followed Jake's routine and checked both the interior and exterior of the house.

"One of the trash cans is knocked over next to the fence on the side of your house. It looks like the guy climbed the fence there to get to your roof. It wouldn't be too hard to get up there," Officer Royce said as he came back in through the front door. "There are a couple of good-sized shoeprints near the fence. They're spaced evenly apart as if someone jumped from the fence. They look like a size eleven or twelve, definitely a man's shoe."

"Are you going to pour in some plaster and make a mold of the shoeprints? Because I could help," Edna offered. "I watch every CSI, and I think I'm pretty current on the evidence- gathering techniques. Should we dust for some fingerprints on the fence?"

Officer McCarthy stood and smiled down at Edna. "Though we do appreciate the generous offer, ma'am, I think we've got this one covered. I'm sure Officer Royce photographed the shoe print, so I don't think a plaster mold will be necessary this time. And we can't really pull fingerprints off the wooden fence."

"Oh, all right." Edna sounded disappointed. "But you are going to talk to the suspects, right?"

"We'll head over and speak to this..." he checked his notes, "Jake Landon now, and we'll check in with this other gentleman, Hank, tomorrow. As of right now, it appears you ladies are safe for the evening."

"Thank you so much for coming by." Edna walked them to the door. She sounded as though they had stopped by for tea or a Sunday visit instead of being summoned to Sunny's home due to an unwanted late night visitor.

"I'm sure you're going to be fine. Probably just a peeping tom. We don't really expect him to be back tonight, but call us if you need anything else, ma'am," Officer Royce said and his eyes lingered on Sunny a moment longer than necessary.

Sunny blinked in surprise, then blushed as she realized this young, gorgeous officer was actually flirting with her. She was glad she had taken the time to put on some clothes, and a bra. Just thinking about answering their questions as she sat half-naked in her silk robe warmed her cheeks further.

"Thank you, I will," Sunny said, smiling demurely. Or at least what she hoped was demurely.

"Take care, now." He gave Sunny a wink and one more flash of his dazzling smile before he pulled the door shut behind him.

Edna crossed to the far wall and peeked through the curtains. "They're going over to Walter's house now. They're knocking on the front door. Oh, there he is. Thank goodness he put a shirt on. Now he's letting them in. Oh, they shut the door." Edna concluded her play by play.

"Well, that Officer Royce was sure a cute one," Edna said, still watching Jake's house through the curtain. "Maybe we could set you up on a date with him."

"Oh, Edna," Sunny scoffed. "He's probably ten years younger than I am. I'm old enough to be his...well, his big sister or older cousin, at least."

"Hog wash. He wasn't that young, and besides, going out with a younger man could be fun." She wiggled her eyebrows and her hips at Sunny.

"I am not going out with him." Sunny laughed, more as a release from the drama of the evening. It felt good to her to think of something normal and safe. "But, he was cute," she added.

"Hey, here they come," Edna said, her attention drawn back to the curtain. Sunny scurried to the window and peeked out with her.

Officer Royce looked toward the window and gave them a little wave before he got into the squad car.

"Dang. They didn't arrest him." Edna let the curtains fall as the cruiser backed out of the driveway.

"Who, Jake?"

"Of course, Mr. Mysteriously-Disappears-When-the-Cops-Show-Up."

"Okay, that was a little odd, but I really don't think Jake was the one who tried to sneak into my window."

They both jumped as the phone rang. The shrill ring seemed extra loud in the still house.

"You want me to get it?" Edna asked. "I'll tell that SOB what to do with his heavy breathing?"

This time Sunny checked the Caller ID. "No, it's Walter's number." She pushed the talk button. "Hello, Jake?"

"Hey, Sunny. You doing okay?"

"I'm fine now. How did it go with the police?"

"Oh, fine. They just asked me some questions, and I told them everything I knew."

The deep timbre of his voice sent warm tinglies to

her special places. "Do you want me to come back over?" he asked softly. "I could just sleep on the couch, if you want?"

*Yes! Yes! Yes! Wait, I mean, no, no, no! Urgh! What did I mean?*

"Let him know I will be sleeping here tonight so we don't really need him to come back over," Edna said, loudly enough that Jake could also hear her.

*Whew, saved by the old lady bell.*

"It sounds like you've got *two* guard dogs with you now." He chuckled. "I get the picture."

"Thanks for the offer though." Sunny turned her back to Edna and quietly said, "I'm really glad you were here tonight. Thank you for coming over."

"You bet."

"Well, good night."

"Hey, Sunny?"

"Yeah?"

"I won't let anything happen to you."

Goosebumps ran up her arms. "Thanks, good night."

"Good night, Sunny. Sleep well."

Sunny put the receiver down and looked up to see Edna giving her that one-eyebrow-raised look that moms and grandmas are so good at. "Cut it out with those ga-ga eyes, girl. I'm telling you, there's more to Mr. Suddenly-I'm- the-Hero guy than he lets on."

"Yeah," Sunny agreed, thoughtfully. "I think there just might be more to him than he is letting on."

"Hrmph." She made another one of those sounds that grandmothers are famous for. "Let's go lock all the doors and go to bed. This crazy night has worn me out."

They double-checked all the door locks, and Sunny got Edna settled into the guest room. Sunny finally fell into bed, but sleep eluded her as her eyes drifted to the bedroom window, now firmly closed and locked. She needed to get her mind off the terrifying part of her evening.

She called Beau up on to the bed and curled herself around his warm furry body. He sighed in doggy pleasure at being allowed to sleep on the bed. Sunny closed her eyes, and her thoughts filled with a different kind of pleasure as she relived the parts of the evening with Jake. She imagined the feel of his hands on her body and his warm lips against her throat. She snuggled deeper under the covers as a sigh of her own filled the room.

"I'll have the Chicken Caesar Salad and a Diet Coke," Cassie said.

"Make that two," Maggie said, "except I'll have the dressing on the side."

"Make that three," Sunny said, "except hold the salad, add a cheeseburger with ketchup and mayo, and I'll have the fries 'on the side'."

"Do you still want the Diet Coke?" the waitress asked humorlessly.

Sunny nodded. "Oh, of course, just like the other girls."

"Just like," the waitress said. She turned and walked toward the kitchen, the popping of her gum in perfect time with the squeak of the white crepe soles of her shoes.

The girls were having lunch the next afternoon at *Happy Days Are Here Again*, their favorite downtown restaurant. It was a fifties-style diner based on the popular TV show. The waitresses wore white smocks over pink dresses and fifties memorabilia from the show adorned the walls. Gleaming black and white checkered linoleum floors led to shiny multicolored leather booths, which were color-coded to the various characters in the show. The red booth was the Richie Cunningham, the yellow was the Mrs. C, and the black was named for The Fonz. The girls sat in their favorite pink booth, the Pinkie Tuscadero, and "*Rock Around the Clock*" played softly on the jukebox.

A long red and chrome counter ran the length of one side of the restaurant, and a chalkboard listed the daily specials of ***Chicken 'Potsie' Pie*** and ***Macaroni and ChaChi-eese***.

As they waited for their food, Cassie and Maggie commiserated over their kids' lack of summer activities and too much time spent on their computers. They laughed and sipped their cokes, and it felt like such a fun, normal day that Sunny hesitated to tell them of her previous evening's adventure.

The waitress appeared at the table balancing three plates on her arm and set them ceremoniously down in front of each woman.

"Your salad," she said to Cassie, as she set a plate, chock full of bright green crispy leaves of romaine and strips of char-grilled chicken, in front of her.

"Your salad." She set a similar plate in front of Maggie, but added a small ramekin of creamy Caesar dressing to the table.

"And your salad," she said to Sunny, as she set her plate before her, the tantalizing scent of grilled hamburger filling the air.

Sunny looked down at the gooey cheddar cheese that dripped over the sides of the burger and the pile of crispy seasoned fries and without blinking an eye, replied, "Thank you, it looks delicious."

Maggie and Cassie laughed, then dug into their crunchy salads. Sunny picked up a fry and nibbled on one end. "So, I hate to put a damper on our fun lunch, but something's happened, and I wanted to tell you about it before Edna called you and blew it all out of proportion."

"Ooo-kay." Maggie's fork full of lettuce stopped halfway to her mouth. A drop of dressing clung to the side of one leaf where Maggie had dipped it into the dish of Caesar. “This sounds serious.”

“No, not really,” Sunny assured them. “It’s not that big of deal. It’s just that late last night, someone tried to break into my bedroom window.”

“What?” Cassie choked on the gulp of Diet Coke she had *almost* swallowed. “Are you okay?”

“Yeah, I’m okay, thanks to Beau. He practically jumped out the window, barking like a crazy dog and scared the guy off. Jake and Edna both came over because they heard him barking and evidently I must have screamed quite loudly.” She looked down at her plate in embarrassment and crammed two more ketchup sodden fries into her mouth.

“Did you call the police?” Cassie asked, just as Maggie said, “Jake to the rescue again, huh?”

“Yes, we called the police,” Sunny said to Cassie, then pointed at Maggie before adding, “and I said Jake *and* Edna came to the rescue. Only Edna was more dressed than Jake- but he was more armed than her. But just barely.”

Maggie set down her fork. “Okay, start from the beginning, and don’t leave anything out, especially what Jake was obviously *not wearing*. I’m dying to know what weapon in Edna’s arsenal she showed up with to save the day.”

“A can of Mace and a Taser gun.” Sunny smirked. “She was ready to shock Jake a good one when she flew into the house and almost caught us making out on the sofa.”

“Oh, my,” Cassie said. “You better tell us everything, and Maggie, put that damn phone away before I break off one of your fingers. No texting at the table. I swear you are like one of the kids.”

Maggie looked up guiltily from where she had indeed been texting beneath the table with a *Who, me?* expression on her face. “Sorry.”

Sunny began with the phone call from Jeremy and told the girls everything that had happened the night before. Between bites of cheeseburger, she calmly replayed the events as if they were a television show she had seen, or as if they had happened to someone else. Because they were her two best friends, she also told them about the couch time with Jake.

"I don't know what came over me," she said. She licked the traces of salt from her fingers. "I don't know what it is about this guy. We haven't even found Walter's body or confirmed his death. My house is almost broken into, I know next to nothing about this man, and what I do know is probably a lie… and yet, every time I'm within three feet of him, I want to jump his bones."

"Maybe you should take a few steps back," Cassie said, a worried look on her face. "It may sound like I'm joking, but I'm not. Sunny, I understand he is seriously hot, but hot equals fire, and I think that's what you're messing with here."

"Maybe I want a little fire," Sunny said. "I've spent the last several years hanging out in dating Antarctica. Maybe a little heat is exactly what I need."

"Well, gosh, I hate to be the voice of reason here, but men *can* lie, and they *can* cheat, and they *can* use you if it helps them get what they need," Maggie said.

"But what could he possibly *need* from me?"

"Besides the obvious?" Maggie asked. "Who knows? Like you said, we don't really know anything about this guy. Why is he here? Where is he *really* from? He is Walter's relative, but why hasn't he planned some type of memorial? Walter does have a nice-sized estate, so he has motive for killing him. Because of the fire, there's no body, so he may have committed the perfect crime and is currently getting away with it."

"Maybe Edna has a point," Cassie added. "Could Jake have been the one who tried to break in and scare you, then showed up as the hero to try to gain your trust?"

"I don't know. That doesn't feel right," Sunny said.

"Why would he need my trust? He keeps telling me he'll keep me safe, and that I should trust *him*."

"Mags, can you use any of your connections to try to find out more about this guy?" Cassie asked. "Surely you know somebody who could do a little digging into his background or find out more about him?"

"I'll give it a try. But if Jake wasn't the one trying to break in, then who was? Do you think Hank the Tank has taken stalking to the next level?"

Sunny took a sip of her soda. "I hate to believe it, but the alternative would mean there's a third unknown man who tried to break into my house, and that *really* scares me."

"Well, I'll talk to Matt again and make sure he's had that chat with Hank." Cassie reached across the table and took Sunny's hand. "I'm really sorry this is happening to you, honey."

"Thanks, Cass." Sunny squeezed her friend's hand. "I'll be fine. I just need to get Jake out of my head."

"I think the recipe for that is one cup of hot cowboy served on a bed of tight Wranglers." Maggie wiggled her eyebrow and gave Sunny a wicked smile.

"Ooo yeah," Cassie said. "Has Levi called you yet?"

"Yeah, he called yesterday afternoon and invited me out to his ranch for a horseback ride this Saturday."

"How does he feel about you bringing a sassy gray-haired chaperone along?" Maggie asked.

"He laughed and said he thought it would be fine. He doesn't really seem to be fazed by much. He seems to have the 'good ole boy' thing going on."

"Piper is really excited for you to meet him," Cassie said.

"Tell her not to get her hopes up. I'm not much of a cowgirl. I've never even ridden a horse before."

"You'll be fine," Maggie assured her. "Even little kids can ride a horse. Go and enjoy yourself and forget about all this other stuff for awhile."

"You girls having any dessert? The special today is

Mrs. C's Cheery Cobbler," the waitress said on her next pass by their table. The girls shook their heads no, and she slapped the check upside down on their table.

"I got this one," Maggie said, as Sunny and Cassie reached for their purses. She pulled a credit card from her immaculately organized leather wallet and slid it under the check.

"Cassie, you made a good point about doing some kind of memorial for Walter. Maybe I'll just stop over at Walter's this afternoon and see if Jake's given it any thought," Sunny said.

"No!" both Maggie and Cassie cried together.

"First of all, the police haven't declared Walter dead yet, so let's wait on the memorial service idea," Maggie said. "Also, I think you need some time to think this through, so as of now, you're on a 'Jake-Break'. Give it a few days before you see him again. Maybe he won't seem so great when you're not in the middle of a stressful situation."

Sunny sighed. "I don't think the stress has anything to do with his smile or his abs or the way he fills out his Levi's."

"Oh, brother," Maggie said. "A few months ago, we could barely get you to even notice men. Now you're dating and mashing with dangerous strangers and talking about how they fill out their jeans. I think we've created a monster."

❀❀❀

*This Jake-Break didn't last long.* He was the first person Sunny saw as she pulled into the driveway and stepped from the car.

Jake walked across the lawn, holding a brown plastic Home Depot bag. "You gonna be home for a little while?" He fell in step with her as she walked up the drive.

"Sure, what's going on?" Sunny asked as she unlocked the front door. Beau greeted her with his usual licking, butt-wagging and running around as if he hadn't seen her in weeks.

"That's quite a greeting." Jake laughed as Beau ran around him, jumping and trying to lick his hand.

"Yeah, if only I could get him to cook, clean house, and put the toilet seat down, he could be the perfect man," Sunny teased.

"I know how to put the toilet seat down, and I make a mean cheese omelet." Jake's eyes conveyed a message her body heard loud and clear.

"Well, uh, what's in the bag?" Sunny stammered as she tried to veer away from that dangerous topic. Didn't she just agree with her two best friends that she should take a step back from Jake and try to look at him more objectively?

"New deadbolts for your door." Jake pulled two packages of shiny gold deadbolts from the bag. "I was in Home Depot earlier today and picked these up for you. After last night, I thought it might make you feel a little safer to have an extra lock on the doors. If you're gonna be around for awhile, I'll install them for you."

"Oh, sure. I was going to work in the yard this afternoon, so I'll be around. That's really nice of you." She wasn't trying to be coy, she just couldn't help but smile at the guy. He had gone to Home Depot for her, after all.

"It's my pleasure," he replied with a grin that might have made her heart skip a beat or two. "I'll be right back. I've got to grab some tools."

He headed for Walter's as Sunny blissfully watched his retreating backside. *Oh, you've already got plenty of tools.*

Sunny giggled at herself and went into the house to change into some shorts. Beau followed, and she shut the door behind her as she tried not to think about the way Jake had said the words ‘my pleasure’.

"What does she see in that fake surfer-boy wanna-be?" he seethed. From in his car parked down the block, he had watched as Sunny had stepped from her car and Jake had come across the lawn toward her.

His blood boiled as she smiled and flirted with another man.

*How could she not see through him?* He had waited for her to get home so he could talk to her and tell her he was sorry for scaring her last night. He had only wanted to watch her. He had no intention of actually entering her house.

But seeing her smile while she talked on the phone, and the way she absently played with that one wet tendril of hair that had fallen loose from the clip on her head, had done crazy things to him.

When she had hung up the phone, he had called her again just to hear her voice. He planned on telling her how much he cared for her and wanted to see her again, but when she answered, the words froze in his mouth. He could do nothing but stare at her. He wanted to say everything right so she would really understand that her future was with him. That instead of petting that stupid dog, she should be caressing him, telling him in her sweet way how much she adored and wanted him.

But her face changed when she answered the phone. She had looked angry and scared as she told him to quit calling her. *How could she mean that?* He hadn't planned to enter her room, hadn't meant to scare her. All he wanted to do was make her understand they were right for each other. But she'd seen his glove as he reached through the curtain. Then that damn mutt went crazy and tried to attack him.

He had gotten out of there fast, but not before he saw the lights go on in Walter's house, and that damn Jake bolted out the door and headed for Sunny's.

*Why did Jake get to go over there and be the hero?* He would probably take her in his arms, and she would just give herself to him.

He slammed his fist against the steering wheel, and then took a deep breath to calm down. If she would give him a chance to explain, she would realize how he felt, and they could put this whole misunderstanding behind them.

But how was he supposed to talk to her with *him* always hanging around? Who was this guy anyway? He needed to find out more about this Jake guy and show Sunny he was no good for her. Then she would see how much he cared for her. He needed to prove that Jake was the one who had planned to kill Walter in that explosion. She sure wouldn't giggle and smile at Jake then. He needed her to see that she was meant to be with him.

Only him.

Saturday morning dawned clear and bright, and Sunny woke with a good feeling about the day. Even if Levi turned out to be a dud, she would get to spend time outside at a real working ranch. And this time, she would have Edna along as a date-buffer. A day with Edna could never be boring.

Levi was supposed to pick them up around two, so Sunny spent the morning putzing around the house doing light housework – which meant straightening some magazines on the coffee table and throwing away some take-out cartons. Then she took a break in her favorite lounge chair in the backyard. There was nothing she liked better than having a Diet Coke and some chocolate while sitting in the sun soaking up the summer. Images of a shirtless Jake ran through her mind. *Well, there are some things I like better.*

A sound rousted her from her daydreaming, and she looked up to see Jake as he pulled the lawn mower from Walter's shed. She waved, feeling a tiny bit disappointed that he was wearing a shirt. "Feel free to cut my lawn next."

He smiled that dang crooked grin of his. Tingles tickled her insides and she couldn't help from grinning back like an idiot.

Sunny did actually get a small Jake-Break because she hadn't seen him since Thursday afternoon. She had worked in the flower garden while Jake had installed the deadbolts. She had really tried to keep her mind on yanking out weeds, but her eyes strayed to the doorway where he worked and to the way his biceps flexed as he used the drill. *What was it about guys and power tools?*

He had finished installing the locks and handed Sunny the keys when his cell phone rang. He answered and his face went hard as he turned from her and spoke into the phone. "Listen, this isn't a good time. Give me a few minutes, and I'll call you back."

"Sorry about that." He turned back to Sunny and tried to put the smile back on his face. Unfortunately, the smile didn't quite meet his eyes this time. "Work," he said, alluding to the caller he had just hung up on.

"Oh, sure," she replied. "Of course. What kind of work did you say you did again?"

"Financial consulting," he replied smoothly. "Did you have some stocks you were interested in?" *And the easy charmer was back.*

*Where had this come from? Financial consulting?* She hadn't heard him say anything about finances, even when she was telling him about her date with Blaine, the boring stockbroker. Another reminder of how much she didn't really know about this man.

"Yeah, all that extra money I make as a teacher," she said, sarcastically.

"Well, I better get going."

"Yep. You gotta return that call for work."

"Yeah. So, I guess I'll see you later." The fun banter they had earlier had deflated into dry small talk.

Not able to just let him walk away, Sunny had reached out and touched his arm. "Thanks again for installing the new deadbolts, Jake. I really will feel safer now."

He looked at her for just a moment too long, as if he wanted to say something, then changed his mind. "No problem. I was happy to do it. I'll see you soon." Then he disappeared into Walter's house, and she hadn't seen him again until now.

Unfortunately, the mini Jake-Break hadn't done a thing to keep her from thinking about him, how he had held her, the way they had kissed on the sofa, the way he had touched her...

"So, today's Saturday. Who's lined up for tonight?" Jake asked, referring to her weekly blind date schedule, and bringing Sunny crashing back into the present. She hoped she wasn't blushing.

"A cowboy," she said.

"Yeehaw. That should be fun. Are you gonna rustle up any 'dogies'?"

"Stop." Sunny smiled a little, in spite of herself. "He gives Piper horse-back riding lessons, and she claims he's 'super-hot'."

"Well, I hope you have a good time. I'll be getting 'super-hot' around here as I mow the lawn and do yard work," he teased, then yanked the cord, and the mower started up with a sputter before it caught.

Jake mowed Walter's entire backyard, but to Sunny's chagrin, he never peeled off his shirt. He caught her staring a couple times and gave her that heart-achingly gorgeous grin.

*What was it about that smile and the way his sandy hair fell across those gorgeous blue eyes?* That tingly feeling was back, and her cheeks were getting warm. *Must be too much sun.*

With that thought, Sunny grabbed her glass and headed inside for a shower.

After running the water slightly cooler than usual, she spent twenty minutes applying some light makeup and blew out her hair. She chose jeans, a floral print button-up blouse, and rummaged through the closet for her only pair of cowboy boots.

Pulling on the second boot, she heard the doorbell ring, then the door opened. Her breath caught as she worried that her intruder had returned. She looked around for a weapon to protect herself. She really needed to buy more dangerous household items. All she saw was a dresser covered in costume jewelry and a closet spilling out a waterfall of too many shoes. Her choices of protection were to poke him with an earring or whack him with the latest style in footwear.

"Yoohoo!" hollered the familiar voice of her favorite neighbor.

Sunny's shoulders relaxed, and she laughed at her own paranoia. Edna always let herself in. "Be right down." She grabbed her purse and headed for the stairs.

"Why, don't you look snazzy?" Edna said when she saw Sunny. "I wonder if I should get some cowboy boots too?" Edna was dressed in jeans, sandals, and a white t-shirt with a pink handkerchief tied bank-robber style around her neck. She had on large turquoise earrings and a pink cowboy hat sat atop her silver curls. "Maybe I don't look Western enough."

"You look great, Edna." Sunny smiled endearingly at her friend. "I think the hat is just the right touch."

A loud engine rumbled as it pulled up out front, and they peered through the door Edna had left open as she came in.

Climbing from a large red Dodge Ram pickup was indeed a 'super-hot' cowboy. From his tight Wrangler jeans to his black felt cowboy hat riding low on his dusty brown hair, he was a tall, cool drink of water.

"Yippee-cai-aye!" whooped Edna. "He could ride my pony."

"Edna, stop it now." Sunny giggled and swatted her playfully.

They stepped out to greet him as he sauntered up the walkway.

"Well howdy, ma'am," he said and extended his hand toward Sunny. "My name is Levi Garrett, and I'm mighty pleased to meet you."

Sunny's cheeks were flushed as she stammered out, "I'm Sunny, and this is my neighbor, Edna." His hand was large and calloused from labor, but warm, and he held her eyes an extra beat before he let go and reached for Edna's.

"Well, pleased to meet you both. It will be my pleasure to accompany two beautiful ladies, such as yourselves, out to my ranch this afternoon."

*Was he for real?* Pulling the door shut, Sunny looked up as Beau jumped into the window and began his, *Please don't leave me,* saga of whining and crying.

"Hey, is that your dog?" he asked.

*No, it's the neighbor's dog, that's why he's crying-to get out of* my *house.* Maybe this cowboy wasn't the sharpest tool in the shed. Good thing he was so cute. "Yes, that is woman's best friend, my lovely Beau-dog."

"You should bring him along," Levi offered.

"Oh, no. He'll be fine."

"Really, you should bring him. There's plenty of room to run around the ranch, and I love dogs. In fact, I have a yellow lab named Duke who would love to have another dog to play with."

"Well...are you sure?"

"Absolutely."

"Okay, Beau! Road trip!" Sunny called as she pushed the door open and eighty pounds of yellow fur rushed past her to get to Levi.

Beau was doing his crying, butt-wiggling dance of, *Please, pet me! I'll be your friend forever,* with Levi, who willingly obliged, bending down to ruffle the dog's coat and murmur sweet doggie nothings into his ear.

*Hmmm. There may be hope for this one. It seemed Piper might have made a good call this time.*

They piled into the crowded pickup, and Sunny's leg rested against Levi's. Her shoulder bumped against his as they pulled out and headed for the ranch. His fingers tapped in time to the radio against his thigh, and Sunny felt the hard muscles in his leg. She looked at the strong outline of his jaw, and her palms began to sweat. He was a seriously hot cowboy.

"Do ya think I could drive?" Edna asked, diverting Sunny's attention from the tall, good-looking man half her body pressed against. "I bet there's some real power in this baby."

"I think I'll drive this time." Levi tried to hold back his grin, no doubt imagining this pink-hatted, five-foot-two granny in the driver's seat of his beastly truck.

They fell into a companionable silence as they watched the scenery go by, the only sound was Beau panting and the light strains of country music coming from the radio.

Suddenly the cab filled with the rotten-egg-sulphur smell of passed gas.

"Oh Beau, how could you?" Sunny leaned across Edna to roll down the pickup window.

As the air cleared, she glanced at Edna who smiled sheepishly, and Sunny swore she heard Edna quietly humming, "Beans, beans, the magical fruit..." which led Sunny to believe who the real flatulence culprit was.

However, she still let Beau take the blame, just to save Edna's pride.

A few minutes later, they turned into a long driveway and drove along a lush green field lined with white fencing. They pulled up to a yellow farm house with a wrap-around porch, complete with two rocking chairs and a kaleidoscope of colored pansies spilling from large white pots that hung from the porch railings.

"Wow. Your house is great," Sunny said as Edna broke into song. "Green acres is the place to be. Farrrmm living is the life for me."

Levi tried to smile but looked a little confused. Evidently, he wasn't a fan of Eva Gabor's *Green Acres* sitcom.

He slowed to a stop, jumped down from the cab, and jogged around to open the passenger door to help

Edna.

Beau flew from the truck and ran frantically from one new smell to another in a nose-sniffing, tail-wagging frenzy.

"Woof! Woof!"

The screen door pushed open, and a blur of yellow raced out in a direct beeline for Beau.

"Ladies, this is my dog, Duke. He's named after…well, ya know, the Duke," Levi said.

"Yeah, I get it." Sunny laughed and shook her head at his feeble description of John Wayne.

The screen door banged again, and out rambled an older version of Sam Elliott.

"And this is my dad, Roy Garrett," Levi explained as the man came down the porch steps toward them with his hand outstretched.

"Nice to meet you, ladies," Roy said, shaking Sunny's hand. He walked with the slightly bowlegged gait of a man who spent a good portion of his life in the saddle. He wore a straw cowboy hat stained brown around the band from perspiration. His gray hair lay straight and fell below his collar, and he sported a thick gray moustache. He smelled of hay, horses, and carried a slight scent of that working-in-the-sun-shoveling-dirt-kind of sweat.

He turned from Sunny and with a twinkle in his eye, lifted Edna's hand to his lips and drawled, "And it's especially nice to meet you, Edd-na." He drew Edna's name out an extra syllable, going deep on the 'na' and pressed a kiss to the back of her hand.

"Well, aren't you just the sweetest thang?" Edna drawled back. Sunny wasn't sure where she had acquired a southern accent in the last three minutes, but it was definitely there as she batted her eyelashes and looked coyly out from beneath the brim of her pink cowboy hat.

A gasp escaped Sunny as she looked past Roy, and they all turned to see what had caught her attention.

A double yellow flurry of super-sonic dog humping was taking place as Duke was evidently really enjoying his new playdate.

"Stop that!" Sunny cried and stepped toward poor Beau. He looked up at her from beneath his new prison boyfriend, with a plea in his eyes of, *Help, make it stop.*

"Aahh, they're just playin'," Levi said, laughing. He swiped at Duke and hollered, "Go on now!"

The lab dismounted and loped off but slowly circled back with a predatory gleam in his eyes.

"It's like getting free HBO," Edna said, "but with dogs instead of people."

Roy looked at Edna in slight shock, then broke into good-hearted laughter. "Woman, how would you like to join me on the porch for some lemonade while these two go for their ride?"

"I'd like to join you for lemonade and a ride," drawled Edna, still in Southern mode.

Again, Roy laughed and held his arm out for Edna to take. They made their way up the steps toward the rocking chairs on the porch.

"Take as long as you like, kids!" Edna hollered over her shoulder. "Roy and I will just be over here gettin' acquainted."

Sunny shook her head and turned to follow Levi to the barn when a streak of yellow ran past her, and the hump-machine started in on Beau again. Duke looked like he was trying to start a two dog conga line, and Beau just hadn't caught the dance fever yet.

"Dad, put this dog in the house, would ya?" Levi called out to Roy as he again shooed Duke off of Beau.

Duke regretfully obeyed Roy's call of "Come here, Boy," and slunk up the steps and through the screen door that Roy held ajar.

"C'mon, I want to show you the horses." Levi took Sunny's hand and pulled her toward the barn.

The horses were housed in a well-maintained red

barn. They stepped through the doors from the warm sunshine into the cool shadowy walkway between two rows of stalls on either side of the barn. Sunny's nose was filled with the barn scents of hay, dirt, horses, and manure, and yet the mixture of them all together was kind of pleasant.

Levi introduced Sunny to his gelding, Star. He was a large black beast with a white marking along his nose faintly resembling a star shape. He brought Star out of his stall and wrapped the reins of his bridle loosely around the top rung of the stall door.

He opened the neighboring stall and led forth another horse that was smaller than Star and had white sock markings on its two front legs.

"And this beautiful lady is...uh...well...Lady," Levi said. Sunny was beginning to get a sense of his creative mind when it came to naming his farm animals.

Sunny stepped forward and reached out to stroke the side of Lady's head and neck. The horse looked at her with gorgeous brown eyes and moved to nuzzle its head into her shoulder. A fly landed on the horse's rump, and she simultaneously stamped her right foot down onto Sunny's toe and shook her head with a huff. Sunny cried out from the assault on her big toe as Lady blew horsy snot right across Sunny's upturned cheeks and into her open mouth.

"That was not very ladylike." Levi tugged on Lady's halter, leading her and Star out into the sunshine as Sunny stood doubled over, spitting onto the ground, wondering if Levi was talking to the horse or her.

After a few minutes, Sunny joined Levi in the arena and approached Lady from the side, questioning how on earth she was going to get from the ground up into that saddle.

"Just put your right foot in the stirrup there, grab the saddle horn and swing up into the saddle," Levi instructed.

*Easy for you to say.* She stuck her right foot up in the air and jabbed for the stirrup. She got her foot into the loop and tried to reach for the saddle horn, in a perfect yoga move of 'Stork Reaching for the Horizon', when something slipped and down she went. Landing hard on her rump, Sunny tried to laugh off her embarrassment and quickly got up to try again.

"Let me help." Levi dismounted from Star and came up behind her. With her foot back in the stirrup, he simultaneously pushed while Sunny pulled on the saddle horn. Between the two of them, she somehow ended upright in the saddle. Levi's help was a cross between a goose and a grab, and his cheeks were flushed pink as he climbed back into Star's saddle, avoiding eye contact with her.

*So far, this date is off to a great start.* Between her gassy dog, her lady-like spitting, and her obvious clumsiness, she'd made quite a great first impression. Whether she liked him or not, the cute cowboy probably wished he hadn't agreed to Piper's fix-up.

Finally, they set off on their ride, leaving the arena, then walking the horses through a meadow. As they crossed the tall grass, Lady must have decided to acknowledge her woman's right to have a snack if it presents itself and stopped dead in her tracks. She proceeded to drop her head and happily munch on the green stalks. Because Sunny terrifyingly clung to the reins, she also proceeded to drop forward.

"Uh, Levi, help, please," Sunny called, as she clung to Lady's neck.

"Aahh, she's just eatin'," he said, and sauntered back to where they had stopped. "Grab the reins and pull back on her head real hard."

"I think I dropped the reins. And I don't know how to sit back up from here," Sunny said pitifully.

Levi brought Star up next to Lady's head and reached down for the reins. He pulled the horse's head up and passed the reins back to Sunny. She pushed back into a sitting position.

But within a few minutes of walking, Lady found a new grassy delicacy, and the process repeated itself again. After several rein-rescues, Levi wrapped the reins around the saddle horn to help keep Lady's head up. He looked a little disappointed in Sunny's horseback riding abilities, so she sat up straighter in the saddle, determined to take control of the horse and Levi's opinion of her.

*Okay. Now I'm getting the hang of things.* After several minutes of riding without any other mishaps, she was beginning to see why Piper enjoyed this so much. They plodded through the meadow and followed a path into a stand of aspen trees, with Sunny's horse in the lead.

Several times Sunny turned to smile encouragingly at Levi and would catch him staring at her behind. Caught, he would look away quickly, his cheeks pink with embarrassment.

A bit smug, now that she had caught the cowboy checking her out, she was a little more confident in herself and her riding abilities. After leaving the meadow behind, she unwrapped the reins and proceeded to lead Lady through the trail.

No sooner did Sunny begin to get comfortable and almost enjoy the ride, than Lady's head whipped back, and the horse took a nip at her leg.

"Hey!" Sunny screamed. "She's biting me!"

"Aahh- she's just playin' with ya," Levi said. "She won't really bite ya."

"Well, she keeps bringing her head back and snapping her teeth at my leg," Sunny cried, now having brought her leg out of the stirrup and hooked her foot behind the saddle horn.

"Hey, stop it!" she shrieked, as Lady turned her head to the other side and tried to nip Sunny's other leg. She pulled that leg up too and counterbalanced, slipping off the saddle. Grabbing for the saddle horn, she began a slow motion descent as her body weight pulled her and the saddle sideways until she let go and dropped unceremoniously onto the ground.

Evidently, her shrieking must have scared Lady as much it did Sunny, because the horse took off like a shot, leaving Sunny in a dusty pile of tears on the ground.

"What the heck? Are you all right?" Levi swung down from Star's back and came toward her. "I've never seen her do that. Usually she likes women."

"Well, thanks. That makes me feel so much better." Sunny wiped her cheeks and tried to untangle herself from the bush she had landed in, her newfound confidence waning with each scratch from the prickly branches.

"I didn't mean she didn't like you," Levi faltered as he reached down to help Sunny to her feet. "I meant she's never done that to other women. Err… I mean…"

"Just forget it," she grumbled and started back down the path toward the meadow.

They silently plodded back to the barn. Levi walked with her, leading Star behind him. Reaching the barn, they found Lady back in the arena, calmly munching some hay from the center trough.

Sunny had realized two things. She did not enjoy horseback riding, and her cute 'cowboy' boots were definitely not made for walking. Her feet hurt, her rump was sore, and she was ready to call it a day.

As Sunny limped back toward the house, she could hear Edna and Roy's laughter coming from the porch. Beau, who had been hiding under the steps, ran cheerfully out to greet her.

"I think we're ready to head back," Sunny called to Edna as she neared the porch steps.

"Already? We were just having such fun." She smiled over at Roy, who winked conspiratorially at her.

"I hate to be a party pooper, but I fell off the horse,

and my feet are killing me. I'm ready to go home now," Sunny explained.

"Oh, honey, are you all right?" Edna came down the stairs. "Did you break anything?"

"She's fine. She just took a little tumble," Levi said, coming up behind them, apparently having taken a few minutes to put Star and Lady back into their stables.

"Oh, shoot! Is that when you sat in the horse poop?" Edna asked, as she circled Sunny, looking for obvious injury.

"What?" Sunny cried, her hands reaching back to feel crusty, dried, horse-poop covering her back side. "When did that happen?" She frantically tried to brush it off.

"I think when you tried to get on Lady, there in the arena," Levi said quietly, as he looked away in embarrassment.

*Ding! Ding! Last straw of the day just joined the party!* Hurt and embarrassed, Sunny's normally calm temperament had been through enough.

"I've had horse-shit on my ass for the whole last hour and you didn't tell me?!" Sunny shrieked, then gasped in humiliation at the memory of his 'stolen' glances at her backside.

"Sorry, I didn't..." he began.

"Son, you better get these ladies on home now," Roy interrupted, trying to save them any more mortification. He began to herd them toward the pickup where they all piled in. Beau jumped into the cab, and Roy shut the door behind him.

"It was nice meeting you, ladies," Roy said through the open window. "I'll be in touch, Edna." He patted the side of the pickup as Levi slowly pulled away.

The ride home was uncomfortably silent, and Sunny and Edna mumbled their thanks to Levi as he deposited them into the driveway.

He pulled away, and Edna sighed. "I would have at

least taken the goodbye kiss."

Sunny shook her head, smiling, and trudged up to the front door, pampering her left foot where she could feel a blister already forming.

Sunny just wanted to climb into a hot bath and forget about humping dogs, spitting-biting horses, sore feet, and her humiliating poop-encrusted butt. In Levi's words, she was done "just playin'."

"There he is," Cassie cried, as she jumped up and down in her seat.

"I can't believe he showed up while we were here," Sunny said incredulously.

"Right? What are the odds?"

"Well, the odds aren't too bad considering we've been hanging around here for the past two days just hoping we'd see him," she answered wryly.

Maggie had to show up at her day job, so Sunny and Cassie had spent most of the day on Monday and Tuesday at the café across from Finney's Investigations, where Piper and Drew had spied Jake the week before. They had wasted hours watching and waiting for Jake's return. So far, they had tried all six flavors of milkshake the café offered. If Sunny saw another french fry, she might vomit.

On Monday, they each showed up to the restaurant in head to toe black apparel, then laughed at each other's silly prime-time idea of spying.

"Maybe the all black is better at night," Sunny said, dragging the black baseball cap from her head.

"Well, you did it too!" Cassie pulled the black leather driving gloves from her hands and stuffed them in her purse. "I just got excited. It's my first stakeout. I didn't know what to wear!"

Their stakeout had gone from exciting and thrilling to dull and boring. So far, it had resulted in watching several women go in and out of the salon and constant full bladders from too many iced teas.

After so many hours of tedious observation, Sunny couldn't believe it when Jake's Mustang pulled up in front of the strip mall. As he climbed from the car, she took in his lean muscled body. His dark aviator sunglasses added an extra air of dangerousness.

Cassie gave a low wolf whistle. "I can definitely see why you're into this guy. He's hot!"

"Told you! Now get down." Sunny pulled Cassie into a squat behind her chair, then reached up to throw some bills on the table for a tip. They duck-walked out of the café and hid behind some low shrubbery, both scrambling to get their dark glasses out of their purses.

Sunny pulled on her glasses then covered her mouth to prevent a giggle from escaping as Cassie looked at her from behind a huge pair of black sunglasses, giving her the impression of a big-eyed fly.

"Cut it out." Cassie swatted at Sunny. "C'mon," she said, and the two ran across the street as soon as Jake had entered the building.

They sneaked in the front entrance just in time to see Jake push open the door to Finney's office. As they crept closer, they could just make out the conversation through the partially open door.

"Hey, Finn, how ya doin'?" Jake entered the office and extended a hand to Jerry Finney. If he weren't so preoccupied with thoughts of a certain curly-haired blonde whose name rhymed with 'Funny', he most likely would have noticed the two women on stakeout across the street. As it was, his mind was busy with thoughts of her in that ridiculous straw hat she wore while she gardened the other day. The way her eyes crinkled as her face broke into a smile…the way her skin had felt as he slid his hands inside that silk robe.

"Jake? Earth to Jake?" Finney snapped his fingers in order to get Jake's attention.

"What? Sorry, man, got a lot on my mind." He took a seat in one of the chairs across the desk from Finn. "So you got the results on the blood-covered shirt of Walter's that I brought in the other day?"

In the hallway, Sunny's eyes widened as she turned to look at Cassie.

"Yeah, I got the results back, and it is definitely a match to the DNA you gave me of Walter's," Finney confirmed.

"The way the blood pattern was arranged on the shirt is inconsistent though. I mean sure they could be from defensive wounds, but they could just as easily have been from the guy cutting himself and bleeding on his shirt," Finney explained.

"So, basically, the shirt tells us nothing except that at one point Walter was bleeding?"

"Basically."

"So, even if the shirt were used as evidence, it bears no proof of any wrong-doing and couldn't be used as proof of guilt." Jake said this as more of a statement than a question.

"So far, there's no real proof that Walter's body was even in the garage when it went up in flames," Finn said.

"But I don't like the effects the detective pulled from the site. The neighbors confirmed Walter was never without that pocket knife and always wore that eagle belt buckle. The wedding ring seems to offer the most proof that Walter's body was either in the garage or that some kind of foul play is involved."

"Again, those things are all circumstantial. I wish I could do more to help you out, buddy. I know how you felt about the old bastard."

"Yeah, well, I wanted him to know how I felt about him too," Jake said with conviction.

"If there's anything else you want me to do, let me know. I ran up an invoice for the lab charges for you."

"Put it on my tab," Jake said warmly. "I appreciate what you've done."

Sunny could tell the conversation was wrapping up. "I think he's coming out," she whispered to Cassie. "Let's get out of here."

In an effort to avoid being seen, they slipped into the closest door and let it shut quietly behind them. Sunny could see into the hallway through the shuttered window as the slats were tilted up and she heard the next door close. The two women pressed against the wall as Jake walked past the window and out of the mall.

"May I help you?" a calm voice asked, which caused them both to jump and Sunny to let out a little shriek.

They turned to find themselves in a room painted purple and gold, decorated with mystical moons and stars, a large mural of a dragon covering one whole wall. A small woman of slight build had come into the reception area and now watched the two women, patiently waiting for their response.

The woman held out her hand as she approached them. "I am Madame Zia, how can I be of service to you today?"

Sunny reached out and shook her hand. Smiling, she quickly tried to come up with a lie. "Ya know, my friend here is worried her husband is cheating on her, and we wondered how much it would be to hire a private investigator to spy on him."

"Oh." Madame Zia's shoulders drooped as she let out a sigh. "You've come in the wrong door. The private investigator is the next door down. But if you ask me, I wouldn't waste your money."

"Sorry to bother you," Cassie said, her eyes shooting

daggers at Sunny as they slipped out the door.

Madame Zia waved them off and headed back into the office as she muttered, "Stupid eye is always throwing people off."

The women looked through the glass to make sure Jake's Mustang was gone before they pushed through the outside door.

"Well, now we know what was in the black garbage bag." Sunny shielded her eyes with her hand as they stepped from the cool interior of the strip mall into the blinding sun.

"We know it was a bloody shirt, and it belonged to Walter, but where does that leave us?" Cassie asked, putting the giant bug-eyed glasses back on her face.

"I can hardly look at you in those stupid glasses without cracking up," Sunny said.

"What? I got them at the goodwill this weekend for our stakeout. They disguise my face plus I think they're kinda cool. Very Marilyn Monroe."

"Try Marilyn Manson. They are hideous. Don't ever wear them again," Sunny instructed.

"Fine." Cassie huffed as she pulled her regular sunglasses from her bag and tossed the too-large glasses in. "Are we gonna stand here talking about my failed stakeout-fashion sense, or are we gonna talk about what we saw in there with your stud-muffin neighbor?"

"Sorry. You're right." Sunny had been using the jokes about the glasses as a way to avoid thinking about the things they had heard Jake telling the private investigator. "Did you hear Jake asking that stuff about using it as evidence in court? Either he was asking if they could use it against the killer, or stating that it couldn't be used as evidence against him– *if* he's the one who killed Walter."

"Yeah, I couldn't tell by his voice how he meant it, but you *could* tell that he doesn't think very highly of Walter. It doesn't sound like he likes the guy very much."

"So you *do* think he killed Walter?" Sunny asked.

"I'm not saying that. Just because he doesn't like him doesn't mean I think he killed him and torched his body in a garage explosion. I honestly don't know what to think." Cassie sighed. "He could be trying to find out who killed Walter just like we are."

Sunny groaned. "The main reason I did this stupid stake-out idea was because I was hoping that we would see something to prove that Jake has nothing to do with Walter's disappearance. Now I am more confused than ever."

"Have you thought about just asking Jake if he knows what happened to Walter?" Cassie asked.

"I have. He just gets all evasive, changes the subject and acts like he is clueless about where Walter is. And then he usually says something charming or funny, and all I can think about is kissing him, then I forget all about Walter." Sunny dropped her head in shame. "I am a terrible person."

"You are not," Cassie assured her. "You are a normal, hot-blooded woman who is a little ga-ga over an amazingly gorgeous man."

Sunny sighed. "The only trouble is, this amazingly gorgeous man may have murdered my next-door neighbor."

I have to see you again. Maggie read the text again as she waited.

It was Monday afternoon, and she sat outside a cute downtown restaurant a few blocks from her office and debated her decision to agree to meet him for lunch. Part of her wanted to get up and run back to her safe law office where she was in charge and had control of the outcomes. Part of her couldn't wait for him to show up so she could see him smile again.

"Are you ready to order?" The waitress set a glass of water on the table before her. A lemon slice floated amidst the ice cubes, and beads of condensation clung to the outside of the clear glass.

"No, thank you. I'm waiting for someone," Maggie replied. "He should be here any minute."

"Oh, are you waiting for your husband?"

"No." Maggie tensed as images of Chad the Cheater filled her head, and she reached for her purse, ready to flee as quickly as she could. "No. I am definitely not waiting for my husband."

"Sorry," the waitress replied, unaware of the social faux-pas she had made as she already moved toward the next table. "I'll check back with you in a few minutes when your date arrives."

*My date?* Fingers of panic squeezed her chest tighter. *What am I thinking? I don't go on dates.* She clutched her purse to her chest and pushed her chair back.

Then suddenly he was there.

She sucked in her breath as she watched him weave his way through the maze of tables, then pull out the chair across from her, smiling as he dropped into it.

"Hi, Maggie," he said.

"Hi, Jeremy," she said and slowly exhaled.

"Am I late? Were you getting ready to give up on me?" He motioned to the purse she still gripped.

"No, you're right on time." She loosened her grip on her bag and scooted her chair back up to the table.

"I'm nervous too," he said kindly as he shook out his napkin and placed it across his lap. "But I'm really glad you came."

"I am too." She relaxed a little as she pulled her napkin free. She wiped her damp palms across the cloth napkin.

"Do you come here often?" he asked.

She laughed at the common pickup line and replied, "Yes, and I'm a Sagittarius. What's your sign?"

His face broke into the grin she remembered and her heart sped up just a little. Jeremy blushed and said, "No, I really mean have you been before, like what's good to eat?"

"Oh, um, they have great sandwiches, and their fries are fresh-cut. Or they have Caesar salads or Cobb salads. And their soup is really good, especially their chicken noodle." She stopped. She was rambling. She could mesmerize a room full of people and speak so eloquently a jury of twelve people would cry, but she couldn't tell this one man what was good at a restaurant. *Pull yourself together, woman.*

"So your date finally arrived. What can I get you two?" The waitress appeared over Maggie's shoulder.

Maggie had been married for so long that the word *date* seemed foreign to her. She looked across the table at this man who smiled freely at her and knew in her heart that she was going to be okay. Whether this date led to another or whether this was it, she could do this. She was still an attractive woman, and she knew she had something to offer. She took another deep breath and turned to the waitress. "I will have the chicken noodle soup with the half turkey and cheddar sandwich."

"I'll have the same." Jeremy handed the waitress his menu.

"Something to drink?"

"Water's fine," he said, his eyes again on Maggie's face.

*Why does it feel like he can see into my very soul?* She couldn't look away.

She wiped her palms against her napkin again. "So tell me about yourself."

He laughed easily, and then he did tell her. He talked about his job and his family, then he asked about hers. He had never been married, but not because he hadn't wanted to. He had just been caught up in his career and hadn't met anyone that captured his attention enough to take his mind off his work.

"Until now," he said shyly. "Now I find myself drifting off at my desk thinking about a dark-haired beauty that I can't seem to get out of my mind."

Maggie smiled as her cheeks warmed. "My thoughts have been doing a little drifting off at work as well."

"They have?" He outwardly flirted now. "Tell me more about these thoughts you've been having."

Their lunch arrived, and they talked easily through their meal. Over coffee and a shared piece of chocolate cake, Maggie found herself telling him how she got married right after high school and the struggles of attending college and law school with a husband and two babies. She told him about Chad and his betrayal and the deterioration of their marriage.

"Wow. I don't know why I just told you that," she said. "I really don't talk about it much." Something about him made her want to talk. Made her feel like she could trust him. The feelings were so foreign to her, she almost didn't recognize them.

"I'm glad you told me," Jeremy said. "It means you're getting comfortable with me." The back of his hand rested lightly against hers as he held his coffee cup.

"It's really not a great first date topic." She felt the warmth of his hand against hers, afraid to move for fear that warmth would end.

"What date do you think would be a good one to bring up your adulterous ex-husband?" he teased.

She laughed. "Oh, probably the tenth or fifteenth."

"Okay, on our fifteenth date, you can tell me about him again." He reached for his wallet as the waitress set the check on the table but kept his eyes steady on Maggie's.

"Okay, fifteenth date it is," she said, losing herself into his dark eyes, and for the first time in over a year, she placed her trust in a man.

He passed the waitress back the check with a twenty and a ten, telling her that he appreciated the service and to keep the change.

*Good tipper, without being pretentious.* Maggie appreciated that, as she had worked as a waitress when she was younger. She followed him through the restaurant and out onto the sidewalk.

"Can I walk you to your car?" Jeremy asked.

"I walked. My office is only about three blocks from here."

"Well, then, can I walk you back to your office?"

"Oh, you don't have to do that," she said. "I'm fine, Jeremy."

"I know, but I want to. I'm not quite ready for our date to end."

"Me either," she said softly as her heart tumbled a little further.

"Shall we?" He stuck out his elbow.

"Okay."

She slipped her arm through his, grinning at his chivalry. He pulled her close to his side and put his hand on top of hers.

"Tell me about your boys," he said as they began to walk. Jeremy threaded his fingers through hers.

She had forgotten the simple act of holding hands and reveled in the joy of walking down the street with someone by her side, their steps in sync as they meandered down the sidewalk.

The three blocks passed in a blur of laughter, and then they stood outside of her building, neither quite ready to say goodbye.

"I had a great time with you today," he said.

"Me, too."

"Please tell me I'll see you again."

She laughed. "You *will* see me again."

He raised his hand and stroked the side of her face, his fingers twisting gently into her dark hair. "I'm really glad I met you, Maggie."

A shiver went down her spine as his thumb caressed her cheek. He leaned down and touched his lips to hers. Something deep inside her came alive, and she found herself gripping his shirt as she pulled his face closer and pressed her lips to his. A passion buried within her came bubbling to the surface, and she pressed her body tightly against him. His free arm came around and clutched her, his fingers splaying across her lower back.

She realized they were in front of her office building and pulled free, her breath ragged, and her body instantly missing the warmth of his.

"Well, I better get back to work." She smoothed down her hair.

"I don't think I'll ever be able to work again," he teased. "When can I see you next?"

"Soon." She turned to the door of the building. Then in a flash of very un-Maggie-like spontaneity, she turned back, grabbed Jeremy's head, pulled him back into a fierce kiss, and pressed herself to his chest. She released him and looked up into his eyes.

"Very soon." She grinned and, without looking back, disappeared into the offices of Wilson, Benton, Grant, and Hayes.

Sunny dipped her finger into the dollop of whipped cream floating in her iced white chocolate mocha. She figured if she could date four different men in one month, she could branch out from her plain vanilla coffee drinks as well. "I liked this book and I love the idea of having an enchanted pair of pants."

"Maybe if you would have had some magical jeans, Sunny, all that horse manure might not have stuck to your butt," Edna said with a cackle.

The Page Turners were gathered around a small table in their favorite Starbucks the following Wednesday discussing their latest book choice. They had let Piper choose a book this time around, and she had picked *The Sisterhood of the Traveling Pants*. It was a coming-of-age novel about four teenage best friends who found a magical pair of jeans in a second hand shop that amazingly fit all of their four different body types and looked good on each of them. The girls shared the jeans, sending them through the mail as they spent their first summer apart from each other. Somehow, the magic of a great pair of jeans spurred their self-confidence and carried them through their separate teenage rites of passage.

Piper had loved the book, Cassie had enjoyed it, Maggie found it boring, and Edna had skimmed the highlights then decided to watch the movie instead.

Sunny had filled the book club in on the adventure

of her last date the previous Saturday, before they had delved into the intricacies of the novel. Edna's last comment produced peals of laughter.

"Maybe if I would have had a magic pair of jeans, one of these dates would be my Prince Charming. Then I wouldn't be spending my time falling off horses, playing video-games, watching baseball, or upchucking onto my lawn after ingesting too much wine and wasting an evening listening to boring dribble about interest rates," Sunny said, which sent the girls into another round of hysterical laughter.

"So if *we* found a fabulous pair of jeans that would help all of us," Piper said, her voice soft and thoughtful, "what would you want them to help you with?" She looked toward her aunt.

Cassie laughed. "I would definitely want some magical, fat-burning jeans that would transform my size sixteen butt into a size twelve butt!"

The women laughed along, but the look on Piper's face made it obvious that she wanted a deeper, truer answer.

"For me," Maggie said, looking at Piper, "I would want a pair of jeans like in the book that would give me confidence, that would help me to be able to give my heart away again, and to be able to trust another man."

Piper's eyes stayed on Maggie for a moment, then dropped to her lap where she was twisting a gold ring around her thumb. "If I had some magic jeans, I would wear them when I could hang out with my mom all day. We could go shopping, and to lunch, and she would laugh with me again," she said all in one breath.

Sunny's heart broke for this precious teenage heart that longed for her mother's love. She could tell by the tears in Cassie's eyes, that her friend was feeling the same thing.

"That day may still come," Cassie said in a soft voice. She took Piper's hand and squeezed it.

"Hey, I have a great idea," Sunny said. "This Friday, let's go to lunch and all go shopping together. We can shop until we find a great pair of jeans for each of us."

Piper beamed. "Oh, that sounds fun."

"Since we're shopping for jeans, let's wait to eat until *after* we try on clothes," Cassie suggested. "Then we could go out for supper and maybe see a movie."

"I can get off by three on Friday, so I'm in," Maggie said, after checking her schedule on her phone.

"Well, I'm in," Edna said. "I need to find a marvelous pair of jeans for my date on Saturday night."

"Your what?" Sunny choked.

"My date."

"With whom?"

"With Roy, of course. Couldn't you see we made a love connection that afternoon at the ranch?"

"Roy, as in Levi's dad?" Piper asked and she wrinkled her nose. "Isn't he kind of old?"

Edna cackled again. "You're only as old as you feel, so some mornings I'm about eighty, but some nights I still feel twenty-five! Hee. Hee."

"What are you all doing for your date?" Sunny asked.

"He's taking me dancing."

"Oh, fun. Are you going to the dance clubs downtown?" Maggie asked.

"No, we're going square-dancing."

"What?" Sunny asked. All of her comments seemed to begin with that word. "What do you know about square dancing?"

"Oh, it can't be that hard. They have a guy up front yelling at you telling you what to do next. Grab your partner, swing her around," she sang in a loud sing-song imitation of a square dance caller. "Do-se-do, Promenade, one foot, two foot, red foot, blue foot. You do the hokey pokey, and you turn yourself around, and that's what it's all about!"

The two couples seated at the next table gave Edna a round of applause, to which she smiled, batted her eyes, and ate up the extra attention.

"You're right." Maggie wiped a tear from the corner of her eye that had eeked out as she laughed at Edna's rendition of a square dance caller. "That does sound easy enough. You'll have to let us know how it turns out." She laughed easily. Shaking her head, she looked at Sunny as if to say, "Hey, she's your neighbor."

"Okay, so we know what Edna is doing Saturday night, but who has a date lined up for Sunny this weekend?" Cassie asked.

They all looked at each other but no one responded.

"Oh, I do," Sunny said. "His name is Beau, and we have a date with a sofa, a bowl of popcorn, and a movie. Hurray."

"Oh, no you don't," Cassie said. "You promised to give us six tries. Doesn't anybody have any ideas for this weekend?" She looked at the faces of Maggie, Piper, and Edna, who stared blankly back at her.

"Well, do *you*?" Piper asked.

"Well, no."

They each picked up their coffee drink and took a sip while Sunny picked at the half-eaten blueberry muffin on the plate in front of her.

"It's fine, you guys," she said. "I don't have to have a date *every* weekend."

"Shh. We're thinking." Cassie stared intently out the front window as if a cute guy might walk by on the sidewalk with a sign reading, CUTE, SMART, FUNNY GUY LOOKING FOR A DATE WITH A BLONDE, CURLY-HAIRED, SECOND-GRADE TEACHER, WHO IS CARRYING FIFTEEN EXTRA POUNDS IN HER HIP AREA.

"Well, how does a nice, single, thirty-something go about meeting men?" she finally asked.

"Maybe you should go to some of the clubs. There should be a lot of guys there," Piper suggested.

"Not," Sunny said. "I've gone out dancing with the other teachers before, and it's a big meat market. You don't really meet or talk to anyone. It's a bunch of horny guys looking for one-night stands, and they are not interested in me when a bunch of gorgeous, skinny twenty-something's are shaking their little bitty butts around on the dance floor. And the cleavage that's on display is crazy. It makes me want to stand on the stairway above the dance floor and toss coins into the crowd to see how many I can get to land in all the boob-cracks."

"Oh, we should totally go do that!" Maggie laughed. "That would be hilarious."

"Okay, so no clubs," Cassie said, keeping them on task. "How about your church? Aren't there some nice men there?"

Sunny attended church with Edna, and though it was a small chapel with a lovely pastor, attendance was minimal with the Sunday crowd mainly the retired, Social-Security receiving set.

"There are lots of nice men there," Sunny replied. "But they are all in their eighties. No offense, Edna."

"None taken," Edna said. "I don't want to date any of those old farts either. Those widowers are just looking for someone to feed 'em, keep track of their pills, and measure out their Metamucil. No thanks."

Cassie chuckled. "Okay. No clubs and no old men from the church. What about your work?"

"There are four wonderful men at my school, but their wives might not appreciate me trying to date them," Sunny teased.

"Geez, this is hard. Where are you supposed to meet men if you're single and work primarily with women?"

"Tara's mom goes out on tons of dates," Piper contributed. "She meets them all online."

"Of course," Maggie said. "Why didn't we think of this before? A couple of the secretaries at my firm are always talking about online dating."

"Oh, c'mon guys," Sunny said. "I don't know if I'm ready to step into that mess yet. I really am fine hanging out with my dog, and I've always got you all."

Going out with men her friends knew was one thing, but the thought of a complete stranger taking her on a date had Sunny's chest constricting with panic.

"Oh, everybody is doing it," Edna said. "I've checked out Cupid.com and the Craig's List classifieds."

"You what?" Sunny asked. There was that word again. Edna just seemed full of surprises today.

"It's fun. You should at least check it out," Edna said.

"Okay, we're moving this party to Sunny's house. Everybody grab your stuff." Maggie pulled her purse strap onto her shoulder. "Let's go see if we can find Sunny a match!"

❀❀❀

"Maybe we should try ETranquility.net. I've heard they really look for someone that you're compatible with," Sunny said. Thirty minutes later, the whole book club crowded around her kitchen table as they waited for her laptop to sign on to the internet.

"You have to answer lots of questions, and then they choose your date. You don't even get to look at profiles," Edna explained.

"You should try the cupid one," Maggie suggested.

Sunny typed in the website address. "All right. Here goes nothing."

Nothing is what Sunny hoped they would find. How had an innocent conversation over coffee morphed into her searching the internet for cupid's match? *How pathetic am I that I can't find my own date?*

A black and red screen popped up with cheesy cupids, hearts, and arrows streaming across the page. The words, LET CUPID SHOOT AN ARROW THROUGH THE HEART OF YOUR PERFECT MATCH, arced across the screen following the path of an arrow and pierced the heart of an un-naturally good-looking blond fireman.

Sunny groaned. "This is not how I want to find a man." Embarrassed by her inadequacies, she considered pulling the plug on this whole idea. Literally, she could pull the plug from the side of the computer and just act like the internet went out.

"You should try the Match one. It's one of the most popular sites, and they offer a one month free trial membership so you're not out anything if you just want to try it," Edna said.

Raising an eyebrow at Edna, Sunny was amazed at the older woman's online dating know-how. Sunny hadn't thought she even knew how to use the internet.

Sunny clicked on the next website address, and a new screen came up with a scene of two good-looking people laughing as they sipped champagne in a hot tub with a backdrop of snow covered mountains in the background. As they watched, the scene faded into a beach setting with another beautiful couple, also laughing while they rode horseback down the sand. That scene faded to still another laughing couple on the patio of a romantic restaurant enjoying a lobster dinner.

"Look how happy all those people are," Piper said.

"Those are the couples who own these websites. They're so happy, because they're making so much money on the poor suckers searching these sights," Maggie said dryly.

"Well, I certainly do enjoy hot tubs, the beach, and eating," Sunny said. "So I should fit right in. And I'm sure my body looks just like that girl in the bikini." Her sarcasm was ignored as the other women intently watched the screen.

"I wouldn't mind being matched up with that one." Edna pointed to the computer as a new scene depicted another gorgeous couple picnicking in the French countryside, their bicycles resting against a nearby tree, and they were, of course, also laughing. The man was dark haired, mustached, and had a muscled tan body. He was pictured feeding a chocolate-covered strawberry to a beautiful blonde goddess. "He looks a little like Clark Gable."

"Who?" Piper asked.

"The guy in *Gone with the Wind*," Cassie said.

"Oh, yeah."

"So, what am I supposed to do now?" Sunny asked. She still couldn't believe she was asking Edna's advice on how to work an online dating site.

"You have to start making choices. Are you looking for a male or female?" Edna asked, teasingly.

"Okay, that's easy enough." Sunny rolled the mouse around to click on Female seeking Male.

"Now put in your age range."

She clicked on the thirty to forty icon.

"Now, put in your zip code, and it will bring up guys in this area."

Sunny typed in her zip and pressed enter.

The screen now held a row of one by two inch pictures, each with a profile title and a short message.

"See, these are the profiles," Edna explained. "You scroll through them and when you get to one you like, you can 'wink' at them."

"Wink at them?"

"It's like a little message to show you're interested."

"Look at this one." Maggie pointed at the screen. "It says, ONLY WOMEN WHO LIKE TO RECEIVE ROSES NEED APPLY and his profile name is *SmoothTalk*. Vomit!"

Cassie laughed. "Wait, look at this one. This guy is called *Got Cheesecake*, and it says I'VE BEEN TOLD I'M VERY GOOD-LOOKING. By who? Your mother?"

They scrolled through the pictures, laughing and hooting at some of the more outrageous profiles.

"*4everLooking* wants to know, WILL YOU COMPLETE

ME?"

"Wait! *Dr. Love* says, I'M A NICE GUY THAT LIKES TO CUDDLE."

"Look at this guy. His name is *Ladylover* and all he wrote was, I'M JUST LOOKIN' FOR SOME TAIL."

"Oh, you better write his number down," Maggie said. "He sounds like a real catch."

"I think we can skip over *Big14U* and *Fun4aNite*," Cassie said.

"Although, you might be interested in *KegMaster*," Piper said, joining in on the fun as she pointed to a beefy guy who wore sunglasses, with his hat backwards sitting in a boat. "He says, LIVED HERE HIS HOLE LIFE, IS AN OUTGOING PERSONE, LIKES DRINKING, HANGING OUT AND NASCAR. And he is obviously a great speller."

"Check out this one. He can't even be bothered to spell. He's just using text language. And he, WANTS TO BE UR SUPERMAN. He says, MY NAME IS JIM AKA LOVERBOY. I LOVE 2 GO TO DA MOVIES N GO OUT 2 EAT AFTER DA MOVIES. I'M VERY ROMANTIC AND LOYAL. I'M TRYING 2 GO BAK 2 SCHOOL...."

Sunny laughed. "Well, *Loverboy* can just go right on back to school. In fact, he would fit right in with some of our fifth graders."

Cassie scrolled to another profile. "How about this one? He LIKES TO WATCH TV AND GET TATTOOS. He sounds like a real winner. No wonder his profile name is *Loner78*."

"But this guy is a CONNOISSEUR OF FINE WINE AND WOMEN," Maggie said.

"Why is this guy on here? It says he's looking for companionship in one sentence and the next he says he works seventy-five hours a week. When would he have the time?"

"How about *HotRockerStud*? That Van Halen long hair is *almost* still in style."

"This is ridiculous." Sunny wiped tears from her

eyes as she tried to control her laughter. "This is why those first people were having so much fun. They had been reading these profiles. Who would go out with these guys?"

Sunny's embarrassment faded with the hilarity of the situation as the laughter in the room grew.

"Now, Sunny, you have to get past the duds and try to find the studs," Edna said, still on the hunt for a good match. "This one looks nice." She pointed to a snapshot of a dark-haired man pictured with two poodles. "His name is *My2doggiesandme.* Now that's kind of sweet."

"First of all, I'm not going out with a guy who has a poodle. Beau would probably eat that little dog. And second of all, I'm not going out with a guy *who has a poodle.*"

"Yeah, Edna, she has some standards." Maggie smirked. "How about going out with *Beefcake*? It says, LIKES TO WORKOUT FOUR TIMES A WEEK."

Sunny laughed and reached to close the laptop. "That's enough for me."

"Wait, I think I might have found one for real," Cassie said, her face intent as she clicked on the picture of an average-looking guy with a blond hair. He looked tan and fit, and his picture was taken outdoors by a stream. He was wearing shorts, a fishing vest, and was holding a fishing pole. His profile name was *Flyfisherman.* "He sounds okay. His message reads, SIMPLE GUY WITH A GOOD SENSE OF HUMOR WHO LOVES THE OUTDOORS, HIKING, AND FISHING. LAID BACK PERSONALITY, LISTENS TO THE EAGLES, AND LIKES TO COOK."

"Likes to cook? Let me call him," Maggie said.

"He sounds pretty good, Sunny. And he looks nice," Piper said.

"Yeah, I guess he sounds okay," she replied. "All right, you can wink at him."

"Now once you let them know you're interested,"

Edna said, “you have to build a profile for yourself so they can reply.”

“Groan. I don’t want to sound as dorky as these guys,” Sunny said, as she watched Edna click through the steps and type in her name, email and description.

“Eyes,” Edna said. “Blue. What color would you call your hair?”

Sunny glared at her. “Blonde.” When Edna didn’t resume typing, she continued, “-ish. Okay, dirty-blonde.”

“Wait. Don’t put dirty-blonde in her profile,” Cassie said.

“Ya, she might get winked at by *Loverboy* or *DrLove*,” Maggie said.

“Just put blonde,” Cassie instructed. “They will see her picture.”

Sunny groaned again. “Oh, my gosh, what are we going to use for a picture?”

“Don’t worry. We can use that good one from Cassie’s BBQ last summer,” Maggie offered.

“Next question is ‘What would you say your weight is?’” Edna read, keeping to her task.

“What would *I* say it is or what would the *scale* say it is?” Sunny asked.

Sunny watched as Edna entered in a weight and height and said, “That’s close enough.”

“Now what is your message going to say?” Piper asked.

“Do you like pina coladas? And getting caught in the rain?” Maggie crooned.

“That’ll get me a lot of dates.”

“Okay,” Cassie said, still serious, “put down kind-hearted, dog-lover, and good with children…”

“Don’t make her sound like a nun,” Maggie chided. “Add in ‘fun and full of energy’.”

“Put that I like to read and watch movies,” Sunny said.

“Put that she likes motorcycles, rock-climbing, and

hang-gliding," Maggie added.

"No, don't do that!"

"Why not?"

"It's lying. I don't do any of those things."

"Oh, everybody spices their profiles up a bit."

"How about, loves to laugh?" Piper put in.

"How about, good hygiene?" Edna asked.

"No! I'll keep my hygiene to myself, thank you," Sunny declared.

They worked another twenty minutes, scanned in the picture from the barbeque, and finally settled on a profile title of *SunnyGirl* and a message that read: FUN-LOVING SINGLE WHO LOVES DOGS AND KIDS. ENJOYS READING, MOVIES, WALKING MY GOLDEN RETRIEVER, AND HANGING OUT WITH FRIENDS. LOOKING TO MEET NEW PEOPLE. LET'S CHAT OVER COFFEE OR LUNCH.

"All right, so I winked at someone, now what?" Sunny asked, leaning back in her chair.

"Now you have to wait to see if they wink back with their contact info," Edna explained.

"But that could take hours."

"Right, so let's switch to the over-sixty crowd and find some men for me," Edna said.

"Okay."

Sunny changed the age group to over-sixty and clicked enter.

Up popped several photos, though not as many as were in the thirty to forty age categories.

"How about this guy, Edna? He's five foot seven, one hundred thirty-five pounds, and he'd like to meet a woman who is shorter than he is but shouldn't outweigh him." Maggie laughed.

"This guy sounds like you." Cassie pointed to a picture of a man with gray hair and an impish grin. "It says: HE'S AN ORDINARY GUY WITH A SLIGHTLY LUSTY MIND, LOOKING TO EXPRESS HIS LOVE IN ROMANTIC WAYS."

"He's nothing like me," Edna said. "He said his mind is only *slightly* lusty."

Maggie, Cassie and Sunny cracked up, but Piper wrinkled her nose in disgust.

"This guy says, I'M 5'9", AND I STILL HAVE MOST ALL MY HAIR."

"This one's a rock-n-roller from way back."

"This guy says, I HAVE NO RV, SO IF YOU NEED ONE, DON'T REPLY."

"Now this one has potential," Edna said and pointed to a man with a handlebar moustache who sat astride a large motorcycle. "He says: I'VE MET WOMEN WHO I COULD PROBABLY LIVE WITH, BUT I'M LOOKING FOR ONE I CAN'T LIVE WITHOUT."

"Ahhh, how sweet. Next page." Sunny clicked the arrows leading to the next page.

Their laughter died suddenly as the photos appeared on the next page.

"What the heck?" Sunny stared at the top photo of the profiles and slowly reached out her hand to touch the picture of the almost familiar man.

"Does this look like…?" she asked, incredulously.

"Yeah, it totally looks like…" Maggie said as she leaned closer to the screen.

"It is him," Edna said. "That is definitely our Mr. Mysterious-Hottie-Neighbor."

They stared at the picture that was Jake's face, yet somehow the photo was enhanced to make him look about twenty-five years older. His shaggy blond hair was trimmed closer to his head and shot with layers of gray. His face still looked tan, but had added wrinkles around his eyes and mouth. The picture was full length, and he was dressed not in his standard ratty t-shirt, jeans and flip-flops, but in khaki's, deck shoes, and a polo with an actual cardigan tied around his neck. He looked ready to head out for a round of golf or at least lunch at the club.

"Why is he dressed like that?" Piper asked. "He

looks like a rich old guy."

"I think he's wearing a Rolex." Maggie's nose practically touched the screen.

"*Gentleman61*," Cassie read his profile name. "Listen to this, it says: I AM A KIND, REASONABLY EDUCATED MAN LOOKING FOR COMPANIONSHIP. I ENJOY GOLF, THE THEATRE, AND EUROPEAN TRAVEL. I AM A WIDOWER WITH NO FAMILY NEARBY, SO I AM LOOKING FOR A REFINED WOMAN WHO IS WELL READ AND ENJOYS BEING TREATED LIKE A LADY. CONTACT ME IF YOU ENJOY ELEGANT DINING AND THE FINER THINGS IN LIFE."

"Well, that sure doesn't *sound* like Jake," Piper said.

"Oh, it's him all right," Edna said.

"How can you be so sure?"

"Because when Mr. Liar-Liar-Pants-on-Fire had that picture taken, he was standing in Walter's living room."

"Oh. My. Gosh. You're right," Sunny said slowly. "That's Betty's antique roll top desk he's standing in front of."

"Maybe someone has the same desk," Cassie offered.

"Maybe someone also has the same hand-made cross-stitched wedding invitation framed and hanging on the wall above their desk too," Edna said sarcastically, then pointed to the screen where about a third of a framed picture was visible above the desk.

Sunny couldn't read the lettering, but she could definitely see the design of the rows of colorful flowers that edged the inscription of the invitation. She knew Betty had spent almost a year working on that cross-stitch project so she could have it framed and present it to Walter for their thirtieth wedding anniversary. Sunny had heard the story many times, and the frame had held the same place of honor on the wall above the desk for as long as she had known them.

"Why would Jake do this?" Sunny asked.

"Maybe now that he's killed Walter, he's trying to take over his life," Piper suggested.

"Why would a young, good-looking guy want to take over the life of an old man?" Maggie asked. "That doesn't make sense."

"There's one way to find out." Edna moved the mouse to click on the wink symbol.

"Aaagh! Why did you do that?" Sunny shrieked and

pushed back from the table. She went to the sink and poured herself a glass of water. It was so much easier believing Jake was a good guy. One click of a mouse could bring out the truth, then Sunny's fantasy of she and Jake being together could come crashing down. "Now he'll know I saw it."

"Exactly," Edna said. "Now he'll know we're on to him."

"He'll know Sunny's on to him." Cassie crossed the kitchen to put her arm around Sunny's shoulders. "So we are purposely antagonizing a potentially dangerous man."

"Uh, guys, maybe you should come take a look at this," Piper said from the table. She had turned the laptop toward her and had continued to scroll through the profiles.

The women clustered around Piper. Sunny clutched her water glass until it almost cracked.

Edna gasped as she recognized the photo Piper pointed to. "Why, that's Walter," she cried.

The picture was of Walter from a few years back. It was also taken inside his house, but this picture's background was his kitchen.

Sunny looked at the picture of Walter from a new perspective as she took in his lean frame and the thick, full head of white hair he still had. The picture must have been taken by Betty because he was wearing a wonderful smile. Sunny sadly realized she hadn't seen that smile on him in a long time.

Piper sighed. "Ahhh, his profile name is *Lonely1*. That is so sad. His profile says: MY WIFE DIED SEVERAL YEARS AGO, AND I MISS THE SOUND OF A WOMAN'S LAUGHTER. I AM AN ORDINARY GUY WHO LIKES GARDENING AND TINKERING AROUND IN THE GARAGE. I HAVE GOOD TABLE MANNERS, KNOW HOW TO DANCE THE TANGO AND AM QUITE GOOD AT BRIDGE. I'M RETIRED AND AM LOOKING FOR COMPANIONSHIP FOR PLAYING CARDS OR MAYBE

GOING OUT TO LUNCH."

"I never knew Walter was so lonely," Sunny said softly.

"I never knew he could dance the Tango," Edna muttered.

"Why do Walter and Fake-Jake both have profiles on this online dating site?" asked Maggie.

"This top line says Walter last visited this site five weeks ago. That's about the time he disappeared, isn't it?" Piper asked.

"Yes, it is." Edna said.

"So, we kind of have a little something to tell you guys." Sunny and Cassie filled the others in on their afternoon of amateur sleuthing.

"Oh, for heaven's sake," Edna said. "Who do you think you are? A couple of middle-aged Nancy Drews? Everyone needs to stop following this guy around. Now, we've got private investigators and blood-soaked shirts involved. What if Jake would have seen you?"

"He didn't see us," Sunny shot back.

"And who are you calling middle-aged?" Cassie wanted to know.

"And who's Nancy Drew?" Piper asked.

"What kind of sheltered life have you led? Don't you ever read?" Maggie asked. "Nancy Drew is a teenage detective who solved about a thousand cases and entertained young girls everywhere with her many mysterious capers."

"Oh yeah, I think I saw the movie," Piper said, and this time Edna was the one who looked disgusted.

"You're not really upset that we spied on him. You're just mad because we didn't invite you along," Sunny pointed out to Edna.

Edna shrugged. "Well, why didn't you invite me? I could have been your lookout."

"Ahh, honey," Cassie said and patted Edna's hand. "We were going to, but we knew you had bridge this week, and Zumba class, and we didn't want you to miss them."

"Besides," Sunny added, "most of the time it was totally boring. We sat around for hours, drinking iced tea and playing Words with Friends *with each other*."

"And trying not to think about how much we had to pee," Cassie added.

"Oh, all right," Edna said, mollified. "But now I'm more confused than ever about what happened to Walter."

"So am I, but I've got an idea," Maggie said. She took the mouse from Piper and winked at Walter. "If there's a chance Walter is alive and out there somewhere, maybe he will wink back, and we can figure out where he is."

"You think he'll answer through the World Wide Web of the Dead?" Edna asked. "Maybe he's doing some online dating from the spirit world."

"He *could* still be alive," Piper cried.

"Of course he could. I'm sorry, honey." Edna soothed the young girl who had grown so attached to Walter. "That was tacky of me, and, of course, you're right. He could still be alive."

*Bleep-bleep.*

They froze as the tiny message envelope appeared on the top of the screen.

Sunny gasped. "Oh. My. Gosh. Walter is trying to contact us from the grave."

"He *is* alive," Piper whispered. "I told you so!" She clicked on the little envelope as the whole group held their collective breath.

Then let it out in several relieved sighs and one nervous giggle as the message came up from *Flyfisherman*.

HELLO, SUNNYGIRL, the message read, I APPRECIATE YOUR INTEREST AND WOULD LIKE A CHANCE TO GET TO KNOW YOU BETTER. HOW ABOUT GOING ON A PICNIC IN THE PARK WITH ME THIS WEEKEND? MY NUMBER IS 555-3276. CALL ME IF

THIS IDEA APPEALS TO YOU. I LOOK FORWARD TO HEARING FROM YOU.

"Soooo, not Walter," Maggie said.

"This night has been too crazy," Sunny said.

"It's about to get crazier, because you are going to call this guy." Cassie reached for Sunny's phone.

"What?" Sunny's favorite word popped out again. "Are you kidding? I'm not calling..."

But it was too late. Cassie had already set the phone to speaker and dialed the number listed on the screen. Sunny reached for it, but Cassie blocked her arm as the connection took, and they heard the operator's well-known line, "Please enjoy the music while your party is being reached."

"I've got a peaceful, easy feeling, and I know you won't let me down..." played from the phone, and then the line clicked and was answered with a pleasant, "Hello, this is Phil."

Sunny stared at the phone, her tongue frozen in her mouth. Maggie nudged her, and she stammered out, "Uh, hi. This is, um, *Sunnygirl* from the match thing..."

"Oh, hi. That was fast. I just sent that email."

"Yeah, well, I was, uh, sitting at the computer and saw it come in."

"Cool. I liked your profile. I'm a dog-lover too. And I thought you had a nice smile, so I took a chance."

"Oh. Well, thanks. You have a nice smile too."

Cassie rolled her eyes, and Maggie mimed sticking her finger down her throat in a gagging motion.

"Thanks. So my name is Phil, obviously."

"I'm Sunny."

"I know your profile, but what's your real name?"

"That is my real name."

"Oh." Awkward silence.

Maggie rolled her hand forward in a 'keep-going' motion as Sunny rolled her eyes. *Really? You missed your calling as a professional mime.*

"So, a picnic, huh?" Sunny asked aloud to Phil.

"Er, yeah, I was thinking we could go on a picnic at Prospect Lake. I could pick you up, or we could meet there."

"Okay, sure. I could meet you there. What could I bring?"

"Oh, you don't have to bring anything. I'll take care of the food. I love to cook. I was thinking we could spend some time outdoors getting to know each other."

"That sounds nice, Phil. How about noon on Saturday at Prospect Lake?"

"That would be great. Do you know where the picnic tables are over by the playground on the edge of the lake?"

"Sure."

"Okay, I will be waiting at one of the picnic tables at noon. You'll recognize me, because I will be the guy with the picnic basket." He chuckled.

"Okay. I'll see you then."

"Lookin' forward to it. Bye."

"Bye." Sunny hung up with a sigh and turned to glare at Cassie and Maggie. "Well, I've got another date now. Are you happy?"

"Yeah, I'm happy." Cassie giggled. "How about you, Mags? You happy?"

"As a clam," Maggie said, grinning. "How about you, Edna?"

"Oh sure, I'm happy," Edna said, distractedly, "but what I really want to know is, when did they make Nancy Drew into a movie?"

❀❀❀

"...fifty-one, fifty-two, fifty-three..." The muscles flexed and strained in Jake's bicep as he curled the barbell up to his shoulder again and again. His thoughts turned to Walter and the pain he had caused Jake's mother. He could picture her sitting in her favorite rocker by the window in her bedroom with that far off look in her eye. He could remember the day he came in to her room and found her crying, the tattered photo album in her hand. The pages were yellowed and frayed from so much use, and as Jake approached, his mother snapped the book shut and quickly wiped tears from her face.

"What are ya lookin' at, Mama?" a nine-year old Jake had asked.

"Nothin', baby," she had replied, putting a smile on her face for her son. "Nothin' but the past."

Jake's chest glistened with sweat as he threw himself into his workout trying to forget the painful childhood memories. There was nothing that hurt a son more than seeing his mother cry.

*Bleep-bleep.*

The identifiable chime of the email notice bleeped from the laptop that sat on the kitchen table, startling Jake back in to the present moment.

He set the barbell on the floor and grabbed his water bottle. Tipping the bottle to his lips, he wrapped a towel around his neck and sunk into the chair.

An errant drop of water ran down his chin, falling onto his chest as he pulled the laptop to him. He recognized the familiar symbol for the online match website. He had so many false hits, yet each time a wink came in, his heart leapt a little in hopes it was *her*.

He clicked on the little envelope and waited for the email message to pop up.

"Ho-ly crap!" He sighed as the profile of a familiar curly-haired blonde who: LOVES TO WALK HER GOLDEN RETRIEVER AND HANG OUT WITH FRIENDS materialized before him on the screen.

*That's great. If she saw my profile and recognized it, she's probably come across Walter's profile too. And that means she'd, no doubt, already told her posse of girlfriends about it. What's she doing on an online dating site anyway?*

He clicked on reply and typed in a short message. I THINK IT'S TIME WE HAVE A TALK. HOW WOULD YOU LIKE SOME COMPANY NEXT TIME YOU WALK THAT GOLDEN RETRIEVER OF YOURS?

Then he picked up his phone and hit the number seven speed dial key.

He listened to the ringing of the phone followed by a gruff, "Hello."

"Hey, it's Jake. I think we've got a problem."

The sun came through the kitchen window as Sunny peered through the glass at Walter's house. Little motes of dust floated and danced through the air, catching the light, and her thoughts drifted to Jake.

He seemed so kind and sweet when they were together, but every so often, she caught this distant look in his eye that seemed to suggest that he had seen things. Things she could never comprehend.

Last night's discovery of the Fake-Jake profile had her rattled. Even after eavesdropping on him at the private investigator's office, she still wasn't convinced that he had anything to do with Walter's disappearance. His actions were like a see-saw of good and evil. On the up end was the way he had cared for her and come racing to her rescue after the attempted break-in, but the down end of the see-saw was filled with menacing over-heard phone conversations and too many unanswered questions.

The phone rang, startling her, and Sunny turned from the window and reached for the receiver.

"Hey, Cass," she said, after checking the caller ID. She was letting all *unknown* and *blocked* callers go to the answering machine.

"Hey, girl," Cassie replied, in her ever cheerful voice. "You ready for your date with Phil the Fisherman?"

"I guess I'm as ready as I'll ever be."

"What are you wearing?"

"It's a picnic, so I'm wearing that cute white sundress with the little pink flowers and my pink mule sandals."

"Do they have a heel?"

"Just a little one, about an inch or so."

"Those will be good. They'll make you seem taller and your legs will look longer. I can picture you sitting on a blanket with your skirt swirled around your legs and a wicker picnic basket by your side. Do you think he'll bring like, grapes and cheese and champagne flutes? Oohhh. Do you have like a big floppy straw hat you can wear?"

"Take a breath there, girl." Sunny chuckled at Cassie's enthusiasm.

"Sorry, I'm just excited for you. It sounds so romantic."

"We'll see. You know he could be a total dud. Or a serial killer."

"Don't even joke about that," Cassie said. "And don't worry, Maggie and I will be there as well."

"You what?"

"Heck yeah. You don't think we'd let you go on a blind date with a strange man by yourself."

"I don't know if Phil's planning on a date with three women. What if he doesn't bring enough food?"

"We're not gonna be *on* the date with you, silly. We're just gonna be *in* the park, you know, meandering around, reading magazines or throwing a Frisbee around."

Sunny laughed. "I would love to see Maggie throw a Frisbee."

"You won't really even know we're there, but we'll be around watching if you need us. We'll be like, your backup."

"Well, that will make me less nervous, knowing you and Mags will be lurking in the bushes watching me on my date. I should be really relaxed."

"It will be fine. We'll be there a few minutes early. If you are in trouble or want us to get you out of the date, you need to text us a *safe* word or give us a signal."

"A *safe* word? Did you see that on a Law and Order or something?" Sunny asked. "And you accuse Edna and Piper of watching too much TV."

"Oh, shut up and think of a word."

"Okay. Okay. How about using 'Beau' as my word? I can try to get out of the date by claiming I need to go take care of my dog."

"All right, that's good," Cassie said. "And we'll try to send you a text or do something to get your attention in the middle of the date just to see how things are going."

"Okay. I have to be there in twenty minutes, so I'm getting ready to take off."

"All right, I'm actually pulling up in front of Maggie's house right now. We'll see you over there. Good luck."

Okay, see you over there. And Cass?"

"Yeah."

"Thanks, Friend."

"You're absolutely welcome. Have fun on your date." Cassie clicked off.

Sunny made one last mirror check and dabbed on a little more pink lip gloss. The color was 'A Day in the Park', so she thought it a fitting shade. She squirted a blast of body spray into the air, walked through it, and declared herself ready to go. Feeling pretty good about herself as she walked out the door, Sunny grabbed her big straw hat, plopped it on her head, then pulled the door shut behind her.

❀❀❀

"Hi. You must be Sunny. I'm Phil." Sunny had found the one guy in the park with a picnic basket, and he now enthusiastically reached for her hand and pulled off his sunglasses at the same time.

She reached her hand out to shake his. "That would be me. Nice to meet you, Phil." His hand was warm, and he had a great smile that went all the way to his chocolate brown eyes.

They both paused as they took a moment to appraise the other one. Phil was probably five-nine and fit. His skin had that healthy tan of someone who spent a lot of time outdoors. His hair was light brown with natural streaks of blond highlights shot through it– which he probably got from the sun instead of paying eighty dollars for them at the salon. He looked comfortable in khaki shorts, Teva sandals, and a t-shirt depicting several fishing flies and a caption that read *THE WAY TO A MAN'S HEART IS THROUGH HIS FLY. Nice.*

Sunny watched his appraisal of her as his gaze roamed over her body, starting at her petal pink toenails and moving all the way up to the floppy straw hat perched on her head. Suddenly, she was rethinking the floppy straw hat idea.

"You look nice." His tone sounded a little confused. "You know it's a picnic, right?" He gestured to the blankets on the ground. He had layered a quilt and a bright green sleeping bag on top of each other. The sleeping bag was unzipped and lay flat. It had green flannel on one side and thick piling inside. On one side of the sleeping bag was a picture of a giant package of gum and the words 'Wrigley's Spearmint Gum' written along the side of the package. Sunny figured he'd had it since he was a kid.

To the side of the sleeping bag sat a well-used yellow fabric cooler, the shoulder strap lying limp across its side. One corner of the cooler was covered in dried mud as if it had sat on the edge of a river bank, and Sunny thought she caught a whiff of dead fish coming from it. She wasn't sure how she was going to eat anything that came out of that cooler.

"Oh, I'm fine." Sunny flounced herself and her straw hat over to plop down on one side of the blankets. She folded her knees under her and spread the skirt out, going for a feminine southern belle look. She smiled up at him. "Fun sleeping bag."

That comment got a grin out of him, and he laughed. "I thought I had a different blanket in the car." He gestured to the green Subaru Outback parked nearby. "But these were all I had. I love this bag. I've had it since the fifth grade."

*Told you so.*

"So, what are we having for lunch?" Sunny asked, eyeing the yellow cooler.

He looked confused as he followed her gaze to the cooler, and then laughed. "That's not our lunch. That's my fishing gear."

Sunny laughed as well, doing an inward sigh of relief– until she realized he said fishing gear. She looked around then, and to her horror, saw he was walking to a canoe that rested on the shore of the lake. A life vest and, *oh, please no*, two fishing poles rested against the side of the canoe. Two poles meant that unless someone else was joining them, he expected her to know how to use one of them.

"I thought it would be fun to try to catch our lunch." He grinned like that would be the most fun idea he had ever had.

"Oh," Sunny faltered and looked down at her pink-flowered sundress and kitten-heeled sandals.

"But we don't have to, if you don't want to," he said, his face crestfallen. "I probably should have been more specific about what to wear. Not that you don't look great."

Sunny sighed. He had obviously put some thought in to this date, and he *had* gone to the trouble of actually bringing a canoe with him. Sunny tried to picture a romantic setting with the canoe gliding through the water, Phil in one end with his muscled arms pulling the oars forward, and she sitting daintily in the other end twirling a lacy parasol to keep the sun off her fair skin. Okay, so she didn't have a lacy parasol or even fair skin, for that matter. But she had committed to this date, and she hadn't actually ever been in a canoe before, and the dress was machine-washable, so what the heck?

"No, I'll be fine." Sunny put a smile on her face and stood up. "This looks really fun."

Phil's smile returned, and he loaded the canoe with the life vest, the fishing cooler, (*thank goodness that wasn't our lunch*), and *both* of the fishing poles. At the thought of lunch, Sunny's stomach rumbled a little, and she realized she was quite hungry. She had had an early breakfast of cereal and meant to grab a mid-morning snack, but in her nervousness over the blind date, she hadn't really felt like eating, until now.

"You ready?" he asked and held out his hand to help her into the boat.

Sunny walked gingerly across the grass to him, her heels sinking into the soft soil. She took his hand and stepped over the side. Her shoe hit a slick patch of mud, and suddenly her foot slipped forward and one arm pin-wheeled as she tried to gain her balance.

"Whoa." Phil grasped his hand tighter and wrapped his other arm around her waist. His quick move saved Sunny from busting her tail bone on the edge of the canoe, but it effectively landed his hand in her armpit while his arm crushed her breast.

"You all right?" He pulled her back upright while doing more boob-crushing with his arm.

"Yes, thanks," Sunny said, regaining her balance and pulling her leg back out of the boat. Her foot came out but the cute pink sandal stayed stuck in the mud on the bottom of the canoe. Sunny might be up for these dating ideas, but she wasn't sure any more of her shoes could handle them.

Phil made sure she was steady before he reached into the boat and plucked Sunny's shoe from the muddy spot. He wiped the shoe on his shorts then held it up for my inspection. "This might not be the best shoe choice for boating. You need some real sandals, not these...what do you call these anyway?"

"They're called mules because you slide your foot into them and they have no back." Sunny straightened her skirt and pulled her left foot free from the other shoe.

"I would think they're called 'mules' because you'd have to be an 'ass' to pay full price for half a shoe," he said, cracking himself up.

Sunny just stared at him.

"C'mon, that was hilarious," he said. "I just made that up right there." He reached for her other shoe and tossed them both back onto the green sleeping bag, still chuckling at his own joke. "Will you be okay barefoot in the boat?"

"Yeah. I'll be fine." Sunny reached for his hand and again stepped into the boat. This time, her bare foot touched the cool bottom of the boat, and the muddy silt squished up between her toes. She kept her balance climbing in and plunked down on the bench seat.

"Here, you should put this on." He handed her the life vest. "All passengers are required to wear one."

"Where's yours?" Sunny slipped the vest over her head and clicked the belt shut, successfully squashing the last idiom of a romantic boat ride.

"I'm a great swimmer." He pushed the canoe away from the bank before he deftly climbed in. Sunny grabbed the sides as the canoe pitched and rocked, but Phil sat down and with experienced ease, paddled toward the middle of the lake.

"Oh, look how pretty she looks," Cassie said.

"She looks great, but why is she wearing that stupid gardening hat?" Maggie asked.

The two women were firmly ensconced behind a large stand of lilac bushes. Between the branches, they had a great view of the picnic site and were fairly well hidden. They had arrived in time to see Sunny pull up and cross the grass to meet Phil.

"He's not so bad," Cassie said. "I like his smile, and he seems pretty relaxed. He said he was laid back."

"Oh, my gosh." Maggie laughed. "He wants to take her in that canoe. She's going to have a fit."

They watched as Phil reached for Sunny's hand, and her crazy slide into the canoe.

"Oh, no! She almost fell," Cassie cried.

"Oh, crap! Wait. He caught her. Good job. Score one for Phil," Maggie said, as she watched Sunny try to regain her balance. "Ahhh. Take off two points. He totally copped a boob- feel."

"What? He did not. He was helping her."

"He was helping himself...to a handful of Sunny's goods."

"No, Sunny, don't put on that hideous life vest." Cassie groaned as she watched Sunny pull the vest over her head.

"Oh, man, she looks like an orange Stay-Puff marshmallow man," Maggie said. "We should have brought a camera instead of this stupid Frisbee."

❀❀❀

"Isn't this great?" Phil asked. "Sunshine, a cool breeze, a pretty girl..." He winked at Sunny. "And goin' fishin'. What could make a day better?"

*Some food. I'm starving.*

Phil pulled the cooler to him, unzipped the top and pulled out a round Styrofoam container.

*Oh, thank goodness, he brought some takeout.* But he pulled the lid back, and to her horror, the container was full of dark soil and wriggling earthworms. She thought she might gag. *Maybe I wasn't as hungry as I thought.*

"Prime night crawlers." Phil pulled a worm from the soil. The worm tried fervently to inch back into the dirt. Phil pulled the worm's body harder only to have it break in half. The first half disappeared into the dark soil, and the other half continued to wiggle, pinched between Phil's thumb and forefinger.

Sunny looked at the half of a worm in disgust. "I thought you used flies."

"Flies are for stream or river fishing," he explained. "Worms are for pond fishin'."

She watched as he settled the pole between his knees, pulled the line free, and threaded the worm onto the hook.

Blood, dirt, and shiny worm-skin goo mingled on the tips of Phil's fingers. *Please don't make me touch that.*

He skillfully tossed the hook into the water and passed her the fishing pole.

"Now, I put a bobber on yours," he explained and pointed to the little floating red and white ball that bounced along the top of the water. "You watch that bobber. When it goes under the water, you've got a fish." He reached down to claim his pole as Sunny watched the little red ball bob under the water.

"It just went under," she said.

"What?" Phil's head popped up. "Are you sure?"

He watched as the bobber disappeared under the water, and the line of her pole started to unreel.

"Set the line!" he cried. "Reel it in!"

She stared at him blankly as she didn't know what either of those instructions meant.

"Start winding that little black crank thing." He pointed to the reel in her hands. "Wind it around toward you."

Okay. She understood 'little black crank thing', and she grasped the little handle and cranked it around.

The more she cranked, the harder it became as the line grew taut, and the fish pulled away from her. The pole bent forward with the strain of the fish's weight.

"Keep cranking!" he hollered. "You've got a big one!" He stood up in the canoe and reached for the pole. The boat tipped and wobbled, but he planted his feet on either side of the boat and steadied the small craft.

Sunny was happy to pass him the pole and she gripped the sides of the canoe. He rocked forward and back, teasing the line, as he tried to reel in the huge fish.

Suddenly, he pulled back, whipped the pole around, and an enormous fish flew out of the water, sailed across the boat and landed...smack dab in the middle of Sunny's lap!

"Aaahh!" she shrieked and jumped up, trying to get away from the giant flopping flounder. In her haste to get away from Flipper, she must have teetered when she should have tottered, because without warning, the canoe rolled sideways and tipped her, Phil, and the massive mackerel right into the lake.

Sunny went under, but the life vest popped her back to the surface where she splashed and sputtered. Through her splashing, she saw Phil swim to the canoe and work to get it right side up again. He hauled himself into the boat and dog-paddled the canoe toward her, then she felt his strong hands grasp the front of the vest and haul her back into the righted boat.

"You okay?" asked a worried Phil as lake water dripped from his clothes and puddled into the bottom of the canoe.

Sunny pushed her dripping bangs out of her eyes and nodded. She took a deep breath and clutched her arms around the fat sodden life vest. She peered over the side of the canoe where Phil's fishing cooler, pole, and her romantic floppy straw hat floated side by side in the water. Phil had already collected his pole and the oars, and he used one now to lift his fishing cooler and pull it back into the boat. He paddled closer and reached for the fishing pole, which suddenly jerked out from under his hand and started to glide across the water.

"Son of a gun!" Phil grabbed an oar and pulled it through the water. "That sucker's still on the line." He paddled by Sunny's hat, reached down, grabbed it and tossed it into the canoe without missing a beat, as he chased after the fishing pole that now *zig-zagged* across the water.

❀❀❀

"Oh. My. Gosh. He handed her a fishing pole," Cassie said from their lilac bush hideout.

"Does she even know what to do with it? Has she *ever* been fishing before?" Maggie asked.

They had set up their soccer chairs behind the lilac bush for a full scale stakeout. Cassie had brought them each a cold can of iced tea that they sipped as they watched Sunny's date unfold.

"Aaaaa! I think she has a fish." Maggie stood up from her chair to get a closer look.

"She does. She's reeling it in," Cassie said. "No, Phil the Fisherman took the pole from her. He must not trust her to pull it in. Geez, he's really working that line, it must be a big fish. Wow, there it is." She watched the fish fly through the air, then gasped as it landed in Sunny's lap.

Cassie leapt from her chair, knocking over her can of tea as they watched the boat capsize, then Sunny's head pop back up over the water. "Oh, no! Where is she? Wait, there she is, she's okay."

She gripped Maggie's arm as they watched Phil pull Sunny back into the boat.

"Poor girl." Cassie felt Maggie's arm tremble in her hand. "She's okay, Mags," she said and turned to her friend to console her worry. But Maggie wasn't trembling from concern. Instead her arm shook from glee as Maggie doubled over in hysterical laughter.

"Why are you laughing?" Cassie asked in a shocked voice. "She could have been hurt."

"Did you see that fish…landed in her lap…she fell out of the boat." Maggie gasped between gales of laughter. She crossed her legs and bent double to keep from peeing herself. "Look at her hair."

"Yeehaw," Phil cried, as if he were a cowboy chasing a steer instead of a guy, in a cleverly worded t-shirt, chasing down a fish still hooked to a pole his blind date had dropped in a lake. With Phil paddling his little heart out, they chased the fishing pole to the middle of the lake where it came to rest. It had stopped several times, and Phil almost had a hand on it, but each time the fish took off again. They watched the pole criss-cross the water as if the fish knew they chased it. The pole sat immobile for several minutes as Phil paddled to it. He carefully reached into the water so as not to startle it and grabbed the pole.

"Got it!" He lifted the pole in triumph. He grabbed for the little crank handle thing and again tried to reel the fish in. The line was tangled and knotted as it came out of the water, and Sunny cringed backwards as she tried to brace herself for another lapful of mackerel.

Phil strained against the line and braced his knee against the side of the boat. "C'mon, you dirty bastard," he coaxed. Suddenly, the line snapped, and Phil fell backwards into the boat. He looked a little stunned as he landed in the bottom of the canoe, then he looked up at Sunny and burst into laughter.

"That was awe-some!" He pushed up from the bottom of the canoe and settled back onto the bench seat.

"I think I'm ab-bout done f-fishing." Sunny's teeth chattered from the cold, wet clothes she wore. The sun was warm, but not enough to dry her out under the wet life vest.

"Oh, sorry." He picked up the oar and paddled them back to shore. "I'm about ready to eat lunch anyway."

Her mouth watered at the thought of lunch, and Sunny hoped for thick sandwiches, some crunchy salty chips and a soda or even iced tea.

The boat slid up to the bank with a thud as it hit the shallow bottom, and Phil jumped out to pull the canoe further up the bank.

He took her hand and helped Sunny over the side of the boat. The bank side was rough against her feet which were pruny from sitting in the watery boat bottom.

She made it to the blanket, and Phil helped her off with the life vest. He pulled it over her head, looked down, and looked away as a blush crept up his neck.

Sunny looked down and gasped, then quickly plopped down on the blankets and wrapped the green sleeping bag around her body. Evidently getting her white sundress, white bra and white panties wet left little to Phil's imagination as to what her body looked like. The cold, wet fabric had her headlights standing erect, and she resisted the urge to rub her chest to get them to go back down.

Phil busied himself with going to the car and retrieving a picnic basket.

*At least he has the good sense to give me a minute of privacy to pull myself together. And he did blush and look away.* Although, she was sure he got quite an eyeful first.

He came back to the blanket, but continued to look off into the park, apparently not quite ready to look directly at her.

"Those gals sure are having fun playing Frisbee."

Phil nodded to two women playing nearby.

Sunny looked over his shoulder to see two familiar women. One held a Frisbee and looked concerned, and the other intermittently clutched her chest and doubled over with laughter. Doing a double take, she realized 'those gals' were Maggie and Cassie. Cassie had said they would be around, but Sunny didn't realize they would be watching her the whole time. She sent a glare at her two best friends, then changed her expression back to a smile when Phil turned back to face her.

"They're probably drunk," she said sweetly. "What's for lunch?"

He placed the wicker picnic basket on the blanket between them. It was lined with a red and white checked cloth, and the price tag still hung from a little plastic ring around the handle of the basket. *Nineteen ninety-nine. Not bad.*

Phil opened the basket and pulled forth two Mason Jars full of a thick green sludge. He handed one to Sunny. "You should definitely start with this. It's a Spirolina shake. I made it myself. It's green algae powder mixed with soy milk and organic bananas. It will give you energy."

She unscrewed the lid of the jar, held it to her nose, and took a discreet sniff. It smelled kind of like seaweed and bananas. Phil watched her with an eager look on his face, as he waited for her to test his home-made concoction. She put the jar to her lips and took a sip. Sunny tried to keep her face neutral as the thick, gritty liquid filled her mouth. *Swallow it. Don't gag. You can do it.* She gulped down the mixture that tasted like banana-flavored grass and put on her best smile for Phil. "It tastes…fine."

His face beamed. "I knew you would love it." He twisted his mouth from side to side and handed her a napkin. "You've got a little something there on your lip."

"Oh, thanks," she said, embarrassed. Sunny took the napkin and wiped the gooey green mustache from her top lip.

Phil pulled more food from the basket, and she watched in dismay as he set small Rubbermaid containers of unknown substances on the blanket between them. *Where was the fried chicken and potato salad? Where are the sandwiches and chips? What kind of picnic was this?*

He pulled the lid back from one container to reveal a super creamy yellow mixture, then handed her a little Ziploc of baby carrots. *Okay, I can do carrots.*

"This is my own recipe for hummus. It's sort of like a bean dip, but made with garbanzo beans. You're going to love it."

She'd had garbanzo beans in salads before and knew they were kind of a bland little mushy bean, so she grabbed a carrot, dipped it in the hummus and took a bite. Her mouth exploded with flavor as the oily dip hit her tongue.

"I put a lot of garlic in my hummus," Phil said. "It's so awesome for cardiovascular, and it has antibiotic properties that cross the blood-brain barrier. Some of my friends think I use too much garlic. What do you think?"

Sunny swallowed the garlicky bite, then crunched more carrot around in her mouth to balance out the flavor. *A lot of garlic was an understatement. I would be safe from vampires for weeks off that one bite.*

"You can definitely taste the garlic," she said, noncommittally.

"On the off chance we didn't catch any fish, I brought along some sandwich fixin's," he said.

*Thank goodness. Finally, a sandwich.*

He pulled the lid off another container to reveal six slices of a thick, dense, dark brown bread. Then he pulled a small can from the basket, popped the top, and used the small ring to pull the lid back to reveal what looked roughly like a can of tuna. Okay, so it wasn't turkey or roast beef, but she could handle tuna.

"This is awesome. It's raw sprouted-grain bread, and it's not actually baked, but made in a dehydrator. And this," he said, and gestured proudly to the little can, "is Tofuna. It's tuna made from tofu. Isn't that great?"

*What? Are you kidding me?* Sunny watched as he spooned the oily 'not-really-tuna' meat onto a slice of bread and passed it to her. It looked like a spoonful of cat food on an old piece of rye bread.

Again, she prayed not to gag as she took a bite from the corner of the bread. The bread sucked all the moisture from her mouth as Sunny tried to chew the thick, dense ball of fish-flavored particle board. She kept trying to chew it, but she was losing the battle.

Phil watched her expectantly, and Sunny tried to smile while she chewed. Her mind said swallow but her throat said, "No. Gates closed. That is *not* coming through here."

Suddenly inspired, Sunny pointed to where the girls played Frisbee in an effort to distract Phil.

He followed her finger, turned toward the park and…

"Ah-choo!" Sunny fake-sneezed the hideous bite into a napkin.

"Bless you." He turned back to her.

"Sorry, it must be these wet clothes." In reality, the sun now beat warmly down on her bare shoulders, and it was quite stifling wrapped in the thick sleeping bag.

"What else did you bring?" Sunny asked lightly, but what she really meant was, *Please, let there be some regular food coming next out of that basket.*

"Last, but not least," he said, and with a flourish, pulled out another Ziploc bag, "chocolate chip cookies."

*Praise the Lord! Saved by the cookies.*

"Wait till you try these. They're delicious. They're made with carob chips so they have less sugar, and are much healthier than your standard chocolate chips."

*Hold the phone. Was he telling me he desecrated all that is holy in the cookie world by using sub-standard chips in these cookies? Why would you put 'healthy' and 'chocolate' in the same sentence?*

At this point, Sunny was starving, and it was either eat a cookie or go back in for another bite of cat food and welcome mat-flavored Tofuna sandwich. *I'll take the damn cookie.*

Soo, it wasn't as bad as she thought. The cookie portion still tasted like cookie, but the chips tasted like really old, vaguely flavored dark chocolate.

"Not bad," Sunny said.

Phil thoroughly enjoyed the picnic food as he filled his mouth and talked around the bites. "I know this great place to go backpacking. You pack in and spend like four days hiking and camping in the forest. Do you like camping?"

"Not really," she answered.

"Oh." Awkward silence. "Well, how about hiking?"

"Not really, sorry."

"Oh."

"I like to watch movies. And I love Survivor. So I like to watch other people camping on TV," Sunny offered.

"I actually don't own a TV anymore," he said. "All it ever has on it is unrealistic drivel and every show seems to have its own political agenda. It sucked at my brain cells and filled my time with meaningless babble."

*Wow. Okay. I'm not sure what political agenda an episode of Friends would have, but he's entitled to his opinion.*

"Watch out!"

The words registered in her head, and Sunny recognized Cassie's voice, but not fast enough to take action before a Frisbee sailed through the air and knocked her right on the forehead. Her head jerked back, and she tipped backwards. Sunny tried flailing her arms to catch herself before she fell, but she was tangled in the thick sleeping bag.

"Are you okay?" Cassie asked, as she ran up to their picnic site. "Sorry, our Frisbee got away from us."

"Wow. That's going to leave a mark," Maggie said as she ambled up to the blanket.

Sunny glared up at her, still trying to untangle herself from the heavy bag.

"Oh, you need to cover that up there," Cassie said, and stepped between Phil and Sunny. Reaching down to give Sunny a hand, Cassie simultaneously tried to rearrange the blanket that had flipped back when Sunny fell. Evidently, Sunny's underwear were having self-esteem issues, because they sure kept trying to attract a lot of attention to themselves today.

Sunny reached back to push herself up and felt a thick gooey substance squish up through her outstretched fingers.

"Oooo. What is that?" Cassie asked, a horrified look on her face.

"Oh, no," Phil said. "You must have knocked over your Spirolina Shake. Shoot, I didn't bring any extra."

Sunny looked at the green goo covering her fingers and dripping onto her dress. *Oh, shoot. That's a bummer. Although I would rather wear the foul drink than actually ingest it.*

Cassie pulled her back into an upright position, and Sunny wiped her hand on a patch of unsoiled grass.

"Are you all right, ma'am?" Cassie asked, innocently.

*Ma'am? Are you kidding me? She was older than me by six months. I'd give her 'ma'am'.*

"Yes, I'm fine." Sunny harrumphed. "Thank you, *ma'am*."

Maggie smirked. "Sorry about the Frisbee. We just wanted to make sure you were all right."

"I'm fine, thanks." Sunny rubbed at the sore spot on

her forehead where she had been hit.

Maggie picked up the Frisbee, and the two women walked sheepishly away.

"They didn't seem drunk," Phil said.

Sunny almost laughed, but instead, with a sigh, told Phil, "I should probably head on home."

"Okay." He put the remains of the picnic back into the basket. "Do you want me to call you again?"

"I don't think so," she said, softly. "I think you're a really nice guy," at this, his face fell, "and really cute." His charming grin came back with that comment. "But I just don't think we have very much in common. You are obviously an accomplished fisherman," Sunny said, stroking his ego a little more, "and I would be good if I never see bloody worm guts again. You like to camp and hike, and I like hotels and television. You like to eat this awesome health food, and I love to eat pork chops and hot dogs and pizza and Cheetos... and I like my steak rare with the blood pooling on the plate." His face had steadily fallen beginning with the word *hotdog*, but he positively blanched when she got to the bloody steak on the plate.

"I see what you mean," he said. "But today was fun."

*For you!* Her day had been anything but fun. She saw it as full of humiliation and awkwardness. But she had to kind of like this guy, with his healthy food and his positive spirit.

Sunny laughed. "Yes, today was definitely fun." She stood and duck-walked toward her car, the bulky sleeping bag still wrapped around her see-through clothing. He carried her sodden straw hat and pink sandals as he followed her to the car where she found a big, hooded sweatshirt. She pulled it on while he turned his back. The sweatshirt was still hot, but wasn't that stifling sleeping bag, and it covered up her girls and the outline of her underwear now creeping up her left cheek.

Phil turned back and gave Sunny a hug and a

sweet, quick kiss on the lips. His lips were smooth, and he tasted faintly of garlic and chocolate.

"Drive safe." He pushed the door closed as Sunny started the engine and rolled down the window.

"Thanks again for today," she told him. "It was an unforgettable date." They both laughed. "And thanks for the picnic lunch. It was very...thoughtful."

He waved as Sunny drove out of the parking lot. She could see Cassie and Maggie jog to Cass's minivan, and then she caught a glimpse of herself in the rearview mirror. *Oh. My. Gosh.*

Sunny's hair had dried around her face in fly-away frizzy curls, and her mascara pooled in black smudges under her eyes. A two inch red mark ran along her forehead where the Frisbee had hit her. *Groan. Too bad I didn't have something stuck between my teeth or a boogie in my nose to round out the picture of the perfect woman.*

She could only laugh as she pulled out onto the main thoroughfare and headed for the nearest Sonic. Sunny's mouth watered at the thought of greasy, hot tater tots and a hamburger covered in cheese and ketchup, followed with an icy Diet Coke.

Phil the Fisherman had the dream of catching the perfect fish, but unfortunately this time, she was the "big one that got away"!

Sunny licked the last remnants of salt and tater tot grease from her fingertips and sighed with pleasure as she pulled into her driveway. Cassie's van pulled in behind her, and she was sure the girl's Styrofoam cups contained their customary cherry lime-ades. Sunny didn't see the big appeal, but those two had been ordering them since they were teenagers.

As she climbed from the car, Sunny heard a screen door slam and looked back to see Jake striding toward her.

"How was the date? I was..." He stopped midsentence as he took in her bedraggled appearance. "You okay?" He tried to contain the grin that was valiantly working to pop out across his face.

Maggie held her hand up to Jake in the halt position. She had spent two weeks filling in for the school crossing guard, so she had the position down pat. Sunny just thought she liked the power.

"Not a good time right now," Maggie said to Jake, her hand still in midair.

Jake put his hands in the air and slowly backed away. "I get the message." He smirked and headed back into Walter's house.

"Thanks, Mags." Sunny threw her arm around her friend's shoulder. "I think I've had enough drama for one day."

The three women walked into the house, and Beau

went into a sniffing frenzy around Sunny as he took in the scents of pond water and Tofuna.

"Why don't you go hop in the shower," Maggie said, in a moment of compassion.

"Good idea." Sunny trudged up the stairs, leaving her floppy hat lying limply on the coffee table.

---

Half an hour later, Sunny walked down the steps to the tantalizing scent of pepperoni pizza. She had spent twenty minutes just standing in the shower, the warm spray of water pulsating down her back.

She had washed the last vestiges of mascara from her eyes, moisturized, and put on her soft cotton Capri pajama bottoms with the matching Tinkerbell t-shirt. Her hair was still wet, but it was clean and combed back from her face. Sunny had used the most scented shampoo she owned to erase the last scents of the lake water from her hair, and it now curled gently as it lay damp across her shoulders.

"Wow, you look a lot better," Maggie said, as Sunny walked into the living room.

"Your candor constantly surprises me." Sunny razzed her as she plopped down into the empty corner of the sofa. A pizza box, a bottle of wine, and three paper plates sat lined up on the coffee table.

Cassie came in from the kitchen carrying three wineglasses and a corkscrew. "Maggie and I ordered pizza, and we put in your favorite Owen Wilson movie."

*I just can't get enough of that guy's curly, mussed blond hair and that crooked broken nose. I could eat the guy for breakfast and still be hungry for him at lunch.*

"Thanks, you guys are awesome. But I gotta tell you," Sunny said, as she took a glass of wine from Cassie and a slice of pizza from the box, "you suck at

Frisbee."

❀❀❀

*Why can't that be me that she's wrapping her arms around?* He watched Sunny embrace Maggie and Cassie at the door.

He had seen them pull up earlier and silently cheered Maggie as she kept that creep neighbor away from Sunny.

Night had fallen as he sat in his car and watched Sunny's house. He had originally parked three doors down on the south side of the street, but now sat only two houses away on the opposite side. He had tried to stay in his original spot, but a thermos full of coffee had eventually sent him to the nearest gas station for a much needed break.

Upon returning, he parked behind a white plumbing van on the street in front of the house next door to Sunny's, which gave him the perfect vantage point to watch her front door while it partially concealed his black car from view.

The light shone through the front windows, and he could see the women talking and drinking wine. The sound of their laughter floated to him through the open front windows. He closed his eyes and let the sound surround him, and he imagined Sunny's laughter as a caress against his skin.

His jeans became more uncomfortable as he imagined her caresses moving along his body and her whispered yearnings in his ear.

The front door slammed, and he opened his eyes to see the three women on the porch as they hugged each other goodbye. He didn't know how long he had sat there dreaming of the time he would finally be alone with her. He watched her friends head to their car as Sunny stood on her front porch in her pajamas waving goodnight, her stupid yellow mutt running back and forth between the women.

It was the same stupid mutt that ruined his chances with Sunny before. He needed to see her, to talk to her, to explain his feelings. Once she saw how much he cared for her, he knew they would be able to get past this misunderstanding and be together. He had to think of a way to get rid of that dog…

❀❀❀

"Thanks again, you guys," Sunny called, as Maggie and Cassie headed toward the minivan. "Tonight was fun. I'll call you. Maybe we can get together again tomorrow. See a movie or something."

"I can't." Cassie simultaneously rubbed Beau's head and clicked the key fob to unlock the van. "Tomorrow is family day. After church, we're watching Matt play football in his Old Man's League, then going for a hike to try to earn Tyler's nature badge for Boy Scouts. I've also got to make four dozen cupcakes for Tiffany's field hockey team. She's got her end of the season party on Monday."

"Oh that sounds fun." A twinge of jealousy nudged at Sunny's heart. She wanted that family life that Cassie had with the husband, the kids, the cooking, and all the activities to fill her time. *Well, maybe not the cooking and maybe not* all *the activities. Didn't we just learn a valuable lesson today about me mixing it up too much with the outdoors?*

"How about you, Maggie? Are you free tomorrow, or are you hiking or making several dozen cupcakes?" Sunny asked.

"As if." Maggie huffed as she opened the passenger door, stuck one foot in, then leaned through the vee between the car and the open door. "I couldn't make a cupcake if my life or even a date with Owen Wilson depended on it. Wait, for Owen, I would probably at least try."

Sunny laughed. "For Owen, I would put on an apron and be right there with you, whipping up the frosting."

"Anyway, I'm on my own this weekend. My boys are both at a three-day soccer camp. They left this morning."

"Oh good, maybe we can do something tomorrow night then. Unless you have a hot date," Sunny teased.

"Who? Me?" Maggie stuttered and her purse fell from her hands and hit the pavement. Sunny could swear she blushed as Maggie ducked behind the door to collect her fallen bag. Maybe not. She seemed her normal composed self as she popped back up and scoffed, "Are you kidding? You know BOB's my only date these days." Maggie loved to tease them about her dates with BOB, her Battery-Operated Boyfriend.

"Maggie, stop that." Sunny laughed. "TMI- too much information."

"Hey, you asked." She shrugged, a devilish smirk on her face.

"Well, if you and BOB aren't too busy, maybe we could catch a movie or something," Sunny suggested.

"Well, I'll have to call you." Maggie looked down as if something in her purse caught her attention. "I've got a lot of work to do this weekend. Big case I'm working on, you know. I'll have to let you know." She smiled and climbed into the car as she pulled the door shut behind her. Through the front windshield, Sunny could see her root around in her purse, then pull her Blackberry free. Sunny watched a funny smile play across her friend's face as Maggie absently waved goodbye.

"I'll try to call you tomorrow," Cassie called through the open window of the van as she backed from the driveway into the street. She dropped the car into gear, gave the horn a little toot, then headed off down the street.

Sunny shook her head and called to Beau to come inside. She didn't know what was so exciting about the mailbox that made it the Holy Grail of Dog Scents, but Beau couldn't go outside without making a beeline for the mailman-scented pole. His eyes looked up at her from where his nose was submerged in a fragrant patch of grass. He took one last sniff, circled the mailbox, lifted his leg to leave a yellow trail of urine running down the pole, then loped toward her, his tongue panting in happy anticipation of the treat he would receive for doing such a great job of peeing.

Suddenly, Beau turned his head and let out a low growl. Surprised, Sunny looked up and down the street but nothing seemed out of place. She took in the Harrison kids playing basketball across the street and the neighbor's white plumbing van parked in its usual spot next door. Everything seemed normal.

Sunny rubbed Beau's head and gave him a soft "Good dog", and he seemed to settle down. Then they headed back into the house and closed and locked the door behind them.

Turning off the warm water, Sunny placed the third wine glass in the strainer and put the bowls from their subsequent dishes of chocolate chip cookie dough ice cream into the dishwasher.

She dried her hands on the dishtowel and squirted a pump of lotion from the dispenser next to the sink into her hand. As she reached to turn the kitchen light off, Sunny noticed the little letter symbol in the corner of her kitchen laptop that notified her 'You've Got Mail'. She rubbed her hands up the sides of her arms to soak up the excess lotion, then moved the mouse to the Inbox.

Sunny clicked the mouse, fully expecting to see another forward from her mom. How many 'THIS ONE REALLY WORKS' and 'YOU'VE GOT TO TRY THIS ONE' make-a-wish forwards could one woman send? Did she really believe if Sunny scrolled down and wished hard enough that a potential husband would pop into her kitchen?

*O-kay. Maybe one of those wishes may have worked.* Sunny must have held her breath just right, stood on one leg, and tugged her earlobe when she wished the last time (*Okay, sometimes I make the wish. What can it hurt, right?*) because the email sitting in her Inbox was from Jake.

It was titled, WE NEED TO TALK, and Sunny got a little chill from the anticipation of him wanting to see her... and from the fear of him wanting to see her because she and her friends had found out about his weird little online dating hoax.

She double-clicked the message and gave a little start as his email began, DEAR SUNNYGIRL. That meant he knew he had been caught on the online dating site. With apprehension, Sunny continued to read, I ALSO ENJOY MOVIES, READING, AND LOVE DOGS. I WOULD LIKE TO ACCOMPANY YOU NEXT TIME YOU TAKE YOURS FOR A WALK. CALL ME. JAKE.

Hmmm. Not 'do you *want* to go on a walk with me?' or '*would* you like to have a talk?' but more of a direct order of we *are* walking and we *are* talking. Sunny wondered if he was trying to be funny or cute, or was this an actual threat?

The phone rang, and Sunny absently answered as she tried to decipher the meaning of Jake's message. "Hello."

Sunny snapped to attention as her hello was answered with nothing but the sound of a deep inhale and exhale of breath on the line.

"Hello," she said again.

More deep breathing. How could the innocent sound of a life-sustaining, involuntary movement cause such a deep fear to rise from the pit of her stomach? The fear was a hard lump in the back of her throat, and she struggled to swallow. Her mouth had gone dry, and the hair stuck up from the goose bumps that pimpled her arms.

She sucked in a deep breath and slowly said, "Quit calling me. I have already notified the police." Sunny clicked the off button as she berated herself for not checking the caller ID before she answered the phone.

*Rinngg.*

Sunny jumped and almost dropped the phone as it rang again in her hand. Her heart pounded furiously, and this time she waited for the second ring to see who was calling.

The phone completed its second ring, and Walter's number appeared in the display. *Is that who had just called me? Was Jake behind these calls?*

She wished she would have waited for the caller ID on that last call. If it had shown unknown, she wouldn't have answered, but at least she would have known if the call was coming from her neighbor's house.

The phone rang a third time. *This is stupid, and Jake is definitely not stupid. He's the one who told me to watch the caller ID in the first place.* Sunny clicked the phone on and softly said, "Hello."

"Hey Sunny, it's Jake. I saw your kitchen light on and hoped you were still up."

"Yeah, I'm up. I just got your email."

"Oh, you did?"

Sunny couldn't see his face, but it sounded like he was smirking.

"That's good," he said. "So, you're expecting me to accompany you and Beau on a walk tomorrow. Because I think we have some stuff we need to talk about."

*Stuff? What kind of stuff? Like 'I want to kiss you again' stuff or like 'you may have seen me on last night's episode of America's Most Wanted' stuff?*

"Okay," she said. Letting her curiosity get the best of her, she asked, "Um, Jake?"

"Yeah?"

"Did you just call me a minute ago?"

"No, I just got back from a run and saw your light on." His voice hardened as it changed from the light-hearted banter a moment before. "Why? Did you get another weird call? Do you want me to come over?"

Sunny's heart leapt at the thought of him coming over to protect her. She thought about the way he would charge through the door and take her in his strong arms. She imagined his warm lips as they kissed hers, then trailed down her neck, alternately kissing and nibbling and sucking... as his hands moved up under her shirt along her ribs, and his mouth moved down toward the exposed flesh of her...

"Sunny? You still there?"

"Huh? What?" Jake's voice startled her out of her reverie. Sunny's mouth had gone dry again, and the kitchen suddenly seemed very warm.

"I said, do you want me to come over there?"

"Um, no," Sunny stammered and tried to collect herself. "I'm fine."

"You sure?"

"Yeah, I'm fine," she assured him, though after kissing him, she was not sure she would ever really be fine again.

"Well, you know the number over here. Will you call me if you need me?"

*I need you right now.* She wished she had the courage to tell him what she was really thinking. *I need you to be my hero. I need you to not have hurt Walter. I need you half-naked, in my bed, and wielding a pirate sword.* "Yes, I will," she said.

"Okay. I'll call you tomorrow, and we'll take that walk."

"Okay."

"Goodnight, Sunny. Lock all the doors and be careful tonight."

"I will, thanks. Goodnight." Sunny hung up the

phone and sighed. How could she want so strongly to add excitement to her life, and yet be so afraid to reach out and grab it when she has the chance?

She spent the day at a park trying to make a connection with some guy she didn't even know, yet she wasn't brave enough to tell the one she did know how she felt. But *did* she really know Jake? That was the real problem.

Sunny checked the lock on the back door and called to Beau. She hit the light switch and headed for the stairs, ready to face another night, with only a shedding, slobbering dog and an unfulfilled pirate fantasy to keep her company.

*Thud.*

Sunny's eyes popped open as she started awake at the unfamiliar noise. Heart racing, she checked the alarm clock. The digital readout shined eleven-forty-eight pm through the dark room.

She wasn't sure what woke her, but her mind registered the fear her body recognized. Something was wrong. Sunny pushed up to her elbows as she scanned the dark room. Her eyes adjusted to the darkness as they took in the familiar shapes of dresser, chair covered in laundry waiting to be put away, lamp...oh God. A huge, dark figure of a man stood silently against the wall of her bedroom. Had her body responded to the sound of his breath as he silently watched her sleep?

Sunny backpedaled into a sitting position and pushed as far into the headboard as she could. Her mouth opened, but she couldn't seem to produce a scream as the dark shape in the corner of the room moved slowly toward her.

A deep resonant voice spoke from the shadow. "Hi, Sunny."

Her body tensed, and Sunny could smell the pungent odor of her own body as fear seeped through her pores and sweat drenched her t-shirt. She squinted in the darkness and tried to see the face that went with the voice.

"I'm not here to hurt you." He moved closer. "I just want to talk to you. I would never hurt you."

He stepped forward into the dim light that cut across the bed from the hallway nightlight.

Hank.

Sunny released her breath slowly, and the mattress groaned as he sat on the edge of her bed.

*It's okay.* It was just Hank. She knew him. Her heart skittered to a stop. She knew he was a big, strong, overbearing, obsessed guy who had pinned her against the side of her house as he pushed himself against her. He had kissed her, and touched her, and she had been powerless to try to stop him. Jake's warning of how strong Hank was rang in her ears.

She tried to pull her legs closer to her body. He dropped his hand to rest on her bare skin, and she was amazed at the size of his hand as it engulfed her calf. He let out a sigh, and his chin dropped to his chest. He looked so sad, like a little lost puppy...*oh no...puppy! Where was Beau?*

Sunny's head snapped to the doorway, and she let out a whimper as she spied Beau's lifeless body on the floor of the hallway, a half-eaten cupcake on the floor by his head.

"Oh, sorry about that." Hank motioned to the dog's body. "I had to take care of him so I could talk to you. Last time he tried to attack me when all I wanted was to see you."

*Last time?* Fear and sadness waged inside of her. *Hank had been the mysterious man that had tried to come through my window! And now he had killed my precious Beau!*

Pushing aside her fear, Sunny could feel the anger in her build over this man who invaded her home, her bedroom, and hurt her dog. Suddenly her paralysis broke. Sunny scrambled forward lashing out with her arms and legs as she hit and kicked at the figure on the bed and she let loose a ferocious scream of rage and terror.

For such a big man, Hank moved with lightning speed as he pinned Sunny back against the headboard, his left hand crushed against her mouth. Her kicks were ineffectual, and he easily held both her wrists in one of his meaty palms as he held her body down with his hip.

Who was she kidding? This man played football. He spent years tackling men double her weight. Her fear returned tenfold as Sunny realized the minimal effort it took for him to completely immobilize her.

Hank leaned his forehead against the side of her head and spoke directly into her ear. "I just want to talk to you. I told you I wasn't going to hurt you. Why did you tell Matt you didn't want to see me? Why are you acting like this?" His breath was hot against her ear, and she could smell the stale scent of coffee on his breath.

Sunny twisted her body and tried to pull away from him. His fingers still covered her mouth, squeezed against her cheeks, as he shifted and his grip tightened on her wrists. She tried to turn her head, but his enormous hand covered most of her face and threatened to cut off her breathing. He moved his fingers from her nose, and Sunny inhaled a deep breath. His hand smelled vaguely of French fries and chocolate, and his class ring cut into the side of her cheek, but at least she could breathe.

Her eyes scanned the dark room for something to use against him or to distract him. Sunny wanted to weep as she tried in vain to come up with a means to get away, but she couldn't move, and she was struck again by how little effort it took him to completely restrain her.

A single drop of sweat rolled down her arm. The beating of her heart tripled. She was powerless against this huge man.

❀❀❀

Jake blearily opened his eyes to find himself stretched out in the recliner. He had one arm thrown carelessly over his head and the other tucked down the front of his shorts, his hand cupping his package to ensure it had neither fallen off nor been penis-napped while he blissfully slept. The credits to *Die Hard* rolled along the television, and he didn't know if the absence of dialogue or something outside had caused him to awaken. The clock on the wall read quarter to twelve, and he knew he should be in bed.

He brought his left arm down to release the recliner and stood to stretch. As long as his right hand was there, it made itself useful and gave himself a full-on package scratch. He pulled his hand free from his shorts and leaned down to pick up his empty soda can and paper plate, the remains of a ham sandwich sliding sideways as he picked up the plate.

Jake headed for the kitchen, looking out the big front window he passed on the way. Something felt off, and he paused to study the darkened street in front of Walter's house. There, that dark car parked down from Sunny's. It had been there earlier tonight.

Hurrying into the kitchen, he tossed the trash on the counter and reached above the refrigerator to where he kept his gun. He grabbed the gun and a small flashlight, then snapped off the back porch light to better conceal himself in the darkness. He pushed his bare feet into his sneakers on the way out the door, the untied shoelaces of one snapping against the driveway pavement as he jogged toward the dark car.

His eyes quickly adjusted to the dark, and he cautiously approached the car, his gun held ready at his side. Peering through the window, he saw the front seat full of crumpled fast food wrappers, a silver Thermos, a red and white baseball cap, and Kit Kat wrappers strewn across the floor. He shined the flashlight into the backseat which held more trash, a gray gym bag, and a child's baseball mitt and ball. The car was empty, and Jake let out a long held breath as he dropped the flashlight into his pocket.

He leaned back against the passenger door of the car and looked up at Sunny's house. He studied each window as he looked for anything out of the ordinary, anything to give him an excuse to ring the bell and make sure she was all right.

Suddenly, a scream of rage and fear pierced the night, and Jake took off running for her house, the flashlight banging against his leg with each step. He leaped the bushes along the side of the house as he headed for the back door where he had seen her use her hide-a-key last week.

He reached the back door and slid his hand along the top of the door frame. His breath was coming hard, and in his haste, he knocked the key free, and it fell into the garden next to her back stoop.

*Damn!* He dropped to his knee, his left leg squishing the pansies Sunny had planted this summer. His right hand still held the gun, and he braced himself against the house as he dug furiously around in the dirt with his left as he tried to find the dropped key.

***

*Calm down. He said he wasn't going to hurt me.*

As if he sensed her calm, he relaxed against her and took his hand away from her mouth. Knowing her strength was no match against his, Sunny switched tactics and hoped that if she could talk to him, she could get him to let her go and leave her house. She tried not to shudder as he smoothed her hair against her head.

"Hank, why are you here?" Sunny asked softly.

Hank dropped his head onto her shoulder and spoke into Sunny's neck. "I just wanted to see you and talk to you. I think about you all the time. After Linda left, I was so lonely, and then you came into my life. You seemed so nice and funny, and your hair smelled so good." His head slowly came up, and he buried his face in her hair and inhaled deeply.

"Linda took Mikey back to stay with her at her mom's," Hank continued, "and I sit alone in my apartment and dream of how my life with you could be. I know I could make you happy, Sunny-D." He kissed Sunny's neck, his breath hot against her throat.

Sunny cringed and pulled her head back as she tried to shrink away from him. Hank pushed closer, and his hands tightened against her wrists as he continued to talk.

"I know I call you too much, but I need to hear your voice and know you aren't out with someone else. But then you answer, and I get all flustered. I can't think of what to say to you, so I just listen to you breathing. I like the way you breathe, Sunny." He kissed her neck again and moved closer to her face. "I can't get you out of my mind. I sit outside of your house. I watch you laugh with your friends, and I want them to be me. I know we could be good together if you gave us a chance. I need you, Sunny."

Hank kissed Sunny's jaw line, and then in an awkward display of passion, his lips crushed against hers. His huge chest pressed down upon her as his kisses became more urgent.

She tried to scoot sideways away from him, but he was too strong, and his large body easily held Sunny pinned under him. A tear slid down the side of her face, and Sunny tried to control the panic that welled up inside of her.

*It's all right. He's just kissing me. I can handle this.* Sunny kept her lips pressed firmly closed, but the feel of his wet lips against her made her want to gag. She could smell his sour breath and feel the moist trail of saliva he left against her throat.

She tried to assure herself that she was going to be okay. But, then she could feel him getting hard against her leg, and the panic had her arching her back against his enormous bulk. He shifted to get his knee between her legs. Using all her strength, she tried to keep her knees tightly together, but he easily forced her legs apart and pressed his knee against her inner thigh.

"I like you so much," he said against her mouth, and he released one of Sunny's wrists to move his hand up to cup her breast.

Sunny gasped as his hand touched her so intimately, and she shook her head from side to side as she whimpered. "No, please, no."

Hank took advantage of her speaking to force his huge, disgusting tongue into Sunny's mouth, and she could taste the flavor of old coffee. Her tears flowed freely, and she used her now freed hand to beat against his broad back. Sunny used everything she had to push him off or to slide free from under him, but he was so heavy and so strong. Her efforts proved useless. His mouth was wet, and she cried out against it as his hand squeezed and groped her breast.

All of sudden, his weight lifted, and Sunny watched in confusion as his body was raised from hers and sailed backwards across the room. She gasped for breath and struggled to get free from the bedspread, then realized a third person was in the room.

Jake!

Hank had not magically levitated from her body, but had been physically thrown across the room. Her savior now stood above Hank, straddling his hulking body as he delivered a punch to his face with his left hand and a solid knock up the side of his head with the gun he held in his right. Hank's head lolled to the side in unconsciousness, and Jake dropped his limp body to the floor. Stepping over him, he crossed the room and scooped Sunny into his arms.

Feeling the safety of Jake's arms around her, the floodgates broke, and Sunny let forth deep gasping sobs as she clung to his t-shirt and cried. She could feel the cool, hard metal of the gun in his hand against her back as Jake pulled her closer. At this moment, she didn't care why he had a gun or what he had to do with her neighbor's disappearance, she was just glad he was here, holding on to her, and keeping her safe from Hank.

"Shh. It's okay now," Jake said softly and gently rocked her back and forth. "He's not going to hurt you ever again."

"He came into my room," Sunny said, between sobs. "I woke up, and he was just standing there, watching me sleep."

"Creepy bastard." Jake pulled one arm free to tuck the gun into the waist band of his shorts at the small of his back.

"Jake, he hurt Beau!" Sunny cried, her heart breaking with each word. "He told me he had to take care of him. Beau is gone."

"What? No, Sunny," Jake said and pulled her face out to look at him. "He's not dead, he's asleep. I heard him snoring when I came up the stairs. I figured he must have been drugged when he didn't wake up when I stepped over him to get to you."

"What? Oh, my gosh, he's okay?" Sunny pulled free from Jake and stumbled into the hallway. She dropped to her knees and buried her face in Beau's thick yellow fur. Jake was right, she could hear the dog snoring. Big, loud, deep, life-sustaining breaths!

"Oh Beau, I was so scared I had lost you," Sunny cried and put her arms around the big mutt as she tried to pull him into her lap. His head lolled toward her, and his eyes struggled to open. In a sleepy haze, his tongue came out and half-heartedly tried to lick her face as his tail did a slow half-wag on the floor. His eyes drifted shut again, and Sunny put her face into his neck and cried some more.

Jake sat on the floor next to Sunny, and she rocked her dog as if he were a big eighty-pound baby.

Sunny jerked her head up at the sound of sirens and turned toward Jake.

“I called the police from my cell phone as I was breaking into your house,” he explained.

The sirens drew steadily closer as the police car came down the street and pulled into the driveway. Jake moved down the stairs toward the door as they heard the car doors slam.

He opened the front door to see Officer McCarthy rushing up the sidewalk, followed by a female officer, her red hair pulled back into a neat ponytail.

“He's upstairs in the bedroom, first door on your right,” Jake said.

Officer McCarthy nodded at Jake, then climbed the stairs to where Sunny still sat on the floor with Beau. He touched her shoulder and looked her directly in the eye. “Are you okay, Ms. Vale?” he asked.

“Yeah, I'm fine.” Sunny wiped the tears from her face with the back of her hand. “Just get that guy out of here, please.”

Officer McCarthy cautiously peered around the door jam, then looked questionably back to Jake after seeing Hank's prone body lying on the floor. “What happened to him?” the officer asked.

“Uh, gosh, I'm not really sure,” Jake said. “I think he fell.”

“Ri-ght.” McCarthy turned and disappeared into the room, and the female officer came up the stairs.

“My name is Officer Delaney. I am here to assist you. Can I help you downstairs?” she asked Sunny.

Sunny was almost afraid to let go of the dog, as if he were a drugged-up, furry security blanket. She looked from the red-haired officer, to Beau, then to Jake, who nodded his assurance at her.

“I've got Beau,” Jake told her.

Carefully, Sunny set Beau's limp body back onto the floor, adjusted her t-shirt and stood up. Her knees were a little shaky, and Officer Delaney took her arm as she helped Sunny down the stairs and into the living room. Sunny sank onto the sofa, and Jake was there, pulling the sofa throw around her shoulders.

He bounded up the stairs to where Officer Delaney had returned. Sunny could see through the stair railing slats as the policewomen placed the half-eaten cupcake into a Ziploc baggie. Jake came down the stairs, Beau's body cradled in his arms. Sunny's eyes filled with tears as he carefully laid him on the sofa next to her so Beau's head could rest in her lap.

"Thank you," she mouthed to Jake. She was so choked with emotion that she couldn't seem to make her voice work.

"No problem." He smiled encouragingly.

Officer Delaney called down to Sunny. "This guy says he just poured Benadryl onto a couple of cupcakes and fed them to the dog to get him to go to sleep. He should be fine after a long nap."

"That's good. Thanks," Sunny croaked out and ran her hand across Beau's furry head.

"I'm going to get you a glass of water," Jake said and headed into the kitchen.

"What in the sam-hell is going on here?"

Edna stood in the doorway, her scrawny legs sticking out from under her plush pink robe. Her eyes were wild, and one side of her hair was smashed against the side of her head while the other stood up in unruly silver curls.

"What did *you* do?" she asked and narrowed her eyes at Jake as he came back into the living room carrying a glass of water.

Before he could answer, the sound of movement caused her to look up the stairs. The two officers pushed and dragged Sunny's attacker from the bedroom, his arms handcuffed behind his back.

Edna watched the officers bring him down the stairs, her eyes narrowed in an accusatory stare. She looked toward Sunny. "Hank the Tank?" she asked.

Sunny nodded and tried to keep her bottom lip from trembling.

Edna walked to the bottom of the stairs to meet them, her Sassy Girl slippers slapping the floor with each step. Fearlessly, she stepped up to Hank. He was at least a foot taller than her, but she tilted her head back and glared at his drooping face.

"You son-of-a-bitch," she hissed and brought her knee up full force to land smack in his family jewels.

"Get him outta here," she directed Officer McCarthy.

He smiled down at her and replied, "Yes, ma'am."

They pulled Hank to the door, and Officer McCarthy stopped and looked back at Jake. "You'll bring her down to the station tomorrow to file a full report?" he asked.

"You bet," Jake answered.

The officers pulled the door shut behind them and dragged Hank to the car. Their voices drifted through the open front window, and Officer McCarthy's laughter as he said, "See, I told you, that neighbor lady cracks me up."

That 'neighbor lady' now turned to Sunny with such compassion in her eyes, her emotions overflowed, and once again, Sunny started to bawl. Edna came to her and perched on the edge of the sofa so she could wrap her arms around Sunny without dislodging Beau.

"What happened, honey?" Edna asked.

"I don't really know. I woke up and he was there, in my room. I thought he had killed Beau, but he just knocked him out. I tried to scream and fight him off, but he was so strong." Sunny's words tumbled together as she tried to explain the events of the evening. A shiver ran through her as she continued, "He had his hand on my mouth, and he was talking into my ear, and he started kissing me, and he pushed my legs apart…" Sunny rubbed her hand across her lips as if to erase the taste of him.

"Did he…?" Edna asked and scrutinized Sunny's pajama bottoms and t-shirt for any rips or tears.

"No, thank goodness. He didn't get that far. But I think he would have, if Jake wouldn't have been there." Sunny turned to Jake and quietly thanked him again.

His gaze never left hers as he nodded. "Sorry I wasn't there sooner. If only I hadn't dropped the damn key."

"Why were you there at all?" Edna asked. "And how do you have a key?" She looked questionably at Sunny, who shook her head that she hadn't given him one.

"I saw this dark car parked by your house, and I've noticed it in the neighborhood quite a bit lately. I checked it out and thought I recognized the Sky Sox hat and the kid's baseball stuff in the back seat. I thought it was Hank, but when I heard you scream, I didn't care who it was, I just wanted to get to you."

"But that doesn't explain how you got in," Edna said.

"The secret hide-a-key isn't much of a secret," he said. "Just being out in the yard, I've seen Sunny use it several times. And if this guy has been watching her, he's probably seen her use it, too. I'm guessing that's how he got into the house tonight."

Edna looked accusingly at Sunny, then Jake turned to her. "And I've seen you use it a couple of times, Ms. Allen, when you've come over to let Beau out."

"Well, shoot," Edna said, sheepishly.

"Well, I'm glad you saw it. You really did save me." The tears built up in Sunny's eyes again.

"Sunny, the hide-a-key was just a convenience. I would have broken down the door to get to you." Jake's eyes never left hers, the sincerity of his statement evident in his look.

And there they went. More tears spilled from her eyes. Edna passed Sunny the box of tissues from the coffee table, and Sunny took one and blew her nose.

"You've had quite an ordeal tonight." Edna patted Sunny's leg. "Do you think he was the one who has been calling you too?"

"Oh, yeah, he admitted he had been calling me. And he was also the one who tried to break into my room before. That's why he drugged Beau, because last time he alerted me and scared him off," Sunny explained.

"Well, that's one mystery solved." Edna looked at Jake with one eyebrow raised.

Unfazed, he turned to Sunny. "Can I get you anything else? You want me to make you a sandwich or get you a bowl of ice cream?"

"No, I'm good." Sunny smiled and gave her nose one last honking blast.

"You want me to stay with you again, honey?" Edna asked.

"Actually, I plan on staying this time," Jake said. Edna and Sunny both turned to him in surprise.

"I'll sleep on the sofa, so you're welcome to stay as well." He nodded to Edna. "But I *will* be staying all night. I want you to feel safe." He smiled that crooked grin and winked at Sunny.

Sunny's heart warmed. *Really, how could a girl say no?*

"Are you all right with Mr. Hide-a-Key sleeping on the sofa?" Edna asked.

"I'll be fine," Sunny assured her. "You go on home and sleep in your own bed. I know how your back gets. I'll call you in the morning."

"If you're sure..." she said and eyed Jake warily as Sunny got up to walk her to the door.

He gave Edna a little wave and took Sunny's vacated spot on the sofa. He stretched his long, tan legs out on the coffee table and threw his arm over

Beau's body as he scratched him along his back. Beau groaned and stretched his legs out, then settled in next to Jake. Sunny thought Jake looked right at home stretched out on the sofa with her dog's head in his lap.

"Go home. I'm sure." Sunny gave Edna a hug before she closed the door behind her.

Sunny leaned against the door and eyed Jake, who watched her as he continued to pet the dog. "You want a pillow or a blanket or something?" she asked.

"Nah, I'm good. I've slept in worse places," he answered off-handedly and pulled the sofa throw onto his lap.

*Worse places? Worse as in messy women's apartments? Or worse like war-torn foreign countries?* There was so much she didn't know about this man. But what Sunny did know was that he was there when she needed him, and that was enough for now.

"Why don't you go on to bed, try to get a little sleep," he said, gently.

"Okay." Sunny climbed the stairs, overcome with fatigue, and felt as if every bone in her body hurt.

She practically fell into the bed, but sleep eluded her as she tossed and turned, feeling as if something were missing.

A few minutes later, Sunny heard a soft knock at the bedroom door. Her heart sped up as she heard Jake's voice. "I thought you might need a little company tonight."

Jake pushed the door open and came in, his arms full of a sandy-haired dog. Sunny scooted over, and he laid the big yellow dog in the bed next to her. She put her arms around Beau and buried her face in his neck so Jake wouldn't see the tears that fell into the dog's fur.

Sunny felt Jake's hand on her head, and he whispered, "Sleep well."

She nodded and looked up to see his retreating back

as he stepped through the bedroom door. Sunny heard his footsteps move down the stairs and the soft whoosh of the cushions as he settled back onto the sofa.

She sighed, curled her body around her dog and slept.

Sunny woke to the smell of freshly brewed coffee and bacon. She rubbed her eyes and looked around in confusion. The events of the previous night crashed down on her, and she looked frantically around for Beau.

As if on cue, the bedroom door nudged open. Beau padded into the room, and jumped onto the bed. If his tail-wagging and face-licking were any indication, Sunny would say he was none the worse for wear from his Benadryl-induced nap the night before. She buried her face in his neck and hugged him. He returned the hug with a lick to her face, and Sunny raised an eyebrow at the dog as she smelled the scent of bacon on his doggy-breath.

She eased from her bed and slipped across the hall to the bathroom. She looked in the mirror and was almost surprised to see the same woman staring back at her. Except for the puffy eyes and lop-sided bed-head, she looked the same as she did before she was attacked. There were no outward signs of trauma on her face. No bruising where Hank's hand had clamped across her mouth. No markings to show the trails of unwanted saliva he had left on her skin.

Looking at her, there were no indications of evidence that anything had happened at all. But Sunny felt the scars in the race of her heart as she remembered the way he had held her captive with his large body, and the fear that ran through her as she thought of the way she awoke to the feeling of an unwanted presence in her darkened bedroom.

Fighting against that fear, she made the decision she would not let some washed up football player with a displaced sense of loyalty scare her. In fact, she decided she didn't want to be scared at all anymore. How many things in her life had she let happen to her just because she was afraid to stand up to them?

*I am stronger than this.* She took another hard look at herself in the mirror. Had she let complacency and the fear of trying something new rule her life? She thought she had craved excitement in her life, but she was too afraid to go out and actually find it. She had let her friends take over her love life because she was too scared to try to find love on her own. And what if love had been right in front of her all this time, or right next-door to her, and she had been too afraid to take the step to find out?

Empowered by courage, Sunny pulled her pajamas from her body and shoved both pieces into the trash. She never wanted to wear them again.

Stepping into the shower, she ran the water as hot as she could stand it. She scrubbed at her body with the soap and shampooed her hair twice. Sunny stood under the steaming spray and let the hot water wash the last traces of Hank from her body as she vowed to let the fear and pain he caused her sweep down the drain with the soiled, soapy water.

Her skin had reddened from the hot water and the vigorous scrubbing. Sunny toweled herself dry and applied creamy scented lotion. She combed out her hair, brushed her teeth, and thought about the man who must be in her kitchen making coffee and feeding bacon to her dog.

She had spent so much time being suspicious of Jake, but when push came to shove, he was the one who came through for her. With all the men she had been dating and spending time with, she found she always came back to Jake. He was the one who made her feel safe and protected and wanted. Sunny knew that it was time to find out the truth about his involvement in Walter's disappearance. She was going to tell him that she knew he was Walter's grandson and ask him about the Fake-Jake dating profile. She was going to tell him that she cared for him.

Wearing only a towel, she crossed back to her bedroom and dressed quickly, choosing a pair of cut-off jean shorts and a simple pink Henley tank top. Leaving her hair wet, she picked up her newfound resolve, and descended the stairs in her bare feet.

"Good morning." Sunny stepped into the kitchen and surveyed the mountainous mess of mixing bowls, egg shells, and greasy paper towels. But, the puddle of drying pancake batter on the counter was easily forgotten as Jake turned and flashed her his killer grin. He must have gone home for a shower, because he wore different khaki shorts and a clean white t-shirt. His hair still looked wet around the ends of his blond curls.

"Hey." He studied her face before quietly asking, "How you doin' this morning?"

"I'm okay."

He cocked an eyebrow at her.

"Really. I'm fine. Or I will be fine," she assured him, her tone portraying the new confidence that she felt. "But I'm glad you're here."

"I am too," he said sincerely. He seemed to understand her brave new attitude, and his grin returned to his ridiculously gorgeous face. "So, how do you like your eggs?"

"Over medium." Sunny came around the counter and peered into a frying pan full of four eggs and a quarter inch of bubbling bacon grease.

Jake flipped the eggs, and another droplet of grease splashed onto the stovetop.

"I like mine sunny-side-up," he said, with that devilish smile of his. Sunny couldn't tell if that was a double entendre and he was flirting with her, or if that was really just the way he liked his eggs.

"Can I do anything to help?" Sunny looked around for any task that would distract her from thinking which of her *sides* would be considered the *side-up*.

He had set the small table in her kitchen nook, and a mug and a small juice glass sat empty on the counter.

"I wasn't sure if you wanted coffee, juice, or milk, so I left those empty." Jake gestured to the glasses. "I found the butter, but I haven't found the syrup yet."

He flipped a stack of pancakes onto one side of a platter and slid the eggs onto the other side. Opening the microwave, he pulled out a plate covered in greasy paper towels which she assumed contained the heavenly smelling bacon. Sunny poured herself some milk, retrieved the syrup from the pantry, then took a seat at the table as he brought plates over and set them down. He stepped back to refill his coffee mug before he joined her at the table.

"Thanks for breakfast." Sunny smiled into his eyes. "You didn't have to do this."

"I know. But I wanted to," he said. "There are a lot of things I want to do for you, Sunny, starting with telling you the truth."

Her chest constricted, and a bite of pancake stuck in her throat as he reached into his back pocket and pulled forth a black wallet that he tossed on the table in front of her.

Sunny set down the fork and took a drink of milk to help the pancake along. She had just told herself she wanted the truth, but now that it was sitting on the table in front of her, was she brave enough to pick it up and face it?

Taking a deep breath, she reached out and opened the wallet. Sunny gasped as she took in the shiny gold badge on one side of the wallet and the Federal Bureau of Investigations ID on the other. The ID had a picture of Jake and the title "Agent Jake Landon" on it.

"You're with the FBI?" she asked, incredulously.

"Yep."

"How do I know this is real?" She fingered the thick gold medal of the badge. The only FBI badges Sunny had ever seen belonged to Mulder and Scully, so she couldn't be sure, but this one *looked* real.

He laughed. "It's real. But you can call them if you want to verify it."

"Who would I call? The Pentagon? Maybe I should dial 1-800-CALL-FBI."

He laughed again, then his eyes turned serious. "It's real, and my feelings for you and your big fat dog are real."

Her heart beat quickened as Sunny looked into his deep blue eyes. Isn't this was she was hoping for? *I like you too* is what she wanted to say, but instead, Sunny said, "First of all, my dog isn't fat, and second of all, so now I know you're an FBI agent. Well now that explains...let's see...oh yeah...absolutely nothing. Except maybe why you have a gun and why Officer McCarthy didn't do anything about you beating up Hank last night. Wait. Does he know you're an FBI agent?"

"Yeah. I told him the first night you had the intruder. Well, I guess now we know it was Hank, who tried to come into your window. That's why I left and went back to my house when the police arrived. So I'd be able to show them my credentials without you and your Murder She Wrote-watching neighbor around."

The wheels were really turning now, and Sunny blurted out, "So that's who you've been talking to on the phone?"

Jake nodded.

"And that's why you were carrying a gun?"

He nodded again.

"But that doesn't explain why you're here, or what your connection is to Walter, or why you took a bloody shirt into that private investigator?"

"Bloody shirt? What? How'd you know about the bloody shirt, and how did you know about Finney?"

"Piper and Drew saw you the first day when you dropped it off. Then Cassie and I followed you the day you picked it up. We sort of eavesdropped on you and the private investigator, and found out the blood was Walter's."

"Why, you little sneaks." A look of almost admiration crossed his face. "I thought I saw Piper that first day, eating lunch at the restaurant across the street."

"But why did you have a shirt with Walter's blood on it? Was he bleeding when you killed him?" Sunny blurted out.

"Killed him?" he asked, incredulously. "Why would I kill him? I'm trying to find the person who *did* kill him. The shirt is evidence and hopefully a clue to finding the actual killer."

"Well, if you're with the FBI, why did you take the shirt to a private investigator instead of a fancy FBI lab?"

"I did send a sample to the 'fancy FBI lab', but Finney's got connections and he can sometimes expedite lab results and I wanted to know if that was Walter's blood as soon as possible. Besides, Finn's a friend that I can trust. *And* he owed me a favor."

"Okay. But, we know you showed up right before the explosion, and Edna saw you drive up in the middle of the night with a briefcase, and a gun, and a mysterious duffle bag."

"Oh, my gosh. I'm dealing with a bunch of wanna-be Nancy Drews." He shook his head in disbelief.

"We're a little older than the girl in the movie though."

"There's a movie? About Nancy Drew?"

*Seriously, both he and Edna needed to get out more.*

"Look," Jake said, "despite all your 'evidence' to the contrary, I did *not* kill Walter. I was gonna tell you this anyway, he's actually my grandfather."

"I know."

"You know? How in the world did you know that?"

"Well, I found Walter's will that day at your house when you were asking me about his computer. And it was drawn up by Maggie's firm, so I asked her about it. She swore me to secrecy and wouldn't give me all the details, but she did tell me you really were Walter's grandson."

"So you've known the whole time?"

"Sure."

"Then how could you still think I killed him?"

"Well, Edna also saw you carrying a mysterious trash bag to your car which we later found out was his bloody shirt. And you always seemed to be around when strange stuff happened. Like me being stalked."

"I was *around* because I was trying to *protect* you. I knew Walter had disappeared, and I was trying to figure out who I could trust in case it was someone in the neighborhood. If I would have known I had the cast from CSI digging into the case, I would have enlisted all of your help a lot sooner."

Sunny kind of liked the idea of being compared to CSI, the real one in Las Vegas, not the knock-offs in those other cities. Did he think she was like that sexy Catherine Willows or was he comparing her to the nerdy, but still cute, lab girl with the ponytail?

"Sunny?"

"Yeah," she said, jerking herself out of the murderous streets of Las Vegas and back into her kitchen.

"Why don't we finish our breakfast, then I'll start from the beginning and tell you everything?" He stuck a piece of crispy bacon into his mouth.

Sunny nodded and cut into her pancake, the syrup making a brown pool around the fried eggs.

They finished eating in companionable silence. Sunny's thoughts raced with a thousand questions. Her tingly spots were on alert as she replayed his words, *I like you* and *My feelings for you are real,* and the fact that he included her dog in his feelings had her heart melting like chocolate in the warm sun.

She still needed answers, though. She took her plate to the sink, and as they loaded the dishwasher, Jake told her the whole story.

"About five years ago," he said, "I was assigned to a case involving a man who was murdered and the prime suspect was his wife. The case was eventually ruled an accident, and that probably would have been the end of it, if another husband of the same woman didn't end up dead about a year later. The woman's name is Mona Masterson, but she has a bunch of aliases. She also goes by Debbie Davidson and Madelyn March. She's been married four times in the past five years, and all of her husbands have died in different ways, so we call her the Black Widow."

"How does she get all these men to marry her so quickly?" Sunny asked, intrigued with the story. She used her fingernail to scratch off droplets of dried pancake batter stuck to the counter.

"She preys on lonely older men who have no family to protect them. And she's also gorgeous."

"But how does she meet them?"

"Usually on internet dating sites." He looked at her expectantly.

"Aaahh." Things began to click into place. "That's why you had that weird online profile that made you sound so lonely. Lonely? Oh no, Walter's profile was Lonely1. He's just asking to be chosen by her. Wait. Are you telling me that this Black Widow is the one who killed Walter?"

"We don't know yet that she killed him, but we do

know that she communicated with him online. We put my profile out there to try to lure her away from him and into a sting operation with me going undercover."

"Why didn't you just go to Walter and warn him? He's your grandpa, for goodness sakes. Wouldn't the FBI let you just go talk to him?"

"It wasn't the FBI stopping me," he said. "Walter is my grandfather, but I've never met him. This is the part where things get a little tricky."

He went to the coffeepot to refill his mug. He held the pot up, and Sunny pushed her cup toward him. He topped off the cup, slid the pot back into the holder, then turned to the fridge to get out her French Vanilla creamer. Sunny grinned.

*What? So he knows how I like my coffee. So what? He's an FBI agent. He's trained to be observant, right?*

They took their coffee into the living room and settled onto the sofa. Sunny took her favorite corner and curled her legs under her, and he sat in the middle and stretched his legs out on the coffee table. Beau followed them in. He jumped up onto the opposite corner of the sofa, circled the cushion twice, pawed at the throw pillow, and with a sigh, settled onto the cushion with his head resting in Jake's lap. He looked up at Jake with big brown eyes as he waited expectantly for Jake to pet him.

Jake absently stroked the dog's head as he continued his story. "My mother's name is Carol Mead Landon. She was Walter and Betty's only daughter. I think she was the typical only child, spoiled and praised for everything she did. According to her, they had high hopes for her future, and she was very close to them. That was until she turned seventeen and found out she was pregnant. She said it broke her Dad's heart. He told her he would help her to 'take care of it', and who knows what that means, but evidently they got into a huge fight and probably both said things they didn't mean. My mom being a teenager and a hormonal one at that, she ran off that night and didn't speak to her parents for twenty-five years."

"What about your dad?" Sunny asked.

"Never knew my dad," he answered. "It's always just been my mom and me. She never told me what happened with my dad, and after a while I quit asking."

"You said they didn't speak for twenty-five years, so they've been in contact the past five..." She looked at him questionably, "...or ten years?"

"Something like that," he said. "My mom finally broke down and called her mom, my grandmother. I was on assignment in another country when all this took place, but according to my mom, the two of them met, had a tearful reunion, yada, yada, yada, and my grandmother begged my mom to forgive her dad and meet with him. Betty explained to my mom that, of course her dad was upset, but if she would have only stayed long enough to finish the argument, they could have worked it all out together. My mom threw back the "take care of it" comment my grandfather had made, and my grandmother explained that Walter had really meant take care of it, as in he and Betty would help to 'take care of' as in 'raise' the baby. She told my mother how her leaving had broken my grandfather's heart. Fast forward thru more weeping and explaining, and suffice it to say my mother and grandmother patched things up just in time for my grandmother to find out she had cancer. My mom took me to meet her before she passed away, but my mom just couldn't face her dad yet."

"Oh, I'm so glad you got to meet Betty, though. She was a wonderful lady. I'm sorry you missed out on knowing her your whole life. And Walter, too. He's really a great guy. Did your mom ever get to see him?"

"She did. She finally called him last year, and the two of them met and were making progress on repairing their relationship. Then I came back stateside and got involved in the Black Widow case. When Walter's name came up as one of her possible next victims, I made arrangements to come out here and meet with him. I had spoken with him on the phone, but we hadn't scheduled an actual visit. He said he wanted to see me, and then all of sudden we couldn't reach him, and I stopped hearing from him. We waited a week or so, and then I flew out and came to his house. I focused mainly on the house and had only looked thru the windows of the garage before it exploded. I was afraid that he could have been in there, either alive, or he could have already been dead when the place went up in flames. I'm still waiting to hear the final results of the arson investigation from Tom Marshal, the detective assigned to the case. He told me it would be several weeks before all the tests came back. I hope to hear something from him soon."

"Did he know you were an FBI Agent?"

"Who, Tom? Not until after your Mini-Ms. Marple threw suspicion on me by telling him I carried a gun. Then I had to fill him in on the investigation."

"Do you really think this Mona-woman killed Walter?"

"I don't know for sure. It's definitely her style of making a death look like an accident. We know he was communicating with a woman on the dating site, but we haven't been able to directly link him to Mona."

"So, what now?"

"I'm not really sure. We wait for the detective to come back with the results, and I keep investigating, and we hope I get a hit from her on my fake online dating match site."

"But what now…for us? Why did you tell me all this now?" Sunny looked into his eyes, and his face turned serious. He slid his left arm behind her on the sofa as he moved closer.

"I told you. I like you, Sunny. I have since the first

day you chucked those frozen chicken chunks at me. I don't want secrets between us, and I sure as hell don't want you to be afraid of me."

Her heartbeat quickened. "I like you, too," she said softly.

He reached under her knees and pulled her legs forward to rest in his lap. Beau lifted his head so Sunny's foot wouldn't kick him in the face. Jake's left arm dropped from the back of the sofa to curl around her shoulders, and his right hand crossed to cup her hip.

He moved his face closer. "You okay?"

*Was I okay?* Okay enough, despite the fact that her heart was beating out of her chest, her mouth was dry as unbuttered toast, and she was pretty sure she was sweating. But this amazing man, who actually was dangerous, but in a good way, liked her enough to divulge his undercover operation to her. And now his hand was running up and down her arm, coming treacherously close to her breast with each movement.

"Yeah, I'm okay," she whispered. Sunny's back arched as she pressed herself to him.

He slowly brought his mouth closer, and took her bottom lip into his with the gentlest of kisses. He softly kissed her again and then again.

He had kissed her before, but this time felt different. Her suspicions were gone, and he had told her personal details about his life. This felt comfortable, more intimate. *And sexy as hell!*

He kissed her once more, his hand running down to her knee, then back up to finger the fringes of her cutoff shorts. Sunny moaned softly into his mouth. His hand tightened on her outer thigh. His arm curled around Sunny's back and pulled her closer. The same arms he had used to gently carry her dog to her when she needed him. The same arms he had flexed as he helped her pull weeds in the flower garden. The same arms that held her when her neighbor's garage burst into flames, and he came running to find her.

Her thoughts ran to images of Jake as he...

*Oh hell, why am I thinking anyway?* Sunny threw her arms around his neck and pulled his mouth to hers as her hand fisted in his hair. She clutched his back and squirmed to get her bottom more into his lap. Sunny accidentally kicked Beau, who acted affronted and stepped off the sofa with a groan.

Jake's strong arm laid her back as he smoothly adjusted their bodies so they were lying side by side. His kisses deepened, and her skin burned as he slid his hand underneath the tank top to cup her breast. He thumbed her erect nipple through her bra, and Sunny groaned again and pressed her hips closer to his. She could feel that he wanted her, and she rubbed herself against him in slow movements.

She sighed as he pulled his hand free from her shirt and moaned with pleasure as his hand ran across her denim-clad thighs to cup the mound between her legs. He rubbed his thumb across her magic button, and she clutched his back tighter.

*BBRRRINNNGG!*

Jake lifted his head, and Sunny tried to catch her breath.

"Let it ring," she said and gasped for air.

He kissed her again as they waited for three more rings and the message to start.

"Sunny, it's Edna. I'm just calling to check on you. Your car's in the driveway, so I know you're there. You better pick up or I'm coming over."

Sunny scrambled from Jake's arms to get to the cordless phone on the end table. She missed and knocked it to the floor. Sliding from the sofa, she grabbed the phone and depressed the tiny on button. "Hello."

"Oh, good, you are home," Edna said. "Are you all right? You sound a little out of breath."

"I'm fine," Sunny answered. Her top half was

hanging off the edge of the sofa, and Jake ran his hand up her leg, sliding his fingers up the back of her shorts. His thumb brushed along the curve of her butt, and Sunny bit down on her lip to keep from moaning.

"I was just checking on you and wondered when you were heading down to the police station?" Edna asked.

"Police station?" Sunny asked. Jake's hand stopped moving and pulled free from her shorts.

"Yes. Remember Mr. Sleep-on-the-Sofa told the police he would bring you down this morning to file a report against Hank the Tank?"

"Oh, yeah." Sunny pushed up to her elbows, and Jake grabbed her arm to pull her back onto the sofa. "We'll head down there in a little while. Thanks for checking on me, Edna. I'll call ya this afternoon." Sunny clicked the off button and set the phone on the table.

Jake smiled and shrugged.

*A call about her stalker was a definite mood breaker.*

"I'm still planning on driving you down there," he said. "When do you want to go?"

"We might as well get it over with. Let me change clothes, and we'll head over."

❀❀❀

"Anything else you can remember, ma'am?" the officer asked. After waiting twenty minutes, Sunny had been ushered in and placed at a desk strewn with folders, Styrofoam coffee cups, and a takeout bag from a local hamburger joint.

A young cop named Officer Ryan had taken notes as Sunny replayed the events of the night before. He took her back to when she first met Hank, and they reviewed the date, the phone calls, and the first time he tried to enter her bedroom.

Jake had sat next to her, his presence alone serving as a source of comfort and strength. Sunny could see his hand clench into a fist against his leg as she gave the officer the details of Hank's assault.

"That's all I can think of," Sunny said.

"All right, we'll be in touch," the young officer said.

"I'm gonna try to find McCarthy for a minute before we take off." Jake stood and scanned the precinct room for the tall, balding man. Spotting him, Jake slipped from the chair and headed across the room.

"That's it for now." Officer Ryan was obviously ready for her to move on. Sunny took her purse from his desk, knocking over one of the Styrofoam cups, the dried brown coffee residue stark against the white of the cup.

Sunny stood and headed for the exit, and a strong male presence fell in behind her, cupping her elbow with his hand. Assuming it was Jake, she turned with a smile only to find herself looking up into the gorgeous face of Officer Royce, her young flirtee from the first encounter with Hank.

"Hey, I was hoping to catch you. I saw you sitting at Ryan's desk. You look really pretty today." His eyes appraised her, and Sunny was blinded with the bright white of his delicious grin.

"Oh, thanks." Sunny tried not to break into girlish giggles. *He was just so cute.*

"I heard about what happened last night. Are you doing okay?" he asked with genuine concern.

"Yeah, I'm fine," she said.

"Well, hey, I wanted to give you my card so if you ever get scared or just want to talk, you can call me. I'll take you out for coffee or something..." He handed her his card, and she read the inscription. 'Officer S. Royce, Amazing Gorgeous Stud, *Oh wait, it actually said*, Criminal Investigations Division.'

"Thanks," Sunny said, amazed at her witty verbal skills.

Even though Officer Cutey had her tongue-tied with his attention, he was still no Jake. No amount of coffee with this young hottie could compare with the passion she had felt for Jake this morning when his lips had touched hers.

"I appreciate the offer, but–" The little card was snatched from Sunny's hand as another male presence came up behind her.

"She won't be needing this," Jake said and passed the card back to Officer Royce. "Thanks, though."

"Okay, man." Royce held his hands up in mock surrender. "I didn't want to step on anybody's toes. It's cool." He nodded, gave Sunny a wink, and one more dazzling grin before ambling off.

"Geez, I leave you alone for five minutes, and you've got half the police squad hitting on you," Jake said as he opened the door for her.

*Half would imply the police squad was made up of exactly two officers.*

"What? He wasn't..." she stammered, the verbal skills again coming up with nothing. Give her a roomful of seven-year-olds, and she could have them rolling on the floor in laughter, but two good-looking men talk to her in the same five minutes, and her brain freezes like chocolate in a Dairy Queen Blizzard.

*Oh, wow.* She could really go for a Blizzard right now. Her stomach rumbled at the thought, and she looked up to see Jake good-naturedly shaking his head.

"You're thinking about food right now, aren't you?" he asked.

She blushed. "Well, it is about time for lunch."

"All right. Come on." Jake took her hand as they walked toward his car. "I'll buy you some lunch."

"And a Blizzard?"

He stopped and raised an eyebrow at her.

"A girl's gotta eat," she said.

He continued to stare at her.

"Well, she does."

"Yes, I guess she does." He laughed and then leaned

down and kissed her. *Right on the mouth. Right on the street in front of God and everybody.*

A warmth spread through her all the way to her toes, and all thoughts of ice cream riddled with frozen chocolate chunks melted from her mind. Sunny knew this man must be special if he could make her forget about a chocolate chip cookie dough Blizzard.

# 26

"Hey, Sunny," Cassie said as she picked up the phone. She cradled the cordless unit against her shoulder as she spread chocolate frosting on the last of the cupcakes.

"Hey, yourself. How's family day going?" Sunny asked.

"Good. Matt's team won their football game and I'm just finishing the cupcakes. Tyler got his dad to take him on the hike, so I was released from scout badge duty. What's goin' on with you?"

"That's what I'm calling about, actually. I've had a little excitement since I saw you last."

"Since yesterday?"

"Oh, yes. But I hoped to get the whole group together and tell you all at once. Edna and I can pick you up, and we can head to Maggie's. She said she was working at home this weekend, so she's probably holed up in her office and would appreciate the break. Can you and Piper get away for an hour or so?"

"Hold on." Cassie stuck her finger to her mouth and licked off the silky chocolate frosting as she looked across the kitchen to where Piper sat. She was curled into the chair by the fireplace, her ears plugged with the headphones from her Ipod. Cassie had to smile as she marveled at the changes in the young girl. Tara had convinced her that her natural blonde color was "ultra-fabulous" and had helped her to bleach it back.

Ever since the Luau party Tara had hosted at the beginning of the summer, the girls had become fast friends, and Tara could be found seated at Cassie's dinner table several nights a week. They swapped music and clothes, and Piper could regularly be seen now in a whole rainbow of colors. The dark black eye makeup was gone, and so was the look of sadness that Cassie was afraid would be permanently etched on Piper's face.

Cassie came around the center island and tugged on Piper's foot as it dangled over the side of the chair, tapping along to the music being pumped into Piper's ear.

Piper pulled one earphone loose as she looked up at Cassie. "What's up?" she asked.

"Sunny's on the phone. She's coming to pick us up. Do you wanna go over to Maggie's with us for a little bit?"

"Is Drew back?" Piper asked and eagerly leaned forward.

"No. It's just the girls."

"Oh," she sighed and her shoulders slumped. "Yeah, I guess I'll come."

"Count us in," Cassie said into the mouthpiece of the phone.

"Okay, see you in ten."

❀❀❀

"Hey, Maggie," Sunny called thirty minutes later, as the group walked into Maggie's office at the front of her house. The front door had been ajar, and they heard music playing, so after they knocked, Edna, Cassie, Piper and Sunny traipsed in.

"Aaahhh!" Maggie shrieked. "What are you guys doing here?"

Sunny looked at the computer screen Maggie had been frantically tapping away at, expecting to see boring word documents full of legal jargon, like heretofore and whereas. But instead of the black and white lines of wording, her screen glowed with the bright blues, greens, and purples of a magical world filled with elves and dwarves and two-handled weapons.

"I think the question is, what are *you* doing here?" Sunny asked with a grin as she stepped closer to the computer.

Maggie's hands fluttered across the desk, and she reached for the mouse to close the screen. Her hair was disheveled on one side of her head, and Sunny didn't think she'd ever seen her so flustered.

Before Maggie closed the screen, Sunny spied the beautiful blonde-haired character of Kynsya, and her huge white tiger, Chaos, prowled the screen behind her.

"Maggie, you're Kynsya!" Sunny gasped. "You're the magical hunter who helped me."

Maggie put her head in her hands in a gesture of defeat.

"Wait. Who's Kynsya?" Cassie looked from Maggie to Sunny and back again. "What's going on?"

"And what the hell is a magical hunter?" Edna asked.

"It's a character in World of Warcraft," Sunny explained. "Remember my date with Jeremy?"

"The cute Clark Kent dark-hair and glasses guy?" Cassie asked at the same time that Edna nodded and said, "Mabel's grandson."

"Right, on both accounts," Sunny said. "Well, remember our date was a whole group of people playing an online video game together?"

"The game where you sucked and got everyone killed?" Piper asked.

"That's the one," Sunny answered. "And I would have sucked worse if I wouldn't have had this other player come in and help me all the time. She was like my guardian angel in the game. Her name was Kynsya, and she was a magical human hunter. I thought she was just a really nice person who could tell I was a beginner. Or in my fantasies, I thought Jake may have signed on and was protecting me in the game. But all along, it was really Maggie."

Maggie looked at Sunny, dumbfounded. "You really thought Jake would go create a character in some obscure game just to protect you from a pretend dragon? You are such a nerd."

"Me? You are the one who actually did that, so you are the nerd. But how did you know I would be playing that game, and how could you be good enough to help me out?"

"All right! All right!" Maggie threw up her hands and stared at the group in defiance. "I know when I'm busted. So, I'm actually a closet video gamer. The boys used to play this game, and one day I sat down at their computer and got sucked into this world of dragons and magic and elves. So I secretly set up my own accounts and created my character, and I play at night when the boys have gone to bed."

"Cool," Piper said and gained a small grin from Maggie.

"Why is it such a secret?" Edna asked.

"Because I am a grown woman who has a successful career. I am a partner in a prestigious law firm, and I waste tons of hours in a fantasy land playing a video game," Maggie cried. "I'm so embarrassed."

"Oh, Maggie." Sunny put her arm around her friend's shoulder and patted her arm. "There's nothing to be embarrassed about. Plenty of women play that game, and I think it's great you found a fun outlet to escape into. We all need that sometimes."

"Heck, yeah," Edna said. "I escape into Springfield every afternoon when I watch Guiding Light on the boob-tube. If I had a way to get in there and hang out with the Spaulding's and the Bauer's, I sure would.

Well, maybe not Alan, he's kind of a crabby old guy, but I sure wouldn't mind hangin' out with those Lewis boys."

"Ewww," Piper said. She wrinkled her nose in an 'old people talking about sex' kind of disgust.

"So, I'm still confused," Cassie said. "How did you get into the game Sunny was playing on her date? Is everybody who plays that game all in it together?"

"Oh no, there are thousands of people who play and several separate worlds. You have to get invited into a raid," Maggie paused as she watched their eyes glaze over in confusion. "It's complicated to explain, but I was over at Sunny's the night of that date, and I met Jeremy. Remember how Sunny spent twenty minutes in the yard with Jake watching her dog puke up her panties?"

They all nodded, and Sunny cringed at the memory, not only out of embarrassment, but at the loss of a pair of eighteen dollar lace panties to her dog's digestive tract.

"Well, while they were outside, Jeremy and I got to talking, and he told me what you were doing that night. How he was taking you to play World of Warcraft. I don't know what came over me, but I found myself telling him how I was a closet Warcrafter myself. We got to talking about the game and our characters, and realized we had been playing together on and off for the last year. He told me where you would be playing that night and invited me to join the raid. But I made him swear not to tell Sunny it was me."

"Well, he kept his word because he never said anything about you to me," Sunny assured her.

Suddenly, the sound of the back sliding door being opened had the group all turn toward the kitchen.

Their eyes widened in collective surprise as the sound of a male voice called out, "The steaks are ready, babe."

Shocked, they looked from the office door to Maggie, then like horses released from the gate, they all sprang into action pushing each other out of the way to see who belonged to this male voice and why he was calling their friend, 'babe'?

They barreled into the kitchen as one unit to see the back side of a dark-haired man wearing khaki shorts and a black polo shirt reach into Maggie's cabinet for some plates. A platter holding three thick juicy steaks sat on the counter in front of him, and Sunny wasn't sure if they began salivating at the delicious scent of grilled meat or at the view of said backside.

The man turned, and his eyes widened in shock at the sight of five women gawking at him from the other side of the kitchen island.

"You must be the Pleasant Valley Page Turners," he said, grinning. His eyes sparkled behind his glasses, and his hair poked up from a cowlick above his right eyebrow. "Hi, Sunny," he said.

"Hey, Jeremy," Sunny said, a smile breaking out on her face as she leaned her hip against the kitchen counter.

"Jeremy?" Edna asked. "Mabel's grandson?"

"I'm really glad to finally meet you all. I've heard so much about you," he said.

"Well, we haven't heard anything about you." Edna folded her arms across her bony chest. "So, somebody better start talking." She looked at Maggie with one eyebrow raised.

"We've already established this is Jeremy," Maggie said, and had the nerve to act pissed at them. "What else do you want to know?"

They stood silent for a moment and looked from Maggie's sullen frown to Jeremy's open-faced grin, and then Cassie stepped forward, her hand outstretched.

"Hi, Jeremy." She reached across the island to shake his hand. "I'm Cassie. I'm so glad to meet you. And this is my niece, Piper." She gestured toward the younger girl.

"Hi." Piper gave a little wave.

He came around the island and extended a hand to Edna. "It's nice to meet you, Ms. Allen. My grandmother speaks very highly of you."

"Well, don't believe a thing that old bat tells you," Edna said as she shook Jeremy's hand.

"She said you were a good friend to her, but she didn't tell me how lovely you were," he said, pouring on the charm.

"See what I mean? She's always leaving out the good stuff."

Sunny turned and watched Maggie as this interchange took place. She saw a look of amusement and pride on her face as Jeremy worked to charm Cassie and Edna. Maggie's face then reddened as Jeremy moved to stand beside her and wrap his long arm around her waist.

"I didn't know they were coming," she whispered to him, though they could all hear her plainly.

"I think it's great," Jeremy said, addressing them all as a group. "I want to meet your friends." He reached down and tilted Maggie's chin up so he could look into her eyes. "I plan on being in your life for a long time."

Sunny swallowed around the lump in her throat and looked at Cassie, whose eyes brimmed with tears. *What a bunch of saps we are.*

"That's fine and dandy," Edna snapped, "but how did you end up in her life in the first place? How did you all get from some magical computer game to cooking steaks at Miss Maggie-I've-Never-Seen-Her-Hair-Messed-Up-Like-That-Before's?"

Maggie blushed again and self-consciously raised a hand to flatten her mussed hair at the same time Jeremy slid his hand up and re-mussed her dark tresses.

"I had known Maggie before, as Kynsya in the game. When I met her in person, she took my breath away." He turned to Sunny and shrugged as he said, "No offense."

"None taken," Sunny replied. "Our Mags is a stunning beauty."

Maggie glared at her as Jeremy continued his story. "I found out that night that she was a lawyer, and it didn't take much digging to find her firm and her email address. I *am* fairly skilled with a computer."

"Yes, we know you somehow eke out a living playing little games on your computer," Edna scoffed.

"He doesn't just play the games," Maggie spoke up in Jeremy's defense. "He designs the games and runs his own company. As a matter of fact, he designed and patented *Call To Action*."

"Really? I love that game," Piper said, finally interjecting into the conversation. "All the kids at my school play it."

"Thank you." Jeremy nodded to Piper. "It's always good to know when one of my games is well-received."

"One of?" Cassie asked.

"He's designed several popular games," Maggie said proudly. "He's really quite brilliant."

"So that still doesn't explain..." Sunny said and gestured to the two of them.

"Right," Jeremy said. "So I started to email her at work, then that progressed to a lot of text-messaging, then nightly phone calls. After a few weeks, she finally agreed to go to lunch with me."

"So that's why you've been so devoted to that Blackberry lately." Sunny grinned. "Here we thought you were working on a big case."

"A big case of tall, dark and handsome," Edna said.

"It was just lunch," Maggie said and pulled a face at Edna. "But then that lunch led to some dinners and then to a movie..."

"And then your boys go out of town, and you plan a special date, and four of your closest friends show up in the middle of it," Cassie finished. "Oh, Mags, we're sorry. We had no idea."

"It's okay. It's been fun having a secret dating thing, but it's also killing me not to be able to talk to you guys about it." Maggie slid her hand down and clasped Jeremy's hand.

"I really like him," she stage-whispered to them. Turning to Sunny, she said, "Sunny, I hope you're okay with this. I know you went on a date with him first..."

Sunny held up her hand to ward off any more of Maggie's comments. "I'm totally fine with this. In fact, I think it's wonderful."

Maggie's face broke into a broad grin, and she looked up at Jeremy as he squeezed her hand. She turned back to the group of women and said, "So just exactly *why* the hell are all of you over here?"

And there she was. That was more like their Maggie.

"Something happened last night, and I wanted to have everyone together so I would only have to tell it once," Sunny said. "But now that we've interrupted your dinner, I feel bad. We can go, and I'll fill you in tomorrow."

"Nonsense," Jeremy said, already moving into the kitchen and pulling down extra plates. "We have plenty of food. We'll split up the steaks, and we have a huge pasta salad, and a full loaf of bread. We're happy to share."

"Those steaks *do* look good," Piper said.

"And they are getting cold," Cassie said.

"I'll get the drinks," Edna said and opened the cabinet door to pull down glasses.

"Is this okay with you, Mags?" Sunny asked her friend, who stood in shock as the book club took over her dinner date.

"Sure, it's fine," Maggie said, breaking her daze. "We can't eat that whole chocolate cake by ourselves anyway."

"There's chocolate cake?" Piper asked, her hands

deep in the silverware drawer.

Maggie laughed, and with a sigh, pulled out a kitchen chair and plopped down at the table.

Through the course of the meal, Sunny filled them in on the events of the night before.

"You mean Hank was actually in your room?" Cassie asked, when Sunny finally wound down.

"And he attacked you?" Piper asked.

"Oh, honey, you must have been so scared," Cassie added.

"Terrified," Sunny agreed and nodded her head. Just talking about it brought forth the familiar tears, and Cassie passed her a napkin to dab at her eyes.

"So how did you get away from him? Did he hurt you?" Cassie scooted her chair closer so she could take Sunny's hand.

Sunny squeezed her friend's fingers and took a deep breath. "No, he didn't hurt me. But I think he would have if Jake wouldn't have shown up and cold-cocked him."

Piper gasped. "Jake saved you?"

"Yes, he literally did. He threw Hank against the wall and punched him into unconsciousness."

"Wow. I like this guy," Jeremy said. Maggie gave him a look as he said, "Well that's what I would have done."

"Worse than hurting me," Sunny continued, "was that he hurt Beau. I thought he had killed him at first."

"Oh, no," Cassie cried.

"Beau's okay. Hank drugged him with Benadryl-laced cupcakes, so he wouldn't bark or growl at him."

"That bastard!" Piper said, with a maliciousness that surprised them all.

Sunny turned to her as Piper said, "Well, there's just no reason to hurt your dog."

"You're right, honey," Sunny assured her. "And Beau is fine. He got a nice long nap out of the deal.

The main thing is, Jake had also called 911, and the police showed up and arrested Hank."

"I showed up right after the police got there, but Mr. Knows-Where-the-Hide-a-Key-Was had already taken care of the dirt bag," Edna interjected.

"Don't worry. Edna still got her two cents worth. She went up to Hank as the police took him out and kicked him square in the family jewels." Sunny smiled at her neighbor with pride.

"Rotten son of a bitch," Edna said.

"Way to go, Edna." Piper reached across the table to give the older woman a high-five.

"Damn-straight," she said and smacked Piper's outstretched hand.

"You should have called me. I would have come over," Cassie said. "Did Edna stay with you again last night?"

"I would have," Edna huffed, "if Mr. I'm-Sleeping-on-the-Sofa hadn't kicked me out."

"Jake slept over?" Maggie asked, her right eyebrow raised.

"Yes, on the sofa," Sunny said, "and he didn't kick you out, I did."

"Hmmm," Maggie said.

"You know her back gets worse if she doesn't sleep in her own bed," Sunny explained.

Maggie chuckled. "So long as you were just thinking of her."

"I wasn't really thinking at all," Sunny said and the room turned serious again. "And Jake was great. He really did sleep on the sofa, after he carried Beau all the way up the stairs and put him in my bed so I wouldn't be alone."

"Aww," Piper said.

"So was he there this morning?" Cassie asked.

"Yes, and this part can't leave this room." Sunny looked at each one in turn.

"Do you need me to leave?" Jeremy asked.

"No." Sunny sighed. "You're in this now, so you might as well stay."

Her fellow diners leaned forward as Sunny told them, "Jake made me breakfast this morning, and he set the table with pancakes, scrambled eggs, and his FBI badge."

"His what?" Edna's fork dropped from her hand and clattered to the floor. The rapid clicking of toenails on hardwood sounded as Maggie's dog Barney raced under the table and gobbled up the piece of steak that had been en route to Edna's mouth.

"He's an FBI agent working undercover to track Walter's killer," Sunny said.

"I thought he was Walter's grandson," Maggie said.

"And he is *also* Walter's grandson." Sunny popped the last curly noodle of pasta salad into her mouth and pushed her plate away.

By now, they had finished eating, but their plates still sat on the table. The steak juice congealed into greasy pools as the group sat transfixed in shock as Sunny filled them in on the conversation she and Jake had shared that morning.

She explained about his sudden arrival, his odd online dating profile, the bloody shirt, and his whole involvement in Walter's case.

"Aren't you going to get in trouble for telling us all this?" Piper asked.

"No," Sunny answered. "I asked him if it was okay if I told you guys, and he said with the way everyone's been meddling in the case, he'd rather have us working *with* him than against him."

"Huh," Edna said, thoughtfully. "So Mr. Shows-Up-Mysteriously-in-the-Night is really working with the Feds?"

"Yep."

Edna looked perplexed as she chewed on the side of her bottom lip.

"Well, I think it's cool," Piper said.

"So do I," Jeremy chimed in, only to get another bracing look from Maggie. "Well, I do."

"The *cool* part about it is that now I know he's investigating Walter's death, not the cause of it," Sunny said. "You should have seen his face when I told him we thought he had murdered Walter."

"I bet," Edna said. "But I'm still not sold. Just because he works with the Feebs doesn't mean he's absolved of the crime. Maybe he just knows more about how to pull off a murder and not get caught."

"Feebs? Really, Edna?" Sunny gave an exasperated eye roll. "How many crime shows do you watch each week?"

"Hey, those crime shows can really teach you a thing or two," she said, huffing in her defense. "I'm just saying I'm not ready to fully trust this Mr. Long-Lost-Grandson yet."

"Well, I am," Sunny said. "I believe him. You guys weren't there this morning when he told me all of this. I looked into his eyes, and I believe him."

"And you like him," Maggie said.

"And I like him." A smile crept across Sunny's face. "I *really* like him."

Sunny looked around the room at the faces of her closest friends and confidants. Maggie wore her usual skeptical look. But it was hard to accept it, when Jeremy sat next to her, his long arm stretched around her back, and his fingers tracing circles along her shoulder.

Ever the romantic, Cassie nodded encouragingly at Sunny, as if she could see her future with Jake shining brightly. Piper's blonde head was bent forward, strands of hair falling across her eye as her fingers worked the keyboard of her phone, Sunny's love life already accepted as she moved forward in her teenage world of friends and texts.

Edna stood and cleared the table, a thoughtful expression in her eyes. Sunny figured she was processing the information of the night as she stacked plates and collected napkins.

"You all will have more of a chance to get to know him this weekend, because I am having a Bayou Barbeque on Wednesday night in honor of our latest book." They had just finished *The Divine Secrets of the Ya-Ya Sisterhood*, and Sunny told them she had been formulating the idea of doing a southern barbeque for their book club similar to Vivi's birthday party at the end of the book. Sunny had visions of fried okra, pecan pie, and Cajun shrimp sizzling on the grill. Not that she knew how to make fried okra, or anything Cajun, but that's what cookbooks were for.

"I thought it would be fun to have the book club bring their families." Sunny looked pointedly at Maggie and Jeremy. "And/or a guest of their choosing."

"I'm free Wednesday," Jeremy said. "What should I bring?"

"She said of our choosing," Maggie said. "I haven't chosen you yet."

"Oh, yes you have." Jeremy picked up Maggie's hand and turned it over to lay a quick kiss on her palm. "You just haven't realized it yet."

A goofy grin crossed Maggie's face for just a moment before she put her scowl back in place. "Oh, all right, you can come," she snapped.

"Because…" he said, a devilish look of anticipation in his eyes.

"Because I choose you," she grudgingly said.

"Yes!" He fist-pumped the air, then turned back to Maggie. "Because honey, I chose you the moment that door opened, and I saw your beautiful smile."

Maggie tried to keep a straight face, but the beautiful smile he had been talking about broke free and her face lit up like a ray of sunshine.

"Ugh. I think I'm going to vomit," Edna said. "That's enough of this mushy crap for me." She closed the dishwasher and rubbed her chest as she let out a loud belch. "I'm ready to go home. That pasta salad made me gassy."

Maggie and Jeremy walked the others to the door, and Sunny reminded them all about the barbeque on Wednesday night. "Everyone should come around six, and I will call you each this week about what to bring."

Maggie touched Piper's arm and quietly said, "I'd appreciate it if you didn't say anything to Drew about Jeremy. I haven't told the boys yet, but I will before the barbeque this week."

"Sure," Piper said. "I'm happy for you. He seems like a great guy."

"Thanks, honey." Maggie pulled the young girl into her arms and buried her face in Piper's shoulder to conceal the broad grin on her face. "And yeah, he is a great guy."

"Pass the salt."

"Matt, you can't put salt on Cajun shrimp. It's already spicy," Sunny admonished.

"Matt puts salt on potato chips." Cassie plopped down on the chaise lounge behind her husband. She ribbed him good-naturedly as she threw her arm around his shoulder and absently rubbed his back.

The scents of grilled meat and vegetables filled Sunny's backyard as the Page Turners and their families milled around.

Cassie had spent the last twenty minutes rearranging Sunny's buffet table so it would *flow*. She'd switched the plates and cutlery to one end next to the napkins, then had Matt bring out an extra card table that she laid a flowered tablecloth across. She filled the table with colored cups and a large pitcher of lemonade. Bright yellow slices of lemon floated amidst handfuls of ice cubes, and droplets of condensation beaded the glass of the pitcher, rolling down the curves as if caressing a woman's figure.

The back door slammed, and Jeremy emerged carrying two Diet Cokes and a BBQ spatula under his arm. The smile that lit up his face was only outshined by the similar one playing across Maggie's. He advanced on her, stopping to pick up a red Solo cup filled with ice from the drink table, already knowing she preferred to drink her soda with a glass of ice rather than from the can. He set the drinks on the table next to where Maggie was stretched out on a chaise lounge. Her white shorts and turquoise halter top offset her tan skin. Her flat black sandals had a round abalone shell and matched the shell at the center of her top that rested in her ample cleavage.

"En Guard!" Jeremy pulled the BBQ spatula from his arm pit and wielded it like a sword. "I am here to slay the mighty dragon for m'lady," he said in his best Old English imitation. "Dost thou fair maiden like her dragon meat rare, medium, or well-done?"

Maggie shielded her eyes from the afternoon sun as she looked up at the tall, lanky man. His mussed dark hair, boyish grin, and blue eyes shining behind his glasses made her heart do a little flip, and she smiled. "Wow. You are such a nerd."

"Yes, I know." He grinned back. "But I am a nerd willing to grill dragon meat and feed it to you on a plate, so how do you want it?"

"Medium-rare, hold the scales," she said and grinned wryly at him.

"Ahh. Dost thy lady have a touch of nerd-dom herself?" he teased.

"Evidently so," Maggie said. "Now, go cook."

He gave her one more pose, swooshing the spatula in a zee motion to mimic Zorro, then stuck the BBQ tool between his legs. With a last nod and a 'm'lady', he galloped to the grill where Jake was laying thick pink hamburger patties across its surface.

Meeting Jake this afternoon, Jeremy had been a little intimidated by his FBI status– and the fact that Jake actually lived out the adventures Jeremy only dreamed and invented imitation digital worlds about. But Jake's easy manner and laid back attitude put Jeremy at ease, and they soon joked and bantered with each other like old college buddies.

Jake took one look at Jeremy and his BBQ spatula stallion and dropped his head in shame. "Really,

Dude?" Jake asked. "The only thing you're missing is the sound effects," he said and mimed the coconut clapping horseless knights of Monty Python.

❀❀❀

"Haven't seen you smile like that in a long time," Sunny said as she pushed Maggie's legs aside and sat on the end of the chaise.

Sunny wore her curly hair in a haphazard knot on top of her head. Her feet were bare and her toenails sported a glossy bubble-gum pink polish.

"I'm glad to know I've still got that smile," Maggie said.

"Who knew it would take an elvin-filled video game and a tall, cute nerd to find it again?" Sunny teased.

Maggie laughed. "Who knew?"

❀❀❀

Drew watched his mom flirt playfully with Jeremy and shook his head as he watched the guy brandish his barbeque spatula sword. *Dude.*

He had been surprised when upon returning from three days of hot, exhausting soccer camp, his mom had sat him and his brother down and explained she had been seeing someone.

"That's cool," Dylan had said, shrugging his shoulders. "Do we have anything good to eat? I hope you went to the store while we were gone."

Dylan wandered into the kitchen, the discussion about his mom's love life accepted and dismissed as he opened the pantry to a fresh array of Pringles cans and Hostess boxes.

"Thanks, Mom," he called back into the living room where Drew still sat, eyeing his mom with suspicion.

"Who is this guy?" he asked. "Where did you meet him? How well do you know him?"

Maggie filled him in on the meeting at Sunny's, her secret video game addiction, the shared encounters with Jeremy in the magical game world, the subsequent phone calls, and the courtship of Jeremy. She was surprised when his first question was, "So you really have a level eighty character in World of Warcraft?"

She laughed. "Yes, I really do."

"That's cool, Mom, but I'm reserving judgment on this guy 'til I meet him. Does he really write video game software for a living? And makes money at it?"

"I guess. Have you heard of the game *Call To Action*?"

He nodded. "Of course. Who hasn't?"

"Well, evidently Jeremy created and designed it."

"No way."

"Way."

"Huh. I'm liking this guy more and more."

And he did like him. Jeremy had come over early to pick up Maggie and the boys for the barbeque, and they had some time to get acquainted.

The *Call to Action* video game had sealed the deal for Dylan, but Jeremy had soon won over Drew as well.

❀❀❀

"You're doing great with them," Maggie had said when they had stepped into the kitchen to get some drinks.

"That's because I *am* one of them," Jeremy joked. "Sometimes I still feel like a nerdy teenage boy, and I created several of my games as an escape where that gawky teenage boy who's hiding in his room can be the hero in an adventure of his own making. They are my test market."

She laughed and shook her head as she loaded a tray with a bowl of salsa, cans of soda, and a glass of ice for herself.

Jeremy opened a bag of tortilla chips and poured them into a bowl. "Seriously Maggie, I think your boys are great. You've done a really great job with them. I was raised by a single mom, and I know what it's like to have a dad that's MIA."

He reached down to touch her cheek and tilted her head up to look into her eyes. "I really care about you, Maggie. I can't believe I found you, and I know how blessed I am to have you. I'm not going to do anything to hurt you or your boys."

Maggie swallowed the lump in her throat as he bent down to lay the slightest kiss on her lips. She felt one more layer of the ice that had trapped her heart crack and melt away as she wrapped her arms around his neck. Twisting her hands into his hair, she pulled his face closer to hers and deepened the kiss.

His arms wrapped around her waist, and his long fingers splayed against her back as he pulled her tight against him.

"Mom! Are you bringing chips or what?" Dylan yelled from the living room.

Maggie pulled her face back, but Jeremy held her for a moment, keeping her trapped with his eyes.

"I sure am crazy about you," he said and pulled her in for one more, hard kiss, capturing her mouth with his as he conveyed his feelings through his lips.

He released her, grabbed a corn chip, and popped it into his mouth. "Now let's go feed those boys." He picked up the bowl of chips in one hand and the tray of drinks in the other.

Drew had watched his mother emerge from the kitchen that morning, her cheeks flushed and her eyes shining, and he couldn't remember seeing her look so happy. The creases in her forehead and the worry lines around her mouth that had appeared after his dad had left seemed to have vanished and been replaced with a softness around her eyes. She almost seemed to glow.

He watched her now, that glow still apparent as she laughed at some story Sunny told her. Their heads were bent together like two young girls on a playground sharing secrets.

He felt a weight lift from his shoulders as he realized his mom was going to be okay. He had considered putting off college this year to work and be closer to home, but he suddenly felt like things were going to work out, and she would be okay if he went to the state university.

The sound of laughter drew his attention away from his mom. His heart quickened as he watched Piper laughing as she and her cousins launched a surprise Super-Soaker attack on Matt.

Cassie yelped as an errant spray caught her along the side of her hair, but Matt had already jumped up and was chasing the kids through the yard. Within seconds, he had wrestled a squirt gun from his daughter and was pumping the handle and aiming for Piper's back.

"Uncle Matt!" she shrieked with laughter as a stream of water hit her squarely in the back.

"Drew, help me," she called, running toward him. He set down his root beer as Piper ran past and tossed him one of her squirt guns. He ducked and narrowly missed a long stream of water coming from Matt's weapon as he and Piper raced around the side of the house, shooting cold sprays toward Matt and Tyler as they ran.

Sunny laughed as she surveyed the scene in her backyard. Jake and Jeremy stood at the grill, beers in hand, watching in amusement as Matt and the kids chased each other with squirt guns. Cassie's voice got higher and higher as she tried to protect the food from the water fight while shouting for the kids to "Cut that out!" and "Put those squirt guns away! Someone's going to get hurt!"

Edna and Roy sat to the side of the mayhem in adjacent lounge chairs. Edna calmly flipped through a magazine, and Roy appeared to be taking a nap, his Stetson leaned low on his face. His arm stretched across the chairs and rested lightly on Edna's leg and in between pages, she would set her hand down gently on his.

Sunny's gaze moved back to Jake, and she smiled as she watched him talking to Jeremy. The highlights in his blond hair caught the late afternoon sun as he causally leaned a hip against the deck railing. He wore his standard khaki board shorts, flip flops and a faded light blue t-shirt that read *I'M WHAT WILLIS WAS TALKIN' 'BOUT.*

He turned as if he could feel her eyes on him, and his face broke into a grin, his teeth dazzling white against his tan skin. The party in the backyard seemed to fade into the background, and all she felt were Jake's eyes on her. Her skin warmed as she felt his gaze caress her body. His smile shifted, and his eyes softened, and she suddenly felt the urge to cover herself up as if he could see right through her clothing.

*Oh hell, let him look.* She pulled back her shoulders and brazenly stared back with what she hoped were her best *bedroom eyes.*

*Dun-Dun. Dun. Dun. Du-du-du.* The musical notes of the theme from Mission Impossible floated through the air, and everyone stopped and turned to Jake.

"Hey, it's my mission, and I can choose to accept it." Jake grinned as he flipped the phone open.

"Landon here," he said. He passed the barbeque tools to Jeremy as he moved to a less populated area of the yard. Sensing it was official business, the party stayed silent and watched as Jake nodded and went through several '*uh-huh*', '*I see*', and '*all right's*'.

He closed the phone and bent his head as he rubbed his eyes, then turned to the group. "That was Tom Mansfield, the detective on Walter's case. He called with some new information on Walter's whereabouts."

"Well, what did he say?" Edna asked. Her magazine slipped from her hands and landed on the grass, the page open to an article offering, *SIX SEX TRICKS HE WANTS YOU TO KNOW.*

The water fight had ceased, and the group moved closer to Jake, surrounding him as if he were a sponge sucking them all in. They were a somber group, each prepared to hear the worst.

"First of all, they've ruled the fire an accident. They pinpointed the ignition point as the back corner of the garage and some faulty wiring. They're assuming the combination of cleaning products and old rags must have caused a spontaneous combustion. Walter had a full propane tank for his grill in the garage and that was the catalyst for the explosion."

"Who cares about the explosion?! What do they know about Walter?" Edna cried.

"At this point, nothing new. The fire was just an odd coincidence that happened around the time Walter went missing."

The group breathed a collective sigh of relief as Jake continued, "They're closing the case on the fire, deeming it an accident with no human casualties."

"Then where is he? Is he dead? Do you still think someone murdered him?"

"Murdered who?" asked a familiar voice from behind them. "And what the hell happened to my garage?"

"Walter," Edna said, her hand moving to cover her mouth as she turned. "Oh, my God in heaven, Walter!"

The group turned, stunned, and stared at Walter Mead, their missing neighbor, as he stood in the entrance to the backyard. He looked tan and healthy in khaki slacks and a yellow golf shirt.

His expression changed from perplexed to shock as Edna let out a sob and catapulted across the yard to throw herself into his arms. Her bony shoulders shook with sobs, and Walter automatically rubbed her back and murmured soft *'there-there's'* and *'it's all right's'*.

He looked at Sunny over the top of Edna's silver-curled head. "*What* is going on?"

Edna pulled back and tilted her head up to his as she caressed Walter's cheek. "You're alive," she softly said. Then she pulled her skinny arm back and slugged him in the bicep. "We thought you were dead, you ornery old cuss. Where the hell have you been?"

The group broke into relieved laughter. Edna stepped back, and Sunny moved forward to wrap her arms around Walter's waist. "We are so glad you're okay."

"Why don't you have a seat, Walter," Cassie said. "I'll get you some lemonade, and you can tell us where you've been the last month. There was an explosion in your garage and for the last several weeks we all thought you were dead."

"Dead?" Walter remained where he was. "I'm not dead. In fact, I've never felt better. I've been traveling and seeing the world, and I've spent the last month with my new wife."

"Oh, no, you married her," Jake said with a sigh.

Walter turned to the voice. His mouth fell open, and his eyes brimmed with tears as he quietly asked, "Jake, is that you?"

Jake moved to stand before his grandfather, his face a mix of longing and reserve.

"Yeah, it's me," he said, the chip almost visible upon his shoulder. "Your grandson."

"Oh, my boy." Walter stepped forward and clasped Jake to his chest. The two men were close to the same height, and Jake's arms hung limp at his sides as the older man clung to him. Jake's hands moved up to clap him on the back as Walter's shoulders began to shake with silent sobs.

Walter pulled back and clasped Jake's face between his hands as he searched his eyes. "You have your mother's face." The tears coursed down Walter's cheeks, and his voice broke as he said, "And your grandmother's eyes."

He pulled Jake back into another embrace. "I'm so glad you're here. I'm so sorry I've missed so much of your life. I'm so sorry."

The group silently watched the tearful reunion until a small sound broke the spell, and Sunny turned to see Cassie blowing her nose into a napkin.

"What?" she asked, her eyes red from crying. "I'm just so happy to see Walter, and it's like an Oprah reunion show right here in your backyard."

Several people laughed, and Walter released Jake, giving his shoulder one last hearty shake.

"I've been staying in your house," Jake said.

"That's fine. I'm glad you made yourself at home. I had no idea you would be here so soon or that anyone would even be missing me."

"Why didn't you tell anyone you were leaving?" Edna asked.

"I did. I left a message on your answering machine the night I left. I told you I was going on a roadtrip and asked you to keep an eye on my house."

"You're kidding?" Edna said. "That damn answering machine hasn't worked in years."

"Why don't you tell us where you've been and what's been going on." Jake took a few steps back and sat on the edge of one of the lounge chairs. Sunny sat beside him, and he looped his arm under hers and clasped her hand. Sunny felt a slight tremble in his hand, and she clasped it tightly between both of hers. She squeezed his hand, offering him her silent support.

Walter took a seat on the closest lawn chair, and Cassie poured him a glass of lemonade and set it on the table in front of him. He gestured for them all to sit down as he took a clean white handkerchief from his back pocket and drew it across both his cheeks before opening it and blowing his nose loudly into the fold.

He took a sip of his lemonade and looked into the faces of his friends and neighbors. The group had settled on various lawn chairs and patches of grass, all anxious to hear Walter's story.

"I'm awfully sorry I frightened you all. That was not my intention. I had been so lonely since I lost Betty, and I felt like my life was in a rut. A couple of the guys down at the lodge were nagging me to get back out into the world and convinced me to try this online dating thing. As you can imagine, there's not a lot of interest in a broken down old man who likes to garden and tinker in his garage."

He turned and looked sadly at the pile of ash and rubble that stood where his garage once sat, the burnt-out shell of his tool cabinet standing tall like a sentinel in the wreckage.

He took another sip of lemonade. "But I did meet

one woman. She seemed interested in the same things I did, and we met for coffee, then dinner, then walks and rounds of golf. She seemed so young, and she was beautiful, and I got sucked into the allure of a gorgeous women's attention. Things were moving quickly, and when she asked me to accompany her on a spur-of-the-moment road-trip to California, I threw caution to the wind and packed my bags. I just wanted an adventure."

"But why did you leave your wedding ring and your favorite belt buckle?" Edna asked.

"And your pocket knife from Betty?" Sunny added.

Walter turned to Edna, a stunned look on his face. "How did you know…?"

"We found the ring, the pocket knife, and your belt buckle amongst the ashes of the fire," Jake explained. "That's why we had at first thought you died in the explosion. But we figured something must have happened to you to cause you to leave your most valued treasures behind."

Walter clasped his face in his hands and shook his head back and forth. He looked back up at Edna. "I'm so sorry I worried you. Before I left, I went out to my workshop and spent some time just talking with Betty. Well, her spirit, I guess. You know how I do that. I explained to her I was trying to move on with my life. I took off my ring and left my knife and belt buckle all in a cigar box on my workbench as a symbol of starting a new chapter in my life."

He looked around at the faces in the group, and again hung his head in shame. "I was a selfish old man. I didn't mean to worry anyone. I don't have any pets to care for, I barely get any mail, and my lawn is set on a sprinkler system. I got caught up in a romance, and when she offered up the idea of this trip, I jumped right in. I was thinking of the adventure of it all, and I just left. I'm sorry. I wasn't thinking of anyone but myself and this gorgeous red-head named

Mona who made me feel young and alive."

He looked at Matt as if for moral support. "She lured me in with talk of sunbathing and margaritas by the pool. She had a bikini, for goodness sakes."

Matt chuckled and nodded at the older man in the universal man-code of understanding that sometimes it all comes down to the allure of the boobs.

"So I get all that," Jake said, drawing Walter's attention. "But why did you have to marry her?"

Walter looked shocked. "Marry her? For heaven's sake, I didn't marry *her*. I would never have been able to keep up with her. Besides, I always felt like there was just something a little bit off with that one. I'm not sure, but I think she may have only been interested in me for my money. Don't get me wrong. We had quite an adventure. We spent a week in Vegas and had some fun gambling and laying by the pool. But that one was sneaky, always workin' an angle, tryin' to get me to buy her this or that. Nah, I tried to hang in there for the whole trip. But after spending another week with her in California, I said '*adios*' and ditched her faster than a cowboy uses an outhouse in January. Yes sir, that woman was trouble with a capitol T."

A loud noise erupted from the chair next to Walters, where Edna sat. The sound was a half-laugh, half-sob and came out as a high pitched snort. "Oh, you are a wonderful man, Walter. I am so glad you are not dead."

He chuckled as he covered his old friend's hand with his. "I am too, dear. I am too."

"I'm confused. If they were traipsing around the country buying gas and staying in hotels, why couldn't you track Walter's credit cards and figure out where he was?" Maggie asked Jake.

"We tried," Jake said. "But he never used any."

"That's because I don't have any of those fool things," Walter explained. "I have lived my life believing that if you didn't have the money, you didn't buy it. I had a stash of rainy day money that I kept in the garage, and I just took that with me. It wouldn't have mattered anyway, 'cause the darnedest thing happened while we were in Vegas. I was playing the blackjack tables one night and someone stole my wallet. I was lucky that I had left most of my cash in the safe in my room, but I lost my driver's license and my AARP card."

"Oh, those are a pain to get again," Edna said. "Why didn't you report it to the police?"

"I told the casino security about it," Walter explained. "But at that time, I was still having fun and playing things loose, so I just let it go and figured I'd have plenty of time to worry about getting that stuff replaced when I got home."

"Now wait, if you ditched Mona in California, then who did you marry?" Cassie asked, still stuck on his earlier statement, which started a chain of reactive questions.

"Yeah, who?"

"Where is she?"

"Are you really married?"

Walter held up his hand. "One at a time. Yes, I really did get married. To a lovely woman named Helen. She just dropped me off. She wanted to stop at her apartment for a few things before she came back over. She should be here anytime."

As if on cue, a dark blue Chrysler pulled into Walter's driveway, and he got up and hurried toward the car.

A tall, thin woman emerged from the vehicle wearing denim capris, walking sandals, and a mint green t-shirt covered by a patchwork quilt vest. She had a short cap of curly white hair, a small nose, and bright, intelligent eyes. She had a beatific smile that she presented to Walter as if bestowing him with a gift as she squeezed his hand. She was close to his height and looked to be in her mid-seventies. They were a handsome couple as they made their way into Sunny's yard where the rest of the party waited.

Walter beamed proudly as he introduced her. "This is my beautiful new wife, Helen."

He moved her through the yard, and Helen shook hands and made comments as he introduced each family in turn. "This is Matt and Cassie Bennett and their children, Tiffany and Tyler."

"Nice to meet you. How cute."

"This is my dear friend, Edna Allen. She has been a neighbor and good friend to Betty and me for many years."

"I'm delighted to meet you," Helen said. "Walter has mentioned you often."

Edna introduced Roy who removed his hat and charmingly kissed Helen's hand. Walter raised an eyebrow to Edna who laughed and waved him off. "He's a harmless old coot. Flirts with anything female and breathing."

Helen removed her hand, smiled at Roy, and moved on to where Maggie stood with Jeremy.

"This is my lawyer, Maggie Hayes. She and Cassie are good friends of my other neighbor, Sunny."

Maggie shook hands with Helen, then turned to introduce Jeremy. He stepped forward to shake the hands of Walter and Helen. "Pleased to meet you."

"You as well," Walter said, giving Maggie a questioning look, which she ignored. He nodded across the yard. "Those two strapping young dark-haired boys kicking the soccer ball around over there are her sons, Drew and Dylan."

"Hey," Drew called, and he and Piper came across the yard to greet Helen.

Walter absently looked at the smiling, happy blonde teenage girl, and then a slow recognition crossed his face. He brought Piper to him in a clumsy embrace as he leaned down and said, "You look lovely, my dear.

Just lovely."

He pulled back to look at her once again, then turned to Helen. "This beautiful girl is Piper. She's Cassie's niece, the one I told you about, who helped me with my flowers this spring. She's become quite a gardener."

"I'm so glad you're okay," Piper said, in a rare moment of affection. "You scared me."

"Sorry about that. I am okay though."

"I see that." Piper looked approvingly at Helen.

"It looks like you're doing okay too," he said.

"Yeah, I'm okay too."

The two generations looked fondly at each other, both sending up silent prayers of thanks that the other one was going to be okay.

A pitiful whine broke the moment, and Walter looked down to see Beau standing patiently by his side. He bent to ruffle the dog's neck.

"And this is Beau," Sunny said, as she and Jake, still hand in hand, approached Helen.

"Oh, I love dogs. I have one of my own. He is just a gorgeous fella, isn't he?" Helen bent to stroke his back, and Beau shook with excitement at all the adoration he was receiving.

"I'm Sunny, Walter's west-side neighbor. This group is our weekly get-together for our book-club, the Pleasant Valley Page Turners."

"Oh, how wonderful. I love to read," Helen said. "I was a high school English teacher for thirty years."

"I'm a teacher as well. I teach second graders," Sunny said.

"What a fun age."

Walter ignored Beau as he continued to nudge his hand in an effort to get him to resume his head-petting. "And this young man is my grandson, Jake," Walter said proudly, grasping Jake by the shoulder.

"I'm so glad to meet you," Helen said warmly. "Your grandfather has told me so much about you, and how excited he is to have you in his life."

"Thank you. It's a pleasure to meet you, ma'am." Jake nodded and took a step back, obviously a little shy about gushy, family reunions.

"Everyone, please sit down," Sunny directed. "Have you folks eaten? There's plenty of food. Can I get you something to drink, Helen? Iced tea or lemonade?"

"Or a shot of brandy?" Edna added. "I think that's what I'm having. What a day."

"Iced tea would be lovely, dear," Helen answered. "I'll keep my options open on the brandy though," she added and winked at Edna, earning a mischievous grin in return.

"Walter was just going to tell us about how you two met." Sunny poured the amber liquid over a pile of ice cubes and handed Helen a red Solo cup.

"Well, we've known each other for years through church and a bridge group we both belong to. It was just a coincidence that I ran into her on a dock in California as she disembarked from a cruise. We got to visiting, and she told me she was renting a car and traveling up the coast for a few weeks before she returned to Colorado. She offered to give me a ride if I didn't mind going the long way home," Walter said.

He stopped and took her free hand gently in his. "Well, I didn't have any ID to rent my own car, and all I had was time on my hands and a stash of rainy day money, so I agreed to go along."

"Oh, we had a wonderful time." Helen's voice was low with a slight Southern grace to it. "We talked, and laughed, and listened to talk radio. We stopped at some beautiful cities along the coast, and Walter would take me out to dinner as if we were on a date. And every place we ate that had a band, we danced." She nodded at Jake. "Your grandfather can really tango."

Jake chuckled, and Walter cut in. "She means I can barely tango. We did visit some amazing places though. We stopped in national parks and hiked to waterfalls. One night we built a fire on the beach and stayed up all night talking. After the first two weeks, we realized we had fallen in love, and we're both too old to waste any more time being alone. So we got hitched."

"On the beach?" Piper asked, entranced by the elderly couples love story.

"Right on the beach," he answered. "The hotel we were staying in offered a wedding package, and we had a little ceremony in the sand by the water. We'll have to make it official here at the courthouse, after I get another drivers license. But the beach ceremony meant something to us. We stayed there a few days then called the last weeks of the trip our honeymoon."

"We also stopped to visit my daughter and her family for a couple of days so I could introduce them to Walter," Helen explained.

"Well, why didn't you ever call?" Edna asked. "Did they not have any phones at any of these beach side resorts you stayed in?"

"Of course they did," Walter said. "But why would I need to call anyone? I had left my neighbor a phone message, or at least I thought I did. And I was having the time of my life. I was living life in the moment and having a great time. I'm sorry that I worried everyone, but I had no idea any one would even be missing me."

"So what happened to Mona?" Jake asked. "No offense, but right now, I'm more interested in tracking down this woman than I am in your romantic seaside nuptials."

"Last I saw," Walter answered, "she had her sights set on another fellow, a Toby something or other, runs some kind of oil corporation. We parted ways at the dock as she boarded a Princess Cruise Line for a month of traveling through Europe with him. That's where I ran into Helen."

"A month? How long ago was that?"

Walter looked skyward and scratched his head. "Oh, I'd say about a month ago."

Jake jumped from his chair and started for Walter's house. "I've got to make some calls. This might be the break we've been looking for." He stopped and looked back at Walter. "Is it okay if I still use your house?" he asked, awkwardly.

"Of course," Walter said. "You're welcome to use anything."

"Thanks." Jake loped to the back door and stepped inside.

Walter looked at Sunny. "What does he want with Mona?"

She explained to Walter and Helen that Jake worked for the FBI and had been searching for this Mona woman for months. Walter's face registered pride for Jake, then blanched pale as she got to the part about Mona being an alleged serial killer known as 'The Black Widow'.

Helen gasped. "You spent weeks with that woman."

"I told you I thought something was off with her," Walter said.

"I'm still confused about something," Sunny said. "What about the bloody shirt? Beau found a flannel shirt with your blood all over the sleeve. That's another reason why we were sure something had happened to you."

"Well, the night before I left, I was out in the garage pulling my stash money from its hiding place and I cut my arm on a piece of metal. It bled like the dickens," Walter explained as he ran his finger over a thin white scar on his forearm. "I remember I got blood all over the shirt I was wearing. I bandaged up my arm and I threw that shirt in the trash. It was an old flannel I'd had forever and that must be the shirt your dog found."

The screen door slammed, and Jake came back across the driveway, a look of triumph on his face. "We got her! Her alias is listed on the passenger log as being aboard the cruise ship, and she used a handprint to board, so we can positively ID her."

"That's great," Walter said. "I'm sorry I didn't contact you sooner. I probably could have saved you weeks of being here. And I missed out on time I could have spent with you. If you have more time, I'd like you to consider staying for a while longer so we have a chance to get to know one another."

"You just got married. Don't you think you should hang out with your new wife?" Jake asked.

Helen waved a hand. "We have plenty of time. We haven't even really figured out where we're going to live. I think Walter should stay here and spend some time with you."

Walter smiled and squeezed her hand. "See why I married this one? She's beautiful and smart." He looked at Jake. "I really would like it if you stayed. I've got plenty of room."

"I pretty much took over your guest bedroom, and I've been living in your house for over a month now anyway. It's going to take some time to wrap up this case, and I have more that I would like to explore here in Pleasant Valley." He looked at Sunny and winked before he turned back to Walter. "Thank you. I would like to stay awhile longer."

"Great. Helen and I can still spend time together. I know you've been here so long already. I'm sorry my actions disrupted your life so much."

"Not a problem." Jake moved back to sit with Sunny on the chaise lounge. He gave her one of his naughty grins as he took her hand. "I found ways to amuse myself."

Sunny watched him look around at the collection of people scattered in the yard. "What are you thinking?"

Jake shook his head. "I'm thinking about this group of women I've come to know over the past month and a half. You've all come into my life and disrupted my investigation. Your friends filled your head with suspicions of me, and now they're serving me plates of baked beans and potato salad. The Page Turners are one crazy group, but they definitely make me laugh. They kind of make me nuts, but I think they're growing on me."

He smiled at Sunny, and she knew a shift had been made. She had yearned for excitement, and it had crashed into her in the form of a scruffy-headed FBI agent and a missing body. She was so tired of sitting still and letting life happen to her. With her new resolve sitting on her shoulder, she knew she was now ready to take charge of her own life, including her own love-life, which now seemed rich with possibilities.

Sunny raised her hand to get the group's attention. "I have an announcement to make to the Page Turners," she declared. "Project Sunny and the Six Blind Dates is now over. No more snobby stockbrokers, hunky cowboys, or health-food-fanatic fishermen. This Saturday night, I get to choose my own date, and I'm going out with Jake."

"Don't you think you should ask him?" Edna asked, around a bite of half-chewed hamburger. Her plate balanced on her knees, piled high with potato salad, grilled shrimp, and red, juicy hunks of watermelon.

"Good point." She turned to face him on the chair beside her. "Jake, would you like to go out with me this Saturday night?"

As if he knew what they were talking about, Beau padded over to lay his head on Jake's knee, looking up at him with sad, brown eyes.

"Change that," Sunny said. "Jake, would you like to go out with Beau *and* me this Saturday night?"

"Arf!" Beau barked and nudged closer to Jake.

Jake laughed. "I guess that's a yes... from both of us."

"Great."

"Great," he agreed. "Now let's eat."

The rest of the week dragged as Sunny waited for Saturday and her date with Jake. She spent most of the day Thursday cleaning up after the party.

Friday afternoon arrived, and Sunny, Cassie, and Maggie sat in their favorite Starbucks indulging in an early afternoon caffeine fix when the door opened and in walked Phil the Fisherman. He was followed by a cute, petite blonde who wore Columbia shorts, a white tank top and a flannel shirt tied at her waist. Thick wool socks bunched at the top of her well-worn hiking boots. With her ponytail swinging, she practically bounced through the door, her melodic laughter carrying through the store.

She and Phil had their heads bent together, deep in conversation. When he spotted Sunny, a sheepish grin crossed his face. He made his way to their table with Perky-Girl following in his wake. "Hi, Sunny."

"Hey, Phil. How are you?"

"Good. This is my date, Stephanie."

Sunny held her hand out. "Nice to meet you."

"Steph, this is my friend, Sunny."

Steph pumped Sunny's hand enthusiastically. "Oh, hi. It's great to meet you."

"Thanks, you too. These are my friends, Cassie and Maggie." Sunny gestured to the girls, and a look of dawning realization crossed Phil's face.

"Drunken Frisbee players?" he asked.

Maggie shrugged. "We couldn't let her go out with a stranger from the internet all by herself."

"Understood." Phil looked toward the barista line. "We better get going."

"Oh yeah, the line's short," Stephanie said. "We're picking up some non-fat Soy-Chai-Teas for now, then Phil made us some awesome energy shakes for later."

"Spirolina?" Sunny asked.

"How did you know?" Steph laughed. "You must have tried them. Aren't they sooo yummy?"

"They sure are," Sunny agreed.

Stephanie waved as she headed for the counter. "Nice to meet you all."

The happy couple finally got their drinks and headed toward the door. Phil turned and gave Sunny a smile and a head nod while Stephanie wiggled her fingers and called, "Bye-ee".

"Excuse me while I barf into my non-soy, mocha triple shot latte," Maggie said.

"Oh, stop it." Cassie swatted playfully at Maggie. "They were cute."

"They were cute, and I'm glad Phil found someone to share his interests. He is a great guy." Sunny raised her glass in the air. "As for us, let us toast to red meat, caffeine, and real chocolate."

Cassie and Maggie bumped their cups against hers. "Here! Here!"

❀❀❀

*What in the heck is that racket?* Sunny slammed the passenger door of the car. Maggie had given her a ride home from Starbucks, and Sunny gave her friend a wave as she headed toward the house.

Weaving between the extra cars in their shared driveway, Sunny followed the sounds of hammering and power tools to Walter's backyard. The yellow ribbon of caution tape had been ripped away from where it had surrounded what was left of the garage, and a loose end flapped in the breeze.

Jake and Walter, clad in soot covered jeans and t-shirts, were cutting away the last pieces of structure and tossing burnt up material into the bed of an old pickup. Their thick work gloves and plexiglass goggles gave them the appearance of strange aliens from Planet Construction Guys.

Jake threw what looked like used to be a weed-eater into the pickup, and must have noticed Sunny standing in the driveway.

He lifted his goggles, revealing his tan skin with a perfect dark soot outline left behind. His teeth were ultra-white against his black smudged face as he grinned and waved. “Hey there. Wanna grab a pair of gloves and help?”

Sunny stepped closer, but not close enough to get the black dirt on her outfit. “What’s going on? You guys look hard at work.”

“We are. Now that Walter is actually alive, and arson has been eliminated, they cleared the garage as a crime scene, and gave us the go-ahead to clean it up. We’re tearing all this out and we’re gonna rebuild a new garage.”

Sunny was glad to hear Jake using the term *we* when he spoke of himself and his grandfather. “Great.”

Walter’s back screen door slammed, and Helen emerged, carrying a tray filled with icy glasses of lemonade. “Who’s thirsty?” she asked. “Oh, Sunny, hi. Can I get you something to drink?”

Jake and Sunny walked over to the deck where Helen had set the tray on the table. “No, thanks,” Sunny said. “I just finished a coffee.”

Walter had thrown a last load of rubble into the pickup and pulled off his gloves as he approached the table. “Thank you, dear. This looks delicious.” He leaned in to give her a quick kiss on the cheek, leaving behind a gray smudge of soot against the side of her nose.

She smiled adoringly at Walter. "Oh heavens, it's the least I can do. Making drinks is easy. Are you sure you won't let me grab a pair of gloves and haul some of the smaller stuff to the truck? I would love to help."

Walter looked skeptically at Jake, who just shrugged. "She's your wife."

"I can help, too," Sunny said. "I just need a few minutes to go home, change clothes and check on Beau. All of us working together should make the job go twice as fast."

"Yeah," Helen said. She stood just a little bit taller.

*Go girl-power.*

After taking a swig of lemonade, Jake wiped his arm across his sweating brow. "I think they could help with hauling the smaller stuff and the sweeping while we tear down the rest of the structure. We're getting that big load of lumber delivered tomorrow, and it could be great to have the demo done and cleaned up before it arrives."

"All right, you girls can help," Walter said. "But, be careful. I don't want you getting hurt."

The younger couple walked to Sunny's backdoor. Jake spent several minutes greeting Beau, who had whined and scratched at the backdoor since he heard her voice across the yard.

Wrapping his arm around her, Jake looked down at Sunny, one of his naughty grins in place. "Need any help with that changing clothes plan?" He leaned close to her ear. "I'm very good with zippers and snaps."

A tingly feeling spread through Sunny's body. One of her special places felt a *snap* of its own as Jake's warm breath caressed her ear, and he placed his lips against her neck. She closed her eyes and tilted her head back as he laid a trail of kisses along her throat and jaw line. A fire ignited in her belly as his lips finally reached hers. Jake's kiss was deep and full of promise. He smelled of sweat and smoke, but his mouth was cool, and he tasted like lemonade.

"Get a room!" yelled the ever-tactful and demure, Edna.

*Reality check.* Sunny pulled back from Jake's kiss. She had been ready to jump him right here in the backyard with the neighbors looking on and her dog sitting next to Jake's leg.

Sunny waved across the yard at her neighbor. "Hey, Edna."

Edna stood on Walter's back porch, a nine by thirteen pan in her hands. "Hey, Sunny. I brought over some chocolate cake for the construction workers here."

Sunny grinned at Jake. "Thanks for the offer, but I think I can handle changing on my own. Can you keep an eye on Beau for a minute? I will be right over, so don't eat all the cake."

Jake was already on his second piece by the time Sunny arrived in a pair of old cut-off jean shorts and a faded red t-shirt.

"This cake is really delicious, Ms. Allen," he said, before he shoveled in another bite.

"If you're gonna eat my cake and make out with my friend on her back stoop, I guess you better start calling me Edna."

He gave her one of his killer grins. "All right, Edna, I will. And both your cake and your friend are delicious."

Edna harrumphed, but Sunny thought she saw her cheeks pinken a little from Jake's charm. He had a way of doing that. Sunny was so happy to see them making headway into getting along. She really wanted Edna and the rest of the book club to see why she was so crazy over this man.

"Well, I'm off," Edna said. "I'm heading out to the ranch. Roy is making me his famous Cowboy Stew tonight. Whatever the hell that is. Probably has an old boot in it. Just wanted to drop by the cake and see how the demolition was coming along." She started back across the lawn then turned and gave a last wave. "Don't work too hard."

Her words fell on deaf ears, because for the next several hours, they worked crazy hard. Helen and Sunny hauled, swept, carried, and fetched, while Walter and Jake hacked, pulled, and sawed the remains of the wreckage down. They worked through the afternoon and into the evening.

When quitting time came, Sunny watched Jake pull off his soot-covered t-shirt and wipe it across his muscled, tan chest. Visions of pirate lust and bodice-ripping filled her head, and suddenly her date tomorrow night couldn't get here fast enough.

*BEEP. BEEP. BEEP.*

The annoying sound of a large truck backing up dragged Sunny awake Saturday morning. She sat up and swung her legs over the side of the bed. A groan escaped her lips as her back throbbed, and her muscles ached as she stood up. With a yawn, she straightened her arms above her head and stretched out her sore muscles.

The whoosh of hydraulic brakes had her crossing the room to the open window to see a large truck depositing piles of lumber and stacks of construction supplies along Walter's driveway.

Sunny could see Jake as he directed the truck drivers where to put the supplies. The sound of his easy laughter drifted through her window as he bantered with the workmen. A tool belt hung low on his hips, and despite her aching body, she couldn't wait to get out there and start to work again.

The coffee had brewed while she dressed, and Sunny held up an empty cup to Jake while she hung out the backdoor, giving Beau a chance to take care of his morning constitution. "Can I bring ya a cup?"

"Good morning, Sunshine," he called and came across the lawn to swoop her up in his arms. He smelled clean like soap and laundry detergent. He hugged her tight, then leaned down to give her one hell of a good morning kiss.

Never one to miss out on affection, Beau loped over and nuzzled his big head between them. Pulling away, Jake laughed, bent over the dog, and ruffled the fur around his thick neck. He scooped up one of the many tennis balls scattered around the yard and sent Beau into a frenzied game of fetch.

Definitely a morning person, Jake looked refreshed and awake. Defined muscles bulged from the cut off sleeves of his shirt which depicted an outline of a drivers license, a rainbow curved up one side and the words, *I AM MCLOVIN', THE 25 YEAR OLD HAWAIIAN ORGAN DONOR* printed across the front.

Sunny touched the front of his shirt and laughed. "Where do you get these shirts?"

Jake looked at the front of his shirt as if he had forgotten which one he had thrown on that morning. "My old college roommate owns a t-shirt shop in California, and he thinks it's hilarious to send me these things for Christmas. He's been doing it for years."

"How amusing."

His chest was warm and solid under her hand. She had the sudden urge to rip that amusing t-shirt off his body, drag him into her house, and tackle him to her laundry room floor. Even better, she envisioned him tugging off her jean shorts and panties as he lifted her onto the washing machine. She could almost feel her legs wrapped around him as the washing machine churned and bumped her against him while his hands pushed up her tank top, exposing her belly while his mouth...

"You kids coming over? There's lots of work to be done," Walter hollered across the yard.

Sunny's cheeks reddened as she looked up at Jake who smiled knowingly down at her. "Hold that thought until tonight." He leaned down and kissed her again, sucking on her bottom lip for just a moment before he released her and headed across the lawn. How did he always seem to know what she was thinking?

Jake had asked to be in charge of their date, telling her he wanted a chance to show up those other guys, but he had told her nothing about tonight except to dress casually. "Maybe bring a light jacket, just in case," he had instructed.

Colorado evenings tend to cool off quite a bit, so she deduced they would be outside for part of the night. She dreamt of the possibilities. A sunset cruise along the river? A romantic dinner at a fancy restaurant with white tablecloths and candles shimmering in gold centerpieces. Wait. Neither of those required her to dress casually and neither would allow Beau to come along on their date. She almost laughed aloud, giddy with excitement over a mystery date with this man who became less of a mystery to her every day.

She had all day to dream about their evening out, but for now, they had work to do, and she knew just where to start.

Her start involved calling in the troops. Matt, Cassie, and Piper were glad to come over and help, and Maggie called Jeremy to invite him as well. Knowing Piper would be there, Drew volunteered to come along.

With Walter and Jake acting as foremen and so many willing hands, the work progressed quickly. Everyone pitched in to hammer and haul, saw and measure. Helen and Edna took over the kitchen, supplying the troops with drinks and snacks.

By six o'clock, they had the garage frame built and were ready to construct the roof. The whole group stood together as Walter thanked them for their hard work, and they all offered to return on Sunday afternoon.

Jake stood behind Sunny, one hand resting lightly on her hip. He leaned in close to her ear. His breath tickled her neck, sending delicious shivers down her spine. "You have exactly one hour to get ready. I will be on your doorstep at exactly seven o'clock."

"I will be waiting with a light jacket and Beau's leash in hand." She grinned up at him. "How about you make it six forty-five?"

"You're on."

True to his word, Jake had rang Sunny's doorbell at exactly six forty-five, and she had indeed been ready. Sunny had showered, lotioned, and dabbed on her favorite perfume.

She decided to wear her hair loose and curly, and had spent ten minutes with the diffuser trying to make it look like it had dried naturally. She wore a light-weight purple floral shirt that snapped up the front, jean capris and a cute pair of low-heeled strappy purple sandals. She held a light zip up jacket, and when she opened the door, it was hard to tell who was more excited, she or the dog.

Jake looked gorgeous in jeans and a light blue button up shirt. His hair was still damp on the ends and curled a little at his collar. He smelled like a heavenly combination of aftershave and masculine soap. He held out his hand to take Beau's leash. "Wow, you look beautiful." He pulled her to him and slid his arm around her waist as they walked to the Mustang. "And you smell amazing."

They made light conversation in the car, and Beau happily hung his head- and his tongue- out the window as Jake drove them to Bear Creek Park. He removed a picnic basket and an old patchwork quilt from the trunk of the car, then grabbed a cooler and slung it over his shoulder before slamming the lid of the trunk.

He led her to a large area of green lawn in front of a pavilion where a big brass band was warming up. The lawn was scattered with several clusters of blankets and lawn chairs.

A family of five sat huddled around a large red and white tub of fried chicken, the kids reaching inside for their favorite piece while the mother scooped artificial white mashed potatoes and gravy onto several plates.

An elderly couple sat side by side in aluminum lawn chairs. They held hands, he tapped his foot to the music, and both wore far off looks as if they were remembering younger days.

Another blanket held a young couple with a gray car seat set between them. They were laughing and eating Subway sandwiches, their drink cups anchored in the folds of the blanket. The young mother absently rocked the car seat with her foot as she chewed her sandwich.

Jake shook the blanket and let it float to the ground before anchoring the sides with a cooler on one edge and a picnic basket on the other. "Have a seat. Tonight is Big Band Night. Warming up over there is Johnny Madison and the Shytown Swingers, and tonight they are playing a Tribute to the Rat Pack."

Sunny sat on one side of the blanket, and Beau curled next to her, laying his head on the side of her leg. "That sounds great. I love that old stuff."

"I know. I checked out your CD's, and I noticed you have a huge selection of this old stuff from the forties and fifties. So I found this concert tonight that played that kind of music. They're playing a collection of Frank Sinatra, Dean Martin and Sammy Davis, Jr."

She clapped her hands in excitement. "This was really thoughtful of you." Sunny was amazed that he had taken the time to try to match a date to something that was important to her.

Jake pulled the cooler toward him, then produced two wine glasses and a bottle of White Zinfandel. He poured them each a glass, then pulled out a saran-wrapped plate of various crackers and little squares of cheese.

As Sunny sipped wine and nibbled on a cheese-covered cracker, the MC, complete in a white tuxedo and red tie, stepped to the mike and welcomed them to the show. The strains of Sinatra's "*Strangers in the Night*" mixed with the cool night air, and as dusk turned to evening, she felt as if she had been transported back in time.

Enraptured by the music, Sunny tapped her foot and quietly sang along to her favorite songs.

Jake unpacked the picnic basket and Sunny *oohed* and *ahhed* over each new item. "I love the way you get so excited every time I pull something out of this basket," he said.

"Me too! It's like Christmas. Like each thing you pull out is a little present," she said. "How did you know to get all my favorites?"

"Because I pay attention to details. And you have given me a lot of details to pay attention to this summer." He leaned down and kissed the spot below her earlobe and a delicious thrill ran through her. "Plus, I think I scored some major points with Cassie when I told her my plans for tonight and asked her advice on your favorite food."

They talked easily as they ate, and Sunny asked Jake how he felt things were going with Walter.

Jake wiped his mouth with his napkin. "I think we're gonna be okay. I feel like rebuilding the garage is a great project for us. In fact, our relationship is kind of like the garage project. It was a mess and mostly destroyed, but it still had a good foundation. With time and a little work on both our parts, and a little help from our friends, I think we can rebuild it into something strong and good."

"I like that." Sunny was glad to see the effort that both men were putting into patching things up, and her heart melted a little at Jake's sentimental analogy.

"The garage isn't gonna be fixed in a day or even a week, but we got the foundation built, and I think the more time we spend hangin' out together and working on it, the better it's gonna get."

"I think so too. Have you heard anything more about Mona?"

"Oh, yeah, I meant to tell you that I got a call from the Bureau tonight while you were getting ready. They said they apprehended Mona as she came off the cruise ship. She was coming out with her new husband, and he was being wheeled out on a stretcher."

"New husband? She already married someone?"

"Evidently so. We knew her bank accounts were running low so we expected her to try something soon. That's why I was so sure she had gotten to Walter."

"But you said he was being wheeled out on a stretcher. Did she already kill him?"

"No, but close. Walter gave us the right information about this guy. His name is Toby Samson and he's loaded. She must have worked some kind of voodoo-sex magic on him to get him to marry her so quickly. She has been steadily poisoning him every day since their blessed union."

"Didn't he suspect anything?" Sunny asked.

"I guess she had him convinced that he had the Swine Flu. She kept him secluded in their cabin alternately caring for him and poisoning him a little more each day."

"So is he okay now?"

"They took him straight to the hospital after they apprehended her, and he seems to be doing fine. She had poisoned him with arsenic which tends to mimic flu-like symptoms. The Swine Flu is so common, I guess she didn't think she'd have a hard time convincing anyone that's what he died of."

Sunny shook her head. "Wow. That woman was some piece of work."

"I'm just glad we got her and that Walter's okay."

"Me too."

"*Everybody Loves Somebody Sometime*" played in

the background, and Sunny licked the final dab of cheesecake from her fork. “That was heavenly. I am so full.”

Jake set a container of Cool Whip and a little dish of strawberries in front of her.

She moaned. “Maybe I have room for a little more.”

He pulled the lid back from the Cool Whip, dipped a bright red strawberry into the luscious cream, then touched the cream to her lip.

She licked at the dab of whipped cream with the tip of her tongue, then opened her mouth to receive the juicy berry. Jake barely touched it to her tongue then pulled it back again, teasing her with the fruit. The backs of his fingers gently touched the edge of her face as he released the strawberry, and she bit into it. The mixture of sweet cream, tart berry, and his touch gave her a little shiver, and she closed her eyes to savor the moment.

When she opened them, she saw the same heat and passion she felt reflected in his eyes. She scooted a little closer to him and Jake’s eyes flashed desire as she wiggled her bottom closer to him. She picked another strawberry from the bowl, dipped it in the whipped cream, and placed it in his mouth. She trailed her finger through the whipped cream, then sucked it from her fingertip. She took another swipe through and held her whipped cream covered fingertip out to him. He moved his mouth to lick it from her finger. She flipped her hand, and deposited the creamy drop onto his nose, then broke out into giggles.

“Oh, I see how this is gonna go,” he said and reached for her. Amidst giggling shrieks, he scooped her up and, with a former wrestler’s ease, had her pinned below him, then wiped the whipped cream from his nose against her chin and neck. She held her breath and closed her eyes again as he nibbled and licked the sweet, sticky cream from her neck. His kisses moved up her jaw line, and she could feel his warm breath against her face. She inhaled his scent of aftershave, strawberries, and ...dog breath. Her eyes flew open just in time to see Beau's big pink tongue coming in for a piece of the whipped cream action. She squealed and pulled her face back, exposing more of her neck, which Beau took advantage of, placing a long slobbery lick up her neck.

"Eww! Beau, get away." She pushed the dog's big head away but couldn't seem to move as she was pinned under Jake's body which currently shook with laughter.

They heard a soft chuckle from above them and looked up to see the elderly couple of the aluminum lawn chairs walking past their blanket. The woman smiled down at them. "What a cute dog."

Jake laughed and rolled off Sunny. They watched the couple move to the dance floor and the older man gently pull his wife into his arms. He led her around the dance floor, and they seemed to float as they glided around the floor with years of practiced ease.

The band played and the lead singer crooned "*Come Fly With Me*" as Jake took Sunny's hand. "Come dance with me?" he asked.

She nodded, and they joined the other couples on the dance floor. Sunny fit perfectly in his arms, and she leaned her head on his shoulder.

Jake seemed comfortable on the dance floor and cradled her to him as they moved around the pavilion. Night had fallen, and the trees were lit with hundreds of little twinkle lights. Sunny felt like she was living a dream as this amazing man held her in his arms. He had put so much thought into tonight, with the food from her favorite places, and the concert with her favorite music, then taking her dancing. All of which she loved.

"I am having the best night," she said and tipped her head to look into his eyes.

"I'm glad."

She wished she could freeze this moment and keep it in her mind forever. Swaying to the music, with his arm wrapped around her, and his hand resting in the small of her back, he leaned his head down and gave her the softest kiss, putting this moment into one of the Top Ten Best Moments of her life.

She leaned her head against his shoulder and looked out over the park. The fried chicken parents sprawled across their blanket, their youngest asleep across the mom's lap. The young couple still sat cross-legged in the grass, a baby blanket thrown over the new mom's shoulder with the tiny feet of an infant kicking out the side.

Sunny's gaze then roamed to their blanket where the remains of their picnic lay scattered around their blanket. Her yellow dog's body lay sprawled across the quilt, his nose buried in the Cool Whip tub as he licked it clean, and a dollop of whipped cream streaked across his ear.

Sunny pushed the front door open, and Beau ran into the house, heading first to the laundry room to see if the puppy-chow fairy had deposited any food into his bowl while they were gone.

The breeze of the warm night caressed her face as she stood in the doorway. The moon was full, and she had yet to turn the house lights on. "Would you like to come in?"

"Oh, yes," Jake said and Sunny's breath quickened with anticipation. He stepped toward her and wrapped one arm around her waist as he swept her into the house with him, then pushed the door shut. He leaned his back against the closed door and pulled her into the circle of his arms.

Silver rays of moonlight shot through the house giving her enough light to see his eyes go dark and a delicious thrill sparked in her belly. Her voice was soft, barely above a whisper as she asked, “Do you want some wine…or something?”

He chuckled softly and reached up to run his fingers through her hair. “Definitely the ‘or something’.”

A nervous giggle bubbled up inside of her, and she looked down at her feet, suddenly shy, all of her insecurities rushing to the surface. “But why?” she whispered. “I’m just a boring school teacher with unruly hair and a crazy dog. I’m ten pounds overweight, and I still love ice cream. I say stupid things when I should just stay quiet, and I cry at the drop of a hat. You live this exciting life of an FBI agent who travels, and I’m pretty sure has been shot. What could you possibly see in me?”

“Oh, babe,” he said quietly and took her face in his hands. He tilted her chin up and wiped away the one lone tear that had escaped as she laid out her soul to him. He looked at her, and she felt he was trying to convey his feelings through his eyes as well as his words.

“I may have led an adventurous life and done some traveling, but having those adventures and moving around all the time hasn’t let me get to know anyone. Adventures mean nothing when you’re alone and don’t have anyone to share them with.”

Jake took a deep breath and wrapped one of her curls around his finger. “I love your hair, and you are anything but boring. In fact, from the moment I met you, we’ve had an adventure of our own. I seem to recall you almost blinding me with breath spray before you launched a bag of frozen chicken chunks at me.”

“And then the garage exploded, and you came to find me after the explosion,” she said. Her hands lay on his chest, and she could feel the hard muscles of his body under the soft cotton of his shirt.

“Oh, man. I was so scared you had been hurt. I couldn’t get you out of my mind that first night. Then you showed up on my doorstep the next day with a plate of brownies and fresh out of the shower. The smell of your hair and your skin as you walked into Walter's house almost drove me crazy. It was weird because I barely knew you, but, Sunny, when I heard that explosion and thought you were hurt, I couldn't get to you fast enough."

"I know. I was so happy to see you coming across the yard," she told him. "Holding on to you made me feel so safe."

He touched her cheek. "Sunny, I have watched your crazy antics over the summer with your friends and those stupid dates. I was so jealous over those guys... secretly I was glad when they didn't work out. I wish I would have known how suspicious you were of me sooner so I could have eased your fears. I can't believe you went all that time thinking I might have killed my own grandfather."

She reached up and laid her hand on his cheek. "I may have had suspicions, but they never felt right. I have been drawn to you since the day we met. I think that inside, my heart has always trusted you."

Jake leaned down to lay his lips against hers. The kiss was sweet and light, a promise of more to come. "Sunny, I love your smile and the way you make me laugh. I love the way your crazy dog wags his tail, and sometimes his whole body, when he sees me. And I love the way you say what you feel." He reached a hand down and caressed her bottom. "I especially love these extra ten pounds, and I will feed you ice cream by the spoonful if you let me."

He kissed her again, this time with more urgency, and he pulled her body tight against him as he spoke softly into her ear. "I can't stop thinking about you, and I can't stop myself from falling in love with you."

"Then don't," she whispered. "Don't stop." She wrapped her arms tight around his shoulders and pressed her cheek to his. "Don't ever stop."

He lifted her then, and she wrapped her legs around his waist, pressing herself against him. He kissed her ear, her neck, her face... then his lips crushed against hers, and all thoughts left her mind except this man, this one glorious man.

He carried her to the stairs, but Sunny was already unbuttoning his shirt and pulling it from his shoulders. Halfway up, he set her down and yanked his half un-buttoned shirt over his head. Her breath caught at the sight of his magnificent body in the moonlight. His tan chest, his slim waist, the line of curly hair that started at his belly button and ran into the waistband of his jeans. Sunny wanted to see, to touch every part of him.

Jake's fingers first unbuttoned, then unzipped her capris. He tugged at them and Sunny wiggled against the steps as he pulled them free of her legs. He slowly unsnapped her blouse, kissing each spot under the snap, her neck, her chest, her stomach.

He leaned back and looked at her. She felt exposed as she lay against the steps, clad only in her bra and thong panties, her unsnapped shirt open and clinging to her shoulders. She could almost feel the heat of his eyes as they took in each part of her body. She couldn't believe this gorgeous man wanted her.

"You are so beautiful," he whispered, then his hands were on her again and finally her skin was touching his. Sunny couldn't seem to get enough of him. She kissed him with a fever and an urgency she didn't know was inside of her. She reveled in the feel of his large hands skimming along her body. Jake reached under her shirt to caress her back and her bare bottom, then slid his fingers along the thin band of her thong panties.

She felt the smooth hard wood of the stair step against her bare skin, then his hand slid between her legs and cupped her femininity. She rubbed herself against his hand, the thin lacy fabric adding extra friction against her already tender area. He bent his head to her breast and nudging the fabric aside, took her erect nipple into his mouth.

Passion flowed through her. Her breath came in quick gasps as she writhed against him. It had been so long since she had felt a man's touch. Everything about Jake excited her. Her insecurities disappeared as he rubbed and stroked her. Then she seized, again and again against his hand, her head thrown back in ecstasy, one hand clinging to his back and the other gripping the stair rail.

Before she could catch her breath, he lifted her and carried her the rest of the way up the stairs, leaving their discarded clothing strewn along the steps. He took her into the bedroom and pulling back the comforter, laid her gently on the bed.

He stepped back and unzipped his jeans, sliding them down his narrow hips. His white boxer briefs glowed silver in the moonlight shining into her room. He pushed his briefs from his hips, letting them fall to the floor, then came to her in all his fabulous naked glory.

He sat on the edge of the bed and brushed her blouse off her shoulders. He unsnapped her bra and slid it slowly from her arms. She had never had anyone undress her before, and she thrilled at the way his eyes lovingly took in every part of her. She lay back, and he slid her panties down her legs before pressing a soft kiss against the delicious spot right below her navel.

His kisses left a trail of fire along her skin as he explored every inch of her naked body. Her hands roamed freely, touched, and caressed all of his magnificent hard maleness.

Finally, he rose above her, and they came together in a glorious union of heat and passion. He filled her, not just physically, but in her heart and soul. Their bodies moved together in a dance both new and familiar, as time was measured in the pulse of their heartbeats. She cried out his name as the sweet, hot flood swept them away.

Afterwards, they lay against each other, their bodies entwined. She ran her hands along the skin of his chest, memorizing every nuance of his body. She rubbed her fingers over the small round scar on his inner shoulder that she was sure was a bullet wound.

He nodded and confirmed her theory. "Yes, I have been shot. The details don't matter. I'll tell you the story some other time, but that bullet put me in a hospital bed for six weeks. In that time, I had a total of four visitors, and one was my mom. I don't let a lot of people in, because I know I'll eventually have to leave and move on to another assignment."

Sunny looked at him, a well of emotions building inside of her. Her eyes brimmed with tears, and she tried to keep her voice steady. "How long are you staying this time?" she asked, her voice barely a whisper.

"Do you want me to stay?"

"Oh, yes."

"Then I'm staying."

"What?" She pushed up on one elbow, a lock of curly hair falling across her forehead. "Just like that? You're staying?"

Jake grinned. "Well, I've been thinking about it for awhile now. My buddy, Finn, has been trying to get me to partner with him in his private investigations firm, and I'm going to tell him yes. After this Black Widow case is wrapped up, I'm going to pull out of the Bureau. I'll stay on as a consultant, so they may call me in once in awhile, but I'll give up my office and all the field work and move out here."

"You will?" Sunny's voice went up an octave with excitement. "But where will you live?"

"Walter and I have been talking about that. He's planning on moving in with Helen and claims his house needs a bunch of repairs. He said I could live there and do the repairs in lieu of rent. He claims I would really be helping him out."

"He just wants you to stick around so he can get to see you more."

His voice quieted as Jake asked, "Will you want to see me more?"

"Oh, Jake, I will want to see you every minute of every day." Her heart felt as if it would burst with happiness. "I'm so excited you're staying. I've been holding back, afraid to really tell you how I felt, because I knew you were leaving."

"*That* was holding back?" He grabbed her by the waist and pulled her to him, rolling up on one arm so she was tucked beneath him. "I can't wait to see what happens when you really let yourself go."

She could not believe this man was naked in her bed, teasing her, and telling her he was going to stay. Her heart soared. She decided she could trust this man who showed up mysteriously in the night and saved her again and again, capturing the loyalty of her dog while he stole her heart. She decided it was time and she did, indeed, let go.

"Jake, I love you. I have loved you from the moment you carried my dog up the stairs to keep me company when I needed him. You always seem to know what I need."

He rubbed his thumb over her bottom lip, and she felt his eyes look into her very soul. "You are all I need, babe. I love you too, Sunny. I love you too."

❀❀❀

"A beautiful woman tried to kill me last night," Jake said.

Sunny looked up from the pan of scrambled eggs she was stirring. She gulped as she took in the sight of Jake, shirtless in her kitchen doorway. His golden hair was mussed, and his jeans had the top two buttons undone, exposing abs so hard she could have cracked eggs on them. She blushed as she remembered running her tongue along that exact area the night before. "Give her another chance, she might try again tonight."

"Why wait 'til tonight? How about this morning?" He sauntered into the kitchen rubbing his belly and slid his arms around her, cradling her back against his firm chest. He nuzzled her neck and kissed that lovely spot right below her earlobe. "Good morning, Sunshine."

Sunny had already showered and made coffee. Strains of an old Elvis song played softly on the kitchen stereo.

She cozied into his embrace. "Good morning. You ready for some eggs?"

"I'm ready for just about anything." He swirled her around and danced her throughout the kitchen.

"Love me tender, love me sweet, never let me go, for you have made my life complete, and I love you so." He sang softly in her ear as they danced, and his hand ran along the back of her silk robe and over her bottom to discover her bare cheek below the hem of the robe.

He stopped dancing and peered mischievously down at her. "Whatcha got on besides that robe?"

She couldn't believe how sexy and brazen he made her feel. "Nothin', but a smile."

He lifted her up onto the kitchen counter, the tile cold against her bare cheeks and stepped between her legs to give her a proper good morning kiss. *Forget scrambled eggs. All I need for breakfast is Jake!*

Jake reached inside the folds of her robe and massaged her bare breast with one hand while the other cradled her neck and entwined her hair through his fingers. He tasted like toothpaste, and she wrapped her legs around him, loving the feel of her freshly shaved legs against his naked waist.

They both jumped at the sound of knocking, and a voice called from Sunny's back door, "Sunny, you awake?"

Sunny unwrapped her legs from around Jake's waist, and he lowered her to floor. Quickly adjusting the folds of her robe, Sunny headed to the laundry room to let her neighbor-with-the-great-timing in. "Good morning, Edna."

Edna took in Sunny's flushed cheeks and kiss-bruised lips and *harrumphed.* She was holding a square cake pan and she eyed Jake sitting at the table forking scrambled eggs into his mouth.

"Morning, Edna," he said. He gave her one of his lop-sided grins and inhaled deeply. "Whatever is in that pan smells like heaven."

"You look like you've already had enough heaven, Mr. No-Shirt-at-the-Table-at-Nine-o'clock-in-the-Morning."

Jake smiled at another of her ever original nicknames for him. "You can't ever get enough of heaven," he said, giving her a wink. "So, what's in the pan?"

"Cinnamon rolls. I thought you all might like some before we start another day of construction."

"You all?" Sunny asked. "How did you know Jake was here?"

"Well, Mr. Lives-Right-Next-Door left his car parked in front of *your* house last night."

"Oops."

"Well, you're going to be seeing a lot more of his car now. Walter is moving in with Helen, and Jake is going to rent his house. He's staying."

Edna gave Jake an appraising look. "Is that right?"

He shot her another killer grin. "That's right, Edna. You and I are gonna be neighbors." He took a bite of a cinnamon roll and groaned in ecstasy. "And I will fix anything around your house if you pay me with another pan of these cinnamon rolls."

It seemed Edna couldn't fight his charm, because she smiled back at him. "Now that you mention it, my kitchen faucet does have an awful drip."

He took a drink of coffee. A drop of creamy icing clung to his chin. "Consider it done."

Edna turned toward the laundry room, hollering over her shoulder, "You two better hurry up. We have a lot of work to do today."

Sunny scooted around the table and followed Edna. Before they reached the back door, Sunny threw her arms around her neighbor. "Edna, I am *so* happy."

The two women looked at the gorgeous man seated at Sunny's kitchen table. Jake was serving himself a second roll, while Beau sat at his side watching him with adoration, waiting for a cinnamon crumb to fall on the floor.

"I can tell, honey," Edna said. "I guess our summer of six blind dates must have worked. It seems Mr. Showed-Up-Mysteriously-in-the-Night turned out to be Mr. Right after all."

The End

# *Acknowledgments*

This book was created through the help and encouragement of many. I want to thank everyone who played a role in making my dream come true.

Always and forever, I am thankful to Todd, Tyler and Nick, for supporting me in this amazing writing endeavor. Thanks for always believing in my success.

I have an awesome group of women that I call friends. Thank you all for listening to plot ideas and proof-reading chapters and sharing in the joy of this dream. I couldn't have done it without Debbie, Melissa, Jennifer, Linda, Pam, Roseann, Mona, Shana, and Marla.

I encourage every writer to get involved in a writing group. I belong to the Pikes Peak Chapter of Romance Writers of America and the support and knowledge I have gained from this group of women has been invaluable. Special thanks to Lana, Michelle, Annie, Jodi, and Cindi for being my cheerleaders, my critique partners, my drill sergeants, and my inspiration.

I am so thankful for the support of my entire family. My appreciation and thanks goes out to the women in my family who encourage me and who all love a good romance. Thanks Mom, Gracie, Coral, Teri, Katie, Chris, and Rebecca.

A special thanks goes out to my beautiful Beta readers, Julie and Carla, who stayed up late reading and correcting and offering ideas. Thanks for not blinking an eye when I said I needed the manuscript back in two days and for being so excited about the chance to help me.

A huge thanks goes out to Kim Killion and Jennifer Jakes and the amazing team at Hot Damn Designs for my beautiful cover design and exceeding all of my expectations in the design and formatting of this book.

I cannot express a big enough THANK YOU to Jennifer Jakes, my editor and friend. Above and beyond doesn't come close to describing the untold hours of help, encouragement and support you offered through my journey of publication.

And thank you to each of you, my readers, who laughed and cried and sighed over the characters in this book. This story was written for you.

# ABOUT THE AUTHOR

Jennie Marts has been dreaming about writing a novel since she was in fifth grade and self-published her first Nancy Drew style mystery to a small readership of family, teachers, and two friends.

She lives in Colorado with her husband, two sons, and two dogs. Tucker, her golden retriever, was the inspiration for the dog, Beau, in this story. Jennie enjoys being a member of (RWA) Romance Writers of America, the Pikes Peak Chapter of RWA, and Pikes Peak Writers. She spends her spare time playing volleyball and reading and believes you can't have too many books, shoes or friends.

Jennie loves to hear from readers. Visit her website at www.jenniemarts.com or follow her on Facebook.

Made in the USA
San Bernardino, CA
21 December 2012